Touc

C000050186

"I completely fell in love with this story from beginning to end. Overall, I was bowled over by Sydney Jamesson's book. I loved it so much, I got to the last page, flipped back and read it again. Don't read the other, more hyped books of this genre ... Read Sydney's, it's incredible!"

~Eryn LaPlant: author of Beneath the Wall, The Blue Lute, Falling for Shock.

"This book is romantic with the right amount of erotica; the love scenes are steamy. The love story of Elizabeth and Ayden takes them to beautiful places. Along with the full sensory descriptions of the places, the music choices make the story come to life and add a certain depth to the story that captivates the reader. I recommend it to those who love a well written romance."

~ Bookish Temptations

"What made this story work for me was the writing style. Sydney Jamesson uses descriptions that I think some writers would be envious of. 'Touchstone for play' isn't just an erotic romance novel of two very different people with sordid pasts. It's a tale of love, heartbreak, danger, fear and mistrust. I loved it and I believe if you enjoyed Sylvia Day's Crossfire Series, you'll love this. "

~All Things Considered Books

"Are you looking for a Fifty Fix? Then this is your series, but not a copy-cat, just a touch of GREY. TouchStone for play and the follow up book TouchStone for giving. Is writing at its best, it sings to you like a song. The characters are so accessible. You will fall in love faster than you can turn the pages."

~ Book and Beyond Fifty Shades

To Chris

TouchStone
for play

*Enjoy the
fairy-tale!*

Sydney Jamesson

*Jamesson
xo .*

First Published by S. J. Publishing, 2013
Copyright© Sydney Jamesson, 2013

A CIP catalogue record for this book is available from the
British National Bibliography (BNB)
S. J. Publishing
P.O. Box 796
ENGLAND
SK4 9DJ

sjpublishing@virginmedia.com
ISBN – 978-09575850-0-3

To the people in my life who mean the most to me, I thank you for your love and support: Barry, Jenna, Mum & Dad

What is love?
Those who play with it, call it a game.
Those who don't have it, call it fantasy
Those who find it, call it destiny.

Touchstone: Noun: a basis for comparison: a reference point against which other things can be evaluated.

The Story of Us...

W hen I was least expecting it, my wish found its way to a fateful star. Someone extraordinary succumbed to the gravitational pull: a mere mortal. That little piece of heaven was Ayden Stone.

In that one defining moment, my life changed forever.

My name is Elizabeth Parker; some would say I'm the luckiest woman you'll ever meet, but today I may be inclined to disagree. The time is 4 o'clock in the afternoon and the rain continues to drizzle; it clings to the glass like tears and mirrors my mood. It's been eight hours, twelve minutes since we've kissed and my lips are already starting to twitch.

I'm sitting here at my desk rolling a red pen between my fingers gazing into space, trying to hold onto a single thought, wondering which set of exercise books to mark first. With time to squander, I surrender myself to vivid memories; blue-green eyes that undress me, a wicked mouth that promises the world and always delivers, and a recollection of this morning's orgasm that has me squirming in my chair. How can I be expected to get anything done?

Regrettably, Ayden has spent the entire day with his mistress, but knowing that doesn't stop him from invading my consciousness; he's my guilty pleasure and a very distracting one at that.

But when did our love affair begin? Was there a single moment when I knew, we knew that Fate was taking us by the hand and leading us towards our destiny? When the planets aligned and the stars came together to form a new constellation? I'm not sure, but what I do know is that Ayden Stone is my heaven on earth, my world. Through memorable days and unforgettable nights, he has been and will always be my saviour, my lover, and my life.

That's all I know, so look and listen and let me tell you the story of us.

1

I can't move. I can't run. There's the stench of stale beer on his breath; he's licking my face and his hands are on me.

"Aren't you a pretty little thing? I've been watching you, princess and I've got something for you ..."

"Please don't hurt me."

"If you're good, then I won't have to, will I?"

He's lifting my dress ... God! No! "... Please don't do this ... please ... please."

One of these frosty, October mornings I'm going to greet a new day with bright eyes; eyes that have not flickered and blinked their way through another restless night. Caffeinated and clothed, I'll temper the noises in my head with distractions: breakfast news, the pages of a glossy magazine, an Aquarian prediction.

'... prepare to meet a tall, dark stranger ...'

The prospect of that lifts my spirits, but that 'lift' is fleeting; like hope and beauty it fades and I am, once more, grounded. Alone.

Until that fateful day, I'll play solitaire with the cards I have been dealt and wish for the kind of flush that comes when two hearts come together.

I wish ...

I've been on my own for too long. Too many nights spent listening to music, reading romantic fiction, experiencing life second hand; characters have lined up to take me to places I'll never visit without them, and I've been content to play chaperone while they have laughed and danced and fallen in love.

For now, it seems my life comes down to the alignment of stars, the roll of a dice or a hand of cards. But, what do you do when your hand is shit? Your prospects are shit and it's Monday. I hate Mondays. There's only one thing I can do: stop feeling sorry for myself and get a grip, or this navel gazing will make me late for work.

Work. A fifteen minute car journey to Harrow Hall Grammar School, one of the best schools in north London – or so it says on the prospectus. Stopping at the traffic lights, I take a quick look at myself in the mirror and smooth on some lip balm, tie back my faded blond hair and re-adjust my glasses: what the hell, I'll do. I amuse myself with a sing-a-long to The Cure ... *Friday I'm in Love* and my mood lifts a little.

I arrive at the school gates at 8.20 a.m., already the natives are restless; shirts in disarray, skirts the size of pelmets and me struggling with a bouquet of cream coloured flowers and a large bottle of spring water, neither of which are for me. They're for our honourable guest speaker who seems quite the diva: even M.D.'s have riders these days. I agreed to cover for Susan on her maternity leave and, although it's a short-term salary boost, offering careers advice to sixteen-year-old adolescents is hardly my forte.

Thankfully, that job rests with Mr. Ayden Stone, a 32 year old media magnate; he has the unenviable task of introducing our students to 'Career Opportunities in a Global Environment' – good luck with that Mr. Stone. Sounds very grand, but it will probably amount to a 20 minute Power-Point presentation and the handing out of some glossy leaflets which will end up on the locker room floor.

By 9.25 a.m. everything is ready, or as ready as it will ever be. I've set up the laptop and the overhead projector, arranged the flowers and provided a glass and his bottle of spring water ... anything else? Oh yes, he's insisted the students are silent during his presentation: if I couldn't guarantee it then he wouldn't come, so I guaranteed it. I'll deal with the fallout later. Someone from the office is going to bring him over and, once I've introduced him to the gathering, I'll leave him to it. He'll have an hour to enlighten and entertain or die an excruciatingly slow death.

There is the sound of footsteps on the stairs; I hold up my finger to the congregation indicating no talking. I fight the urge to nibble my thumbnail and instead occupy myself by realigning my glasses and straightening my skirt. There's a hushed silence. So far so good – welcome to the lion's den Mr. Stone.

The door opens and Margaret from the office limbos her way into the auditorium, carrying a box of what I assume are hand-outs. I'm not sure how to read her expression but, when the owner of the outstretched arm and the masculine hand appears, it hits me.

He's ...

I'm nailed to the spot by a vision. Before me is the recreation of a heavenly body; male beauty personified and deliciously wrapped like an expensive gift in navy blue.

Wow!

My eyes appraise him like a lift making its way from the lobby to the roof and I extend my hand; manners, yes manners, I remember those.

Ping! I just reached the penthouse ...

"Miss Parker?" He presents a heart-stopping smile that makes its way to an ocean of sea green eyes causing the skin around them to ripple slightly. It renders me temporarily senseless; for in those eyes I catch sight of a memory, something forgotten, a wish maybe? He's reaching out for my hand and I'm offering it instinctively. As we touch, I feel a kind of tingle that reaches down from my little finger to somewhere below my waistline and I forget to pull away.

"Mr. Stone, hello. Thank you for coming. Our students have been looking forward to your visit," I gush, hoping my welcome will disguise my nervousness. But we're not moving, we're standing, I'm still holding onto his hand, or is he holding onto mine?

"Please make your way to the stage. I have everything ready for you."

With a confidence born of wealth and achievement he descends, leaving a trail of Christian Dior or something just as evocative in his wake. I resist the temptation to lift up my head to get a whiff of sheer opulence and totter behind him as he strides fearlessly onto the stage.

"Good morning everyone. Thank you for waiting so patiently. I'm Ayden Stone and I run a company which you may have heard of called 'A.S. Media International.' He claims the stage, talks with confidence, and pours out a glass of spring water; he's even admiring the flowers, caressing the petals with his forefinger and thumb. I'm happy to watch.

There's a snigger from the back row and, with a nod of his head and a weighty pause, silence is restored. "You need to listen carefully because what you'll hear today may be a turning point for you or, at the very least, think of it as an hour out of the classroom."

There's that smile again. If I'm not mistaken, I think every female in the room is starting to swoon and that includes Margaret who is still perched by the doorway, holding what must now be a weighty parcel. I usher her down and she stomps her way to the front, places the box by the stage and leaves.

Mr. Stone doesn't miss a beat. I'm impressed and so is his audience: he's a gifted speaker. From the moment the first word leaves his mouth, he has their attention and gets right down to business by introducing his 'Pay Back Programme.' He spares them the customary rags to riches tale, assures them there are opportunities out there for the taking and, from their expressions, they believe him. That has a lot to do with the subject matter but even more to do with him being the kind of man who exudes power; he's become the centre of attention without even trying.

Half an hour in, I sit down and feel comfortable enough to take off my metaphoric teacher-in-charge hat. He has them eating out of his hand.

I steal a moment to take stock of him; he's very well-manicured from head to toe, but not so much that the rough edges have been filed away. Everything about him reeks of money and expensive taste. From the top of his raven black, just got out bed hair, rippling around his ears and licking at the edge of his collar ...

I swallow noisily and become aware of a quickening pulse.

Moving on ... his middle section isn't too bad either. His navy blue suit fits his lean frame like a glove and I wonder what it would be like to squeeze myself inside that glove. I tug at my skirt and glance round grateful my thoughts are my own. If ever a man personified male perfection, it's Mr. Ayden Stone.

Susan had arranged the event months ago and I never thought to check him out beforehand but, I'm checking him out now and what a feast for the eyes this man is, moving unselfconsciously around the stage. Right on cue, he draws his presentation to a close by answering questions which reflect some degree of intelligence and genuine interest.

I make my way to the stage. "So everyone, I'm sure you'd like to show your appreciation for Mr. Stone ..." There's spontaneous applause and I think he's quite taken by it; he attempts a theatrical bow and the students start filing out of the auditorium, some stopping to shake his hand.

"Well, that went well, Mr. Stone," I say with a polite smile, straightening my skirt and pulling down my blouse, feeling self-conscious. "You've done this before."

"Yes, a couple times," he answers, smiling in a way which might have a younger woman in a quiver.

"Can I get you anything, a coffee or some water maybe, or do you have places to go and people to see?" My weak attempt at humour forces a half smile, so I extend my hand to direct him off the stage.

"No, no places, no people. I'm all yours Miss Parker."

What a strange thing to say ...

Strange or not, that declaration is causing my body temperature to rise ever so slightly. I'm grateful I have my back to him. My sixth sense tells me he's checking out my derriere. I only wish I was wearing something more flattering.

"Great, then let's get something to drink." In one graceful movement he's at my side, making me feel a little intimidated, I'm not sure why. Perhaps it's his height and his self-possessed manner.

Once in the cafeteria, I pull out an inexpensive, lightweight chair for him. Clearly it's not what he's used to but this is my world and he's just visiting. I place down our chilled bottles of water, two paper cups and shake out my hands, pretending to warm them but really it's just a helpless attempt to stop them from trembling.

Instead of pouring out his water he sips it from the bottle, slowly tipping his head back to catch every drop. For some reason, this simple act of drinking and swallowing is so erotic. I try not to look but for two, maybe three seconds I'm staring. The water is bubbling and tumbling into his mouth, the rim is touching his exquisite lips and his tongue is coating his bottom lip with wetness, making it moist and glossy. Lost in the moment, I try to tear myself away, shifting my focus to *my* bottle top which is welded on. Damn it! Now is not the time to look ineffectual.

"Please let me ..." His perfect mouth forms into a flat line as he takes the bottle from my hand.

The touch of his fingers across mine is feather light, sending an electric current the full length of my arm and beyond. I detach my hand and pull my tingling fingers into a fist, allowing him to pour the water into my paper cup.

"Thank you, Mr. Stone. The art of chivalry is alive and kicking it seems," I say smartly, then wish I hadn't.

He does a kind of shrug that I have neither the concentration nor the skills to decode. Thinking on my feet, I fill the space with a compliment. "I must say, you've made quite an impression on our students today. They aren't usually that enthusiastic about careers advice."

"Thank you, not many teenagers know what they want to do at this age, they need guidance and for their talents to be recognised and nurtured."

That's a sensible answer.

"True. Is that what happened to you? Did you have someone who recognised your potential at an early age?" I'm genuinely interested and he seems eager to explain.

"No, not exactly. I came across an opportunity that others didn't recognise, modified it to improve the performance of existing applications and turned it into a profitable business, that's all. Wasn't it Machiavelli who said, "Entrepreneurs are simply those who understand there is little difference between obstacles and opportunity and are able to turn both to their advantage?""

"So you're a Prince among men?"

He sniggers at the suggestion. "Hardly."

"An entrepreneur then?"

"Yes, it's in my blood, but now I'm able to harvest the necessary blend of talents to expand my business, and that allows me to remain competitive. I strive to be good at everything. I like to win."

I'm happy to let him talk, transfixed by his stare; those azure eyes can make you forget every thought you have in your head - and they have. I feel my breasts heaving and I just know the skin around my neck is starting to glow. Silently, I'm praying the flames don't make their way to my cheeks.

What's happening to me?

"I see," is all I can conjure up out of nothing.

"What about you, how long have you been teaching?" His enquiry seems sincere enough and, what the hell, I've got all the time in the world.

"I came straight out of university into teaching so it's, what, six years now." I smile responsively.

Pull yourself together, he's a professional, you're a professional ...

"And do you think you'll remain in teaching or do you have other ambitions?"

He's asking me about ambitions? How can I think straight when he's playing around with his bloody bottle top. Keep still!

"I, I'm not sure. I enjoy teaching. I'm only 27, so I think I'll stick with it for now." I look anywhere but at him. I don't think he's noticed.

"Good, you should do what makes you happy. So much of my life is centred on my company. I envy you." After a thoughtful pause he continues with what feels like honesty. "That's why I started up the 'Pay Back Programme.' It's a small gesture but I like to think I'm making a difference, if only in a limited way. Of course I'm not educating the next generation like you ..."

"You're a fine role model for them, Mr. Stone: a capitalist and a humanitarian." I'm finding my feet in the conversation and justly rewarded with an amiable smile.

"If you say so, Miss. Parker." Discreetly, he checks his watch which probably cost him more than I earn in six months.

We've only been talking for ten minutes and already I'm boring him? I take hold of my paper cup and bottle. "You've been very gracious, Mr. Stone. I've taken up enough of your time. I'll let you go ..."

"Only if that's what you really want to do ..."

Did he just say what I think he said?

He's directing a molten stare my way; it's igniting the air around us and causing a rush of blood to my head, my face. "Well ... I suppose I could stay and chat ..." I pour out another mouthful of chilled water to douse the flames. Thank God I'm wearing my reading glasses because my pupils must be the size of footballs by now.

"Good, I'd like that." He repositions himself on the flimsy wooden chair directly in front of me, laying out his hands on the table in a kind of predatory stance, ready to pounce. "Tell me what interests you have, other than teaching."

Me? I swallow hard, shifting my focus between his hands and his eyes. I must look like a rabbit caught in the headlights of a Ferrari. I feel like one. "Oh, I like to read, listen to music, watch movies, visit friends, you know, the usual kind of thing. What about you?"

I follow his right hand, keeping my eyes on it as it leaves the table and settles on his chin. He's massaging the cutest dimple with his forefinger, contemplating his response. "Let me think ... I like to travel, go to the theatre, to keep in shape, and to fuck beautiful women ..."

He leaves those words hanging like a hot air balloon caught on electrical cables; they crackle and circulate the room, before creating a moment of uncomfortable silence. And that's when it hits me: you're toying with me Mr. Stone.

You arrogant bastard!

"Is that so? That must make you The Playboy of the Western World then, Mr. Stone?" I smile sweetly and tip my head to one side. The ball's in your court.

"I'm not a fan of Synge but I take your point. You're an English teacher, I presume?"

"Yes, full marks, I'm an English teacher, you know, plays, prose and poetry." I hold up my arms in a kind of ta da and he rewards my animation with a sexy smile.

"That's surprising," he muses, sounding so self-assured I could slap him, if only to feel a chiselled cheekbone against my palm. He leans over to my side of the table, forcing my back to straighten reflexively. "From where I'm sitting there seems to be more chemistry than poetry."

Bang! What a line!

I give him a well done smile and roll my eyes. He looks quite pleased with himself. "Did you make that up on the spot or is it one you save for occasions such as this?"

"No, it was a one off just for you, Miss Parker." He leans back in the seat, forcing it to creak under the strain, taking great delight in watching me squirm.

"Then thank you, Mr. Stone." I offer a formal nod and try to suppress a smile. Another comment like that and I'll spontaneously combust and my insides will cascade across this table like spaghetti.

"Ayden, my name's Ayden," he states. "And you are?"

"Elizabeth, Beth."

"I like the name, it's solid, traditional."

"I suppose it is, but Beth's fine."

It's just a name ...

"May I ..."

Just when I think I'm holding my own and I've got the measure of him, he hits me with a sucker punch. He removes my glasses with both hands without touching my face, breathes on the lenses and proceeds to clean them with his blue, silk tie. Even without the glasses I feel his eyes on me, sharp and scrutinising, stripping me of my self-imposed disguise.

He looks at the lenses against the light. "There you are, that's better. Now you can see things more clearly."

Things, what things?"

"You have beautiful eyes, Beth, the colour of a summer sky. You shouldn't hide behind your glasses." He hands them back.

Summer sky? Where is he getting these lines?

"I'm not hiding," I answer defensively. "I can't read without them and that's quite important for an English teacher." I settle them more comfortably on my nose.

"Indeed it is, forgive me." He tilts his chin and launches a rocket of a stare my way. I try to launch one back but he's too skilled in what feels like verbal foreplay and, defeated, I glance away. I chew my thumbnail and breathe ...

"Can I get you anything else ... Ayden?" I ask, brusquely. "I'm afraid I have a lesson in 10 minutes and I need to prepare for it." Looking purposeful, I gather the bottles and stand.

He seems unsettled by my assertion. "Yes ... of course, I hadn't realised. What are you teaching?" He stands and fastens his jacket, once again adopting that model pose.

I throw the cups and bottles into the rubbish bin and head towards the door. "The sonnets, you know, 'Should I compare thee to a summer's day ...'" I stop, realising what I've said and smile coyly.

"How apt. 'Thou art more lovely, and more temperate'" He smiles broadly, enjoying my look of genuine surprise.

"You're fond of the sonnets?"

"Not especially, I'm more of a Romantics man myself."

"I find that hard to believe," I huff, starting up my mouth before my brain is in gear.

I'm met with a bemused smile which only lingers for a second, but it's there. I change the subject quickly. "I assume you're parked at the front of the building?"

He nods. Before reaching the door, he stops abruptly and I turn to see why. He's rubbing the back of his neck with his right hand as if there's a tense spot that he can't reach. "Look, Beth ..."

"... Please Mr. Stone, Ayden ... you don't have to say anything. It's been a pleasure meeting you, really it has. I've enjoyed the 'I'm all yours,' the smouldering looks, and the chemistry thing was very clever but, if you don't mind, I have to go back to my world now, and you have to go back to yours."

For some reason he is taken aback by my directness. In fact, a veil of sadness has descended upon his face, sharpening his stunning features. "So you think we're worlds apart do you?" There's that scorching stare again.

"Well aren't we? In your world, people react to you in a certain way and I get that."

"... You mean women?"

"Yes, I mean women. You know what you're doing and you do it so well. What can I say?" The words ricochet out of my mouth but I'm not entirely sure I want them to find their target.

"But sometimes Miss Parker, worlds collide." There's only the trace of a half-smile, but his sparkling eyes are intense and questioning.

"Yes they do, but it usually ends in tears." I reinforce my declaration with a carefree shrug and look away.

"Touché," he concedes, pressing his lips together, nodding but not appearing entirely convinced.

I reach out to shake his hand, prepping myself for another power surge. I've done myself proud ... if that's the case, then how is it this man is affecting me so, is tormenting my senses and breaching all my defences?

"It's been an interesting morning, Miss Parker. *How* was it for you?" His crooked smile reaches up to the corners of his eyes which now, in the morning sunlight, have taken on a kind of cerulean iridescence: they bewitch me. The cool morning air has breathed new life into his handsome face and I'm spellbound, caught up in his ethereal beauty. We're sharing a private joke and the space between us has become incredibly intimate.

"It's been ..." I take a dramatic pause, adopt a thinking stance and turn to face him. "Entertaining."

"I won't argue with that." He nods his head in agreement and I realise he still has hold of my sweaty palm and his thumb is brushing across my hand, stroking my feverish skin, creating a silent but not unfamiliar bond. He leans into me and kisses the corner of my mouth, and I find myself moving into him. My lips are parted, anticipating something more.

"It's been an education, Miss Parker," he whispers softly, so close I can feel the warm air leaving his mouth, caressing my cheek.

Standing on my tiptoes I reciprocate and kiss the corner of his mouth, catching the essence of masculine heat and expensive cologne: it's an intoxicating mélange. Breathless, I put my lips to his ear and say softly. "But you didn't win, Mr. Stone."

When I pull away I am met with an expression I can't read; it looks a lot like affection, but there's mischief lurking in those eyes and a silent promise of ... something.

The school bell sounds and I focus my attention anywhere but on him, it'll be easier that way. "Saved by the bell," I say in an airy whisper. "Goodbye, Mr. Stone. Have a safe journey." Leaving him in the safe hands of his chauffeur, I turn and walk away.

My classroom door closes behind me with a slam. What just happened? With that whisper of a kiss he has awakened something in me. I feel as if a great weight has been lifted from my heart, a spell broken. I feel alive.

I'm cooling in the afterglow, having been charred by the scorching rays of something hot and unbidden. I'm gasping, moisture oozing from my body, heat flaying my skin. Dear God! This can't be normal. Two words are forever etched into my consciousness: Ayden Stone.

The day comes to a welcome end. All I can think about is climbing into my car and being alone with my sensual thoughts. For some reason, I'm exhausted but unsure why. Who am I kidding, after the morning I've had and the inquisition I faced at lunchtime, I'm lucky to still be standing.

Margaret had gone to great lengths to spread the word: Ayden Stone is a babe magnet, or was it a fine specimen? Probably both. Female colleagues were Googling him and a thousand photos appeared, 70% of which included stunning women of five foot ten plus, draping themselves over his arm or around his shoulders like poison ivy. What could I say: he hit on me, he took off my glasses and cleaned them with his tie, and he even mentioned chemistry for God's sake? They wouldn't believe it - I don't believe it. Instead, I said he was self-assured, polite and cultured. I wasn't lying, but I did fail to mention I'd probably lost three pounds in perspiration.

Thankfully, the rest of the day passed without further incident and now I'm grateful to be left alone to my own devices, to drive home with only Sting urging my beating heart to still. I relive our conversation over and over: 'I could have said this' and 'I should have said that.' But I'd had my fifteen minutes and blown them in sterling fashion.

When I enter my ground floor apartment, there's the fragrance of fresh flowers. I think nothing of it until I set foot in the kitchen. There, placed in my biggest vase, is an enormous bouquet courtesy of my obliging neighbour: blue hydrangeas, crème roses, lilies, lavender limonium, and salal in cobalt blue: so it says on the card. My first thought is, whose are these? My second thought is: Ayden Stone.

Unable to contain a cry of unparalleled delight, I throw down my bag, lift out the card from its envelope, and read the hand written note:

Where true Love burns Desire is Love's pure flame;
It is the reflex of our earthly frame,
That takes its meaning from the nobler part,
And but translates the language of the heart.
X

There's only one person who would send me flowers, and there's only one person who would think to include a poem called 'Desire' written by Coleridge. That would have to be a self-confessed 'Romantics man.' It's a powerful message, so romantic and - it's for me!

I put the card next to my lips and think of where it's been: in his hands, between his finger and thumb, perhaps he even blew across it to dry the ink? He knows I'll recognise the poem and, more importantly, he knows I'll understand it.

It must be the heady perfume from the bouquet that causes my head to spin: I'm stunned. I realise I'm holding my breath and, for fear of actually fainting, I exhale. I catch my reflection in a pane of glass and come face to face with a young woman with wide blue eyes the colour of a summer sky and an 'O' shaped mouth: it's me.

Time for a reality check: is this just a game, an attempt to draw me in, to have me fall at his feet, merely to satisfy his ego? In the space of five minutes my feelings go from elation and sheer delight, to rock bottom disappointment. I should know better, men don't respond to me *that* way. But he has ... and the flowers are so lovely and, besides, who hand writes a poem like that just for fun? Maybe Ayden Stone does?

For the hundredth time, I run through our conversation and I'm smiling. I'm also a little flushed just remembering the way he threw his head back to drink and how the thick band of platinum wrapped around the middle finger of his left hand, and the way he played with the bottle top and ... I shudder myself out of the memory, feeling a twinge of something that simply isn't decent at 5 o'clock on a Monday afternoon. No-one has ever made me feel quite so out of control.

I pour myself a tall smoothie and nibble on a quiche. On my kitchen table is my copy of Pride and Prejudice and on my mind is my favourite quote: *"The very first moment I beheld him, my heart was irrevocably gone."* What am I thinking?

I quickly rid myself of that foolish thought and begin my research. Let's see who you are Mr. Stone.

As I read his biography, I realise he really is a self-made man: born 1980, London; spent most of his childhood in a residential care home and wasn't adopted until he was 12 years of age. Young Entrepreneur of the year 1998, having been the brain child of 'A.S. Media International.' Included in the U.K top 20 Rich List in 2000 and set up the 'Pay Back Programme' in 2010. There are rows and rows of achievements that just fill the page: he's the real deal.

My eyes fill with bubbling tears. I'm overcome with regret, not because of a missed opportunity but because I behaved unforgivably. Towards the end of our conversation, he tried to speak but I wouldn't let him. Was he trying to articulate the words he has so eloquently included in a poem? Will I ever get the chance to say I'm sorry?

My mind is in turmoil. He was right, sometimes worlds do collide; it might end in tears but, who gives a fuck? I've spent my whole life waiting for a 'collision' just like this.

Bedtime brings little rest. I wrestle with my pillow and struggle to find a settling thought. I have visions of a neglected and broken boy and my heart aches. I find solace in the fact that he's tough and he's come through the flames like a blazing phoenix. Nothing fazes him, not even the possibility of rejection. What did I whisper in his ear? "You didn't win Mr. Stone." I want to take it back.

Scattered on my carpet are pictures of him; they're like fragments of a puzzle I may never get the chance to piece together. That's the thought that has me tossing and turning for most of the night.

***

Dan Rizler takes a cigarette from the packet, taking care not to crush the filter between his finger and thumb. He's a former boxer; he claims to have the strength of two men and considers his hands to be his weapons of mass destruction. No-one messes with Dan.

It's 0500hrs. Most mornings begin the same way, with a hard on. The trick is to keep his eyes shut tight; his special girl lives behind them, in that secret place that only they know. If he peeks, their precious moment is lost and the image of her vaporises, leaving nothing more than a fading ghost.

The cold shower purges him of his brutish notions and leaves him to shave unhampered by further hauntings. He takes his time shaving, tracing the outline of his firm jaw, watching the brown hues return to his eyes. There was a time when the ladies found those dark brown magnets irresistible. They would do anything for him. All it took was a nod and a wink and they'd be his for the taking. The recollections of backroom antics and bouts of all night boozing, make his mouth twitch. Wiping the foam from his cheeks, he reassures himself, "You've still got it, Danny boy."

At 39, he's the youngest of a four man team of maintenance men at The University of Cambridge. He takes his job seriously, likes the shift work. He considers checking out the 'pretty young things' a perk of the job, that and the free lunches.

He leaves early to beat the rush hour traffic, knowing the A10 will be clear and he'll be able to make good time. He prides himself on his timekeeping. He's never late. That's something he learned in the army: be punctual and be prepared. It's his mantra and his guiding principle.

First stop, his locker. Speaking to no-one in particular he mutters, "I bet that bitch in E4 has put another complaint in about me ... you know what she needs? A good seeing to. If I had the time, I'd pay her a visit one night and wipe that fucking smile off her face." He's straightening his back, lifting his head to gain extra inches, increasing his physical presence: being six foot four and 15 stone just isn't big enough.

He spits out something under his breath, it sounds like "bitch," but his footsteps cover the sound and it becomes nothing more than a hiss.

With a kick and a tug, his locker door opens and he checks to see if anyone is around, there's no way he's going to share *her*. Tucked away under a prospectus is a photo. The faded picture is of a pretty, dark haired girl in her late teens, wearing a pair of jeans and a black sweater. He rubs his thumbs over the sweater and his breathing quickens at the thought of sliding his hand up inside. He knows what he's doing, he's seen it on the internet; getting her hot and ready won't be a problem for him. The snapshot is one of his favourites, that's why it's there. How could he be expected to start the day without her? It's one of hundreds he took with an expensive camera with a zoom lens that cost him over a week's wage. "Worth every penny," he growls, salivating over her delicate frame.

A short burst of adrenalin triggers his breathing and those accustomed feelings travel at the speed of light to his groin, making him hard, again. He slides his hand down inside his boxers and touches himself, smiling and whispering, "I'm saving this for you, princess."

The sound of approaching footsteps ends his special moment. He scowls and slams the locker door shut.

A cheerful looking fellow of around fifty with thinning brown hair and glasses sidles up next to him. "Alright Dan? You're early?"

"Mornin' Ernie, traffic was light, made good time." He doesn't like to chat, but he's known Ernie a while and they've had a few laughs.

They undress, keeping their backs to each other and put on the required black work pants and T-shirt, with the added bonus of the University insignia. It's not what he'd wear given the choice, but it gets him into all kinds of places that an everyday outfit would not. How many times had he been called upon to unblock the toilets in the ladies' changing room at the gym and forgotten to mention that he was in there? The prospect of scoring another job like that gets him through the day.

"Hope we've not a lot on, Monday's can be busy. Fingers crossed, eh?" Ernie closes his locker.

"Yeah, but I think it'll take more than crossing fingers to stop this fucking lot from making work for us."

"You're right there. Do you know what the buggers did outside Lamont? They filled the sculpture with cans and bottles. And they're supposed to be the bright ones?"

"You don't have to tell me, Ernie. I was called over to the undergrad dorms and some bastard had busted a shower, torn it right off the fucking wall. Took me half a day to put it right."

"And I bet you didn't get so much as a kiss my arse?"

"Wouldn't have been so bad if I had. There were a couple of nice little arses I wouldn't have minded kissing or bending over a desk." That thought touches a nerve and he sits down to fasten his laces, giving himself time to settle.

Ernie pats him on the back. "I'll leave that to you champ. I'm a bit too old for that kind of talk."

"No problem, I can handle your share," Dan calls out after him, still feeling the after effect of something sweet between his legs.

"I'll check the jobs list and we'll draw straws for toilet duty. Ladies or gents, you're welcome to it. Gets my guts rollin' that smell. Puts me right off my lunch." He's sticking out his tongue like a lizard tasting the air.

"Leave it to me, Ernie. I'm used to clearing up other fuckers' shit. I hold my breath and count to sixty. By then, the worse bit's over." Dan stands tall, his chest fills out his work shirt; he's fearless.

Ernie checks his watch and compares it to the one on the wall. "You're a good lad, Dan. We'd better make a move. Can't stand here, chatting all day. Shit happens." They share the joke and stroll towards the office, Dan at the rear and Ernie in his shadow.

It's 1500hrs, the journey home to Ely only takes Dan forty minutes but he can do it in thirty on a good day, minus the tourists.

"Hello. Honey, I'm home," he calls out to his golden coloured cat, the only female he has ever cared about, bar one.

His one bedroom, ground floor flat is no more than two rooms and a bathroom, slotted together into a tidy matchbox shape. For a man of his size it's adequate, or it would be if it wasn't for the piles of newspapers and magazines stacked like stalagmites along every wall. There is only one special area, his favourite place, facing his cork noticeboard where he stands and remembers.

His face casts a ruggedly handsome reflection in the window pane as he fills the kettle with water. A mug of hot tea, that's what he needs. He relaxes a little, feeling Honey weaving herself around his ankles, not for attention but for food. His awesome frame towers above her but she isn't intimidated by his size. He gives her what she wants and her behaviour is merely instinctive.

"There you go, Honey." He amuses himself with the endearment. "Get your teeth into that and I'll tell you all about my day." He scrapes out the remains of a half empty can of cat food and leaves it by his feet. "Let's have half an hour to ourselves. Then I'll get to work. We've a job to do, I feel lucky tonight."

He places the day's newspapers and magazines on the battered sofa, throws yesterday's take-away box off the single chair into a black bin bag and plonks himself down. On his knee rests a new pizza box: it's cheese and pepperoni. He hits the news channel on his TV remote and lets it wash over him; he lives in the present, but his thoughts reside in the past. Distant memories are as vivid now as they were seven years ago. Letting go simply is not an option.

Fifteen minutes later, with the sizzling taste of pepperoni and cheese tingling his taste buds, he prepares to start the night shift. He is not a man to shy away from work, especially when it's the same thing he did yesterday and the day before, and the day before that ... looking for her.

The chair seems to give a grateful wheeze when he eases himself out of it and makes his way over to the kitchen table, carrying today's purchases under his left arm. They drop onto the pine table with a thud and sit patiently waiting to be scanned for any trace of her. Laid out on the table is his equipment, tools for the job: a pair of scissors, a pad and a pencil at the ready to take notes to plan, to orchestrate an abduction or, at the very least, the consummation of a sexual encounter left unfinished.

An antiquated computer stands tall at one end of the table. Any minute now it will be coughing and spluttering its way around the internet, pausing to catch its breath on social network sites like Facebook and Twitter. It may have been almost seven years but that's nothing to him; he's determined, ruthless, and unrelenting in his search for Frances Parker.

Before starting his labour of love he glances up at his noticeboard at the hundreds of faded photographs, held up by coloured stickpins. Some of the photographs have become frosted and blurred over time, others have yellowed around the edges but, there is no mistaking one fact, they are of the same person: his obsession, his girl, his princess.

Around the board is a length of dusty, gold tinsel, a left over from six Christmas' ago. The memory of the Christmas he spent with her in his head, in his bed, it's on replay. So much so, it shifts and changes with every new recollection, each time there's a new addition; each time a confirmation of their festive union. How does something that was once fantasy become corporal - it just does!

It's 0100hrs and another wasted night. No sign of her, but he knows she's out there, thinking about him, waiting for him. Every night he gets one step nearer to finding her.

He stands eye to eye with her faded image, remembering her smell, her voice and that look in her eyes. It excites him, makes him hard and ready. His mouth opens slightly and his hands unwrap, pinning her to the noticeboard with human hand cuffs.

"I'm going to find you, princess."

2

I drive to work, weary from lack of sleep and emotionally drained. Every time I catch my reflection, my eyes are saying 'sorry.' Adele sings on the radio, *Don't you Remember?* I sniff and take her words to heart. How will I ever get through the day?

When I get to my classroom, I give myself time to regroup. I switch to autopilot mode, with no sense of purpose or direction. I rummage through my bag and find a couple of painkillers to ease the self-inflicted agony.

Please let the day pass quickly...

After my final lesson of the day, I head home and wish for more strength and less regret, or at least an equal measure of the two. My upstairs neighbour is waiting to ambush me.

"So who's the lucky fellow then?" she asks cheerfully. "You must have an admirer, Beth?"

"Hello, Pat, I suppose I must but I can't imagine who." I fiddle with my key and push open the door to my apartment. "Thanks for taking the flowers in for me, I appreciate it. Bye." Not soon enough, I close the door.

Dinner is a simple affair, a small tuna salad and an apple. Not a lot of sustenance but all I can force down under the circumstances. For some reason, this empty house seems like a vacuous space, there is no air. I barely have the strength to breathe, so heavy is the weight on my chest. Everything I own resides here, rests on the floor, covers the walls and sits in drawers; and what do my meagre possessions say about me? Alone with a capital 'A'.

I collect my mail and throw the bills to one side. There's a plain lemon envelope which looks like a birthday card or an invitation. I open it and there's a ticket to the new production of Romeo and Juliet at the Apollo Theatre in the West End for tomorrow evening. It's a single ticket and I think I know who has the other. It has a tell-tale cross in the bottom left hand corner, much like the soft kiss that lingers at the corner of my mouth.

Maybe it's the effect of the salad, but I feel suddenly energised. For the first time today I exhale; it seems like I've been holding my breath for far too long or, maybe, I've been holding out for something, for someone?

I collect the photographs off the floor and slip them into a drawer. This time tomorrow I'll be face to face with the real thing but there's so much to do before then, like finding something to wear.

I switch on Britney singing *Piece of Me* and skip off into my bedroom. Before she hits the chorus I'm dancing in my one designer dress and stomping in heels I've never worn, hoping I'll find something that won't reveal my ordinariness to this prince of a man.

Just to be on the safe side, I want to enlist the help of my best friend Charlie. She's an urban firecracker with flaming red hair and a perfect smile; a city girl who's paid too much and knows how to spend what she earns, usually on socialising and herself. I'll need her help if I'm going to pull this off.

All it takes is a phone call and she's knocking on my door in 50 minutes. Over her arm are what look like 20 dresses of varying colours and lengths: what a lifesaver. Under sufferance, I try, twirl and discard until we have two contenders; a red smock dress that sits just over my knee or a fitted silver, grey cocktail dress that's slightly shorter but with a less revealing neck line.

"It's a winner," Charlie announces, seeming even more excited than I am. Some things never change, she's the same red headed girl I knew at university but slightly taller with straighter teeth.

Caught up in the excitement of it all, she blows a stray piece of hair from her face and issues another round of instructions: "Hair, nails and legs," and I wonder if it might not be easier to give her the ticket. So much to do and so little time - on a school night too!

By 9.30, I'm almost done and I'm sitting in a bath with a face mask on while she's giving me a manicure. The bath is filled with bubbles and the oils ripple around my softening skin like a luxury spa. I'm enjoying being pampered. It's a new experience for me.

"There, all we need now is two coats of varnish and you're done and dusted." Charlie is proud of her handy work. She goes to refill our glasses with more chilled Chardonnay and I step out of the bath; the soft folds of the bathrobe glide over my baby soft skin and I hug myself. The bathroom is a sauna and I can't see for steam, but I know I'm glowing and that has something to do with the oils, but more to do with the thought of seeing Ayden Stone again. I'm getting a second chance to shine.

Once again sleep doesn't come easily, but for different reasons. There's a trace of regret, but I hold onto the promise of redemption and it comforts me. I dream of wild azure eyes and soft kisses, and awake to the sound of an angry alarm clock. It's a new day.

Wednesday is a blur. Every lesson takes care of itself and I'm totally preoccupied. From midday onwards I have butterflies in my stomach and, at one point, actually feel I might bring back my lunch. It's like being 16 again, only I was never like this at 16. I consider myself to have been what my father reliably called 'an ugly duckling' and I trusted his judgement. Most of my boyfriends developed out of friendship and when romantic liaisons came to a natural end, I'd suffer the indignation of losing both a boy and a friend. But, I'm captain of my own ship, so come hell and high water, I'm ready for you, Ayden Stone.

It's 6.15 p.m., I'm almost done and Charlie has arrived to give me the once-over. She finishes off my hair and make-up and leaves me to dress. I take a look at her masterpiece in the mirror and I'm pleasantly surprised. By choice, I've put myself on the back burner for almost seven, long years and here I am all fired up and full of anticipation. I take one last look. "Welcome back, Beth." An undetectable smile caresses my lips and I head off to make my dramatic entrance.

Charlie gasps and holds her hand to her mouth in mock horror.

"That bad, eh?" I screw my face into a grimace.

"No, no, Beth. You look amazing. Who knew, under all those stuffy shirts and pleated pants was a babe just waiting to get out. He'll have such a hard on when he sees you."

Oh! Now there's a thought ...

She runs over and gives me a hug. "I'll drive you to Shaftsbury Avenue. I want you to stay just like that: gorgeous. Put your glasses in your bag honey, we both know you don't need them. Let this lucky bastard get a look at your sexy blue eyes." She swerves her hips at me and we laugh like a couple a teenagers. I really like her, she's more like a sister than a friend and I can tell her anything. She knows all my secrets. I catch a shawl she throws over to me and head out in the direction of her new Audi, giving my sorry looking Fiesta an apologetic smile.

En route, she lists the dating do's and don'ts and I pretend to listen, but I have my own thoughts to contend with. She has us singing along to her hits of the 80's CD and, as luck would have it, Shalamar just about set the tone with a *Night to Remember*.

By the time we reach the theatre I'm feeling nervous, not the frightened kind, but the kind that comes from having high expectations. Could he be the one I've been waiting for? Has he found me?

Charlie bolsters my resolve. "Look, you can do this, Beth. I know it's been a while but friggin' hell, any guy should be lucky to have you. Just look at you! You're Cinderella! Now go to that friggin' ball and knock him dead."

I check my simple make-up, ensure there's nothing stuck between my teeth and step out of the car. I call out, "Thanks, Char, I couldn't have done this without you." And it's a fact.

"You know where I am if you need me. See ya."

I wave her off and head towards the crowd, considering at what point my life became a hopeless fairy-tale: that would be the day I learned there are wolves out there, I suppose.

I can see him, but he has no idea I'm here. I've entered by the side door and I really think, for once in my life, lady luck is on my side. I blend myself into the flock wallpaper and digest him from the shoelaces up. He seems taller than I remember and he isn't wearing a suit but black, tailored trousers that must have been made to measure. He has a lean body, broad shoulders and there's the suggestion of muscles, taut and firm in all the right places. His right hand is in his pocket and the front of his blazer pulls back slightly, drawing attention to his crisp white shirt and the firm package underneath and ... is there a hint of chest hair on his collarbone? I can feel myself blushing and imagining what he must look like naked; I wish I'd brought a fan or something to waft away my carnal thoughts. I lick my lips lasciviously at the thought of his mouth on my skin kissing, licking, tasting ...

My God what am I thinking?

I manage to control my breathing, but the air leaving my body is so much hotter on the way out than on the way in. Forcing down a lump in my throat, I continue my visual exploration of Ayden Stone and here comes the best bit: his flawless face. The light in the foyer isn't stark; it's created by two stunning chandeliers hanging to his left and right. Hampered only by limited shadow, I'm able to focus on his eyes; framed by heavy brows, they're darting from left to right, catching every speck of light like polished glass, shimmering with an incredible luminosity. Even from this distance they're dazzling and hypnotic. How will I hold onto a rational thought when I'm being ensnared by them like a tiny, helpless creature? He'll chew me up and spit me out and take no delight in the snack. Even his liquorish coloured hair serves to frame his staggering manliness; it's carelessly dried and may still be wet, and I fantasize about how those black flicks will feel between my hot fingers.

I'm sighing ... just look at him, he's breathtakingly gorgeous.

But, I'm so out of practice. It's been a year since I went on a date and even then it was arranged *for* me. Talk about diving in at the deep end ... what should I do - leave?

I glance over to him again, he's checking his watch; it's now or never. I take one last look and make the mistake of examining his bone structure and that makes walking away even harder: a sharp and well-defined jawline, a Romanesque nose and an upper lip that forms into that perfect pouting 'v.'

Be still my beating heart ...

Classic sculptures of the male form come to mind, Michelangelo's David or Prometheus: he could give them a run for their money. If she were alive, my mother would tell me to be careful what I wish for, but he *is* what I wish for and I thank my lucky stars he's here, impatient and waiting for me.

I exit the building, taking in the fresh evening air, preparing myself for my grand entrance. I re-enter via the foyer, pausing to look around. I catch his eye and he removes his hand from his pocket and fastens his jacket. He's all smiles and fuck-me eyes and my heart starts to beat through my clothes. I've simply got to calm down.

Dodging the other theatre goers we move toward each other; I feel like a moth being drawn to an irresistible flame that will incinerate me with its smouldering beauty; but I refuse to give in to the temptation to skip or run, I refuse.

This is it.

He reaches for me with both hands and takes hold of my shoulders so I can't look away. Just as I knew they would, his eyes burn into me; he's assessing me like I'm some kind of precious object or oil painting. His gaze rests on my face and I can't shake free. It's like a gravitational pull and, as hard as I try, those dazzling flecks of blue and green hold me captive.

With a thankful sigh, he declares, "Miss. Parker, you look stunning." Before resting his mouth a millimetre from mine, he says softly, "I knew you would."

Another great line, he's really good at this.

I find my voice. "You look pretty good yourself, Mr. Stone. Thank you for the invitation and the compliment."

He offers me his arm. "Would you like a drink before the play starts?" He places his hand over mine as if we're an old married couple. It feels warm, firm, protective.

"That would be nice." I'm becoming more self-assured with every step. He seems to think we look good together, and who am I to question his judgment. I lick my lips, anticipating the drink. My mouth is so dry, I can feel the moisture leaving the corners and a sticky residue forming.

"What would you like to drink, Miss Parker?" His words have such a rich cadence that I can hear them ringing in my ears after he's spoken. I'd forgotten the refined way he articulates his words, like they've been cultivated over time; the English language is in safe hands.

"Dry white wine please, and it's Beth."

"Very well, it's dry white wine and it's Beth from now on," he declares, brushing my left arm with the knuckles of his right hand.

His touch causes the hairs to stand up on the back of my neck and my back to straighten.

Is he doing it on purpose?

He hands me the wine, turns to face me and offers a toast. "To new beginnings ..." Strangely, as if on cue, we present matching smiles.

"To new beginnings ..." But I so want to say, 'Look, I know I was rude the other day ...' but before I can get the words out ...

"... You've managed to get here in one piece without your glasses, I see." He seems to be finding something rather amusing.

"Yes, who knew... just don't ask me to read you anything off the wine list."

What a stupid thing to say. Why would he ask me to do that?

"I'll try to remember." He winks at me, so I sip my wine and try to avoid those probing orbs of iridescent light.

I remember the flowers. "By the way, thank you for the lovely bouquet and the Samuel Taylor Coleridge poem; that was a surprising addition. It gave me something to think about." I'm feeling a little braver and turn to engage him. "But I suppose that's why you included it?"

He refuses to be baited. "I'm glad you liked the flowers and enjoyed the poem, it's a favourite of mine and, before you ask, no it's not one I save for occasions like that. It was a one off, just for you."

I try to stifle a smile. "I see. Then I'm very flattered." Blown away would be nearer the mark. Nervously, I play with my rings and prepare to make small talk. "So, how's your day been, Mr. Stone?"

I can't believe I just said that.

"Pretty good, although I have to say it's getting better by the minute, and please call me Ayden."

I love the way those two syllables come together, Ay-den ...

When the bell sounds for the start of the play, I sigh with relief. I'm fighting to hold onto my composure and that's virtually impossible with my insides insisting on doing somersaults.

"That's a nice thing to say, Ayden."

He leans into me and, startled, I tip back a little. "What can I say, I'm a *nice* guy." He throws that out there, just waiting for me to catch it.

"I don't doubt it." I pull my lips together, forcing myself to say no more, but Mr. Stone there's so much more I could say in response to that. You're toying with me – again. "Do you come to the West End often?"

Now I'm really scraping the barrel.

"Not as often as I'd like. What about you?" He has me in his sights again.

"Not as often as I'd like, parking can be a problem."

"Yes it can. But that can be said of so many cities around the world. Thankfully, I don't have *that* problem."

"Why, don't you drive?"

His mouth twitches slightly. "I have a chauffeur, Beth, parking is his problem, not mine."

"Lucky you," I reply, much too tersely.

He broadens his smile in such a dangerous way it almost causes me to fall of my chair. "Indeed, lucky me. I feel *very* blessed."

Now he's teasing, making me laugh or is it a giggle? He's laughing softly too and his eyes are alight with amusement. I'm no expert, but I think we just connected. Then again, what do I know? Either way, I'm becoming more physically aware of him by the second. He's doing something very indecent to my libido.

I think I'm being seduced.

With a playful glint he massages his chin with his forefinger, letting it roll in and out of that delicious dimple. "Perhaps we should carry out a kind of survey and check out the parking arrangement in other cities?"

Is he being serious?

With girlish enthusiasm I play along. "I hear Rome can be quite congested."

"Well there we are, let's go to Rome and check." He stands and takes my arm.

Remaining seated, I offer a down turned smile. "No, I can't. I'm sorry."

"Why ever not?" He mimics my expression.

"It's a school night."

"Of course," he says, as if he should have known. "Nevertheless, I hear Rome is nice this time of year."

I'm finding it impossible to conceal just how much I'm enjoying his company and partaking in our silly conversation. In fact, I can't remember when I *ever* had this much fun with a man, with or without clothes on.

"Rome's nice at any time of year," I say confidently. "Or so I've been told."

He ushers me towards the door, stopping to whisper in my ear. "Then we'll have to go."

Effortlessly, he takes my hand. With a spring in my step I accompany him through one door and then another and up a flight of stairs, until we enter a private box overlooking the stage. It's red and plush and beautiful.

"A box to ourselves? This is lovely, Ayden."

He directs me towards the seat on the left overlooking the stage while he moves towards the seat on the right, next to an ice bucket with the neck of a rather expensive looking bottle of something sticking out of it.

"Can I pour you a glass of champagne, Beth?" he asks with so much self-assurance it makes me think, *you've done this before.*

"Why not, you seem to be going to such a lot of trouble on my behalf and, I have to say I'm a little taken aback." It's true, who does this?

"Believe me it's nothing, I didn't want to ... overwhelm you." He considers his words carefully.

"Then you've succeeded. I'm flattered but not overwhelmed." I flutter my eyelashes and dismiss the idea with a hand gesture which makes us both smile.

"Good. Let's watch the play and then we can get to know each other."

With that, the curtain rises and I'm left with a full glass of champagne and a brain working overtime, analysing the word 'know?'

Does he mean in the Biblical sense?

Every so often I turn out of politeness to share a moment and catch him studying me, but I'm so consumed by the events in the play I let it go. I start to worry when the interval approaches at the end of Act 3 Scene 1. Both Mercutio and Tybalt are dead and my heart starts its relentless, palpating reminder that I'm here with the most charming and seductive man on the planet.

"What do you think of the production?" he asks, moving closer to top up my glass of champagne.

I realise something ... he knows this is my thing, he wants me to feel comfortable around him, not squirming and simmering like before. He wants to see the real me. I like that. "Well, I've seen this company before and what they lack in experience they make up for in enthusiasm. A lot of attention's been paid to the fight scenes, with some improvisation, but there just hasn't been the right degree of sensitivity. The young protagonists are teenagers, it's their naivety and disregard for mature decision making that brings about their tragic death, but I wish they were more credible as star crossed lovers ... "

"... And breathe." He has a glint in his eye and my suspicions were right. He holds onto my fingers to steady my glass and tops up my champagne. His hand feels hot to the touch, but not as hot as mine.

"I'm sorry, but you did ask," I respond innocently, forgetting myself and allowing my thumb nail to edge into my mouth.

"No, please continue." He removes my hand from my mouth, places it on my knee and gestures for me to go ahead, but I've lost my nerve now.

"I like watching you when you're not self-conscious." He strokes my arm with the knuckles of his left hand and I turn away, giving my body time to recover from the double dose of his touch.

Finding some semblance of self-control, I ask, "Why do you like watching me?" I'm not sure I'm ready for his answer, but I have to ask. He pins me in my seat with a look I cannot recollect ever having to decipher before. I can't look away.

"Why? Because I'm drawn to beautiful things, Beth, and you are beautiful." He takes a dramatic pause. "What makes you all the more desirable is the realisation that you have no idea just how lovely you are." Words leave his mouth smoothly like icing from a piping bag, creating swirls in the air. He moves to stroke my arm again but he rethinks his gesture when he sees my reaction.

"I think you're toying with me, Mr. Stone. I've done my homework and I'm not deluded enough to think you're being entirely genuine when you say things like that to someone like me. They're fine words, but please don't ruin a wonderful evening. No games." He wants me to find my voice, and here it is.

There's a serious look! "You think this is a game? What would be my motivation?"

"Motivation?" Here goes nothing. "To seduce me, I suppose." The words leave my lips like droplets of water on blistering metal and he seems to visibly sizzle before me.

"I see." He contemplates his next question, leans into me and studies my face for clues. "Do you want to be seduced?"

Of course I do, yes please.

His stare burns through me like hot lava, causing my insides to ignite; he's started a fire in me. "I don't know." I return my attention to the stage.

"Don't look away, look at me!" He's stern and his tone is austere. He tips up my chin with his forefinger so I have nowhere to hide. "I'll only ask this once. What do you feel when you're with me, I need to know?"

How can I begin to explain? I inhale deeply and breathe him in. "I ... I'm nervous around you because you're so handsome and I'm not used to being around men like you." I pause timidly, unsure of myself. "You're very charismatic and the things you say to me and the way you look at me are intense." I'm losing my nerve. "Y ... you make me sweat and I imagine doing things with you but I know I can't have you, and that makes me think you're being cruel by playing a game I have no hope of winning. That's how I feel." There, I said it.

His mouth falls open and his eyes soften in response to my confession. My honesty seems to have floored him. I feel his left hand taking hold of mine, causing my breath to hitch slightly.

"I could see that in you, Beth, that's why I felt compelled to send you the note and to invite you here tonight."

I shake my head from side to side. "That's all very well, Ayden, but it's a pointless exercise." I wriggle my hand free, put down my champagne flute, and prepare to take my leave. "I've carved out a life for myself here and it suits me. There was a time when I thought I wanted more but ..."

He's shaking his head. "But you and me, Beth, we're the same."

I stand to leave. "I think you're confusing me with someone else."

"I don't want anyone else, Beth." He takes me by the wrist and eases me back. "Sit down ... please. Let me explain." There's a gentleness to his voice and it beckons me.

Obediently, I sit.

"You're a strong willed person but, like me, you're cursed."

I attempt to speak but he places his fingertips over my lips and I resist the temptation to open my mouth to taste them.

"We're both attractive individuals, people are drawn to us. I use my sexuality in so many ways, I always have and that's my weakness, you know that. I know no other way. But you, you're much smarter. You conceal your beauty behind unflattering clothes, untamed hair and glasses you don't need, just so people will look beyond the exterior and see the beauty within."

My mouth must be making that O shape again. I feel his thumb touching my cheek to wake me from my daydream.

"But I can see beyond all that, Miss Parker, and I see you as you really are; smart and sexy as hell. I WANT YOU."

The words are tumbling from his mouth but I'm not processing them, I'm descending with each syllable. I only hear the word 'curse.' But he doesn't know me; he can't know the nature of my curse. He thinks I'm concealing beauty? I'm hiding much more than that.

He reaches over and slides his left hand behind me, taking hold of my neck while positioning his other around my waist until it is outstretched across the small of my back.

What's he doing?

"You see me for what I am, so I have a proposition for you." Gently, he pulls me towards him and I can't help but arch my back and lean in his direction.

I try to speak.

"Don't speak," he urges. "Let me show you how I feel."

Tenderly, he tips my head over to the left; he's kissing my throat, his kisses are soft and land like snowflakes on my skin. He's moving to my ear and wrapping his tongue around my ear lobe, making the muscles in my groin tighten. I open my mouth to take in air and his lips find my neck, my chin and hover over my face, only brushing my parted lips on their voyage of discovery. I'm swept away.

My God!

Both of his hands are gripping my chair and dragging me forcefully towards him, finding the shadows at the back of the private box. He's slipping his knee between my knees and taking my face in his strong, hot palms.

"Open your eyes," he orders. "Tell me what you see."

He's licking my lips with his tongue and I'm starting to tingle everywhere; heart racing, breath quickening.

"Tell me what you see."

I'm trying to say something, but I'm panting and speaking is difficult. "I see you ..." He continues to ravish me with no more than fingertips in my hair and his devilish tongue. "I see you ..."

For the first time I steel myself and stare into his eyes. The green flecks are dancing and his pupils are as dark as the night sky, depthless; he looks almost wild and unbroken. I pull back, but he has my head in his hands and I can feel his tongue entering my mouth, pushing its way through lips and teeth, penetrating me. I want to run.

I grab his upper arms and try to push him away but he's like marble; hard, muscular biceps too big for my nimble hands to hold onto. I push against the arms of his chair and his right hand moves down my back holding me firmly, I'm anchored to him. There's no escape.

My fear dissipates, I release my hands from his chair and I touch him, afraid that if I reach out he'll disappear and be no more than a figment of my imagination, a fantasy come to life, a wish come true.

I feel sinews flexing beneath his shoulders and timidly stretch out my fingers to touch his perfect face, caressing chin and cheekbones. Feeling my embrace, his urgency melts, his movements are less fraught and it's as if a moment of complete calm folds in on us. There's an understanding, beyond words, beyond space and time. This is where we belong.

With trembling hands, I let my fingers ease their way into his hair; the soft curls fold over my thumbs and I take hold of them, fulfilling a need in me to claim and possess this exquisite man. I pull his head closer to mine, forcing him to thrust his tongue into me, giving myself to him as I have never done with any man before. My jaw relaxes, our tongues touch, there's an explosion of sensations; he enters me, body and soul.

Growling, he releases me. "The power you have over me, Beth ... you feel it don't you, tell me you feel it?"

The air around us is spinning. "I feel it, Ayden." My heart beat is whooshing in my ears, yet there's a gentle stillness between us that comes from accepting our fate. I want to frame this moment, to put it up on a wall behind a curtain so only I know it's there; the moment when our two worlds actually collide.

I take his face in my hands and allow my senses to take in every pore. Ayden Stone you are so incredibly beautiful, why would you consider this gift of loveliness a curse?

Instantly, his firm hand is on my chin, his fingers along my jaw and his thumb skimming my lower lip. "I want to be inside you," he mutters, sliding his thumb into my mouth. His lip twitches momentarily as my tongue finds the soft pad of his thumb and circles it slowly. He shifts in his chair and I sense his arousal. I feel my own; I'm wet and my underwear is sodden and I know my dress will be stained from sitting.

"Suck hard, Beth, take all of me," he instructs, before moving his thumb in and out of my mouth in a sort of hypnotic incursion. His other hand is moving down my dress, his fingertips are tracing spirals across my collarbone and still I suck and lick his insistent thumb.

He removes it from my mouth and trails it down my chin before filling the vacant space with his tongue. Like magic, he breathes life into me; his breath enters my mouth and I inhale him like oxygen. I push back with my tongue, I want to taste him. He takes me inside his mouth and groans at my fevered invasion.

I'm so preoccupied with his mouth I barely feel his hands on my breasts. He's cupping me, searching for my nipples with his thumbs through the silk material. I feel them hardening and rubbing against my bra, so I push them forward, encouraging him, urging him on. I'm so aroused. I want to be touched, I need to be touched, and I desperately want to touch him.

I lower my hands from his face, feel the damp pleats of his shirt against his skin and let my hands come to rest on his knees. But my hands are rigid and I hold onto his hard thighs, afraid of traveling further into unknown territory.

"Do it," he gasps. "I want you to do it."

"I can't, not here."

He moves his hands to my waist and moans into my mouth, "I'm so fucking hard for you."

I know where this is going but I'm powerless to stop it. His hands rest on my hips and he rocks me back and forth in a kind of rhythmic embrace, but I can't tear myself away from his passionate kisses.

My stomach muscles start to tighten when he places the palm of his right hand just below my navel. I feel his fingers spreading wide and his thumb skimming my pubic bone; it feels too good. My arousal steps up a notch, it's hovering dangerously in the red zone.

This is wrong!

What's he doing to me?

This is wrong!

I'm starting to panic ... he's got to stop, I've got to stop. This is too much. "Ayden," I gasp. "Ayden ... stop, please stop." When the words leave my mouth, I sound as if I'm pleading.

He pulls back, removes his hands from my trembling torso and scoops up my face in his sizzling palms. "I'm sorry," he whispers, kissing my forehead. "It's too much I know, but I can't help myself."

He tips my face to his so we are staring into each other's eyes; blue and green hoops orbiting bottomless pools of blackness. Our breaths are shallow and we come slowly down, down.

"I didn't intend for this to happen, not this way, but you're like a drug to me. I lose all self-control around you."

He seems vulnerable and unguarded. I want to kiss him, to feel the plump moistness of his lips on mine, but I hold off and stroke his face with my thumbs, letting him speak.

"I've been thinking of nothing else but you since Monday... I like order in my life, but you've come along and everything's been tipped on its head. I don't know what the fuck's happening to me!"

In my flushed state I can't think straight, but I have to say something. This is not the time for untruths. "I've been a wreck too. If you hadn't sent the invitation, I don't know what I would have done."

His confession comes out in a rush. "It's as if there's something pulling us together. Everything about you is magnetic." There's sincerity in his voice; his admission leaves him exposed and that makes him all the more desirable.

"I've tried to be invisible for so long, Ayden. You've come along and you see me and I'm so thankful for that." Before I can say another word, he pulls me to him with such force I think I'll fall from my chair.

"How could I not see you? You're beauty personified." He relinquishes his grip and brushes away a single strand of hair from my face, taking in every line, every pore.

"But, Ayden, I don't understand what it is you want from me."

"I want to possess you and be possessed *by* you, in every possible way. That's what I want."

My heart quickens in response to those heartfelt words. I can tell from his expression he is utterly sincere, but there's an edge to his assertion that seems a little unnerving. Sexual attraction is one thing, but possession? I stiffen slightly. Where's this going?

"How do you think I can do that, Ayden?" Am I so inexperienced, should I know what he means?

"If you let me love you then we'll find out together."

For some reason, that doesn't satisfy me. I'm suddenly alert and captivated by him at the same time. "Ayden, I've loved tonight and this thing we have is, well, mind blowing, but what is it you're not telling me?"

Before my eyes, this sexy, self-assured God of a man is fading and in his place sits a lesser figure who seems to have the weight of the world on his shoulders; he's wrestling with an unfathomable dilemma.

I'm drawn to his tormented features and gently tip up his chin with my fingers, forcing him to look at me. "No games, Ayden, remember?"

With unexpected softness he says, "I want to ..." He stops, looks into my wide eyes, the colour of a summer sky, and reconsiders his words. "I want to be your... submissive ..."

"... My what?" I try not to appear shocked but inside I want to scream. "I don't know what you mean."

A single brow lifts in response to my declaration. "I want *you* to take control, Beth; to be sexually dominant, with me." He's scrutinising my face for evidence of understanding. He won't find it there. Why does this stunning, wonderfully talented man want to be dominated by me? Me?

Fuck!

"Ayden, look at me."

He lifts his head and so forlorn is his expression that it cuts me to the quick.

"I can't imagine what makes you feel you have to be dominated. I don't know what to say to a request like that. Truly I don't."

A little too quickly, he regains his composure. I see him transforming, reverting back into the self-possessed man I saw framed by crystal light only two hours ago. It's as if he's made a bad call, misjudged the situation somehow. He's settling into the back of his chair; he's becoming fierce and remote. "I see."

But he doesn't, he's pulling away, out of my reach. "No you don't," I answer sternly. "I didn't say no, you took me by surprise, give me a minute ..."

There's an urgency in my voice that comes from a colossal surge of emotion stirring inside me. It reaches down to the depth of my soul and I am powerless to control it. "Do you think I would let anyone dominate you or treat you that way? Of course, it *has* to be me." I take hold of his hands in mine and rest them on my lap.

The gravity of the situation hits me; this is one of those moments in life when a promise made is a promise kept. "I promise to take care of you, Ayden, in whatever way I can and however you want me to. If you want to call that being dominant, then so be it. Can I make it any clearer for you?"

"No." For some reason, he treats me to a victorious smile and moves closer so we can feel each other's breath against our lips. He's intoxicating and, by all accounts, so am I. His pupils are like dark pools of rainwater; in them I can see myself reflected and I know I belong there in that dark, secret space.

"What should I call you?" he asks with a sexy glint in his eye.

Call me?

I'm thinking on my feet. "Behind closed doors you can call me Elizabeth, but only then. Right here and now I'm Beth."

"OK. Sounds good to me." Confidently, he takes hold of my hand, preparing to leave then halts abruptly thinking through his actions. "Are you ready to go?"

I swallow deeply and prepare for my command performance. "Yes, if we're starting tonight then you should take me home so I can tie you up and fuck you." I assume that's the right thing to say and, by the look on his face I think I've hit the bullseye.

His smile lights up the private box, it stretches to his eyes and the warmth of that light makes us glow like a constellation of undiscovered stars. He upturns his hand and reaches out to me.

"Let's go, I'm all yours."

***

By lunchtime Dan has had enough. He makes himself scarce and goes for a smoke behind the north exit door, remembering to keep the bin between the door and the latch. He got caught out by it once before and it took him seven minutes to walk all the way around the building and to re-enter through the double swing doors. That was the day he caught the eye of Sandra clearing the bins in the back office. The memory of that encounter has stayed with him like a bad dose of indigestion. "What a fucking mistake that was," he recalls with a sneer.

"Oh you're a big boy, aren't you," she called out when he passed, causing him to clench his fingers into a fist. She was trying to embarrass him in front of her workmates, but he was having none of it.

He sauntered over to her and positioned himself against the door jamb, blocking her path. "Are you talking to me, sweetheart?" He could be charming when he wanted to be.

"I might be," she said.

He hated the way she came onto him, fluttering her eyelashes and flashing her tits. "Then, decide if you are or if you're not because I haven't got all day." He had her on the ropes.

"What if I am?"

"Then you should be here at 5.30 ready and waiting for me." He knew exactly how to handle her sort.

"And what if I'm not?"

"Then you'll never know, will you?"

"Never know what?"

"Whether I'm a big boy or not," he said, throwing her a wink over his shoulder. He left her with that thought, knowing she was gagging for it. He could hear the peals of laughter as he turned down the corridor, and could already feel the bile forming in his throat. It took a visit to his locker to see his girl and a couple of strokes to make him feel better.

When he turned up as arranged at 5.30 p.m. in the foyer of the main entrance she was there, fussing with her peroxide blonde hair and straightening her blouse which was easily two sizes too small. Her face lit up when she saw him and he even managed to manufacture a reciprocal smile to reassure her, before he hit her between the eyes with a knockout punch.

"You're here."

"I am."

He watched her wiggle her arse and straighten her skirt, leading him on. From the way she was holding her mouth, he could tell she was expecting to be kissed. But there was no way that was going to happen. Almost choking on cheap perfume and cigarette breath, he rocked forward into her. "Then fuck off, I don't date slags!" Her face was a picture. He wished he'd brought his expensive camera along, even without the zoom lens it would have been one for the photo album.

Leaving her standing, mouth agape and ashen faced, he walked away muttering, "Why the fuck would I settle for a witch like you when I've got a princess at home?"

At the end of his shift, he made the forty minute journey back to Ely, grinning for the entire 16 miles at the memory of her disintegration.

3

I n one swift movement, we are trotting down stairs and gliding along marble floors. Ayden is pressing the screen on his iPhone and, after only two rings, puts it away in his pocket. For a matter of seconds, we linger at the bottom of the foyer steps, avoiding a passing vagrant of gigantic proportions. A sleek, silver Rolls Royce comes around the corner to the left of us, registration number: ASMED1A. It pulls up outside the entrance.

A smartly dressed man with a number two haircut and a stance that belongs more on a military base than outside a theatre steps out and walks around the car to open the passenger door. I glance over to Ayden and we share a look, yet say nothing about the chauffeur driven car. It's our private joke.

"Good evening, Mr. Stone, Miss Parker."

"Hi Lester. Just drive." This is a side to Ayden I have yet to see; him giving commands so effortlessly. "After you, Beth."

I step into the sumptuous interior; there's the sweet smell of leather cleaner and polish and it reminds me of my mum's house. How strange that a fragrance can evoke such a powerful memory.

"Where to?" Ayden asks, shaking me out of my absorbing recollection.

I'm too taken with the night's events to have even considered where we're going, but I'm supposed to be taking charge so I issue an order. "To my apartment, please." Realising he doesn't know where my apartment is. "Sorry, the address is ..."

"He knows the address," Ayden states as a matter of fact and throws me a 'what did you expect' look.

"He does?" I return fire with a surprised look. I wonder what other information he has on me. There's a kind of uncomfortable silence, making me feel on edge. I want to laugh. He looks so debonair and I can't believe my good fortune; this kind of thing doesn't happen to women like me. I put my hand to my mouth to contain a giggle.

"That's one way of breaking the ice." He grins and leans into me expectantly.

Is he assuming I'll take the lead?

I look out of the window and try to devise a plan of action, but nothing comes to mind. "Ayden ... what are you expecting when we get to my apartment?"

He has a dead-pan expression. "I'm expecting chains and whips and a selection of bondage gear."

"What! Have you had them delivered?" From his reaction, my face must be a picture; I'm startled beyond words.

"Beth … I don't know what I'm expecting when we get to your apartment. I'm in the dark here." He is shaking his head, but his eyes are laughing; he's fooling around.

"That makes two of us," I say, thinking out loud. "I would have some explaining to do if my neighbour had taken *that* parcel in." I bump against his shoulder affectionately, we share the joke and the ice melts in the warmth emanating from his smile.

When we reach my ground floor apartment, I'm suddenly reminded of the mess I left behind in my eagerness to get ready. He'll be lucky if he can find a space to stand. When I put my weight behind the front door and it opens, I'm stunned to see it's immaculate. "Charlie," I say quietly.

"Who?" Ayden looks about the apartment furtively, fearing our discovery.

"There's no-one here, come in." I watch him taking it all in.

"It's very tidy and … homely," he comments, making his way over to the marble fireplace. His eyes are drawn to my framed piece of Papyrus. "Have you been to Egypt?"

"No. Charlie my best friend went as part of an incentive programme. She was 'Top Biller' or something like that for three months. She brought it back for me."

"Is it authentic?"

"I think so. It came with a certificate, saying 8th Century AD. It looks authentic." I lean in to take a closer look, our faces reflect in the glass before it steams over with our combined breath.

"So much of this stuff is banana paper, but you can usually tell if it's real by the quality of the script. I have a couple of wooden masks at my place that date back to around 440 BC."

"Are you're a collector?"

"No, but I like lovely and unusual things," he states coyly, shifting his attention to me. "Do you want to show me round?"

I nod, hoping he can't sense my awkwardness. My heart begins to flutter. The bedroom is only thirty feet away, soon we'll be heading in that direction and he must have all kinds of expectations.

I push him around with my hands on his back as if he's an inanimate object. "So this is the kitchen." All he can do is nod and keep his hands in his pockets. We approach the bedroom and instantly his eyes are drawn to the two framed prints on the walls; one to the side and one over my bed. Both are by Nobert Gerstenberger.

"Interesting artwork." He tips up his head to each one in turn.

"You like?"

"I'm not sure."

"They're only prints. I was drawn to the contrasting images of romanticism and cruelty."

He spins around, forcing me to take a step backwards. "Cruelty?"

"Yes. Here these two women were with so many dreams, so hopeful and yet they've been overwritten, coloured over and have faded into the background. It's as if they never existed."

"Why do you have them if they make you melancholy?"

"They make me reflective. That's not the same as melancholy."

He takes a closer to them. "You're right, it isn't. They have a dreamlike quality but there's something sinister about them."

"I think you're reading too much into them." I take his arm. "I simply like the artistry."

He doesn't budge. "And what of these women, do they get their happy endings?" He turns around to face me, making me feel shy and uneasy.

I have to look away. "Happy endings are a construct, Mr. Stone. Everyone knows that." I laugh softly but receive only a flat-smile in reply.

"Do they have titles?"

"Yes." I point out each one in turn. "The Love Letter and The Princess."

He sniggers at that, but I'm not entirely sure why. "How apt."

Did I miss something?

I try to lighten the atmosphere with good humour. "You see, us Cinderellas like to live in hope."

He circles my chin with a single finger, then returns his hand to his pocket as if he hadn't moved. "In hope of what, exactly?"

Words don't come easily. "Of being loved by prince, of course." I feel very unsophisticated right now; I have absolutely no idea what I'm saying. "The Prince Archetype was the focus of my dissertation," I say much too hastily, trying to regain some semblance of credibility.

He folds his arms and props himself up against the bedroom door. "Tell me about it."

"Alright. Fairy-tales are like portals into another world, another reality..."

"... Escapism?"

"Yes, for some, but they're part of our oral traditions, a shared consciousness; a way of connecting the imaginations of living people."

"I didn't know that." I really think he's listening.

"... I'm sure it all sounds very juvenile to you, but these kind of stories go back centuries ... they're full of real emotions and they have a distinct symbolic and metaphoric language. People used to understand that language but these days, all we get is the Disney version."

"You're passionate about this, aren't you?" He scrapes back a stray tendril of hair from my face and so gentle is his touch, I think I may have imagined it.

"I always have been, since I was little ..." That memory makes me smile.

"Some things stay with us, even as we grow older and mature," he says with total authority. He reaches out suddenly, grasps my hand and twirls me around, winding me into the carpet like a tight, little corkscrew.

I stumble into him, quickly regain my balance and point at the bed. Feeling so nervous I fall back on an outdated cliché. "And this ... is where the magic happens ..."

He throws me a look I can't quite decipher, or perhaps it's better I don't.

"Please ..." He walks off into the kitchen but I can tell, just from the angle of his head, he's smiling. Stifling laughter, he calls out, "Can we have some wine before the magic happens?"

Oh please God yes, lots of wine.

He turns his nose up at the inferior wine and hands me a glass of everyday Shiraz. "You look like you could do with a couple of glasses of this stuff. Maybe then you'll calm the fuck down."

He's trying to be firm but his mouth is soft and his irises are sparkling in a kind of teal green. In spite of his assertions, he's relaxed and taking great delight in watching me squirm. I ask myself: in what universe does a man like this become submissive?

Dismissing my unease, I sense my cue. "I don't think you should be talking to me like that, Mr. Stone, after all I'm the one in charge, remember?" I feel more confident now. I'm finding my feet, or it might be the effects of the half glass of wine I've gulped down. "You shouldn't be so rude, or I may have to punish you." I hear the words, but I'm not sure where they're coming from.

I'm about to laugh when I realise I have his undivided attention. He looks crestfallen and I want to go to him, to say 'I'm only teasing,' but his body language has altered. He's less authoritative somehow, less intimidating. His head is bowed and his free hand is hanging limply by his side. I stroll over to him, place down my glass on the counter, take his and position it next to mine.

I summon up a firm voice from somewhere. "I don't like it when you're rude to me, Ayden." And before I can finish my sentence, he says softy...

"I'm sorry, Elizabeth." His eyes don't leave the floor.

My hand rests against my mouth, concealing my horror. What have I done? He's like a small child who's been scolded, caught cheating in an exam, broken a window ...

I don't know what to do, what should I do?

Here and now I decide to do the one thing I wanted to do from the very moment I saw him at the top of the stairs in the auditorium, that moment when our eyes met and our hands were welded together; to take him to bed. But this is not the time for seduction, it's about something else. It's about me making him feel safe and cared for, I think. I lift his face to mine, gaze into those khaki pools of light and take his hand. "Come with me, Ayden, we're going to bed."

I turn on the bedside light and watch how it catches his cheek bones, dazzled by his innate beauty; there's no air brushing here. I stroke his shoulders and push off his jacket, feeling a kind of reverence for him as an air of serenity circles him, mimicking his mood.

Unbuttoning his shirt, I find myself talking about nothing in particular. I don't know what I'm doing but I can sense he's totally relaxed and willing to let me care for him in the softest of ways. I scan my iPod resting in its deck by the bed for something appropriate and settle for the soothing voice of Sade. She sings of *No Ordinary Love* and I let the album play.

With nimble fingers, I undo the double buttons on his cuffs, push back his shirt, and try to contain a gasp. His upper body is sculpted and toned; washboard abs and that V shape etched into his hips. There's a sprinkling of chest hair between his pectoral muscles that I can't help but stroke and rest my cheek upon. How long has it been since I felt this close to someone? I can't recall a time – never.

I trace the outline of defined abs with my fingertips and breathe him in. He's every inch the man I imagined him to be. I come to a stark realisation; this is about self-control, his *and* mine. Willingly, he's transferred every decision, every ounce of his power to me. He is my submissive and how amazing is this?

Sitting him on my bed, I remove his shoes and socks. He is content to watch me. I catch his eyes darting from left to right, tracing every tender move I make.

"Stand please," I ask and he does.

With nervous hands I focus on the stylish fastening on the top of his trousers, feeling my breath quickening and my pulse racing, but ... I *can't* undress him. I hardly even know him. What the hell am I doing? I look up to him, seeking permission or is it guidance? He knows ...

"*You're* in control, Elizabeth."

Is he reading my thoughts, is my inexperience so obvious?

"Go ahead, it's okay." His voice is soft and coaxing.

Our eyes meet and there's a sensual craving there that's flickering like glowing embers, I'm fighting to contain myself and I suspect he is too. With shaky hands I pull down his fly and lower myself to lower his trousers. I stop to take in all his manliness. His erection shifts and strains against his boxers and I feel as if I could climax here and now. I fall to my knees, happy to worship at the altar of Ayden Stone.

"S... step out please." And he does. I throw his trousers onto the chair by the wall and try to regain some semblance of rational thought, but my brain is fried and my clitoris is aching for him.

Dear God. Why did I ever agree to this?

The man of my dreams stands before me like an unwrapped gift, perfect in his passivity and aroused state. What's he waiting for?

I know the answer; he's waiting for my command. "Ayden, I want you to get into bed now."

"Yes, Elizabeth."

He slips under the duvet and lies on his back. Beneath the duvet I can see him rigid and primed, and it's taking every speck of willpower I have not to launch myself onto him. But that wouldn't be fair; he's played his part to perfection. Now it's my turn.

Against every inclination I have to turn off the light, I leave it on. Taking my time, I remove my shoes and unzip my dress, knowing he is watching me. I thought I would struggle with this but, the further down the zip goes, the more I'm getting turned on by the fact this gorgeous guy with an enormous hard on is lying in my bed, watching me. As I wriggle out of my dress, I feel my pants sticking to my crotch. I'm sodden and stimulated beyond measure.

I let my dress fall to the floor and start to remove my stockings slowly, scandalously. I'm not just undressing, this is a striptease. I'm the exhibitionist and all the time our eyes are locked together closing the distance between us, intensifying our connection. I throw my stockings onto the chair and they float slowly down and settle on the carpet by the bed. But ... my confidence is waning. I'm almost naked before this stranger.

What am I doing?

Just as I'm about to lose my nerve, his movement draws my attention away from my bashfulness. He lifts up the sheets and holds them up for me. An understanding smile forms and I move towards him willingly, with gratitude, and position my body next to his.

No words are spoken but for all of Ayden's apparent calmness, I feel his heart racing against my palm. I'm certain he will not touch me, but I so desperately need to be touched. I remember my promise and I know what I must do. I reach over to my stockings and straddle him.

"Give me your right hand, Ayden." He lifts up his arm so I can gently wrap the stocking around it. I lean provocatively across his face and feel his involuntary jerking as I do so. His breath is hot and shallow against my bra, triggering an aching hunger to be tasted and enjoyed. Once his hand is secure, I sit back down onto him. His breathing is laboured and his chest is lifting, but he makes no sound.

"Give me your left hand, Ayden." He does and I rock forward again, trying to find purchase for my needy clitoris on his taught abs. His jerking begins again, as does my deep craving for his hands on my body; but he's bound by my stockings to the wrought iron bedhead and I must satisfy my yearning another way.

I lower myself onto him and his rate of breathing intensifies. Arching myself forward, I push out my breasts so he can taste the perspiration forming between the cups of my bra. He licks and traces the top of each cup with his tongue. The thrill of letting him see me so scantily dressed burns in my throat and finds its way to my groin. Every sensation finds its way to that place, the most sensitive part of my body.

I lean into him once more, gripping his shoulders for support. His teeth tug at my bra and he rolls his tongue from one breast to the other, seeking hardening flesh. He pulls on his nylon restraints and I long to release him into my arms but I daren't. I want to say his name. I want to hear him say *my* name.

"Ayden, say my name, please say my name."

In no more than a half whisper, he says, "I'm all yours ... Elizabeth."

The sound of his fractured voice touches me and his declaration spurs me on. I have to give him what he wants: to be taken. Against my deepest desires I move to his ear and whisper. "I want you to lie still and stay hard while I fuck you."

Like a powerful aphrodisiac, my words ignite his passion and he begins breathing frantically, arching his back and pressing his throbbing cock into me, desperate for liberation.

Keeping my hands on his shoulders I lower my thighs, so I am perfectly placed to rub myself against him. In quick response, his stomach muscles tense and flex and I place my hands there to experience the undulating movement beneath my fingers. I so want to feel his perfect body against mine and I flatten myself across him, pinning him to the mattress; hot flesh on hot flesh.

I envelop his face in my hands and suck the steaming breath from his body. My mouth finds his and his hunger for my tongue is insatiable. He rocks his head, tugs and pulls, straining his arms to reach me. I pull away to prolong his sweet agony.

Watching this remarkable man coming apart before my eyes is too much. I have to taste him, devour him. Without thinking, I lower my head onto his chest and lick his flexing muscles, relishing every precious inch. His chest hair tickles my nose, and I brush my face against it to savour his faultless physique. I move lower to the firm centre of his core and brush my cheek against soft skin and pubic hair, feeling him quivering under my instruction. I'm not myself, I don't know how to do this ... but Elizabeth does and she is, thanks to this benevolent God of a man.

"Fuck, this is insane," he calls out and I have to agree. I don't know what I'm doing but it feels too good to stop.

Making it up as I go, I brush against his pubic bone with my nose and nibble the elastic waistband on his boxers. His desire is peaking and he's groaning and lifting his body in search of my moist tongue. I run my hands across his boxers and become aware of an aching need in him to release. I can't take him in my mouth, not yet, I'm not ready for that, but I offer him my hand.

I trace the rigid grooves and the veins with my thumb before folding my fingers around his throbbing cock and begin fisting him, gently at first and then at a faster rate; up and down, from tip to base using seeping pre cum to lubricate my fingers.

"Let me come ..." he begs, for some strange reason.

As gently as I can, I acknowledge his neediness with an intimate smile and watch as his breathless panting dissolves into feverish moans of pleasure.

He calls out, "What-the-fuck!" in broken words and ejaculates into his boxers.

After a breathless interval, I sit astride him and suddenly become aware of my semi-naked state. Snuggling down, I pull up the covers, tucking my hands against my breasts. It feels wrong to touch him now. I ask tentatively, "Are you alright?"

"Yes, I'm great, Beth."

My change of name takes me by surprise; he's back and the role-play is over.

"Do you want to untie me?"

I turn to face him. I've forgotten about the stockings. There he is strung out over my pillows like a scarecrow; a gorgeous one at that. Forgetting my inhibitions, I jump up and go in search of scissors. It isn't until I'm on my way back from the bathroom I catch myself in the full length mirror. I'm virtually naked.

He follows my approach with a lecherous stare, making me feel awkward and shy, wondering how the hell I'm going to get the stockings off without thrusting my breasts in his face. I climb onto the bed. "Excuse me," I mumble as I lean over him. It seems the polite thing to say but clearly it's inappropriate because he finds it hilarious.

I sit back down, wave the scissors around and playfully remind him, "Aren't we forgetting who's tied up and who has the scissors?"

He pretends to be silent. "Alright, I'll be good." But then he bursts into laughter again and it's a real heartfelt giggle that makes me giggle too.

"I've known people die this way. Their bodies aren't found 'til months later, not until the neighbours start to complain about the smell."

"Is that so, then we'll have to come to some arrangement won't we?" He rolls his eyes theatrically. "You set me free and I'll get you off. How about that?" He means it and the laughter is still visible in his eyes. It's highly infectious. "Just don't say "excuse me" again or you'll crack me up and I'll have to start renegotiating."

I cut him free; he rubs his wrists and grabs me by the waist, pulling me down from the top of the bed to face him.

"I like being around you," he says with a grin, pulling up the covers around me. He's so warm and that just 'come' look is playing havoc with my libido. "I'm going to clean up. Don't move." He kisses my nose and jumps out of bed.

Now it's my turn to ogle. I watch him go and inside I'm saying, please hurry back, but my thoughts turn to more intimate matters; what does he want to do to me? Now the shoe's on the other foot, I think I prefer him passive and restrained.

He returns, gloriously naked and excitable. When he positions himself next to me I'm aware of the smell of sex on skin; it's laced with pheromones. My heart flutters, more with apprehension than desire.

He wraps his left arm over me and pulls up the duvet to keep me snug. "You're full of surprises, Beth. Who would have thought ..." He draws his hand to my face and tenderly brushes back my hair.

"I didn't know what I was doing, but you relaxed and went with it, and so did I." Lifting out a crumpled hand from under the sheets, I caress his lovely face. "You know why I used my hand, don't you?"

"Yes I do. It's early days." He turns away and a smirk crosses his lips.

"What's so funny?"

I hope it isn't me.

"I'm just replaying what you said before. "This is where the magic happens" ... you weren't wrong." He places a wet kiss on my nose. "I don't usually get that worked up, but it's you, you're exquisite and you don't even know it. I've not been touched like that since ... I can't remember when."

I want to return his cheeky smile but modesty prevents me from saying anything.

"You even smell great." He nuzzles into my neck and it causes a twinge of desire to circulate around my body. "Let me get you off, I want to hear you come."

What! My God!

When he says things like that, I start to lose it. "I'm okay. I'm really tired. Maybe next time."

He raises his right elbow to support his head. "Are you kidding?"

I shake my head from side to side. He has no idea what I'm like or what I've been through, and I'm not about to get into that now.

He caresses my lower lip with his thumb. "Don't go all virginal on me. You just undressed me and gave me a hand job. You show me how you get yourself off and I'll improvise. I'm good with my hands."

I bet ...

The gleam in his eyes makes me want to say yes, but something is holding me back. "I want you to, I do, but not now." I settle my mouth on his and our tongues mingle in wet confusion. My chest is tightening and the sensation of his hand on my back urging me to give in to him is so persuasive ... but I draw back and sweep unruly curls off his forehead. "I know what you're trying to do, Mr. Stone, so stop. Be good."

Another wet kiss ends his enticement and we lay comfortably together in a kind of afterglow. I place my head on his shoulder and he enfolds me in his right arm, and I feel safer than I have for a very long time.

"I've got to go, so I'll leave you to get some sleep. You've been busy and on a school night too!" I feel his smile on my head and a kiss brushes against my hair. "I've got a plane to catch at 7.00 a.m. to New York, so I'll call you later."

I nod my acceptance, hoping he will.

He swivels out of bed and starts to dress. "I'm going commando but don't tell anyone." He's so unself-conscious; it's as if I'm not here. I treat myself to the sight of immaculate manliness. He climbs into his trousers and casually slips into his shirt. "I'll shower at home, pick up the paperwork, and make my way to Heathrow." *He* has everything under control now but, I suspect, he's been navigating all night. I've simply been following wordless direction.

"I know. It's okay. Don't miss your flight."

He picks up his jacket off the floor and haphazardly throws it over his shoulder. Even after having expended all that sexual energy, he looks fresh and even more adorable. Before leaving, he pauses and returns to sit by me on the bed. His hand is in my hair. He leans in to kiss me deeply, and I feel a longing that makes me wish I'd taken him up on his offer.

His gazes into my weary face. "We're good, right?"

"Yes, Ayden, we're good." He stands but, before he can get out of the room, I slither out of bed and stroll over to him provocatively, wanting to give him a closer look at what he's walking away from. I feel shameless. I unclip my bra and throw it on the bed, pinning him to the door with my nearly naked body. In true Dominant style, I raise his hands above his head and kiss him within an inch of his life.

"Have a safe flight and hurry back." I feel the stirrings of an erection by my hip and it's my parting gift.

"Christ, Beth! I'm going to have to jerk off in the shower now ..." He rubs his neck to ease the tension and leaves, slamming the front door behind him, but not without a parting word. I catch a three syllabled utterance, "sub-miss-ive?" but it's said more out of disbelief than a statement of fact, leaving his mouth in one long hiss.

I return to bed smiling from ear to ear. I think I did pretty well under the circumstances: mission accomplished.

***

It's 1445hrs on a wet Wednesday afternoon. Ernie is wiping his brow with an off-white handkerchief his daughter and that less-than-useless son-in-law sent him for his birthday, with a book on wine making.

He turns to Dan. "I've worked like a slave today, if they stick a bloody brush up my arse I'll sweep up!"

"You don't have to tell me. I've split a gut shifting and sweeping for this lot." He's done himself proud: stacked the furniture into the warehouse out of three dorms, cleared the leaves from the quad and carried over the stationery to the main office. "How much fucking typing do they do in that office?" he asks Ernie. "There's enough A4 to go around the planet ten times over."

He's ready for his 3 o'clock tea break but Mr. Crowther, his immediate boss, has other plans. "Dan," he calls out with the kind of authoritative bite that has Dan grinding his teeth. He pretends he's not heard and keeps walking.

Ernie gives him a knowing look. "Better see what he wants or he'll only come after us with his bloody whip."

Dan knows Ernie's right, but there's just something about that guy. When he hears his name being called for a second time, he chooses to acknowledge it.

"Yes, Mr. Crowther, what can I do for you?"

"I'm hoping you can fill the breach tonight and take the minibus down to Shaftesbury Avenue, you know, off Piccadilly Circus."

"I know where Shaftesbury Avenue is." Inside, Dan is seething. *Does he think I'm fucking stupid?*

Slightly out of breath, he explains in more detail. "Leslie's had to drive to Birmingham, apparently her father has been taken into hospital with a heart attack and there really is no-one else with your level of expertise." From the way Mr. Crowther is massaging Dan's ego, it's obvious he's his last port of call.

"Why, what's happening on Shaftesbury Avenue?" Dan asks, as if he doesn't know. *Not another bloody musical?* He can't stand all that prancing around. Just the thought of it makes him want to strangle someone with their own fucking tights.

"No, no. It's the English under-graduates, they're going to see a production of Romeo and Juliet at the Apollo; an opportunity for them to see the Bard's work up close, so to speak."

His words leave Dan cold. "I did have plans," he says with a shrug. "But, I suppose I could help out if you're desperate."

"That's the spirit. You can always rely on an army boy when there's a crisis."

Who the fuck is he calling a boy?

Ernie comes to his rescue. "It's the training you know, 'Eris Optimus,' Be the Best."

"Yes, yes, well done, Ernie." His patronising tone has Dan reconsidering his good deed. Sensing he has overstepped the mark, his attention quickly shifts to the man of the hour. "So, Dan, are you up for it, a trip into the city with sixteen of our brightest freshmen and women?"

It all seems too much trouble until he mentions 'women.' Something is stirring in him: the possibility of coming into close-contact with some 'pretty little things.' Now, it's turned into a mission, he's not putting himself out at all.

"It would be my pleasure, Mr. Crowther." He seals the deal with a handshake. "It won't be as challenging as the infantry but I'm your man."

Mr. Crowther can't believe his luck. For a moment, he thought Dan was going to say no. "You certainly are." With him on side, he alters his approach. "Now you need to be at the Old Schools entrance at 1800hrs." He gives himself a well-done grin, believing he has got the better of the big man. Both Ernie and the man himself know different.

"Yes Sir," Dan answers, presenting an exaggerated salute and turning it into an insulting example of face pulling by pressing his thumb onto his nose and wiggling his fingers as if he's playing a flute.

"Yes, yes very funny, Dan. Very entertaining." He walks away, shaking his head, feeling a little dispirited by Dan's impertinence.

"Ernie reaches up and pats Dan between his shoulder blades. "Daft sod thought he was pulling the wool over your eyes."

"Yeah, little shit."

"Anyway, what did you have on tonight?" Ernie asks, curious to hear what he gets up to on a Wednesday night.

"Not a bloody thing." He grins more for his own pleasure than for Ernie's

"I didn't think so."

"No, but he doesn't know that. And now he owes me."

"That's right Champ. Keep your friends close and your enemies closer."

"Always do Ernie, always do. Come on. Let's get that bloody kettle on, my mouth feels like a pair of whore's drawers."

At 1800hrs on the dot, Dan is handed the keys to the sixteen-seater minibus. He checks his watch, knowing the passengers should all be on board by a quarter to.

There are a couple of 'pretty little things' who take his fancy, and he keeps a close eye on one through his rear view mirror. He knows she's not a patch on *his* girl, but she'll serve as a 'stand-in' until he and she are reunited.

He takes stock. The 'stand-in' has a similar body type, slim but shapely, easy to pin down and position with one hand, leaving the other free for ... whatever. She even has that untouched look about her he likes so much: she's probably a virgin. Every time he stops, he can see her lurching forward, her breasts are pert and rise to the occasion like a couple of ice-cream cones. He's thankful the traffic is heavy and it's stop-go all the way.

When a cyclist pulls out in front of him, forcing him to slam on the breaks and to curse, he calls out, "You stupid sod! You nearly got yourself killed."

Watching her eyes widen and her mouth opening like that sends a rush of blood to his twitching cock. He savours the feel of it and makes a silent promise to sort himself out later. He'll press rewind and mentally relive the moment, all it will take is a couple of hard strokes and he'll be as good as new.

He delivers the excited passengers at their destination in plenty of time. They disembark and bask in the glow of the Apollo's after dinner light show. Romeo and Juliet are emblazoned across the front of the building and the 'star-crossed lovers' invite them in for a spectacular night of Shakespearian drama. He takes a sharp left and follows the slowly moving traffic into the car park.

With the heater turned up full and music playing in the background, he's feeling relaxed and proud of himself. He *was* the best man for the job and he'd make sure Mr. Crowther didn't forget it.

By 2050hrs he's feeling a little peckish and beginning to wish he'd brought a snack or at least a packet of crisps. Having not eaten, he prepares to go on the hunt for food. He steps from the minibus and gives a yawn, he's feeling stiff and is rolling his neck clockwise and then in an anti-clockwise direction to regain his flexibility. His hands find their way into his pockets. He isn't cold but the wind is starting to pick up and the spitting rain is beginning to ride it in horizontal waves. His bare skin is taking the brunt of it.

The theatre is quite a sight, all white and formidable, illuminated in shades of red and gold. It reminds him of two enormous pillars of salt with screw-off tops on either side of a sparkling, chalk faced mansion.

He's so busy looking down Shaftesbury Avenue that the young couple holding hands, trotting down the theatre steps have to swerve to avoid bumping into him. He turns, "Hey! Watch where you're ..."

The air rushes into his lungs when he sees her. She's beautiful: every bit the princess in her little silver dress and party shoes. Sure, she's a little older and she's changed her hair colour but ... there's no mistaking her.

He pulls his hands out of his pockets and takes a step in her direction, but thinks twice when the tall, well dressed guy she's with turns and gives him a condescending look. Is he squaring up to him? Does he think he can take him? He wishes he'd try.

'Fucking tosser,' he's thinking. 'Got his fucking hands on my girl.' His lips are separating from his teeth in a kind of snarl.

Thinking on his feet, he scans the street for witnesses. There are too many people about. 'I can't deck him here and get away with it.' He assesses the situation; holding back the impulse to hit him and grab her is agonising.

When the time is right and he's mentally prepared to act, a silver Rolls Royce pulls up sharpish at the curb. A big guy in a suit is opening the door. The toff in the suit lets her get in first and turns again in his direction and looks down his nose at him. 'He's getting in. She's getting away. Fuck!'

He watches the car ease into the traffic and makes a mental note of the registration: ASMED1A. That's easy enough to remember. To make sure, he takes out the key to the minibus, rolls up his sleeve and scratches it into his arm. It hurts like hell, but duty calls.

As the silver car disappears into the night, the pavement moves beneath him like he's on an escalator. "What the fuck's going on?" he asks himself, unsure of exactly what he's feeling: anxiety, exhilaration, arousal?

In a second, the dizzy spell passes and he puts it down to dehydration or hunger and checks his watch again. It's only 2100hrs. Taking long, assertive strides he heads off in the direction of a food source thinking, planning and feeling the familiar ache in his groin.

"No time for that," he whispers, censoring sexual urges. He considers his game-plan: 'A snack to keep me focused, get the kids back to base and then ... I'm all yours. I've got your fancy boyfriend's number and ... he'll lead me straight to you. '

4

Thursday is always a slow day in any school. It's better than Wednesday but you just can't beat that Friday feeling. After a brief assembly, it's business as usual. More prose, plays and poetry: no Chemistry. I think back and smirk. By anybody's reckoning, that's an impressive line.

By lunchtime I'm pining for Ayden and, by the end of the day, I'm crawling up the walls. I check the time in New York: it's not even lunch and he'll be involved in a meeting. I'm consoled by that thought.

Finding myself with some extra time on my hands I decide to give Charlie a call. She's quick to answer. "Hey, Char, I'm on my way home and just wondered if you're still a size small?"

She's confused. "Why, do you want to borrow more clothes?"

"No, I'm thinking of getting you a French maid's outfit, you've done such a good job with my apartment." I can't contain my laughter.

"Oh, I get it now, yes very funny."

"I can't thank you enough. I was dreading bringing him back, but everything was perfect. It must have taken you hours?"

"No, just over an hour but you're going to have to get some marigolds because I've had to have a manicure to get rid of the smell of bloody polish."

I visualise her giving her nails the once over, blowing on make-believe varnish. "Sorry about that."

"No probs honey, but you owe me. That's all I'm saying."

I detect a smile. "Yes I do, I won't forget."

"So, *how* was it?" She puts emphasis on the how and I know she's itching to hear every sordid detail.

I think before I speak, and decide against lying. I've got to tell someone before I explode. "Great. I think I'm going to marry this guy."

There's a two second silence. "Friggin' hell! That good, eh?"

"Not quite, not yet, but he has potential."

"Potential? That's a good sign, especially coming from you. Most of the dorks you've dated have had a lot going for them but definitely no potential." She gives a disgruntled moan and continues. "So when do I get to meet Mr. P?"

"Mr. P?"

"P for potential, if you won't tell me his name then I'm going to have to call him something."

"Right, Mr. P." I like the sound of that. "You'll get your chance, but we're still just getting to know each other, so I think I'd like to keep him under wraps for now."

"Okay, but you know by doing that you're just going to make me more curious, don't you?" I sense a hand on a hip.

"I do, but I think it's for the best."

"Suit yourself, it's your call. But you can at least tell me where he works, or is that top secret too?"

"He works in the city."

"So he's a banker?" I don't reply. "A broker?" I don't reply. "An ad man?" She's getting exasperated and quickly running out of professions. "What the hell is he then?"

"He owns his own company, he's the MD." I have to give her something or I know she'll keep at it until I confess.

"*Nice.* Then he's a keeper?"

"I think so."

"Is he fat with bad breath and a limp?"

I have to laugh. "No, not quite." In my mind's eye I see Ayden lying beneath me, tethered to my bedstead and I feel a shudder of sexual yearning scattering through the length of my body. "Look, I've got to go and I've loved the interrogation, can we do it again soon?"

"You can count on it."

"Thanks again, Char."

"No probs honey, catch you later, bye."

"Bye." I end the call and put my phone away: still no message and still no call.

When I arrive home there's a parcel on the kitchen table. I imagine it being full of all things relating to our 'special' relationship but, when I open it, I'm wrong. Wrapped in purple tissue paper is a lamp with a delicately cut glass shade, a perfect match to my bedroom decor. I lift it out of the box carefully, letting the lead unravel itself. I see the attachment: it's a dimmer switch. How thoughtful.

I reach down and there's a book. '*The Beginners Guide to Seduction.*' It makes me smile. He seems to have spent some time thinking about my amateurish attempt at seduction, and that's not a bad thing.

Next out of the box are two first class tickets to Rome. I gasp and hold them to my chest, excited at the prospect of strolling hand in hand down The Spanish Steps with the most attractive man I have ever seen.

I delve further into the box, wondering what untold treasures are tucked away inside the crisp tissue paper. I grapple with what feels like a box of some sort. When I open it, I'm aghast. It's a platinum chain and the pendant is a small cross, a kiss; a reminder of that first encounter. It's so delicate and so exquisite: it's perfect.

Just when I think my day can't get any better, my fingers stumble across a leather item. It's soft to the touch and I'm curious to check it out. I lift the wrapping and it's a small, leather wallet. I flip it back and inside is a velum business card with embossed print in midnight blue: it's Ayden's. I turn it over and there in his hand writing is his mobile phone number and email address. That's a nice touch. I like the idea of being able to get hold of him at a moment's notice.

I'm about the push the card back into its snug little pocket when I see another card underneath it. I slide it out to take a closer look. It's a black Visa card in my name. It's rather unimpressive to look at but that's the point, isn't it; people who have money don't make a song and dance about it, they just spend it.

I'm taken by surprise. I love everything in my box, but this takes the edge off what is a very thoughtful surprise. My joy is mitigated by the feeling I'm being paid for my services, maybe not by the hour but it feels like that somehow. He won't see it that way but, what we feel, or what we're starting to feel has been soiled by its association with money.

I walk away from the table and turn on the TV, still trying to fathom why he should give me such a thing. Does he think I'm impoverished? I scan my apartment. Granted it's not five star accommodation, but it's comfortable and ... it's my home. The TV draws my attention away from my reflection. It's the news.

There's talk of another terrorist bombing in Iraq and the Euro crisis, then a piece on Anglo American trading and special friendships. A Bill Gates look-alike called Ryan Stadler is shaking Ayden's hand and together they're smiling for the camera.

I draw the platinum kiss to my mouth and feel where his soft kisses were. It's hard to put our past and his present together. He's smiling, but it's uncharacteristically broad and exaggerated; he's simply not conveying any genuine emotion. He's under pressure, going through the motions. But, for all that, the camera loves him and I know, if I allow myself, I will too.

I have a plan. I won't confront him about the Visa card, not now, but I will disturb the order in his life with some very sexy thoughts. He looks like he could do with a distraction. He said he wanted to 'gift' himself to me ... well he'll be my final gift of the day.

I lift out his business card and punch in the number of his London office. I clear my throat and prepare for my performance.

A smartly spoken woman answers my call. "A.S. Media International, good afternoon."

"Good afternoon, I'm trying to get hold of Mr. Stone. Can you tell me what time you expect him to complete his meeting in New York?"

"Of course, can I ask who's speaking, please?"

"It's Elizabeth Parker."

"Ah, yes Miss Parker." I'm momentarily stunned that she knows my name. "If you can bear with me for a moment, I will check his schedule for you." There's a brief pause. "His meeting is scheduled to end at 3 p.m. and then he is planning to return to the Carlton to do some work before attending a charity dinner at 7.30p.m. Can I get a message to him from you?"

"No, thank you ..."

"Charlotte, Miss Parker."

"No, thank you Charlotte, I'll contact him myself later. Thank you for your help."

"My pleasure. Please feel free to contact me again if you require any further assistance."

"I certainly will."

"Goodbye, Miss Parker. Have a pleasant evening".

"Thank you. You too, goodbye."

That has got to be one of the strangest conversations I've ever had with a complete stranger. What had Ayden said to her to make her so ... helpful? I check the clock, it's 6.30 p.m., I've got a couple of hours to kill before I take to the stage.

After a bite to eat I settle for a long soak in a hot bath, listening to the Sugar Babes singing '*Press The Button*:' my sentiment exactly. The combination of steam and scheming leaves me feeling dozy and ready for bed but I'm resolute and so prepare myself for Act 1 Scene One. I turn down my iPod and pick up his business card and dial the number on the back. On the third ring he picks up.

"Yes!" he snaps, not recognising my number.

I find my most innocent of voices. "Hi, Ayden, it's Beth."

"Oh! Beth! Hello. This is a pleasant surprise."

"I hope I'm not interrupting anything, I just wanted to hear your voice."

"... Really ... no, I'm back at the hotel. What are you up to?"

"I was about to get into a bubble bath but all I can smell is you. You left your boxers in my wash basket and your smell has got me feeling ... well ..." I can sense his surprise. I actually believe he is lost for words.

"W... ell, I'm sorry about that. What do you want me to do about it? I'm three thousand miles away."

I'm sure you'll come up with something.

"I just thought, after what you offered last night that you might be able to help me out." I pause, giving him time to assess the situation. "But, if you're busy ... it's just that, I'm stood here wearing your lovely platinum necklace and kiss pendant and ... by the way, thank you for all my presents. It isn't even my birthday."

"It doesn't have to be your birthday, I can buy you gifts any time," he says, briskly.

"I realise that, but it was very thoughtful of you. I'm just so hot and wet ... but I can always go to bed."

"Whoa, just take it easy, Beth. You don't want to go rushing off."

At last, I think the penny has dropped. I hear him swallowing and taking a couple of extra breaths. "Alright, what should I do?"

"What you usually do."

"I usually go to bed and sleep it off." I'm enjoying this so much I pull up a chair and make myself comfortable.

"That's never a good thing to do. We can't have that now, can we?"

I hear something or someone in his room and I catch my reflection in the bathroom mirror. I stand.

"Wait a minute. Room Service is here." There's a pause and I sit myself down again. *"Yes ok, just bring it in. Right, take the money. No I don't want you to pour. No thank you. Can't you see I'm on the fucking phone here?"* There's the sound of a door being slammed. He's back.

"Sorry, that was room service, some arsehole wanted to pour wine." For some reason he seems a little agitated and out of breath.

"I'm still here, Ayden."

"I have an idea." *I thought you might.* "We can have phone sex. How would that be?"

"I'm not sure what you mean." I contain my amusement.

"Take off your clothes and put me on speaker phone. I'll talk you through it."

I place down the phone and wait. He actually believes *he's* initiating this. "Okay, I'm wearing my panties."

"Now lick your fingers."

"Which hand?"

"I don't know, either hand, you decide. Whichever you think will do the job."

I purposely take a couple of seconds to add a little drama. "OK. Now what?"

"Slide your fingers down your panties, so you're touching yourself. What can you feel?"

For some reason, this game is getting serious. I don't believe it, I'm starting to tingle. It's getting so I really *do* want to follow his directions. I lower my right hand until it's between my legs, seeking out my clitoris. Through gentle gasps I answer, "I'm warm and wet ... I'm sort of aching inside."

"Fuck! Hold on, Beth ..." I think I can hear the sound of a zipper coming down and the fact he's masturbating to the sound of my voice is a massive turn-on.

I start to moan. "Talk to me, Ayden, I need to hear your voice."

"I'm here, Beth, I'm feeling you." His breathing is ragged and his words are broken into syllables. "I'm right here with you. I'm hard for you, baby."

"Ayden." I feel the room stating to spin and there's a burning sensation which is mounting and overpowering me. Maybe, I'm recalling the way he looked last night, tied to my bed, coming apart ... but my breathing is frantic and my heart is pounding in my chest.

"I'm with you, Beth, I can feel you. You're so close."

I start to spasm wildly, and my orgasm has me falling to my knees. "Ah!" I'm helpless. I throw my head back and give in to it.

"Argh!" A deep guttural roar comes from the phone and resonates around the bathroom, letting me know he's had a spectacular orgasm. "Fuck!"

Gradually, his breathing eases, he sounds exhausted but settled.

I take a minute to gather my thoughts. This isn't the way I saw this little scene playing out at all. There I was, so sure of myself and here I am having *real* phone sex.

"Are you there, Ayden?"

"Yeah, I think so, just about." I still hear his breathing. "Make me a promise, Beth. You'll never do that to me again. What if I'd been in a meeting?"

"I knew you weren't."

"How did you know?" He's eager to hear my answer. I've roused his curiosity.

"I called Charlotte to check and you should give that woman a raise because she was very helpful." It feels good to explain.

"Aren't you the resourceful one? How did you know I would go along with it?" I picture a wary expression.

"Because I saw you on TV and you looked very handsome, but your smile was a little too forced and it didn't reach your eyes. I thought you might like to take some time out." That's what this was really about. Not a power trip for me but a way of taking care of him. I just had some fun along the way.

"You're very special, Beth, fancy you knowing that." There's a heartfelt sincerity in his voice, it transcends the distance between us. At that moment we are inextricably connected.

"You're very special to me. I want you back here in my bed." The truth spills out of me like hot steam from a kettle.

What am I saying?

"I can catch an earlier flight tomorrow and land around nine. Do you want me to come over?"

"You'd better, or we're going to have to do this all over again." I catch myself in the steamed-up mirror: I'm flushed but I have a self-satisfied smile on my face.

"Should I bring anything?"

"Only a change of clothes and anything else you think you might need. I'll provide the entertainment."

"Then I'll look forward to being entertained."

I see his boyish smile. "By the way, why are you eating, you have a charity dinner at 7.30?"

"I never eat at those things, and you can stop now. You've had your fun. Let me get back to work. I know my schedule." How quickly his armour plating is restored. All that softness is tucked away, zipped up and he's back to being fierce Mr. P. Not for potential but for powerful.

I sense it's my cue to leave. I decide to exit stage left. "Have a good night, I've some bedtime reading to catch up on. See you tomorrow." My briskness is uncalled for and the second the words let fly from my mouth, I regret their departure.

"You too, sleep well, Beth ... we're good, right?"

"Yes, Ayden, we're good."

"Beth ..."

"Yes?"

"Check your mail."

"Okay."

"See you tomorrow."

"I'll be here."

I end the call, feeling a little disappointed but not to the extent I will let it spoil my evening. It has been fun, after all. I'm about to head to bed but, instead, I fire up my laptop, copy out his email address off the back of his business card and send him something to lift his mood.

Prior to meeting him, my only companion and flat mate was my music. I have welcomed it into my home with open arms like an old friend who has given me comfort when I've needed it, and been here for me at the end of my working day. Through good times and bad, I have found solace in the melodies and lived my life to the beat of chorus' that resonate throughout the tracks stored on my laptop and on my iPod. They make up the soundtrack to my life. I want to introduce Ayden to it, I think they are about to become very good friends. Welcome to my world Mr. Stone.

From:	songbirdBP@hotmail.co.uk
To:	a.s.mediainternational1@global.com
Date:	15th October 2012 21.45
Subject:	WHY THE SERIOUS FACE?

HOT!

I'm off to bed with my book and jiffy bag in hand. I wonder what's inside.
Have a great evening ... be good!
See you tomorrow.

Beth. X

I can visualise Avril Lavigne strutting her way through the song and that thought makes me smile. He won't be mentally prepared for this kind of email and it will throw him temporarily off track. But isn't that the idea?

Before turning out the lights, my curiosity gets the better of me. I Google *Sex and Submission* and, my God, have I been wrapped-up in cotton wool? Unsure of what to think, I shut down. My head is filled with the kind of images of domination which make me shudder and flinch. Is this the kind relationship he wants? Is he that kinky or, more importantly, does he think I am?

Up until now, all I had was a recollection of Justin Timberlake singing about 'shackles' and 'whips' in *Sexy Back*. But now, I don't know what to think.

The laptop pings. I have an email. I wonder who from?

From:	a.s.mediainternational1@global.com
To:	song.birdBP@hotmail.co.uk
Date:	15th October 2012 16.55
Subject:	WHAT SERIOUS FACE?

(VERY) HOT!

I've had over 96 personal emails today and yours is the only one that's made me smile. Thank you. Get to bed!
Enjoy the gift ...
Ayden x

Now it really is time for bed, although sleeping with the after effects of *that* orgasm still rattling around my insides will not be easy. If his voice has that effect on me, what will he be able to do with those hands, or any other part of his perfect anatomy?

And what the hell's in this bag?

I tear it open. Inside it is a rectangular black box. It's jewellery, a necklace perhaps?

Oh! That's unexpected ...

It's a black silicone, egg vibrator with a charger and a remote control. Ha! A wicked smile is sweeping across my face, stopping only when it threatens to split it in two. A giggle escapes from my throat and a surge of arousal finds its way to my nether region, causing my breath to quicken at the prospect of using this aesthetically pleasing and fully functional sex toy.

I snap my phone free of its charger and compose a message.

Mr. Stone, your gift is making me blush. You are a Very naughty boy who is turning me into a Very naughty girl ... B. X

Thanks to the power of modern satellite communications, courtesy of A.S.M.I. no doubt, I have an immediate reply. With excited fingers I click 'read.'

Miss. Parker, you have no idea ... Sleep well! A.X

Time for bed, I think.

***

Despite the icy wind, Dan is sweating, looking like a man who has done ten rounds with a sparring partner. He's driven home like a man possessed by some intangible force of will and determination, having been distracted all day. He's feeling exhausted due to a combination of physical exertion and fatigue, brought on by lack of sleep and nervous energy.

Having had an extra, large lunch to compensate for the fact he would be too busy to have an evening meal, he's reading through last night's notes. For the first time in six years, he's had a break-through; he was in the right place at the right time. Last night's encounter with *her* was no coincidence. He'd been feeling as if something was about to happen and, the fact it had, has him feeling pretty pleased with himself. His instincts were good.

The day's delivery of newspapers has been dumped onto the sofa. He decided to forgo the scanning in favour of a personal approach. He has to follow up his lead, pronto. His most important detail is written down in big letters on his pad, it's also etched onto his left forearm: ASMED1A.

On his phone there are only ten contacts. One of them belongs to Jack Simpson, a fellow infantry man with a knack for computer hacking and all things electronic. The operation Dan has in mind calls for teamwork and specific skills. Jack's just the man.

His phone rings four times. "Hello Jack, it's Dan, Dan Rizler. How are you, mate?"

"Fuck me! I thought you were out for the count. How long's it been champ?" The voice at the end of the line is uncultured but friendly.

"Nah, I'm still alive and kicking. Need a favour." Dan doesn't believe in beating around the bush.

"Sounds serious mate. You in a spot of bother?"

"No, but I know a fucker who's about to experience some."

He's sniggering down the line. "Oh yeah, who's that then?"

"You still cleaning the cop shop on Bolton Street?"

"Yeah, has its perks. Why?"

"Wondered if you could give me some info on a Reg? Some smart arse clipped my car and did a runner. Got the Reg. though and thought I'd pay him a visit."

"Poor bastard."

"I hope not, because I don't accept cheques." They both laugh cruelly.

"What's the damage?"

"I'd say a monkey would cover it."

"Right. Sounds like a piece of piss. So what do you need?"

"What are you offering?"

"I can supply you with a name, an address, date of birth. What else do you want?"

"Nothing. That's more than enough for what I need."

"Let me get a pen." There is silence down the line and Dan is growing impatient. "Right, let's have it."

"ASMED1A"

"That's it?"

"That's it."

"That's a fancy Reg. What sort of motor was it?"

"A Silver Rolls."

"Fuck me! You want to hold out for more than a monkey. Sounds like you've got yourself a rich bastard."

"Yeah." Dan can barely speak he's so overcome with a temper which is fast becoming an incendiary device. "Looked like a right poser. You know the type?"

"Oh yeah. It's always the pretty boys who think they can get away with it. He'll shit himself when he finds out he's about to become your new sparring partner."

"Oh, I think he'll give me what I want without a fight." The sneer says it all.

"No can do tonight, but I'll get back to you tomorrow. Got your mobile number, so I can text details or call. Either way, I'll get the job done."

"Good man. I'll give you a ton for your trouble, if it works out."

"Have I ever let you down before?"

"No, but there's always a first time."

"You're an ungrateful bastard, Dan."

"That's me, Captain Cautious."

"Right Captain. For a ton I'll get straight on it. I'll be in touch."

"Tomorrow?"

"Tomorrow."

Dan ends the call, feeling very pleased with the progress he has made. The game is in play and he knows all the moves. He trusts no-one, but has some faith in Jack. Since Iraq they have stayed in touch. When Jack had needed someone to throw their weight around, he was there. So now it's payback time.

A hungry cat is weaving in and out of his ankles, trying to gain his attention. "Evening, Honey, you ready for your tea? I'm late tonight, had something important to sort out." He reaches up to the top shelf and lifts out a fresh tin of cat food. He spoons it into her dish. "There you go, eat up."

The bowl falls to the floor with a clatter and he gives it no more than a cursory glance; his mind is on other things. He pulls the tab off a can of lager and makes his way over to his comfortable chair, feeling optimistic about the prospect of getting back together with his girl. His Cheshire Cat grin wouldn't be quite so menacing if it was directed at someone or something in particular. The fact that it's merely a manifestation of his inner thoughts makes for a disturbing expression.

He snatches one of the newspapers off his daily pile and glances at the headlines: more economic doom and gloom and concerns about the threat of war in the Middle East. The information is of no interest to him. He rests the paper on his lap and throws back his head, feeling chilled lager trickling down his throat. It's been a while since he allowed his lips to touch a drop, but today's a special day. He has cause for celebration.

He glances over at his cork notice board and the faded photos, contemplating his next move. "Maybe we should tidy up a little, Honey. Make this a palace fit for a princess. What do you think?"

Taking no notice of his address and having eaten the food, Honey saunters over to the cat flap and makes her escape. She's had what she came for and wants nothing more from him, which is just as well as he has nothing to give. He only has room in his heart for one female and, once he catches up with her, she'll need more than a small hole in a door to make *her* escape.

The TV lights up the dusty room, but it's still unwelcoming and oppressive; the net curtains are held together by dust and cobwebs, even the coffee table wobbles and is sticky to the touch. This is not a home, it's a store room. An overcrowded storage depot inhabited by memories and endless nights searching, longing for sexual gratification at the hands of a helpless, blond haired woman.

Feeling somewhat sedated by the lager in his bloodstream, Dan drops off to sleep. The newspaper on his lap slides down his thighs, over his knees and lands on the floor. It lies open, four pages in. There is a picture of two businessmen; one is wearing a grey, pinstriped three piece suit. The other is tall, wearing a well-tailored designer suit in midnight blue and smiling. They are shaking hands and the headline reads: *Big Apple Agreement for Stadler & Stone.*

The sound of his snoring drowns out the TV and echoes around the shadow-filled room. There's no-one to nudge him into wakefulness and he sleeps until dawn.

When he stirs, it's with a burgeoning sense of arousal. He breathes deeply, letting his senses resurface. Before his shower, he strolls over to his favourite place. A lewd sneer slithers across his face.

"Not long now, princess, not long now ..."

5

F riday morning sunlight drizzles through the curtains and makes its way across my bedroom, bringing light to every gloomy corner and crevice. I rise from my bed a good half hour before my alarm goes off, still tingling from the after effects of my fingers, his words and his gift: what a wicked combination.

After a morning's teaching, I spend my lunch nibbling a sandwich and typing up stickers for seats in alphabetical order. I have to help with the planning of a presentation evening that's three days away. All the students who have completed exams are returning to collect their certificates. It's a night of celebration. By the time the bell rings for afternoon lessons, they are done and ready to go.

Making the most of a free period at the end of the day, I've headed into town. I'm enjoying the sunlight on my face and the bustling crowds remind me of how I've been hiding myself away for too long. Like a character from a fairy-tale, my self-imposed exile has kept me safe from harm; insulated but alone. Not anymore.

I head in the direction of the local Ann Summers shop in search of something suited to the role of a Dominant, what exactly, I have absolutely no idea. Something will come to me. I'm starting to take my role seriously and finding shopping for such a man a real eye-opener. Who knew these kind of toys existed on the high street, tucked away behind dare-devil lingerie and dildos.

I buy all the basic provisions: Danish pastries and orange juice for breakfast, on the off chance he stays the night. I'm secretly hoping he'll be overcome with jet lag and collapses in my arms, but he travels first class and I shouldn't rest my hopes on sleep deprivation.

When I arrive home with my selection of goodies, I struggle to place the bags down, hearing my phone ringing in my bag.

"Hello."

"Hello to you too." It's Charlie. "I'm on my way over, should I bring anything: wine, ice-cream, tissues?"

"No, just yourself."

"See ya in five."

Her call triggers my dilemma. Do I reveal who my secret lover is or not? I decide to tell her, she'll be the one to catch me if and when I fall. She'll be my shoulder to cry on, as she has been for the past nine years.

"It's 6.30p.m., it's Friday night, and it's wine time!" Charlie announces. She is in the mood to party and has better things to do than listen to me fawning over my beau, but I sense another inquisition.

"So are you ready to tell me yet? I'm losing sleep wondering who the hell he is."

"Okay. It's Ayden Stone."

"Who?" I hand her the print outs and the info. She reads through his biography, captivated by both words and pictures, stopping only to fan herself with his photographs. "He's friggin' gorgeous. Where did you meet him? It must have been at school or at the supermarket because you never go out."

She's stunned and I'm not sure I should tell her any more but, what the hell. "He was a guest speaker at school and we kind of hit it off." That's not entirely true but it's close enough.

"And he asked you out, just like that?"

"No, he sent me flowers and a poem." The memory of the poem brings a smile to my face. *'Desire is love's pure flame ...'*

"A poem? What is he, bi?" She tucks a flaming strand of hair behind her ear.

"No, he's not bisexual, he's straight," I retort, coming to his defence much too readily.

She takes a closer look at the photographs. "He looks too ..." I wait for the rest of it. "... Too well groomed to be straight."

I start to laugh. "Charlie, I can confirm he is definitely a hot blooded, heterosexual male."

"You've been laid!" she calls out clapping her hands together. "My God, I take my hat off to you, Beth, you've been holding out for someone special and here he is." She lifts up one of his photos and plants a noisy kiss on his face. "You're a very lucky guy, Mr. P."

She passes me my glass of wine. "Let's toast to you getting laid and me finding my Mr. Right tonight." Our glasses clink and we revel in my good fortune.

I haven't the heart to tell her our relationship has yet to be consummated, why ruin my fun?

By 7.30 p.m. Charlie is preparing to leave and on her phone to someone securing VIP tickets to a fashionable club. She leaves in a flurry and it's like waving off a whirlwind. I love her like a sister but sometimes watching her leave is the best part of a catch-up.

I'm soon in familiar territory and have three hours to clean, cook and calm down. It's only 7 o'clock but I want everything to be perfect.

I scroll down my iPod nestling comfortably in the kitchen dock and select Kate Walsh. I need a remedy for my anxiety and her soothing tones are like valium to the senses. '*Animals on Fire*' is a fair assessment of the state of play. The gentle distraction is momentary. It occurs to me, I know so little about the man I'm so eager to have in my life. I've read his biography, but that can only tell me so much. He was my best kept secret until an hour ago and I wonder how many of *my* secrets I'll be able to keep to myself after tonight.

I make a mental list of the things I know and smile when I admit to myself, it's purely physical: his breath on my throat, his hands on my skin, his mouth on my mouth. With every recollection of him comes a breathless sigh and a flicker of desire that cannot be extinguished. I want to touch myself and to have his hands touch me, to fulfil a yearning I have repressed for so long. But thoughts of the flesh must be shelved for now; coq au vin won't make itself.

Next on my 'to do list' is my bedroom. With reluctance, I strip off the sheets, clutching them to my chest like a sail from an ailing yacht. I catch his scent and I'm all at sea. The wicked combination of feral masculinity and sex reignites the embers and my head spins. I quickly bundle the linen into the washing machine with his boxers and start a hot wash. Every trace of him is locked away behind tempered glass and soap suds, for now at least.

With a visitor's eye, I carefully scan the whole apartment. It's so small and compact and doesn't take more than five minutes. It isn't much, but it's mine, my world and his welcome invasion is fast approaching.

It's 9.50 p.m., I'm ready and waiting, showered and shaved. I sit on my sofa with my hands on my lap but my thumb nail keeps finding its way to my mouth. I stand, then sit and stand again. Why am I so friggin' nervous? The external buzzer sounds at 10.10 p.m. and I stumble to answer it. "Hello?"

"Hi, Beth. It's me," he declares, sounding unsettled.

"Who is it?" I ask, for my own sadistic pleasure.

"Just *open* the door!" An invisible smile finds its way to his voice.

"OK, push." I press the release button and move to open my front door. When I see him standing there, he takes my breath away. He's come straight from the airport, suited and booted with a tie roughly pulled from his collar. How could I have forgotten the colour of his eyes and the shape of his mouth? He's exquisite. For a split second I cannot move, I cannot speak.

"I can't come in if you don't invite me," he says with a devilish grin.

I tip my head to one side and find my voice. "I thought that only applied to blood sucking, over-sexed, stunningly attractive vampires?" I can't hold back a smile.

"Darling, I'm home." He throws down his overnight bag and walks me backwards to the wall. A picture wobbles against my back and the door slams shut, courtesy of his fancy footwork. Without so much as a 'Hello', his hands are on me; hot palms move upwards from my neck into my hair, finding their resting place on my warm cheeks.

"That has got to be the longest flight in history. Ten hours with a fucking hard on!" Each word is spoken between hurried kisses.

I become aware of his physical longing and pull his body into mine. "You smell delicious." I lift my hands to his fragrant hair and inhale his luxurious cologne.

"I showered on the plane." His passionate kissing hitches up a notch, and his tongue wraps itself around mine.

"They let you do that?" I ask, still unconvinced about actually being able to shower on a plane.

"First class, Beth. First Class. Forget the shower, focus!"

In need of no further prompting, I melt into him and nibble his bottom lip. He groans and the reverberation from that groan, arrows its way to my core and beyond. The sounds this man makes do something to me.

How can this be happening? We've only had one date and we're acting as if we've been doing this for months, forever. I give myself to the moment and feel my breathing starting to quicken. I become aware of urgent hands descending to my buttocks, grabbing, lifting me so his straining fly is pressing against my moist panties.

Oh Christ!

He leans back and is about to speak. "I know I said I wanted you to take the lead but right now all I want to do is get down and dirty with you."

He sounds so desperate, I want to say, "Me too!" but something I cannot fathom is stopping me. He continues to press his rigid mass into my crotch and the folds of his trousers find my clitoris. It would be so easy for any woman to say 'yes,' but I'm not any woman. I have issues, and fucking me now really is not an option.

"Undo me," he urges, still taking my weight on his muscular arms.

I can't

"Undo me, Beth."

I can't.

I'm suddenly breathless, not out of desire but with blind panic. My heart's racing; muscles are becoming rigid and knotted. I'm afraid.

Sensing my shift in focus Ayden lowers me to the floor, but is so wrapped up in the moment, he forges on at an unstoppable pace.

Oh no!

He's undoing his zip. He's pushing down his trousers. He's devouring my mouth with his ravenous tongue. I want to say stop, but he's sucking every breathless word from my lips. Only when I feel him hitching my skirt do I find the strength to say his name.

"Ayden!"

I feel the tip of a rigid mass against my flimsy underwear and I want to push him off. My fingernails press into his flexing shoulders through his jacket. I start to push harder, but I've tried this before; he is made of granite. I look at him. All I can see are eyelashes and a man driven by a savage urge to penetrate me. I tell myself, 'I want you' but my silent assurance is no match for my darkest fears.

Misreading my frenzied embrace, he takes my hands, bends my arms at the elbows, and slams them left and right, either side of my head. It's all I can do to stop myself from screaming. Instead, I fight him with all I have. I call out his name and so wild is my cry it stops him dead.

"Ayden. No!" Panting and frantic our eyes lock. He sees horror and I see disbelief.

"No?" Never has a man been so stunned by a single word.

"I can't. I'm sorry." With a heaving chest, I look away. I feel such a fraud.

It takes several seconds for things to register. He pulls down my skirt and the noise of his zip fastening is a sobering sound. He cannot take his eyes off me.

"No?" The word has a fierce inflection. This is not a man who ever hears the word 'no' from anyone, especially not from women. His face is expressionless.

I shake my head, struggling to come to terms with my own behaviour. "I thought I could, but I can't." I take his serious face in my hands, hoping he can hear the sincerity in my words and take pity on my plight.

"There's a word for women who play this kind of game," he points out, lowering my hands from his face and straightening his jacket. "And it isn't very complimentary."

My body sags at the thought. "I'm not a prick tease if that's what you're suggesting, and this is not a game."

"No?"

"No." I'm having to choose my words very wisely. He's come here straight from the airport after a long flight, expecting 'entertainment.' What a terrible disappointment I must be: me with my issues. Before he comes to his own conclusions, I swallow hard and try to explain myself. "I don't want you to simply fuck me

Ayden, not like this. I'm better than that, for Christ's sake you're better than that."

He looks lost, disbelieving my assertion, unconvinced. Risking rejection, I nervously raise my hands to his face. "You're very special, there's so much goodness in you. It's all I see."

He manufactures a half smile. "Then maybe you're not looking hard enough. It's all smoke and mirrors."

What a strange thing to say ...

"There's no smoke and mirrors here, just us." I hold him so close to me I can feel his heart still fluttering against my shoulder. With his desire contained and affection returning to his eyes, he smiles and brushes a strand of hair away from my face.

"Something smells good, I'm starving." A chaste kiss and he takes my hand. "Let's eat."

I pull him back.

"What?" He looks anxious, unprepared for another surprise.

"They have showers in first class, but they don't feed you?"

His crooked smile lingers for a second. "I was too excited to eat." He pulls my knuckles to his mouth and brushes them with his lips. "But I think I've found my appetite now."

Out of relief, my hand finds his cheek and my face cracks into a grin: he's back.

We eat coq au vin with French bread and enjoy each other's company, later nibbling on cheese and crackers. Ayden opens a bottle of Chateau Mont Redon and the zesty white wine goes down easily. Feeling more relaxed I decide to test his humour.

I relate Charlie's observations about him being too attractive to be straight, and all I get is a raised brow. I let him down easy and explain how I came to his defence, but there's still a discernible awkwardness about him and I suspect he's wondering where this night is going. Will I ask him to stay? I come to his aid.

"Ayden, about before ..."

He won't let me finish. "I'm sorry, Beth, I'm used to taking what I want and I wanted you. Can you forgive me?" He wraps his hand over mine and caresses my heart with his words.

"I can forgive you anything, Ayden. What I can't forgive is myself." He tries to interject but my fingers on his soft lips quieten him. "Something unpleasant happened to me in my final year at Uni. Some guy grabbed me in a car park one night and attacked me." I try to make light of it but he is so attentive and I'm searching for the right words.

"Christ, Beth."

I palm his face, accepting his compassion. I feel the need to explain myself, and perhaps purge myself of my demon in the process. "I can remember him pinning my hands above my head and gripping my wrists really tight. Thank God some guy came out of one of the apartments opposite to walk his dog. When the security light came on the bastard got scared and let me go."

"Thank God!" He seems visibly relieved and sighs. "Did you call the police, did they arrest him?"

"No I went home and I thought I'd be able to laugh it off, but it took a while."

"I bet." His grip tightens.

"A few months actually. Charlie was a rock. She got me through it ... I think it brought us closer together." I squeeze his hand gently. "You should meet her, she's nothing like me. All fire and sparkle."

He aims a perceptive look in my direction. "Oh, I don't know, I've seen you all fired up." A seductive smile kisses his lips and I wish it would kiss mine.

"Please, you're making me blush." I look away with images of our nocturnal antics after the theatre and the phone sex replaying in my visual cortex ... and the gift!

Don't even go there...

From the look on his face, he has a recollection too. "I seem to recall someone who was rather hot and wet on the other end of a phone last night!"

When he gives me that look I am lost; come to bed eyes are the least of it. It's his sensuous mouth, to kiss it isn't enough. I want it on me, tasting me, claiming every inch. And ... those distracting hands, powerfully masculine with almond shaped nails, just a touch too short but perfect for exploring and probing. Everything about him is a feast for the senses. He holds me, spellbound.

"Or were you just playing games, Miss Parker?" He gives me such a probing stare, I'm defenceless.

"I don't know what you mean." I smile so sweetly and put my thumb nail to my mouth, feigning school girl innocence.

"Take your thumb out of your mouth, or you'll have me hard again and we both know that's going to get me in all kinds of trouble."

I do as I'm told. "Trouble might be fun, if it doesn't involve holding me down?" I look away and rethink my approach. "But I like the idea of holding *you* down."

For the first time I feel confident enough to play him at his own game. "But, *you* said you wanted to modify our arrangement, and *you* said you wanted to lead. So where does that leave us?" I observe his brain working with the precision of a pocket watch, the mechanics of his mind formulating a response. He's considering the switch.

He has a solution. "Then perhaps we should reflect on the error of *my* ways and resume normal service." There's a seriously naughty twinkle in his eye that almost has me crawling over wine glasses to get to him.

"Service? You consider what I do a service?" I won't look away, I won't look away. He seems a little ruffled.

Wow! Now there's a look! Ayden Stone ruffled?

"I may be having some difficulty doing and saying things the right way tonight, but I'm hoping you'll put that down to jet-lag and blue-balls ..."

I laugh out loud. It's been a while since anyone made me laugh like this, two nights ago in fact. That frozen lake in me is cracking and beginning to thaw.

"Oh nice, laughter, that's right go ahead. I'm dying here and you're laughing." He's holding back a smile but the skin around his eyes is wrinkling; fine lines like the wings on a humming bird are visible on his cheek bones. In this natural state, he's flawless.

I do believe he's finding me 'entertaining.'

"I'm sorry, I'm nervous. I need more wine." I go to fetch another bottle but he takes hold of my wrist and stands so close our bodies are touching. My nose is filling with the delectable aroma of expensive cologne and it's making me light-headed. He raises my chin so we are eye to eye.

"No more wine, Beth." He kisses my cheeks left and right. "Tell me what I can do to make up for my atrocious behaviour. Come on, anything. Be bold."

I gather my thoughts. "There's one thing I want you to do for me." I take hold of his tie and slowly pull him to my mouth. He leans in, so close his breath tickles my nose. "I want you to go into my bedroom and take off your clothes in front of me, very, very slowly." I pause then issue a stern command. "Do you understand?"

He nods his head.

"Do you understand?" I ask again.

There's a hint of a playboy smile. "Yes E. LIZ. A. BETH." He spells out my name, floors me with a stare of such intensity it makes me hold my breath, and edges his way into my bedroom.

I reach over and finish *his* glass of wine and follow, my insides full of butterflies, hot and excited little butterflies.

When I enter the bedroom, he is standing five feet away to the side of the bed, still dressed, waiting; eyes fiery and alive. I reach over to the bedside lamp he bought for me and dim the light. He gives me a grateful smile even though he's happy to exhibit himself, and why wouldn't he be with a body like an athlete?

Perched on the side of the bed, I begin our game. Trying to sound as dispassionate as possible, I give him his first instruction and, in response he loosens his tie. He pulls it slowly from left to right until it ends up on the floor.

"What else can I do for you, Elizabeth?"

"Unbutton your shirt and take it off." His crisp white shirt goes the way of the tie. I'm getting into my stride but I have an idea. *"Be bold,"* he said.

Deliberately I make space between my knees, a centimetre at a time. His focus shifts from my face to the hem of my skirt and back again. I have *his* attention now.

"Remove your socks and shoes, Ayden." I half expect him to make a spectacle of himself, to fall over and for this spell I have cast to be broken, but the task is completed with perfect balance and poise.

"And now...?"

Experiencing a longing which starts at my thighs and finds its way to my mouth, I utter, "Take off your trousers and place them on the chair."

His strong fingers pull at the fastening and make short work of the belt and the zip, but he's eager and I want to whet my appetite with this visual feast.

"Slowly."

He obliges and, as a reward I start to hitch up my skirt. I place my hands just above my knees and edge towards my damp thighs. His striptease falters as he catches sight of my provocative movements; his chest is rising and his breathing is visibly quickening.

He pauses. "Are you ready for this, Elizabeth?"

"I'm very ready." I'm trying not to smile but I know my eyes are betraying me: pure joy radiating from them and making its way to his side of the room. When he steps out of his trousers, it's as if all my birthdays have come at once. He is every woman's aphrodisiac: unkempt hair, taut muscle and an impressive erection that threatens to make its escape from his Calvin Kleins.

"Are you sure?"

My God, you are so self-assured.

In response, my fingers screw up the hem of my skirt and I pull it higher so he can see my moist underwear. This is a tortuous game for us both, but I'm determined to follow through: he's daring me to see it through. I go for broke. Let's see if I can't ruffle his feathers, just a little ...

"Show me how you please yourself."

At that, he looks a little surprised but, after a moment's hesitation and a failed attempt to mask a sexy smile, he slips his right hand between the elastic and his hard abdomen. His eyes betray his mounting arousal and his heaving chest is a giveaway.

I incline my right hand towards my lacy pants and trace the edge with my thumb. How I wish it was his thumb seeking me out and rescuing me from this torture. But he's suffered enough and if I don't tell him to stop he's going to jerk himself off.

I meet his dancing irises with a fierce stare. "Stop! Come here to me."

Was there ever a man more grateful for a command? He's trembling and I sense the relief in his bones. I contain a gasp when I see the sweat gathering on his upper lip and between his forefinger and thumb: he's taking this role play very seriously. Now he stands a little off balance but passive, his hard torso inches from my mouth: a perfect specimen. I'm finding it almost impossible to construct a coherent sentence. "... Put your hands behind your back and grip your wrists. If you try to touch any part of me, I will stop. Do you understand?"

He swallows deeply and answers with a quivering whisper. "Yes, Elizabeth."

I feel as horny as hell and knowing I can do anything with his amazing body causes me to throb with desire. I feel empowered; this has got to be the boldest thing I have *ever* done.

Holding his attention, I trace the top of his boxers with my fingertips, front to back, testing the elastic as I go. His stomach muscles ripple and flex at my touch and I am encouraged. It hits me: I've never seen this gorgeous man naked. I have held him and run my hand the length of his cock but this is a whole new level. The thought of seeing him in all his primal glory makes my hands shake. I play for time and caress the rod of throbbing muscle with my palm and, feeling the need to attach myself to him, put my cheek against the steaming cotton material. He leans into me, aching for my mouth and I stop.

"Don't move, Ayden. Let me do this. You have to be good or I'll stop. Do you understand?"

"Oh, fucking yes, Elizabeth!"

The neediness in his voice makes me smile. When I look up at him he is teetering on the edge; his face is glossy with perspiration and there's that sexy, 'fuck me' smile that has me creaming my panties.

"Good."

Having regained my control, I pick up where I left off, but this time I start to lower his boxers. I feel his arms straining and the grip he has on his wrists, tightening. He wants to grab my head and fuck my mouth. Not tonight Mr. Stone.

With as little pressure as possible, I roll down his boxers and he steps out of them effortlessly. His bulging cock springs into action and I cannot hide my surprise when its proximity to my face makes me lean back. My astonishment does not go unnoticed.

When I glance up, he manifested a look which combines self-satisfaction and amusement at my naiveté. He tilts his head to one side, silently saying. 'What did you expect?' Our connection is profound; there's no embarrassment and no fear, simply trust.

"Be good," I caution, and he adopts a more obedient stance. I take him in two hands. From crown to base, he's beautiful, captivating. I lick the tip with my tongue, tasting a pungent fusion of hot saltiness. As a reflex, he pushes forward and, realising his mistake, pulls back slightly.

I take him in my mouth and deep, guttural noises emanate from his throat. Or is it his chest? As I quicken my movements, his mouth opens and the sounds become louder and less controlled: more animal than human. I fist the base with my right hand and allow my lips to trace each bulging vein, feeling myself blushing as an internal flame finds its way to my cheeks.

He's about to orgasm so I intervene. I release him from my mouth. "Don't come." Isn't this what Dominants do, withhold orgasms, didn't I read that somewhere? "Count back from ten and come on one."

"Yes, Elizabeth," he pants, his body trembling in front of me.

When I take him again, I force the tip to the back of my throat, so far I can feel my eyes starting to water. He lets out an aching moan which causes every muscle inside me to tighten and contract.

"Seven, six ..."

By five he's coming undone.

"Three, two ..."

And he's calling my name. "Eliz-a-beth!"

One is lost to a ferocious relay of pulsating muscle and ejaculation. My mouth fills and I swallow unsure of what other course of action to take.

"Holly fuck, Beth!" Is all he can manage; clearly Elizabeth has done the dirty deed and left the building. He falls to his knees, head bowed, wasted.

He raises his eyes to meet mine. "Where did you learn to do that?"

I explain simply. "The Internet."

"Then God bless the internet." He grins, boyishly. "That's got to be the best blow job I've ..." He stops himself before finishing the sentence, but the damage has been done. I feel a crushing hurt forming; it starts in my chest and reaches my eyes. Disgust and anger builds in the space between us like a seething monster.

"Finish the sentence, Ayden. 'That's got to be the best blow job you've ever had.' Have I got it right?"

He looks mortified, and so he should.

I push him away from me and he falls backwards onto the carpet. I stride into the bathroom and slam the door shut behind me. Does he have any idea how difficult it was for me to do that?

When he enters the bathroom, I'm cleaning my teeth. I won't look at him. If I do I know I'll cry. He's turned something so intimate into a vulgar act and I feel cheap and humiliated.

He approaches me, taking cautious steps. "Beth ... look at me."

I won't. I can't.

"Beth, I'm so sorry. It was meant to be a compliment but it came out all wrong."

He expects me to speak but I continue to clean my teeth, I'm sure he can guess why.

"Stop!" He takes the toothbrush and throws it into the sink. "Look at me while I'm talking to you."

I wipe the toothpaste from my mouth with the back of my hand and look directly at him. On witnessing my hurt, he turns away.

He composes himself. "Look, you can't expect the habits of a lifetime to stop overnight."

I watch and listen but I don't speak.

"You've done your homework, you know my reputation. I don't do dates and I'm not Prince fucking Charming. You asked me what I like to do in my spare time, and I told you. 'I like fucking beautiful women.' That's because beautiful women like to be fucked by me, any way I choose."

"Thanks for the news flash, Ayden, and that's supposed to make me feel better how exactly?"

He begins to wrestle with himself and his right hand finds its way to his neck, he rubs it to ease the tension. "It's ... it's you, you've got me hooked. I was a bastard earlier and I've been an insensitive bastard now but it's because, in my own fucked up way, I care about you."

He reaches out for my hand and I offer it as a lifeline.

"I should be in New York now, I've crossed time zones and haven't a fucking clue what day or time it is; I've cancelled meetings to be here with you. I don't do that, business always comes first." He strokes my knuckles with his thumb. "Do you seriously think I would ever do what I just did, like that, with anyone else?"

He hits me right between the eyes with a wide, sea green stare. "I know it's the same for you, but you've got to give me some leeway because this is a steep learning curve for me too and I'll fuck up, not because I want to, but because I don't know any better."

His strung out expression holds my attention. As the seething monster leaves the room, it's only me and this naked Adonis that remain.

I sniff back tears. "But comparing me to some bitch who's had your dick in her mouth was hurtful."

"I know, baby." He takes me in his arms. "I know." He's stoking my hair and his naked body is so hot and damp to the touch, I can feel his odour permeating my clothes.

"I would never compare you to them. No-one has ever come close to what we have." He dusts away a tear. "Now this is what we're going to do." He presents my face in front of him and I cannot break away.

"You're going to go back to bed, get naked and I'm going to shower and get rid of ..." He looks to the ceiling, seeking out the right words. "... the after effects of your spectacular BJ, and then ..." He tips up my chin. With each word he kisses my lips chastely. "I'm going to make love to you. I'll do whatever you want me to do to make up for my indiscretions and you're going to come so hard you'll be begging for more by morning. Do you understand?"

I nod.

"Do you understand, Beth?" He is waiting for me to say the words.

I answer with a wide-eyed stare. "Yes, Ayden."

"Then go."

I turn in the direction of my bed and he softly slaps my behind as I leave.

Walking and stripping isn't something I normally do but now it's all I can think about. In ten seconds flat, I'm in bed waiting. When I close my eyes all I can hear is the shower and the beating of my own heart. Anyone who has been in a position like this will know; it's the fear of disappointment or failure that affects the performance. My only consolation is that Ayden cannot fail me. I have so little experience and no expectations. Whatever he does will have me in orgasmic heaven, I have no doubt about that. All I have to do is let him get close to me. But that's easier said than done.

He makes his entrance, and what an entrance; tumbling hair the colour of wet tarmac, a low slung towel and a 'coming to get you' smile.

Thank you God!

"Are you naked?" He asks casually.

I nod my head shyly.

"Good." He throws off his towel in a single movement and slips between the sheets on the left side of the bed. He's next to me and I'm not sure if it's the look, the hair or the fact that he smells so good that causes my pulse to race.

"Hi," he says, brushing away a strand of hair from my face.

"Hi," I answer sweetly, touching his nose with mine.

"Did you miss me?" He bowls me over with a smile and I'm suddenly bashful. "No? Then I'll have to do something about that."

Gently, he strokes my hot cheek and finds my mouth with his minty tongue. I can do no more than move to respond.

"I want you, Beth, but not like before. I want to do this right. Whatever happened in your past put it behind you." His hand takes hold of my hair in a kind of ragged promise. "You're safe with me, I won't hurt you."

I'm pinned in place by his stare. "I trust you, Ayden." And it's true - almost.

"Let me make love to you, try not to fight me." He repositions himself and his tongue finds that spot just beneath my ear.

"I'll try," I whisper, experiencing the kind of tingle that makes your toes curl.

"Don't do anything, let me do this." He redirects my words back at me and I smile into his hair, it's wet and like silk against my lips. I feel his showered body pressing down on mine for a second before he sits up and shifts his weight onto his knees. He is straddling me and finding my hands, locking our fingers together. I'm grateful for the dim light and catch him exploring my breasts with covetous eyes.

"You're so beautiful, Beth." He kisses the tips of my fingers, one after the other and continues along my arms, crossing over my neck as if it's a kind of bridge from west to east. It feels divine.

He continues to explore my body inch by inch, lingering on my breasts long enough to force my nipples to stand to attention in response to his gentle sucking and licking. All the time he holds my hands and I feel bound to him.

When he finds my navel I am so wet and ready, I want to roll him over and take him inside me, but I control my desires and give him his wish because, if I'm honest, it's my wish too.

He looks directly at me and I see something new, something raw; this isn't like any look he's given me before. He's fucked beautiful women and they've blown him, but this is new to both of us: this is serious.

"What do you want, Beth, tell me."

I'm breathless, but I still have enough self-control to speak. "I ... I want to feel your hands on me."

Without further encouragement, he releases his fingers from mine and spreads them across my stomach. His hands are naturally powerful but his touch is soft and patient. With a gentle push, he opens my thighs and kisses the smooth, damp flesh. I can feel his hot breath on my crotch, and it makes me arch my back. His fingers stretch over to my most sensitive of parts and I voice my pleasure but find myself clutching his head, pulling him away.

'Stop' is the word I hear in my head, but he touches me so delicately I think I will come apart. 'Enough,' I say silently.

Unconsciously, I'm pulling his hands away and starting to fight him.

"Beth, it's okay. Look at me."

I turn my face from the wall and meet his kind face. There's a softness there like that of a long-time lover, a forgotten memory, and it soothes me.

"You're safe with me." He releases my hands and I rest my fingers in his hair; this is a safe place, a place I know. His hand cups me and I move my body to meet it. When he slides a finger inside me, I fold in around his exploring hand. We move in unison.

"Good girl, let's see how sensitive you are."

Oh ...

"You're so wet, my fingers are all over the place. Is this normal for you?"

"Normal," I pant.

"So tight and moist." He slides in a second finger and moves them in and out in a slow, rhythmic dance that I rock and arch to follow.

"I suppose so. "

"You know, I'm so hard for you, I could slide right inside you and you'd hardly even notice."

I pant more. "Oh I'd notice."

His hot breath brushes against my thighs. "You'd notice, but it would be so easy."

"Then do it."

He's moving his head very slowly from left to right. "No not yet, you're not ready."

"I though you said I was."

"Down here you are, but..." He's climbing my body like a praying mantis, stopping only to kiss my forehead. "But up here you're not."

"Aren't you the expert?"

The smile he gives me is simply indecent. "You have no idea. Close your eyes and relax while I slide into you, ready?"

My head is moving up and down so enthusiastically he gives me a cheeky smile that only makes me want him more. I feel the push of his two fingers into my most private of places and arch my back to absorb the sensation. The fiery glow in my groin is so strong I grip his fingers so tight, he flinches.

"Whoa ... breathe into it ... wait for the spark."

I'm so saturated, I think I can hear as well as feel his fingers pushing deeper. I arch my body higher. When his thumb finds my clitoris, I convulse into him.

"Good, that's it ..."

My senses are over-stimulated I come so hard onto his fingers that he calls out, but his words are drowned out by my breathless whimpers. The red-hot throbbing of my first orgasm with a man is unspeakably intense.

He slides his fingers from my vagina in a single slippery movement and I want to pull him to me, either to thank him or to hide. I'm not sure which.

"Fuck, Beth, I think I just came on your sheets." He kisses me with a ferocity I have never experienced before, kisses fuelled by lust and pure desire. "When's the last time a guy got you off?"

I can only manage a whisper. "There's never been a last time."

He's shocked. "Never?"

I shake my head. "No."

"Then I think you've got some catching up to do." He repositions himself; his head is on my stomach, his right hand is caressing my pubic hair. "Let's do that again, I want to get to know your body."

My body!

If it could speak it would tell him, he's made an impressive introduction already! He's like a teenage boy, full of sexual fervour and excitement, eager to repeat the process. But surely I haven't the energy to do *that* again? When I feel his hands gently opening my thighs I find the strength from somewhere.

"I want to do this right, tell me what you want." I know where this is coming from. *'I want to be the best,'* he had said.

Surely not at everything?

"You're doing pretty well without any help from me, Ayden," I gasp, feeling his thumb circling my clitoris.

"Count back from ten, and then come."

"From ten?" I'm already panting.

"Come on, you can do it, make it last."

What!

I can't hold out until one! He's playing my game. That's *so* unfair.

His game starts with "ten" and I pick up the countdown. By the time I get to four, waves are lapping around my ears. Three and I can barely speak for gasping. Two and I'm about to spontaneously combust. One is an ecstatic blur.

When I finally come down to earth I'm breathless, whispering his name and fisting his hair.

My God!

After five minutes I regain some composure. He settles himself besides me, nuzzling into my ear and wiping the sweat from my brow.

"Well, well … I'm pleased to report that you are a very responsive woman, Miss Parker."

As hard as I try I can't stop grinning, inside and out. "Beginners luck."

Now he's grinning. "Oh, we'll see about that."

We drag our exhausted bodies closer together and I hold on tight. We kiss and I can smell myself on him; when he strokes my face I want to say thank you but it's unnecessary.

He's exhausted. He could count the hours of sleep he's had in the past three days on two hands. I turn away from him and pull his left arm across me, kissing his hand. We spend the rest of the night spooning. We slot together perfectly, conjoined and connected.

***

With no more than a name to go on, Dan Rizler pieces together a simple biography of his adversary. He's got his work cut out. "Fuck me, Stone, you move around more than a ferret with fleas," he says with a sneer, shocked at the 1,947,320 results that roll out before him on his aging computer screen. Ten minutes in and he realises his opponent will not be an easy guy to get close to. He doesn't seem to have a routine that will put him in any given place at any given time. There is only one certainty, wherever he is, there she'll be. Stone will have been around her long enough to know how special she is and gone all out to steal her from him, making her forget the time they spent together.

For a treat, he takes out the cardboard box hidden under shoes in his wardrobe. It's about the size of a cereal packet, only a little deeper. "What have we here?" he asks, as if he doesn't know.

The film of dust that has formed across the lid is thick enough to write in. He drags his forearm over it, sending the dust particles cascading onto the floor like shards of broken glass. The contents are priceless; everything he stole from her is wrapped in newspaper and arranged in the box like buried treasure. To the outsider, the contents are innocent enough but, upon close inspection, they become a terrifying reminder of what happened on that unforgettable night.

With unaccustomed tenderness, he peels back the yellowing newspaper and marvels at his cache; four items, small, inexpensive but worth more to him than the crown jewels. His eyes are unguarded, etched on his face are powerful emotions, tell-tale reactions to assorted tactile, visual, aural and fragrance filled images that would disgust any other person, but not him. He would be the first to admit it, to take it on the chin. The way he feels about his girl is beyond normal: she's his obsession.

He takes out her small shoulder bag; the chrome fastener has become tarnished and the nap of the black suede is flattened and faded. Even so, it's soft to touch and when he strokes his face with it, he can imagine her tiny hand brushing against his chin, held in place at the wrist. With every item comes a memory, a fantasy that makes his head spin and his cock twitch.

Next is her Nokia 6230. It sits in the palm of his hand like a ten pack of cigarettes, not much heavier since he removed the battery. The screen has become opaque, like a square eye clouded over with an unsightly cataract. But, that doesn't detract from its power to excite. Very softly, he brushes the buttons against his lips. Some of the letters have faded but that doesn't matter, his mouth is against her mouth. With his eyes closed, he visualises her lips parting, meeting his, swollen from crying, aching to be kissed, supressing a helpless voice, pleading. He licks his lips and enjoys the feel of her responsiveness. She knows she can't fight him, can't fight the urge and gives into him, gratefully accepting his advances. Her whimpers become defenceless moans of pleasure.

Like leftovers from a jumble sale, the two items are displayed on his duvet waiting to be added to.

Next: her small leather purse. It has fared better over the years. The patent leather has not lost its sheen. When he holds it up to the light, keeping his forefinger and thumb either side, he can see her fingerprints, imprints of nimble fingers and thumbs that trace the lines on his face, the stubble on his chin and the flexing muscles below. Every innocent stroke takes him closer to orgasm, leads him on to a fantasy world where he is king and she's his princess.

But, he's saved the best until last. With trembling fingers he delves into the crumbling newspaper and lifts out a pair of white lacy panties, unwashed, untouched by hands other than his own. They are his best kept secret, his prize possession; the one item he stole from her apartment all those years ago. He could have taken anything, but he was drawn to the delicate lace, the pungent smell, the stained crotch, evidence of her arousal, her neediness. It all amounted to subtle seduction then, and nothing has changed in almost seven years.

Never has one man envisaged so much from so little. He sits on the side of the bed, the three items drawing his eye, laid out in a row, having served their purpose. The delicate, lacy fabric covers his left hand like a silk glove, resting over his mouth and beneath his nose. He inhales deeply and breathes her in. His other hand stokes and teases, until he is fully erect: hard flesh against a rough hand. With his eyes closed, he conjures up her ghostly image out of the darkness. "There you are, there's my girl," he whispers, almost tenderly. "Have you missed me? Yes? Good."

His movements quicken, his breathing becomes ragged and grunts of pleasure emanate from his throat. "My special girl's been hiding from me, haven't you, been playing hide and seek, but I've found you now and it's time for us to play another game."

The images and the souvenirs combined are a powerful stimulant. He jerks himself off and falls backward onto the bed, utterly depleted. "My, my, I have to give it to you, princess, you never disappoint."

6

I wake to the sound of bread being flicked out of a toaster. My senses combine and the images in the present are overshadowed by images from my recent past. Last night's events linger in my mind, just long enough to create a longing to do it all again.

Ayden's side of the bed is cold, so he must have been up for some time, doing God knows what. I dive into the shower and wash away that tell-tale smell of sex on my skin and catch myself in the mirror. It's still me, but I detect a sparkle that wasn't there a week ago and a rosy colour in my cheeks. I look as if I've had a tonic or a metabolic boost: it's the Ayden Stone effect.

I apply a little tinted moisturiser and lip balm, slip on a pair of Levis and a sky blue T-shirt to match my eyes, quick dry my hair and tiptoe into my kitchen. He has his bare back to me, his dark blue jeans are hung seductively low and he's barefoot. Even from the back, he looks out of place: too refined, too sculptured for such a humble abode.

He's opened up the French doors and the October light is streaming in; my shadow-filled world is bathed in autumn sunlight, transforming it into a Garden of Eden. Ayden has taken me out of the darkness in every way and this feels like a symbolic gesture.

I saunter over and wrap my arms around his waist, pressing my breasts against him. "Good morning, have you been up long?"

He pulls my hand to his lips and kisses my palm. "Only a couple of hours, I thought I'd let you sleep." He turns and lifts me onto the work top so we are eye to eye. "You had a busy night."

I try to conceal my embarrassed smile but he plants a marmalade kiss on my lips and I'm no longer self-conscious. "This is true," I reply, using a turn of phrase more suited to him than me. He hears the inflection in my voice and raises a brow before turning to face me.

"What can I get for you?"

"Nothing. I'll get some cereal, that's all I want for now." I lean in and kiss his cheek. "I'll let you know if I want anything else."

"Please do." He kisses my nose and returns to my laptop on the kitchen table.

I switch on the kitchen iPod and flick though until I find JLo. *'I'm into You'* plays in the background while I lean against the open doors eating cereal, moving to the beat and singing along. Does life get any better than this?

When I look at him, he's engrossed in something and typing away frantically. I almost choke when I see the small, leather wallet sitting on the middle of the table. I tiptoed out in the early hours and slipped it into his overnight bag. I felt uneasy just having it in my possession, but I feel even more uneasy now it's found its way back to me.

"What are you doing?" I ask casually.

"Checking emails and finishing some paperwork, I can remote access my desktop computer in my office." He's talking but still entirely focused on his work.

"That's cool." I wiggle to the beat. *'I'm into you.'*

"Yes, it's very cool." He smiles, swapping formality for my vernacular phrasing.

I'm so content, humming, crunching and looking at this fine example of the male form partially clothed in my kitchen. I want to take a photograph, to capture the moment ... but he breaks my concentration.

"Are you watching me, Miss Parker? Am I being assessed?" He doesn't even lift his head. Does he have a sixth sense?

"No, not assessing. Just enjoying."

"Me too." He raises his eyes to meet mine and smiles that smile. I stop spooning food into my mouth and feel my heart racing. Does he know he has this effect on me? *'I'm into you ...'* Of course he does.

The music stops and I place down the remaining cereal on the worktop. "Will you be working all day?" I enquire casually. "Or do you want to do something?"

"I've already made plans."

"Oh, okay then, maybe we can meet up later?" I sound desperate. Did last night mean so little to him?

"I'm taking you shopping." He slams down the laptop lid and pushes it aside.

"Oh, Shopping? Shopping for what?" I take a seat.

"For clothes, for you, for Rome." He places down his palms onto the table and his fingertips touch the leather wallet.

All I can hear is 'clothes,' 'Rome.' Clearly my expression is as good as a thousand words.

"You already have the tickets, remember? We just need to check our diaries, choose a date and synchronise our watches."

"Well, my diary is pretty full," I tease. "I'm not sure I can fly off to Rome, just like that." My broad smile belies my words.

"Then go get it and we'll confer," he orders, flicking out his smart phone.

"OK, you show me yours and I'll show you mine." I smile cheekily.

"Oh, you've already seen mine." He holds up his smart phone for added theatricality.

"Yes I have," I say, biting my lip. "And very nice it was too." I hear myself saying the words but feel myself blushing.

"You're very bold this morning, Miss Parker. Are you up to the 'A's' in your new book?"

"Only just, although I keep getting stuck in the A's. You know: ankle, arse, and arousal." I try my hardest to force a seductive stare and the quickness of his breath tells me I've hit the target. I saunter over to him and sit across his lap, positioning myself between his abdomen and the table.

"What do you think I'll find in the B's, Ayden, any ideas?"

He outstretches his hands. "You're the one with the English degree, why don't you enlighten me?"

"Well, there's breath." I kiss him softly and allow the hot breath from my body to caress his lips. "There's bottom." I slide his right hand under my right buttock. "And let's not forget being bold. That's your favourite, I think." I feel his grip tightening around my cheek and his fingers reaching out in all directions like a wayward compass.

"I don't have a favourite, Beth. It's all amazing with you."

A compliment indeed, for one as inexperienced as me.

I feel his hand gripping my neck, forcing our mouths together. Breathless, I try to speak. "So who am I now - Beth or Elizabeth? I can be either one for you or both at the same time. We know that don't we?"

"Yes we do." His tongue enters my mouth.

I take his wondrous face in my hands and hold him still. "I know what you've done, Mr. Stone."

"Oh really, what have I done, Miss Parker?" He's fisting my hair and pulling me to him with increasing intensity.

"You've brought me back to life, no less; kissed me and woken me from a great sleep."

"No I haven't, you were only hibernating, sitting out a cold spell. Anyway, what does it matter?" He lifts my left leg over, so I'm straddling him; he's becoming hot and restless beneath me.

"It matters to me." I pull away from him. "I need you to hear this, Ayden."

He's twisting his head to find my mouth.

"Be good. Listen. You know, the Dom/Sub thing, I get it now and I've read up on it - but my... *our* version of it is, well, it's a pale imitation compared to some of the stuff I've seen." I blow out a gust of air and look to the heavens. "You and I both know I could never cause you pain." I think he's listening so I continue. "Okay, I might buy some toys, but that's all they are, toys."

He's scraping back my hair, examining my face, planning where his next kiss is going to land.

"Ayden! Focus!" Now I have his attention, but I'm looking at a frown. "So I think I know what you've done."

He leans back in the chair. "Alright, I'm listening. What have I done?"

"You're a planner, a strategist, that's the way you make your money. You make lists, you tick things off: Elizabeth, submission. That must have been one you haven't had to tick off before?"

He tips his head to one side, says nothing, just smirks.

"You've orchestrated this ..." I struggle to find the right word. "... this relationship, you've been very naughty. If you'd come onto me, full onto me playboy style, I would have run a mile." I can't help but throw him a wide-eyed stare.

He's smiling so wickedly, I'm having to look away to maintain my equilibrium. "Anyway, I get it. You've given me your body to play with, to explore, to get use to by creating Elizabeth." I frame his face with my hands. "I don't have a problem with it. This is me saying thank you." I kiss him hard and squeeze his face. "Thank you, Ayden."

Unfortunately, my words don't have the desired effect. When I lean back and look at him, he's still and serious, lost somehow.

"I don't deserve you, Beth," he mutters, stroking my hair so softly it feels more like petting than caressing. "What happened last night was, what can I say, unexpected, especially as we didn't get off to a very good start. It was more than I deserve. I felt so relaxed and turned-on. It was a new experience for me."

I feel his thumbs stroking my cheek bones with a kind of devotion and it's a humbling experience. Why would such a man be so taken with a novice like me?

He wants to explain. "It was a first for us both and that's what makes us work. Do you know what I mean?"

"I think so." I'm really just guessing. "You're saying that you didn't mind it, but you don't really want to be dominated by me or anyone else?"

He's shaking his head from left to right with such a force I'm rocking on his knee. "I've tried the real thing." He smiles, caught up in the recollection. "I paid some leather clad bitch with a whip to tie me up and to do the business, to make me forget myself for a couple of hours."

"And ..."

"And, I didn't relax. I wanted to beat the shit out of her when she'd finished with me."

"And did she get you off?"

"No, she didn't, not even close, and I didn't want her to. It was the least erotic experience of my life. I paid her £1,000 and never went back."

I'm confused and I don't know what to think. "So where do I fit in?" My tone is terse but, good news or bad, I need to know.

"You fit perfectly into my fucked up world. I need you, Beth."

I blink away thankful tears. "And what about Elizabeth?"

"I like Elizabeth - you like Elizabeth a lot, you like being her. She creates a safe place for us both."

"But, what if she decides not to play fair and she's not sweet, will you like her then?"

His face is alight with raw emotion. "How could I not - she's you?!"

I wrap my arms around him and hold on tight. His strong arms enfold me like a protective blanket. "But ..."

He laughs softly. "Here comes the 'but'." A warmth radiates from him and finds its way to my heart, making me hot and restless too.

That's all it takes: a smile, a look, a touch, a word ... I want him *now*, anyway I can have him. "But what if I want to initiate something, to be bold, can I still be Elizabeth?"

"I'd be disappointed if you weren't, isn't that part of our game?" His tongue is skimming my lips and easing its way into my mouth. I long for that invasion.

I press my body down onto his hard thighs and tighten my grip around his hips. I've waited my whole life for you, Ayden Stone. I want to be bold. "Then fuck me, right now." It's a whisper, but I sound desperate and that's exactly how I feel. I'm fisting his hair and easing my tongue between his teeth, circling, tasting.

This is what he does to me, he chases away my demons, releases my shackles; he's shown me what it is to be free. Now I want to feel him. Inside me. Now.

He looks into the deepest depths of my soul. "But, Beth, I can be brutal and I don't want to subject you to that."

He says that, but his hands are moving towards my crotch and his thumbs are starting to search for soft flesh beneath. He wants this as much as I do. "I need to know what it's like, Ayden. I trust you to show me. I'm not made of glass."

He's shaking his head. No. "You have a fragile beauty, Beth, like a snowflake and I must handle you with care; too much heat and you will melt in my hands."

"That's what you think?"

"Yes." There is a lifetime's worth of sincerity in his words.

I have no choice. I have to test our theory. I whisper in his ear. "I could always make you."

Has a man ever looked so utterly wicked and so utterly gorgeous at the same time? "Then make me," he says, and my theory is proven.

This is our own, private game and I can take the lead whenever I want. It's now or never. "Then pick me up and take me to my bed and fuck me." I sense some hesitation and add an empty threat to my command. "If you don't, I'll beat the living shit out of you." I lick my lips and try to contain my unquenchable thirst for him. I've been wandering this barren desert long enough. "Are you motivated now?"

A lascivious smile takes shape. "I'm *very* motivated." As if I'm a sack of feathers, he lifts me and, with my hands still caressing his face, carries me into my bedroom.

The room is awash with sunlight and I'm about to lose my nerve when he slams me down onto the side of the bed without pleasantries or permission. Roughly, he undoes my jeans and yanks down both my jeans and my underwear in one swift pull. When I look at him, his eyes are wild and fierce and I'm a little intimidated. I should have thought this through.

He drags his belt off and pulls down his jeans and boxers. To describe his cock as firm would be an understatement; it's rigid and bulging and ready to impale me.

What happened to foreplay?

But no, he's over me in a second. His left hand feels for moisture between my legs, while his right hand takes the condom from his pocket and savagely tears the wrapper apart with his teeth.

I start to pant noisily. I'm breathless and wanton, writhing on the sheets, edging back.

My God, he's taking me at my word!

Before I can stop him, he's manhandling himself, finding my sex. I feel the tip of something firm against me, like steel wrapped in velvet, but only for a second before he edges into me; gently at first, allowing me to accommodate his size, and then in thrusting, jerking movements until he is deep inside me. I cry out more from shock than discomfort. My opening is tight and I can feel him pushing me to my limit; it's excruciating but what a glorious turn-on.

My mouth falls open and I reach for him, but he denies me his mouth, instead he positions his muscular arms left and right of me to support himself. I want to feel his wet tongue, to conceal myself in the shadows beneath his chin but there's nowhere to hide. I am exposed in the most intimate of ways.

We find each other with our eyes and augment our connection. I place my hands on his arms and feel the hardness of his biceps; inhale his virile scent and watch him work up a sweat. Even if I wanted to, I couldn't stop him now. But why would I want to?

He is lunging into me, but still holding back. "You feel so tight, Beth."

The fact he uses my name ignites something deep inside me: he's not simply following an instruction, this is free-will fucking and yet, he's treating me like I have fragile stamped across my forehead.

"Stop holding back, Ayden. I said fuck me!"

He has my permission to let go, and let go he does. I feel him dipping his hips to find more length; his penetration is starting to feel primitive and savage.

I'm desperate to come. "Please ..." I grab his hips and pull him into me, my nails digging into the fleshy part of his buttocks. He winces and throws back his head in wild abandon.

Until now I have not known what it is to ache for someone. To have this flawless man inside me is more than I could dare to wish for. To have him here, filling an emptiness inside me, chasing away the loneliness, I would give him anything.

I'm arching my back and breathing in the pheromone filled air between us, taking all of him. Every inch of my body is tingling and boiling. This is what Ayden meant when he talked about being possessed and taking possession. He's locked deep inside my body: I am his and he is mine.

"Fuck, Beth, you're crushing me."

I prolong his wondrous agony and pull in my internal muscles tight.

"No!" He feels my every movement. "Stop, it's too much!"

I release him and allow him to push me further. I suck him in deeper and deeper to the throbbing rhythm of J Lo's, '*On the Floor*' playing in the kitchen. This isn't love making, it's something else, much more lustful and primal. I had asked for this, dear God I had insisted on it. Whatever *it* is, I know I'll want it over and over again.

"Come now, Ayden, come now!"

"No."

"Come ..."

"No. I'll come when *I'm* fucking ready," he snarls. With that he lifts my left leg and pushes into me so deeply, I can feel his steaming body against my straining folds.

"Ayden!" I call out, allowing his passion and my panic to race on to fever pitch. There is some discomfort but it's surpassed by my need to orgasm with him still inside me.

In a contorted voice he hisses, "Come on, Beth, let's hear it ..."

His words do something to me. I'm starting to tremble, my breathing is frantic and I feel the heat of his flesh radiating over me. I'm at my limit, about to explode.

With grinding passion, he calls out. "You're burning up inside ... give it up for me."

And I do. I jerk upwards and come so hard I crush him with my ecstatic clinching. He watches me with a seething stare and, with a final thrust that fills every centimetre, I watch him lose all self-control, lose himself in me. He orgasms with a roaring release that shocks me. It rips him apart and every pulsing thrust presses against me like a heartbeat. Instinctively, I pull him to me, calming him with soft words.

When he raises himself he is drenched in sweat and his body glistens with a moist second skin. Still breathless, he tries to speak. "I'm ... I'm going to think very carefully about the way I phrase this but ... you're one hell of a fuck, Beth."

"And that's you saying it nicely?" I grin with mock indignation.

"It's all I can manage." Once he settles, he turns to face me with a captivating stare. "That was our first time."

As if I didn't know. "Yes it was." I smile softly, concealing in that smile an intimate connection that will never be broken.

We're both naked from the waist down and our faces are soaked with perspiration but, in the cold light of day, he's everything I have dreamt of, wished for ... waited for.

"You're so beautiful inside and out, Beth. I like being around you." He pulls me to him and our foreheads touch.

"I like being around you too." I stroke his face, feeling the heat of his exertion searing my skin. "It's all about you and me, our two worlds *have* collided, and I was wrong." I recall our first conversation.

"You don't think it will end in tears?" He holds my hand to his face. He remembers too.

"I hope not."

"Me too." He brushes my lips with his thumb, sealing in those words and follows through with a kiss. "I'll run you a bath. You'll feel better after a soak." He dashes off to the bathroom, pulling off the condom on route.

Realising I'm only partially clothed I wriggle myself off the bed. It isn't until I stand that the after effects hit me.

Ouch!

My legs are wobbly and my head is fuzzy, I may need to sit down for a minute.

After a quick soak, I feel much better. When I join Ayden in the lounge, he's still busy working on *my* laptop and consulting his iPhone at regular intervals. I pour out two glasses of Rioja and hand him one but whatever it is that's holding his attention is far more important than wine.

"This will only take a couple of minutes," he says, maintaining his focus on the screen. "Then I'm all yours."

The promise of that keeps me still and silent for a while.

He slams down the laptop lid. "I'm done." He's taking a long, lingering look at my face, I assume for any signs of discomfort or pain. I offer a cheerful smile and he seems relieved. "What are we celebrating?"

"I don't know. You decide."

Where to start?

He's happy to oblige. "Alright ... to you Beth." He reaches out to touch glasses.

"Me?"

"It has to be you, Beth." Our glasses touch. "Apart from the sex which, incidentally, was mind-blowing, I have to say I've never met a more charming and alluring woman than you. Thank you for inviting me into your home." He pulls me to him. "How are you feeling?"

Better for hearing that ...

"Good, a little sore but good." I kiss his hair and stroke his head with my free hand, even up close he's a sight to behold.

"Let's go and spend some money." He reaches over to the small leather wallet and wafts it in front of my nose. "This seems to have found its way into my overnight bag."

I try to walk away but he keeps hold of my hand. "I have money Ayden, I don't need yours," I say, sounding insulted.

"I know, and I can guess why you gave it back." He lowers his chin and observes me through long eyelashes. "It's not payment for anything. It's a gift." He places the Visa card in my hand and folds my fingers around it. "I have lots of money too but, what's the point of having it if I can't share it? I want to share it with you and this is a start. Please take it."

"But ..."

"Stop with the but's: it's a fucking gift. Not a gift for fucking." He gives me a grim look. "You'll make me very unhappy if you don't."

"I don't want you to be unhappy, but don't do this again, not without asking me. OK?"

"Yes, Miss Parker." He stands and twists me around, holding onto my hand. "Let's get you ready for Rome. The pin's your date of birth."

Of course it is.

***

Dan woke to a crisp, icy morning fired up by the prospect of carrying out some under-cover work. He has been parked up on Grosvenor Crescent, opposite Stone Heath since 0800hrs with no more than a flask of tea, two cold pasties and an empty bottle to piss in. He's carried out surveillance work before. It's another of his 'skills.' The heater is blasting out hot air and the radio is blaring out rock music. Suspicious locals and early morning dog walkers are drawn to the vehicle: it looks out of place at the upmarket address. No self-respecting resident would be seen dead driving an ancient, silver BMW in Belgravia.

Feeling in the mood for gadgets, Dan snaps a couple of photos; zooms in on the alarm box and the windows checking for locks. The impressive, three storey property is not that pretty to look at but he knows it's worth around three mill, maybe more: three floors, two garages and a roof top terrace. "Very nice," he remarks to no-one in particular. "You've done alright for yourself, Stone."

He swaps the camera for a Dictaphone, anticipating he won't be able to scribble down notes *and* drive at the same time. After a quick test, he clears his throat and begins his report on the job he's decided to call, 'Operation Snatch Back.' He thinks it has a punchy ring to it.

"It's 1045hrs Saturday 20th October. Operation Snatch Back is underway. Carrying out surveillance at Grosvenor Crescent, permanent address of Mr. Ayden Stone." He glances up and down the road. *"There's limited access from the south and multiple entry points via ground floor garages and doors, front and rear ..."*

As his mouth forms another word, a silver Rolls Royce edges out of the right hand garage, forcing his lips into a sneer. He reaches for his binoculars and confirms the registration number: ASMED1A.

"It's 1045hrs. The vehicle in question is exiting the premises and heading in a northerly direction. I'm in pursuit, maintaining maximum distance to avoid detection." The key clicks in the ignition and his car splutters into life. "We're on."

From his 'maximum' distance, he is unable to see who is in the car. He makes an educated guess that the chauffeur is driving and that Stone is either in the back or about to be picked up. He knows where from, and that sneer becomes a grin that stretches from ear to ear at the prospect of an early Christmas present. He thrums the steering wheel excitedly; it's been a while since he was on the receiving end of good tidings.

The driver takes the North Circular Road and heads out of the city in the direction of Kingsbury. Five roundabouts later, Dan turns off at the Pinner exit: he's clocked 17 miles before he ends up in Harrow. The silver Rolls pulls up outside a three story block of tidy apartments. The chauffeur gets out. He waits.

To Dan's utter delight, it's the same attractive couple he saw leaving the theatre on Wednesday night: he's hit the jackpot. They're hand in hand; she's glowing, just like he knew she would and he's smiling as if he's just cracked a joke. *"Note for records, the address is 53 Elm Gardens, Harrow. Three story building with double security to front. Will double back to check possibility of rear entry.*

It's decision time: does he follow the Rolls or stay and focus on target address? He has nothing to gain by following them. Now he knows where they both live, he can pay them a visit anytime.

"Time check: 1125hrs, target address secured. Remaining on site to assess security arrangements and entry points." With a predatory instinct, he watches the silver vehicle disappear out of sight with its three passengers. It's time for a drive-by.

He slows to a stop, noticing the top apartment, 53c is for rent. *"Note: apartment for rent, top floor. Estate Agents: Taylor and Main telephone number 02086114327. Call to arrange viewing asap."*

Wanting to strike the iron while it's hot, he punches the number into his phone. "Hello, I've seen an apartment you have for rent in Elm Gardens. I'd like to take a look at it asap, please." His sinister intentions are undetectable so skilled is he at deception, he's had years to perfect it. He's so close now; he can almost smell her in the air.

A friendly sounding woman with a London accent called Miss Richards arranges to show him the property at 1300hrs. Perfect. That gives him enough time to eat, buy what he needs and to smarten himself up.

With the pride that soars from feeling clever and disingenuous comes that same old twinge in his groin; he cannot suppress the agonising need to touch himself. Beneath Thursday's newspaper lying across his knees, a single, hot and heavy hand tightens around his cock, the zip catching on the cuff of his black sweater, shredding the material as he fists himself. Only a couple of pumps away from ejaculation, he spots Ayden Stone smiling back at him, stops, reads the opening paragraph of the article and picks up where he left off with violent, self-abusive jerks that merge pain with pleasure. His guttural moan is drowned out by the music and he spurts into his half empty milk bottle. Not having thought to pack tissues, he uses the article to wipe himself off and tosses the crumpled image of Stone onto the back seat. Taking a lingering look at himself in the drop down mirror, he spells out exactly how he feels. "Thanks for that, Stone, how does it feel to have my cum smeared across your fucking face?"

He's laughing and singing along to Black Sabbath, feeling satisfied and cheerful; he loves it when a plan comes together.

***

I had no idea that shopping could be organised with military precision, but then I've never been with Ayden Stone. By 1200hrs I'm ready to go into battle, destination Bond Street. Usually, it's my favourite place to window shop, but he insists I use the Visa card and I feel the need to indulge him.

Apparently, today's the day I'm being introduced to my personal shopper - a freelance Fashionista who writes for the broadsheets. She is going to help me match clothes and accessories. Isn't that Charlie's job? Why Ayden should go to the expense of employing a professional is beyond me.

Lester pulls up on Bond Street and I'm reminded of just how high-end the clothes are in this part of the city. A striking, dark haired woman in her mid-thirties comes over to meet us. From the way she regards Ayden, I can tell she knows him quite well. I assume the worse and take an instant dislike to her. She's all trussed up in a leather biker jacket and knee length britches and boots. I feel awkward and under-dressed in my Levis and smart white blouse. Sod it! Let's get some retail therapy.

My personal shopper is called Celine, and she's been working in fashion for 15 years, apparently. When I ask her if she has done this sort of thing for Mr. Stone before, she is initially hesitant but, in a typically French response, explains. "Mr. Stone has required my services before for special occasions, for his special friends."

As a rule I wouldn't care either way about those words but, today, they make my skin crawl. The words 'special' and 'friends,' have all kinds of unsavoury connotations when they are used in the same sentence.

I press her. "Often?"

"When required. Mr. Stone has very particular tastes." She regards me with suspicion. Has she signed a NDA? Or has it got something to do with the fact that I'm decidedly un-model like; too tall for the circus and too short for the catwalk.

Momentarily, the judicious look fades and I see an understanding, a woman to woman thing. She guesses what I must be feeling. "If it is any consolation, Miss Parker, Mr. Stone always gives me specific instructions and a limit: four thousand pounds maximum and one dress."

"I see." Obviously I don't.

"However, today his instructions were not specific. He said 'clothes for Rome and no limit - just buy everything and assume nothing.'" She touches my arm. "So you see, you are special, Miss Parker."

"Beth."

"Beth. We should have much fun today."

I offer an appreciative smile but don't expect to have *much* fun today at all.

After spending 20 minutes grappling with boredom, Ayden made himself scarce. He's going to wait for my call when I'm done, come and collect me; we'll go and get something to eat and then go sight-seeing together. That's the plan. Lester will take my purchases back to my apartment. Ayden has everything under control. Just the way he likes it.

When he returns to collect me, there are no pleasantries between him and Celine. She is an employee, I realise, and nothing more. He rattles out an order, "Bill me Celine." His hand is on my arm. "Let's go eat."

Before moving away I turn to Celine. "Je vous remercie beaucoup, vous êtes très utile." We kiss cheeks right and left.

"Ce fut un plaisir, Beth, Bonne chance." She offers Ayden a respectful smile and walks away.

"She likes you," he states, taking my elbow and leading me across the road. "I know a great French Bistro round the corner. You can translate the menu for me?" He winks.

I nod, link his arm and squeeze it with both my hands. What a great day.

By 1500 hours we're sipping Marques de Murrieta Capellania and enjoying Lobster with brassicas and pink grapefruit in a fashionable bistro called L'AutrePied. Ayden's giving a master class in how to order food and I'm struck by his flamboyant confidence; it's as if he has an aura around him that people unconsciously respond to, especially women. He orders food that isn't even on the menu and the waitress appears hypnotised. I'm tempted to click my fingers and say, "Pull yourself together, woman." But I doubt it would make any difference.

So this is what he meant when he said he uses his sexuality to get what he wants? He claimed not to be Prince Charming but he seems to be a pretty good imitation. It makes me wonder if he hypnotised me. Our amorous encounter at the theatre involved a steamy exchange of passionate kisses and promises, and that could hardly be classed as my usual modus operandi. Was I thinking straight, was that me?

Maybe not, but my thoughts are my own now and from what I can see …

He notices my contemplation, thankfully unable to read my thoughts. "Assessing again, Miss Parker?"

"No, just enjoying."

"One of these days, you're going to tell me what's going on in that head of yours."

"But not today."

He kisses me softly. "No, not today."

When Big Ben strikes four, we are queuing for the London Eye. The air is crisp and the sky is clear, it's as if the sun has come out just for us. Ayden hands the student on afternoon duty £20 and guarantees us a pod to ourselves. I've visited the attraction before but he has not, even though it's visible from his office; these small amusements have passed him by, it seems.

When the pod reaches the highest point, I press my nose against the glass and take in the incredible view: the Houses of Parliament, Big Ben, and even Buckingham Palace: an English history lesson in a single glance. I feel him standing behind me, his presence is tangible, a protective force at my rear: Master of all he surveys. Instantly, I lift up my arms into a flying position.

"This is a Titanic moment, Ayden," I declare, without a shadow of a doubt.

"A what?"

I pick-up on an uncertain tone. "A Titanic moment, you know, like the film." I turn my head to regard him over my left shoulder.

"No, you've lost me."

I'm horrified. "You didn't see Titanic? Kate Winslet and Leonardo Di Caprio?" I suddenly feel very foolish with my arms outstretched and begin to lower them to my sides.

Sensing my disappointment, he places his hands beneath my forearms and outstretches them until our fingers are locked together. I lean back into him. This just became a special moment shared for posterity.

"This is our first Titanic moment, Ayden."

"If you say so, Beth, then it must be true." He kisses my neck and I know right here and now, this is the man I've been waiting for: he gets me.

We step out of the pod but I say nothing, even though I'm thinking I'm one step closer to love. It's my secret.

***

Dan inspects himself in the mirror over the sink in what the company likes to call their 21st century megastore. Overhead a female voice, much too indistinct to be taken seriously, announces two for one on Coco Pops and the deal of the week on washing powder, but to him it's just noise. He is preoccupied with his own, less homely thoughts. He takes one last look at his checklist before giving himself the once over.

Get petrol

Draw £250 out of bank.

Acquire tripod for camera.

Buy drill, knife, wall attachment, chain, masking tape, leash and latex gloves.

He puts the top back on his biro and folds away the grubby sheet of paper, feeling prepared and satisfied. "All present and correct," he declares, saluting himself in the overhead mirror.

His attention shifts to his other purchases: a new pair of jeans and a check shirt which is probably a size too small, and a white T-shirt. He's about to meet Miss Richards from the Estate Agents, she is showing him 53c Elm Gardens, so he's dressed to impress.

After checking he has removed the tags, he leaves the stark lighting of the men's lavatory and weaves his way through mothers with babies, shopping trollies piled high with washing powder and Coco Pops and the occasional lonesome shopper with no more than a microwave meal and a four pack of lager, advertising their loneliness. Dan knows only too well how that feels, but not for much longer. Soon, very soon, he'll be shopping for two.

Elise Richards is a thirtyish woman who looks her age; she's around five foot six with blond hair with roots that could do with a touch-up. Dan likes what he sees. She's not his usual pert type, but she has an innocent smile and he likes that. She's waiting for him outside the apartment block at 1300hrs exactly, he likes that too. Be late or be warned, is one of his favourite mottos.

"Mr. Rizler." She reaches out her hand for him, smiling like the saleswoman she is. "Have you had a chance to check out the area?" She nods her head to one side, expecting a response.

He plays along. "Yeah, it's quiet, just what I'm looking for."

"Oh good. Let's take a look inside, shall we?"

He follows her to the security door, using his height to look over her shoulder to read her notes. She punches in 1459.

"Has the apartment been on the market long?" he asks, knowing that's what a prospective tenant would ask.

"No." She starts the climb up the stairs. "It only became available a week ago and we haven't even produced the spec yet. So, you're the first to see it."

"Great," he replies, checking out her arse and the way her skirt lifts when she takes the next step up.

She fusses around with a set of keys, checking the tag. "Right, here we are." When she opens the door they walk into what could only be described as an empty shell.

"As you can see, it has a spacious living area. The lounge is located at the front and the kitchen at the rear, with ample space for a table and chairs, ideal for breakfast or even for entertaining."

"So I see." Dan suppresses a snigger. He won't be the one doing the entertaining here.

"And this is the bedroom." She walks into the empty room and stretches out her arms wide to emphasis the space. "There's room enough for a double bed and there are fitted wardrobes too."

Dan nods his head, seeming as if he needs persuading. In fact it's a done deal, and it was even before she opened the front door. "How much is it a month?"

"Just let me check." She consults her notes and follows the line on the page with her index finger. "It's £600 per calendar month."

He wanders into the bathroom. "It's a little small but I'll take it."

Suddenly animated, her face breaks into a broad smile. "Wonderful. When are you looking to move in?" She has her pen in her hand, making notes, hoping for a signature.

"Monday."

"Monday the ..."

"The 22nd, two days time?" He holds her attention with a serious stare.

"Oh, I see, *that* Monday. That's very soon."

"Yeah, I've been bunking with a mate for the past month and it's not, well, it's not working out."

"I see."

"Is that a problem?" He folds his arm and waits.

"No, not necessarily. Although we will require a reference from your current landlord and from your employer, as well as a credit check, of course."

Fucking red tape.

"Of course. That won't be problem. I've worked at Cambridge Uni for over eight years, and I was with my last landlady for over six years. I can supply references, no problem."

"Well ..." She is wavering.

"If you give me your email address, I'll get them to you by Monday and then you can get on with your credit check. I just can't face another night of Jack's bloody partying. All I want to do is come home from work and wind down, watch a film then go to bed." He lets out a dramatic sigh. "You know what I mean?"

"Oh yes." She really does.

He considers her response. He was right about her, she's not the type to put herself about, she's got class. Not much but some. "I suppose you'll be wanting a deposit and a month's rent up front?"

"That's usually what we ask for and we have a small administrative charge." She looks at him apologetically.

"No problem." He makes it easy for her.

Her expression brightens when he accepts the admin charge, no questions asked. Usually she has to explain. "I'll have the Tenancy Agreement drawn up for you."

"Six months."

"Right."

"I'll probably renew after then but I'd prefer to check out the neighbours first." He smiles at her in such a way she cannot help but respond.

"Yes, that's a good idea." She's leading him towards the door. "And we'll need you to come down to the office and fill out some forms, if that's alright? Name, current address, employer etcetera. Perhaps we could arrange a time for tomorrow?"

Dan takes the initiative. "What's wrong with today?"

She's taken aback. "Oh! Nothing, nothing at all." She slams the front door behind them and side by side they descend two floors. "If you want, you can follow me back to the office."

"That would be my pleasure." He holds back the security door and allows her to exit first. He's pushing the boat out and she likes the attention, he can tell.

"Thank you," she smiles, unacquainted with common courtesy. "Follow me."

He takes a second to look back; number 53a is only a couple of feet away. Against every impulse he has, he concludes his Oscar winning performance with a role clinching display of self-restraint and walks away from *her* door. But, from Monday, he will only be two floors away and, when she and he are under one roof, he'll be able to give a blow by blow account of her submission; store it on his machine, keep a record of every whimper, every plea.

Imagine...

7

I t's 6.30p.m. and I'm kicking shoes off aching feet. Every bag is a reminder of the money I've spent: DKNY, Prada, Louis Vuitton, Armani, Vivienne Westwood, Harvey Nichols and Selfridges and not forgetting Victoria's Secret. The sexy range looks and feels delicious, and my new baby doll nighties in white and black are luxurious and indulgent. Naturally, some personal favourites have crept in like Zara, Oasis and Jimmy Choo; every girl needs accessories.

Ayden hasn't been shopping, he's been working. He needs to relax, but I doubt he even knows the meaning of the word. I pull him onto the sofa.

"I have a great idea. Why don't I order Chinese food, put on Titanic, and make some popcorn? We'll chill and enjoy a movie together. What do you think?"

He forces a half smile but appears disinterested. Are my Saturday nights that tedious?

"I'm up for the Chinese food, but not too sure about the popcorn."

I'm aghast. "You can't have a movie without popcorn, Ayden, everyone knows that."

"Everyone but me, it seems." He looks away, still detached from the idea, engrossed in emails on his phone.

"I have a menu somewhere." I scoot off into the kitchen and retrieve a battered menu from my local take away. "Let's take a look, what do you fancy?" I shuffle closer to him and casually pull my feet under me.

"I don't mind, anything," he answers, still disinterested. "I don't want anything sweet."

I slither across his lap so he can't view his phone. "But you want me?" I think I have his attention now.

He raises his eyes so they are level with mine and I'm rewarded with a flat smile. "This is true."

Hello relaxation … time to play a game we'll both enjoy. I pull my thumbnail into my mouth, anticipating a visceral response. "But sometimes, you like me sticky and hot?"

"You got me there." He's beginning to thaw, so much so his phone is relegated to the sofa.

"Then why don't you stop ignoring me, tell me what's on the menu for tonight and maybe I'll be able to serve it up on a platter for you?" I trace the outline of his bottom lip with the forefinger of my right hand while my left hand teases his hair. He looks so casually coifed and yet so damn sexy. I can't keep my hands off him.

I grab his phone and snap a picture of him. He's not accustomed to this kind of playfulness, and that's the look I've captured. "Send it to me."

"I will." He takes his phone from my hand, pulls me to him so our faces are touching and stretches out his right arm. I look into the tiny lens and smile. It flashes. He looks briefly at it and then back at me. "The picture doesn't do you justice, Beth."

"Let me see." I'm moved to tears, we look so close, so together, so ... I daren't say the word for fear I may jinx this bud of an affair. "You can send that to me too." I return his phone to the sofa and focus all my attention on him. "So what do you want to eat?"

He says nothing and he doesn't have to, his eyes say it all. The blue-green iridescence that usually catches the light has been replaced by smouldering grey hues. This is a man who is having very wicked thoughts and that idea makes me feel extremely needy all of a sudden. His erection is stirring beneath me and making me wriggle on top of him.

"Have you been reading your new book?" He smirks. "What are you up to, C for cute?" He raises his brows and tips his head to the right. "Well, I can't fault your reading skills." He brushes a strand of hair behind my ear. "You must be an excellent teacher, Miss Parker."

His hands are moving slowly down my body, over my shoulders, down my arms and under my buttocks. He's manoeuvring me into a comfortable position.

"I'm an excellent teacher, but I'm very strict." I'm trying to keep a straight face.

"I'm very pleased to hear it." His pleasure is palpable and he even directs my focus to his crotch, just in case I hadn't noticed.

I take a lingering look at his fly and the bulging mass, and a salacious smile finds its way to my lips. When I raise my eyes to his there's the look, the one that makes me weak at the knees, the look that could floor you and turn your brain into a vacuous space.

I place my hands on my knees and fold my thumb into the creases of his stretching seams. "I can see just how pleased you are." I lick my lips anticipating my next sentence. "Maybe we should go try out some of your new 'toys'?"

He's genuinely surprised. I sense a mood shift. "You bought *toys*? This should be interesting ..."

Apparently, he finds the idea of me using 'toys' on him quite amusing. I hate it when he uses that tone. It reminds me of how I'm way out of my league with him; that he's indulging me, probably more than I deserve.

"That explains your browser history."

Whoa, gear change. I try to look shocked. "Ha, you've been spying on me."

"I was bored, you were sleeping, what else was I going to do?" He shrugs his shoulders and tries to look innocent.

"You said you were working?" My voice is half an octave higher than usual; my eyes are wide with amusement.

"I was, but I got distracted, what can I say?"

"And is there anything else you happened to stumble across on my laptop?"

"Only your extensive music collection. I synchronised my iPhone to your library, that's all."

"Oh, that's kind of cool, find anything you like?"

"It's an eclectic mix, I'll give you that. There's music there for every occasion."

"It's the soundtrack to my life," I confess, creating stillness in the room.

He strokes my hair. "Yes it is. We'll have to add some new tunes and update it."

"We will." I caress his face with the backs of my fingers. "Maybe I'll add some music to make love to?"

"I think you should." He enfolds my face and pulls my lips onto his. "I do appreciate the 'toys' but I don't want you to do anything you're not comfortable with. Let's face it. You're never going to be a Dominatrix are you?"

I shake my head and roll my eyes.

"When you take charge, you do it with so much gentleness, you take care of me. I need that. That's what I get off on." He plants a lingering kiss on my lips and I feel myself melting. "And also the fact that you're so damn sexy."

"Thank you." My mind drifts and I remember our first kiss, the urgency, the desperation. We've come a long way. "I'll never hurt you, Ayden."

"I know."

I feel his erection starting to fizzle like a firework left out in the rain. Unwittingly, I have quelled his desire and softened his mood; time to stoke the fire.

"Anyway, even us novices can be quite skilful with our toys, Mr. Stone. Give me ten minutes and you'll be putty in my hands."

He's roaring with laugher and I'm having to steady myself on his lap.

What did I say?

"I hope not, or this is going to be one almighty anti-climax for both of us."

I giggle, realising my faux pas. When I rest my gaze on his face, I see only tenderness there. It's as if he can see into my soul: we are connected. Time stands still, the way it always does.

"I like being around you, Miss Parker."

"I like that you like being around me, Mr. Stone. Do you want to play?"

"Only with you Elizabeth, Titanic can wait." He picks me up and, with my legs still around his hips and my arms around his neck he carries me into my bedroom.

He sits down on the side of my bed. I can see flames of passion starting to ignite around him like a blazing aura: he's so damn hot. He's taking in every inch of my face, preparing the way for his lips but, when he comes in for the kill, I pull back. He tries to kiss me again. I pull back.

A mischievous smile sweeps across his face. "What game is this, Elizabeth?" he asks, gifting one of his cheeky smiles.

"Let's get you into position," I say as decisively as I can, feeling a breathlessness that I can barely contain.

I slide from his knees and reach into the drawer in the bedside cabinet and lift out a blindfold. It's black, silky and elasticated. I slip it over his glossy hair and secure it over his lids. He helps me, moving his head to make this highly erotic act all the more harmonious. "Can you see me?"

Between unruffled sighs, he answers, "No. What *are* you going to do to me?"

I gently push him backward, until he is lying across my bed with his knees bent over the side. "You'll see, or maybe not ... Put your hands above your head and weave your fingers together."

As he does so his grey T-shirt lifts and exposes his clearly defined abdomen. His muscles tighten and contract and that sculpted V shape from his hips to below his low slung jeans draws my attention; it's distracting. Visually, I trace his arms from biceps to wrist and marvel at the speed at which every sinew responds. I'm not sure whose heart is beating fastest, probably mine.

My next toy rests in my sweating palm; it's a length of soft restraining cord. I walk around the bed and examine him from another angle. He's fully dressed, but it doesn't matter, he still has the same effect on me. Something about this beautiful man stirs my soul. I want to tie him up and keep him prisoner, to never let him go and this is step one of my wicked plan. Rather than simply tying him up I decide to have some fun, after all isn't it all about anticipation?

I lean over him and stretch out my arms, beginning at his hands. I hold onto his wrists and ease my way to his shoulders, my nimble hands struggling to contain his muscular biceps. I feel his hot breath on my face as I rest my head by his intertwined fingers. I move further over him and allow his fingers to stroke my breasts; the skin over his knuckles whitens but he stays obediently in place. I reward him with a chaste kiss and feel a ripple of pure lust surge through my body as his tongue reaches out, anticipating more contact.

I tie his hands in a glorified bow. "Can you feel the rope, Ayden?"

"Yes, Elizabeth. You have me at your mercy." I watch as his chest lifts and falls, just the thought of being restrained and taken has made him hot and hard.

"I do." And it's an almighty turn-on. I crawl over him, over his arms until his head is beneath my crotch. I lean forward and very, very slowly start to undo the belt on his jeans.

"Are you going to blow me? I do hope so ..."

"Hush." I feel his breathing starting to quicken, his chest rising and falling beneath me. He senses the proximity of my body, yet is powerless to touch, taste or even see it. This is my form of gentle dominance.

Before lowering his zip, I place my palms on his abdomen and lower them until I reach his pubic bone. Rather than stopping I keep going, until the thumb on my right hand hits his erect penis. I push against it with my thumb and forefinger, knowing he can't move but it's the pressure against my skin that is making his stomach muscles quiver and causing soft grunts to escape from his mouth.

I pull down his zip and lower his jeans and boxers, he lifts his buttocks to ease the movement and, with a grateful moan, his cock frees itself and points to the ceiling. It's rock hard and beautiful, and I want to taste it.

With a sensuous craving, I lick my lips and reposition myself for the task, still with my back to him with my knees either side of his hips. He responds instinctively when I rest my hands on his thighs by thrusting himself towards me, desperate to be sucked and enjoyed. His breathing is irregular but there's a kind of rattling sound coming from his throat, a sort of trembling excitement.

"I want you to ask me nicely, Ayden. Do you understand?"

"Yes." A muffled cough escapes his mouth as he gathers his thoughts. "Fuck me with your mouth, Elizabeth ... please."

I hear the words and they are a powerful stimulant. How could I refuse when I'm finding unimaginable joy in his surrender? "Lie still, calm your breathing, just feel." He takes deep breaths and I can tell he's enjoying the fact that I have it in my power to control his orgasm; he must capitulate completely to me.

I slide my hands towards his knees and lick the tip of his rigid cock. It tastes of salty sweat and sex on skin. He lets out a single grunt in gratitude and that's enough to spur me on. I bend down and take him in my mouth until the crown is touching the back of my throat.

An appreciative "Oh." leaves his lips.

I start to move up and down, paying special attention to the tip as I rise. His body is starting to jerk and lift and I remove my mouth.

"If you keep moving, I'll stop, Ayden."

"No. Don't stop! For fuck's sake, don't stop."

His plea moves me - he is so aroused, it causes a torrent of emotion to flood through my body. I resume my position and take him into my mouth again. I feel him straining beneath me, fighting to keep still, gluing himself to the mattress. It's all I can do to take the strain, so I attack him with more ferocity, sucking, licking, enjoying him.

"Oh. You suck me *so* good."

Glowing with pride, I lower myself as far as I can go and he detonates in my mouth. His orgasm discharges in a roar and a hiss and he spurts into the back of my throat. His spasms ease and when I turn around to see his face, he is lying open mouthed, breathless. I slide off the bed and bend down to kiss him whilst he's still wearing his blindfold.

"See how you taste." I push my tongue between his teeth and he responds by drawing it into his mouth. Still devouring him, I untie the bow restraining his hand and rub his wrists. There are no marks where the ligature has been and it wasn't tight, he could easily have freed himself. The blindfold comes off easily and I look down at him as he blinks and assimilates to the early evening light.

"Welcome back," I smile. "Are you okay?"

"I'm better than okay." He pulls my head down to him and kisses me forcefully, his lips are on fire and mine are swollen and moist. When I open my eyes he is staring at me, lost in some indecipherable thought. I pull away, suddenly shy.

To conceal my nervousness, I collect the 'toys' and walk around the bed towards the cabinet. I glance at him on route. He's still naked from the waist down but not completely lifeless. He pulls up his boxers and jeans, reaches over to me and grabs me by the waist. Before I know what's happening, I'm lying flat on my back with him at my side, gazing at me. I can't look away.

"I like my toys, simple but *very* effective."

"I like your toys too." I ruffle his hair.

"Now it's my turn to play."

I recognise that look, it's unbridled lust and I think I know what he has in mind.

"I can't believe you didn't even undress. I imagined you naked and your bare ass over my head, and all the time you were fully clothed."

"Blindfolds can have that effect on a person."

Like I'd know...

Holding me in place with a searing stare that stops oxygen finding its way into my lungs, he speaks. "You like doing this don't you, Beth, the role play? You don't feel pressured?"

I shake my head, but I want to explain. "I like that you trust me to *play* with you like I do. I have little experience and I feel more ..." I search for the right word. "... liberated, doing it this way. I'm getting to know you and your body and it's your gift to me."

There's that smirk I love so much. "I think you're under-selling yourself, Beth, I'm the one on the receiving end." He kisses me with a softness that makes me want to squeeze the life out of him, but I desist. "Do you think you'll ever get to the point when you'll trust *me* like that?"

"To tie me up?" I look to the ceiling, unsure of what to say.

"Yes."

"Maybe, but not tonight."

"That's good enough." He kisses my nose, slips over to my right side and lifts my chin to face him. "But for now I owe you an orgasm." That look spells trouble.

I start to laugh. "I wasn't counting, but if you must." I love his playful side, he seems so relaxed and just oozes sex appeal; it ripples over me like melted ice-cream.

"Oh, I most definitely must and, I'm going to take your lead and leave my clothes on."

I present a down-turned smile. "Where's the fun in that?"

"I'm going to get you to talk me through it."

I don't like the sound of that, telling *him* how to get me off? "I'm not sure ... I think you may be getting instructions from the wrong person. I'm hardly qualified to give you direction."

I'm met with a piercing stare. "But you know what feels good?"

"Well yeah, but you seemed to be doing pretty well all on your own last night, without any help from me ... as you said, you're good with your hands."

"I want to be better, help me be better," he implores, feigning schoolboy innocence.

A soft kiss wafts across my lips and I'm spellbound. How can I refuse a request like that? "I'll do my best, but if I stop giving instruction, then you're either doing pretty well, or I've run out of suggestions."

He starts to fiddle with his zip and belt. "Good enough."

"What are you doing?"

"Getting dressed, I don't want to distract you."

"You having your pants undone won't distract me," I lie.

"Maybe not, but I don't want you getting any ideas about reciprocating. You've done your bit and so skilfully too." He brushes a strand of hair from my face. "It's all about you now. Lie back and let *my* lesson begin."

He takes my left arm and bends it back so that my hand is next to my ear. He does the same with my right hand. "Now hold onto the pillow." He kisses my neck between words. "You won't be fighting me, not tonight." Another kiss underneath my ear. "Not tomorrow night." Another wet whisper. "Never again."

With his right hand, he starts to undo my jeans and slowly slips his hand down over my panties. I let out a little moan when his finger meets my sodden crotch.

"Jeez, you're so ..."

What?

He cups me and I put my head back and bite my bottom lip. This is high school fondling but, what the hell, it causes a gush of pleasure to radiate through me.

"Take deep breaths, there's no rush."

He lifts out his right hand and puts his fingers just inside my mouth." Now tell me, did you like my gift?"

Gift?

I know exactly what he's talking about. "Which gift, there have been so many?"

He taps my bottom lip. "Now, now. You know what gift."

I swallow and watch the colours dancing and shifting in his eyes. "Oh *that* gift."

"Yes, *that* gift. Did it do it for you, or do I need to find something else to get your motor racing?"

I'm blushing. "No, no, there's no need to do that. It's a perfectly good gift."

"And does it do what it says on the tin?"

"Er ... Yes."

"Do you want me to use it now?"

Now?

I'm thinking yes, but shaking my head and saying no.

"Are you sure? Because I'm not averse to using electronic devices, when needs must."

"Me too, but my needs must be attended to by you at the moment, if you don't mind?"

He swaps his fingers for his lips and devours my mouth with a kiss of such ferocity, I'm left breathless and needy.

"There's nothing else I'd rather do, but you will let me know if you change your mind?"

In a high pitched voice that surely doesn't belong to me, I answer, "Yes, you can count on it."

"Good girl." I watch him drag his moist fingers down over my T-shirt. Now he's easing his hand down, across my pubic bone and inside my panties. His hand is still, but against me. "Just breathe, I'm not doing anything - not yet."

I was doing fine until the 'not yet,' and now my insides are a quivering mess.

He's resting the fleshy pad of his hand against my clitoris and kneading it very gently. A sound leaves my lips, no words, just an extended "Ah" telling him he's found the spot. This is so erotic, his hand discovering my very sexuality and his eyes never leaving mine. There are no ropes or ties but I am bound to him. I cannot move.

"How am I doing?"

What?

My state of arousal makes it virtually impossible for me to speak, let alone give instruction. "Let's ... just assume you've ... you've got it covered."

"Is this fast enough?" With total concentration he's massaging my swollen clitoris.

"Jesus Ayden ..." I grip his chin with my left hand and pull his face to mine. "Do I look turned on to you?" My chest is heaving and I'm visibly liquefying. "Don't wait for instructions, just do!"

He smiles indecently, inches down and slides one finger into me so I can feel him inside. "You're so warm. I know this is supposed to be for you but fuck me ..."

Yes please...

He rests his head on my chest to watch his hand move beneath my jeans and, I suspect, to monitor my breathing and my heartbeat. He circles his probing finger and rocks me as he moves in and out. With an extended out, he slides in a second finger.

I call out, I'm so turned on. Here we are, fully clothed like a pair of young lovers and he's inside me. He lifts his head to watch me come and I turn to the left and search for cool air and invisibility.

"Do you want my mouth?"

Oh please don't say things like that ...

"No, I'll come." My voice is hoarse and unrecognisable.

He stops moving his fingers and whispers in my ear. "Not yet missy, this is a game two can play."

I turn to face him, unsure whether to be angry or more aroused. Is he switching? When did I become the sub?

"Just hold on." He seals his command with a fierce kiss and a penetrating tongue claims my mouth.

I pull him to me, sinking my nails into his T-shirt and offering myself to him. His fingers are moving in and out and the slightest bend is finding my G-spot. I lurch forward spontaneously, giving in to a throbbing hum as he increases the pressure on my clitoris.

I'm pleading. "Let me come, I have to come." He pushes deeper and I convulse, holding his fingers.

He slows. "No. Not yet, Beth, I'm going to stretch you."

No!

He pulls out his fingers and tries to push three fingers into me. It hurts a little, but then it feels so good.

"Breathe into it ...."

"Ayden." I'm losing all self-control, it's agonisingly good.

"Good, you can feel the spark now can't you?"

"Yes ... yes." I'm so stimulated, my body is trembling, I'm so close. "Ayden." I cry out his name.

"There it is ... let it go..."

My insides explode and there's fireworks and a deep burning in my groin that goes on and on. My insides throb. I can't get my breath.

"Fuck" He's pushing into me and I'm coming hard onto his fingers. He swallows up my cries with his mouth until my orgasm subsides. My breathing starts to slow and he eases out. He's staring at me with a look of total veneration.

Still panting I bait him, "Mr. Stone, perhaps you should have used one of your electronic devices after all. I think you need more practice."

His face cracks wide open into a full, self-satisfied grin. "Oh, are you assessing my performance Miss Parker?

"Yes ... and enjoying. I think you have a lot of potential but could try harder." He starts to nibble my ear and my post orgasmic daze turns into a giggle.

"Oh, you want me harder do you?"

"That ... that's not what I said. Don't misquote me."

The rough and tumble of the next five minutes is almost as much fun as the previous five minutes, almost. After a restful silence I prepare to speak. "What are you thinking? Anything you want to share?"

"I was just thinking how my life has changed over the past week."

I turn my body so I can face him square on. "I know that feeling." I nuzzle into his chest hair.

"I've got some really important business coming up in the next few weeks. I'm going to L.A. then Hong Kong. Why don't you come?"

I feel his fingers playing with my hair. "That's a wonderful invitation, but no. You have to be a different person out there. In here, with me, there's no pressure. It's best if we separate the two. You'll have me to come back to."

I move my face up to his and kiss him softly. I see disappointment in his eyes; the dancing flecks of green have been replaced by cloudy streaks of khaki.

Reluctantly, he accepts my explanation. "You're right. It was a crazy idea. It's just, I feel so ... relaxed and invincible when I'm with you."

"Even when you're blindfolded and tied up?"

"Especially then."

"Wait!" I'm feeling impetuous. I jump up and head for the bathroom.

After five minutes, I return and position myself next to him crossed-legged. I feel a little giddy with excitement. I can actually give him something he doesn't have: a gift that money can't buy. I hold out the jewellery box my kiss necklace came in.

He sits up. "What is it?"

"A gift."

"Another gift, you're spoiling me."

"You're worth it," I grin. "Open it."

He opens the box and spiralled around inside is a long lock of my blonde hair. It's held together at one end by an elastic bobble.

He looks puzzled.

"It's my hair. So whenever you feel stressed or unhappy you can take it out and wrap it around your fingers. It's like the restraining cord or my body or me inside: I'm holding you, keeping you safe, empowering you."

He lifts it from the box carefully, as if it's spun gold.

"Now, you can travel the world, be powerful and invincible and I'll be with you."

His head falls and his eyes are fixed on the lock of hair; he wraps it around the fingers of his right hand and pulls it tight.

"See." I fold his right hand into a fist around it. He licks his teeth and bites his bottom lip but says nothing. Shit! I've misjudged the situation; it's too much, too soon. "Of course, you don't have to keep it, I just thought ..."

I'm captivated by his serious eyes; their glistening flashes mean only one thing. "Oh, Ayden." I hold him to me and he hugs me back so tightly I can barely breathe. "I never intended to upset you, I'm sorry."

He edges back. "Don't be sorry, Beth. It's a very special gift. The most amazing gift I've ever had. I'll treasure it and take it everywhere I go." He stands and leaves the room.

He's on the phone. Is he calling a taxi?

When I enter the lounge, he's poured out two glasses of red wine. He hands me a glass, still seeming a little unsure of himself.

"I've ordered Chinese food," he announces, moving over to the sofa. I follow, but there's an invisible barrier between us and the air has shifted in the room.

"OK," I respond cheerfully. "I'll eat anything." His hand is on his knee and I place mine on top of it affectionately, but he lifts his hand and rebukes my gesture. Suddenly, after a fantastic day, I feel bereft. I could cry.

"Beth ..." He struggles to articulate his feelings. " ...we've not even known each other a week and I ..."

I know what's wrong - he thinks I'm taking this relationship far too seriously, cutting off my hair? What was I thinking?

"Look Ayden, don't sweat it. I'm a big girl and I won't put any demands on you."

He's watching me speak but doesn't seem to be registering the words; he has the look of a man tortured by something so painful the mere mention of it has him in pieces.

"If you think the hair thing was too much then give it back." I reach out for it

"No, it's mine now," he calls out impulsively.

His declaration rocks me. He's a frightened child, he's my broken boy! I feel the muscles around my heart tightening.

"You can't go giving things to people then take them back! That's just cruel."

"I don't want it back. I thought you didn't want it." I'm shocked beyond words.

"I need it, Beth."

I'm close to tears. "Then fucking keep it. What's wrong with you? You think I go cutting off my hair for every guy I meet? No! I don't. So it's yours, from me: a gift."

His head falls into his hands and he seems lost.

"If you don't start telling me what's going on, then you can leave because I'm not sitting here letting you make me feel like shit for doing something with good intentions."

"I'm sorry." His voice is small and helpless.

I pull him to me, he's tearful. "Ayden." My Mr. P is coming apart at the seams. What have I done? "Please don't be upset. I didn't mean to shout." I swallow back tears. I'm so desperately sorry.

"It's not you," he mutters, sniffing and wiping his nose with the back of his hand. "I never talk about my childhood but something like this is a trigger, it brings it all back." He looks to me for understanding.

I let him talk.

"I didn't get gifts; no-one cared enough to buy me presents. If I wanted something I'd either work, steal it or trade what I had for it. I was the kid who got left behind on trips; the cute kid who got more attention than was good for him, especially off the wrong kind of girls and then there's the pervs who ruffle your hair and offer you sweets in exchange for fuck knows what - you soon learn to give them a wide berth. So ..."

He holds onto my lock of hair as if it's a lifeline offering some kind of salvation. "So, to get such a special gift like this with no strings attached is unexpected. It's like a mind-fuck for me." He looks into my sad face and I can't even fake a smile.

"That's all, it's not you." He holds my face in his free hand. "It's me." He places the softest of kisses on my flat mouth.

The images I had days ago, all come flooding back; picturing that lonely and neglected boy tears me apart. "Ayden, I'm so sorry."

"I'm not after sympathy." He's regaining his composure and offering a smile of sorts. "But this." He kisses the lock of my hair circling his fingers. "This I'll keep right here." He places his hand onto his chest, onto his heart.

I manage to hold back my tears somehow. "Good!" I exclaim. "That's where it belongs." I plant a noisy kiss on his hand.

He nuzzles my hair and we embrace for several minutes. I count every second and listen to his decreasing heart beat while my own heart continues to race.

Like a man possessed, he stands and begins to pace the floor. "Where the hell's that food?"

In the blink of an eye, he's back. He's on the phone and I barely recognise him. His body language, the tone of his voice, everything about him reeks of authority. I reach for my glass of wine and gulp down virtually the whole glass. Unintentionally, through my innocent act of offering him a gift, I have unearthed some disturbing memories. I realise, for all his wealth and status, he's just a man, a very special, self-made man. All I can do is offer him my understanding and love. I just hope it's enough.

***

It's Saturday night, the TV is on, creating a kaleidoscopic backdrop to the main event; a half-eaten pizza is starting to curl around the edges, looking like pantomime shoes and Honey has long since left the premises. Only Dan remains, packing his newly acquired equipment into his rucksack with the excitement of a schoolboy embarking on a camping trip or starting a DIY project. One at a time he ticks each item off, knowing there's no room for error; he lost his bottle and fucked it up last time, he won't make that mistake again.

He's made an addition to his checklist and added a box of sedatives; he told the doctor he was having trouble sleeping years ago and has kept the Tamazepan tablets, just in case. Of course he'd never take them, he's made of stronger stuff, but they may come in handy if his little girl plays hard to get.

The drill comes with a selection of drill bits, making it possible to chew up any kind of material and to secure a fixing, although he suspects the walls of the apartments in Elm Gardens will either be breeze block or plasterboard. He places the mighty tool carefully into the bag, ticks it off and moves on.

The heavy chain has links the size of pound coins. It seems solid enough but, not taking any chances, he's checking it for weakness; pulling and tugging at each one, taking the strain, inspecting the metal for fractures.

The double width, masking tape gets a cursory glance; he's used it before, there's not much can go wrong with that. Same for the box of latex gloves, size large, a necessary accompaniment but not something he intends keeping on. He's waited long enough to touch her, to feel her soft skin against his. He throws the box into the rucksack. "Fucked if I'm doing it with gloves on," he announces. "You can't leave fingerprints on skin."

He pulls the knife out of its brown, leather sheath; it's a Browning Backcountry Hunting Knife almost nine inches in length, lightweight, easy to handle and very, very sharp. He catches his face reflected in the stainless steel blade and presents a distorted smile. "Dan, Dan, the dangerous man," he chuckles, waving the blade in front of him like a luminescent sparkler. He balances it across his palm, slips it into the sheath, then into the waistband of his jeans and pulls his shirt over it. It feels a little uncomfortable but empowering. With bare knuckles and a blade, he'll be invincible.

The folding tripod takes some manoeuvring to fit inside the carrier and, even after several attempts, it sticks out of the top, looking like a 60's TV aerial. He isn't worried, it could be anything; no-one will suspect its real purpose. He checks the camera is fully charged and slips it into an inner pocket for safe-keeping. It fits perfectly onto the tripod. Unable to contain merciless laughter, he gives in to the idea. "A couple of home movies to add to the family album. Why not?"

Finally, he frees the leash from its packaging and wraps it around his hand. The strip of leather will serve as a training tool; absolute submission and obedience are what he expects and that's non-negotiable.

With the evening's entertainment out of the way, he turns his attention to the TV but, disinterested, returns to the list, sensing he has forgotten something. It comes to him slowly, taking shape out of the mists of time. He scuttles off into his bedroom, returns holding something small and fragile in his right hand. Unhurriedly, his fat fingers unfold like the petals of a prehistoric plant, revealing a tiny ring. It has little monetary value but, he suspects it's the kind of ring only a princess would wear for sentimental reasons. After all, she put up such a fight to keep it.

"With this ring, I thee wed ..." He loves the way that sounds. "... for richer, for poorer, 'til death us do part ..."

The ring nestles into a small zip-up pocket. He secures the fastening, places the heavy rucksack on the floor and leans back in his chair feeling proud of himself. Reaching into his jean's pocket, he pulls out the receipt for one month's deposit and one month's rent in advance for 53c Elm Gardens. Tucked beneath the folded paper, is a cream business card:

Miss. Elise Richard
Residential and Commercial Sales/Lettings Negotiator
Taylor and Main,
Tel: 02086114327

He taps the card to his lips. "Why not, nothing ventured, nothing gained."

8

When I wake, I'm stretched out between Ayden's legs on the sofa; we'd fallen asleep and missed the end of Titanic. Trays of uneaten Chinese food are scattered on the coffee table: there's still enough left over to feed an army. I slither off the cushion and begin clearing food away as silently as possible, leaving him to rest.

Twenty minutes later, the job is done. My freezer is full and the kitchen is tidy. I select George Michael from my iPod. *Jesus to a Child* softly plays.

Carrying what's left of the Rioja I return to his side, moving stealthily to sit on the sofa in the curve created by his body as he rests, side-on. The music is a gentle lullaby and the words resonate and create the perfect backdrop for my moment of veneration. And why not, he has the face of a prince – my prince? In his repose, he is at peace with the world, serene and untroubled by dark memories. What a rare treat this is to see him in this unconscious state. I lean over him, resting my weight on my elbow and brush back the hair from his forehead, taking a mental picture. This is the man I love, this is the man I've been waiting for; he's found me at long last.

I brush my lips against his. "Awake my beautiful prince, awake."

He stirs, scratches his head and swings his legs into a sitting position, unaware of my secret proclamation. "Hey, I must have fallen asleep. How long was I out?"

I hand him his glass of wine. "A couple of hours. I've only just woken. You missed the end of the film."

He offers a phoney sigh. "Oh no! At least I got to see your Titanic moment." He holds his glass up to mine.

"*Our* Titanic moment."

"I stand corrected." He's still sleepy. His hair is ruffled and he looks a little dishevelled but still a wondrous sight: a gift from above.

I ask tentatively, "Are you planning to stay over?" I don't want to make any assumptions.

"If you want me to." He seems a little surprised I even ask the question.

I nod.

"Then I will, besides, I have plans." He's found his second wind; his libido is fuelled by something inflammable. Is he concocting some kind of sexual assignation?

I do hope so ...

"That sounds like fun." I smile cheekily. "But before you put your plan into action can I ask you something?" I'm afraid I might have handed him a fire blanket but there are things I need to know, things he's said and done that are floating around in my head like flotsam.

"Fire away." He sits back and folds his arms, preparing for an inquisition.

I put down my glass of wine on the coffee table. "It's about before, you know, when we were fooling around."

He nods and I see his mouth twitch; he manages to stifles a full smile.

"Well, actually I have two questions."

"Two?" He looks faintly amused. "Okay. But before we start, what's my motivation?"

Oh, I hate it when he plays this game.

"What motivation do you need to answer a couple of questions?" I give him a baffled stare.

"Buttons."

"What?"

"Two questions, two buttons." He holds his forefinger to his chin as if contemplating his words and then points to my shirt. "That's my best offer."

"Oh please, you're like an adolescent boy!" I undo the top button of my shirt revealing the top of my white lacy bra. "Now will you stop negotiating and just listen?"

He nods acceptance "I'm all ears."

"Before, you seemed to know what you were doing when you were ... you know..."

"Getting you off."

"Yes that. When I Googled you and selected images, there were hundreds of pictures of you with beautiful women. I just wondered ..."

"... You wondered if I'd fucked them all."

I nod and concoct a half smile. He knew this conversation was brewing.

He lifts his chin and begins. "Just for you, I'll explain. In my position, I'm invited to at least three functions a week: Award ceremonies, movie premiers, book launches, charity functions and so on. To keep up appearances, I have a list of people - women - who I get my secretary to call, so they can accompany me to these events. I buy the dress, we smile for the cameras and Lester takes them home."

"And that's it, with every one?"

He interjects. "I didn't say that, not … *every* one. I'm not made of stone." He smiles at his own attempt at a joke but, for some reason, I don't find it amusing.

"So you've slept with …"

"Slept with, no - fucked yes, there's a difference."

I feel myself becoming agitated. Have I opened an exploding can of worms? "So, you've fucked how many?"

"I don't know. I don't keep score." He starts to laugh but I'm not sure it's appropriate.

"More than 20."

He nods yes.

"Less than 100?" Does he actually have to think about the question?

"Less than 100." He is primed and waiting for my next question. He knows what I'm getting at but he's making me work for it.

"Fifty?"

"Look. Beth, I don't know. Does it matter?" He's becoming a little defensive.

"It matters to me," I assert with too much humility.

"Why?"

"Because …"

He waits for the rest of the sentence. "Because …"

"Just because."

"That's not a reason, Beth, besides, I could ask you the same thing."

At this precise moment, I feel the room folding inwards. I should have got out before he turned the question on me. I look down at my hands before taking a sip of wine.

"How many guys have charmed their way into your panties, missy?"

I don't like where this is going. I won't look at him.

"More than ten?"

I shake my head: no.

"Eight … six … four?"

I can stand it no longer. "What is this? A bloody rocket launch?"

He laughs, but soon that happy face is replaced by a serious frown. He takes me by the shoulders and lowers me back so he is lying on top of me on the sofa. He has me pinned with no means of escape. "You started this, Beth. You're asking me some really personal questions here." He brushes my cheek with his thumb. "Two?"

"No."

He withdraws and supports his body weight with his hands. "Don't tell me you were a virgin, not after this morning." He looks horrified.

I try to sit up. "No, I'm not! I wasn't a virgin, not really."

He's astounded. "Not *really* ... what does that mean?"

I'm blushing. "I've been with someone, of course I have but ..."

"Yes ..."

"But not properly, not like this morning."

He rocks back and his right hand reaches for his neck. "Fuck!"

He's finding this difficult to accept. Why didn't I keep my big mouth shut? "Please don't do the neck thing." I reach out my hand to touch him.

"The what?" He has no idea what I'm talking about.

"You always rub your neck when you're anxious or stressed about something."

"And why would I feel anxious or stressed?" Sarcasm oozes from his lips like butter melting on a crumpet. "I could have hurt you, Beth, I mean really hurt you."

"But you didn't, Ayden, you didn't. I enjoyed it. Shit! I want you to do it again." The words ricochet out of my mouth, but he's not listening.

"Thank God I held back."

I cannot hide my surprise. "You held back!"

Christ! That's holding back!

"I didn't want to, but you were so fucking tight, I got scared that I might tear you. I felt like I was breaking you in."

I launch an indignant look in his direction. "That's not very nice."

"You know what I mean. Christ, Beth, you've got to be straight with me. If something isn't right, tell me." He lifts up my chin and plants a tender kiss on my lips. "I don't want to hurt you."

"I know. I'll tell you if something's bothering me." I pull his face to me and take his tongue in my mouth, briefly. He's eager to continue but I push him off. "That leads me to my second question."

"Buttons."

I reach down and undo another button so that my push up bra is clearly visible. "Have you any idea how ridiculous you sound, trading answers for buttons, Ayden?" I raise my voice. "Ayden! Eyes, up here."

He takes one last look at my heaving breasts and returns his attention to my face.

Oh dear!

Those wicked, dark pools of desire betray his every thought. We share a straight smile which stretches the width of our faces. He leans right, folds his elbow and rests his head on his upturned palm. I take a lingering look at him.

My God. You are exquisite.

Momentarily, I lose track and the question goes out of my head. He's doing it on purpose. He needs reprimanding. "Stop trying to distract me. Don't look at me like that." I shake my head to ease the fog and clear my throat. "I got a little scared when you said you were going to stretch me, is that because I was so tight?"

He rubs our noses. "I didn't mean to scare you, but I could tell you were inexperienced this morning so I wanted you to get used to feeling me, that's all." He laughs quietly. "If I'm honest, it's a massive turn-on. I mean, every guy wants to think they are the first to bust their girl's cherry. It's a guy thing."

I dismiss it as a nonsensical idea. "I thought that was an urban myth?"

"It ain't, baby. Us guys still think with our dicks most of the time. Can't you tell?" He leans into me with an imminent erection. He starts to laugh and it's a rude kind of giggle that has me heating up all over.

He sees my brain working. "Tick, tock, tick, tock. What now?"

"Back to my first question."

"Buttons." He leans back anticipating a full strip-tease.

"No, it's the same question and therefore doesn't constitute the undoing of any more buttons." I slap his hand. "What did you mean when you said you'd just fucked, what about foreplay? So many women, so many bodies to practise on."

"I don't know why you do this to yourself, Beth." He manoeuvres me so he can lay me flat; he sits at my side, as if he's perched on a hospital bed. With his right hand he's stroking my hair like I'm some kind of treasured possession.

"Outside these four walls, I'm a different person. I have ..." He rethinks his words and alters the tense. "I *had* no other reason to exist other than to make money. I employ around four thousand people worldwide and that's a massive responsibility. I get up, I get dressed, I work. I come home, I get dressed and, when the mood takes me, I get laid. And that's it. It's old news, Beth. I've fucked beautiful woman who have been only too pleased to be fucked by me. I've not had much occasion to indulge in foreplay. I haven't needed to." He faces me squarely, assuming he's drawing a line under the matter.

"Then how come you're so good at it?" I venture to ask.

"I can read. And I can watch."

"Oh!"

"Oh. That's it? Oh?" He kisses my forehead and grins. "You make me smile, Beth Parker. You really want the truth?"

"Yes, of course."

Here it comes...

"I've not met anyone as ..." I wait with bated breath. "... As inexperienced as you. I want to be the one to introduce you to a more erotic, sexy kind of relationship. Besides, just the thought of you gets me in the mood for sex."

"Really?"

Wow!

"Really." He tips up his chin, pondering what my next question will be.

A tiny shiver of satisfaction ripples through my body; how is it possible I have this effect on him? Just the thought of me ...?

I accept the accolade with modesty and prepare to launch an offensive strike. "Have you been in love with any of them; the women you've fucked?" I ask timidly.

He shakes his head. Takes hold of my hand and languidly sucks on each finger, beginning at the smallest. Just watching is causing me to tingle all over.

"Look. I'm not sure what's going on between us. I don't have all the answers." He sandwiches my hand between his until it becomes an invisible slice of something hot and moist. "All I know is that it's not about who's done what, how often and with whom. It's about being connected and, I think, it's blatantly obvious that we are. Don't you?"

I give him a wide eyed stare and nod in agreement.

He kisses me softly. "So, stop looking for hurdles to climb over. There are none. I'm not making comparisons. I have no benchmark for this, for us ..."

"Me neither."

"Well then." He leans into my face so close I can hear him breathing. "Maybe, we should intensify that connection right now?" He tips his head to the side and scrutinises my face, holding me in place with what looks a lot like adoration. "Any more questions?"

"No."

"Are we done?"

I nod yes.

He brushes my bottom lip with his thumb, the way he always does when our conversation is at an end. "Good. Let's go to bed." He sets me on my feet, plants a kiss on my forehead, and leads me into my bedroom. I have no more questions - for now.

The bedroom is crowded with shadows, only the light from the kitchen and from outside manages to inch its way into the room. Ayden moves to the window and draws the curtains, before gently sitting me down onto the bed. This has been an eventful weekend for all kinds of reasons, not least of all because of the way he has confided in me; he's opening up. The more I hear, the more I want to rescue him; from what exactly, I don't know. The one indisputable fact is that he has changed. The man I met less than a week ago no longer exists, not within these four walls. He is my Mr. P for Perfect.

"I'm going to make love to you, Beth, and it won't be like this morning," he utters in the half light. "Stand up." His voice is like a hypnotic drug, everything about him is potent and charismatic.

When I stand I can feel his hands moving upwards from my waist, he's undoing the remaining buttons on my shirt. This takes me back to our first night together, how relaxed and passive he was. I know that feeling, now I'm *his* for the taking.

His beautiful face is partly in shadow and the light from the kitchen circles his head like a halo. My first thought is to undress him, but I shelve it. I want him to undress me, to enjoy me the way I have enjoyed him; to take pleasure not only from physical intimacy but from total surrender, my surrender.

"Beth," he whispers with so much tenderness, it's like a passing breeze caressing my face. He peels off my shirt and lets it fall to the floor, his eyes never leave mine. "I don't want you to do anything, let me take care of you."

He pulls off his grey T-shirt and throws it across the room, missing the chair. I reach for him but he lowers my hands and places them next to my hips. I'm not sure I can do this without actually touching him. He unfastens my jeans and pushes them down to my knees, following their journey to the floor with a moist tongue. As he does so, his mouth grazes my navel and then my panties, feather light kisses tickling my skin. My heart is starting to race; he's doing so little, yet I'm drunk and euphoric. I step out of my jeans and wait for his sizzling touch.

Nose to nose he raises his right hand and tips my head to the left; he traces the line of my jaw, paving the way for his lips. I moan when he finds that spot beneath my ear that connects directly with my insides. It's heavenly.

He skims over my mouth and repeats the process and I oblige him by tipping my head to the right to give him access. I close my eyes and savour the sensation. No-one has ever made me feel so cherished.

His journey of discovery continues downwards to my breasts; he's tracing the edge of my bra with his fingertips. "You have a perfect body. It's getting so I can't get through the day without thinking about being inside it."

Christ!

He's lowering my bra straps and I help by reaching behind and undoing the clip. He catches my bra before it hits the floor.

"Good reflexes." I smile, pulling my lips together to stifle sound before it becomes a giggle.

"You have no idea." He grins mischievously and I realise I have my arms across my breasts. I turn my hands around and place my palms onto his chest, feeling muscles flexing and stirring beneath my fingers. With dexterous hands he cups my breasts, rubbing his thumbs across my tender nipples until they are hard to the touch, ripe for tasting. I hold his head to me and weave my fingers through his hair. I feel the heat coming off him; he's melting any cold spots inside me, fanning the flames in my groin.

With me well and truly tasted, his attention shifts; he senses my need for close contact and offers me his mouth. I fist his hair and feel the dampness at its roots, as he holds my face in his vice like grip and devours me with such ferocity I think I will need reviving. I lower my arms, reach for his jeans but he takes hold of my hands and wraps them around my back.

"No, Beth." Instantly, he releases them and pushes me slowly backwards onto the bed. I feel his heart beating against mine and his hands removing my lace panties. It's all happening like a dream, like an out of body experience. I can hardly catch my breath.

I'm lying naked beneath him, breathless and so turned-on he could talk me into an orgasm, but I want him. I need him inside me, this angel of mine.

He leans up and draws an invisible line down my body with his right forefinger, from cheek to breast to hip to groin. His masculine hand cups me and I am shamelessly exposed.

"You're perfect, in every way."

His fingers scissor out to spread me and I hold onto the bedding and push upwards into his hand. I know his stare is burning into me and searching out my intimate places, and I turn instinctively and cover my face with my right forearm. It's too much.

His hand is on my wrist, pulling my arm from my face. "Don't hide, Beth, you don't need to hide. Look at me." I open my eyes and he's inches away from my face. "If you want me to stop, tell me."

I nod, so desperate to be less self-aware and more accepting of his attention. I want this. I do.

"I want to make love to you, but you have to want me."

I take hold of his despairing face. "I want you, Ayden. I want to give myself to you, but this is so intimate. I've never experienced anything like it before."

He puts his forehead to mine. "Me neither." His hand caresses my face. "We're both virgins when it comes to this." He lifts me off the bed and pulls back the sheets so I can slip under them. Whilst I crawl inside he takes off his jeans and his boxers and then positions himself next to me. We're eye to eye.

My hair folds over his hand and he starts to speak. "I can't tell you how much I enjoy being with you, Beth."

I don't believe what I'm hearing. These heartfelt words coming at a time like this?

"And, you know what makes this even more special?" I shake my head in reply. "You don't want anything from me. Nothing." He kisses me and it's a long, drawn-out kiss that leaves a sticky residue on our lips, gluing us together. But it's only the beginning.

He launches himself at me and his kiss is so savage I think my lips might bruise. His full weight presses me into the mattress and I am enveloped in his dark shadow. I feel for features, muscle and slide my hands down his lean torso; he's tacky and damp against my palms and the smell of virile perspiration and cologne makes me light-headed.

I'm parting my legs to accommodate his waxy body as he travels southward sucking, nuzzling and ravishing me. I'm clenching and tugging at the sheets, lost in a myriad of sensations. I don't recognise my own voice; I'm hoarse and lusting for his touch, his penetration.

When his head dips below my navel, everything stops and is captured in a freeze frame. Every muscle inside me knots in anticipation of his tongue. I want to give myself to him, without reservations, without fear.

With infinite gentleness, he spreads my folds and prepares to lick my sensitive skin. "I'm going to use my mouth on you. I want to taste you."

I'm so aroused by that thought, I forget to respond. He takes my wordless answer as consent and dips into me. The tip of his tongue finds my clitoris and I call out involuntarily while his hands grip my hips, holding me in place. His breathing is fast and hot on my skin; his moaning a powerful aural aphrodisiac, taking me to a place of unspeakable joy and ecstasy.

I lurch into him and let go: every fear, every bashful moment, every scrap of self-doubt is banished. I tip back my head and take everything he can give me as he leads me to the point of orgasm.

When his tongue finds its way inside, I call out his name. "Ayden" But it's lost in the deep, guttural roar of primal hunger coming from him.

"You taste so sweet," he growls.

With frenzied hands, I pull his head to my clitoris and start to writhe and groan. "I have to come ..."

The tip of his tongue strokes me over and over and I feel a warmth rushing through me like an electric current: a wave of indescribable pleasure surges and builds. I climax hard. So shocking is my orgasm that it scares me. I'm trembling and in a state of shock.

He wraps himself around me and I nuzzle into his neck while he rocks me. "Oh, Beth."

When I come down to earth, I can barely speak.

He's looking at me with awe. "Welcome back."

I manage a shaky smile. "Hi." I pull him to me.

"Feeling better?"

"Yes." I flatten my body against his and pin him to the mattress, covering his face with kisses, sucking on his ears, listening to the guttural sounds he makes when he's aroused. I take his face in my hands and look down at him. "I'm so glad you've found me, Ayden."

"Me too. I thought I'd never find you."

With that, he's on top of me and again I'm spreading my legs for him. He positions his rigid penis by my wet opening and kneels up to slide on the condom waiting for use at the bottom of the bed. He resumes his position, watching my face as he pushes into me, but I'm slick after the foreplay and he enters smoothly. I can't help but moan, he's snug but there's no discomfort. We savour a glorious connection.

I arch and move to the tempo of his movements and hold him with my clenching, but there's a gentleness in his movements; he's being cautious, he's afraid to push too hard or thrust too deep.

I lift myself up off the mattress and reach out my hands; he pulls me to him so he is kneeling and I am riding him. I wrap my legs around his buttocks, feeling them against my calves. He starts to move.

I plead. "Make love to me, Ayden."

Instantly, I feel the quickening of breath and I tighten my grip around his body, urging him to seek me out, to fill me. I'm ready. He's prepared me and I can take anything. I lean back and face him, holding on to his biceps while he grips my neck and lunges again and again with carnal craving.

"Yes, Oh fucking yes!"

With every piercing thrust, my own breathing is quickening and I'm echoing his passionate cries. "Yes, yes."

"That's it. Find your voice … let me hear you," he urges.

Now I'm squeezing and lifting myself off him to feel the full length of his stiff cock sinking into me; I'm rolling and rocking and coming again with such ferocity I think I will pass out.

"Yes!" I throw myself back and with a final thrust he pumps everything he has into me, growling my name over and over.

We fall together, sprawling onto the cold sheets exhausted and desperate for sleep.

When I rouse from my slumber, Ayden is sat beside me, stroking his chin with his thumb. What is he thinking about? I turn to face him, but my body is stiff and I stretch out my arms and circle my neck to ease the aching in my limbs.

"Hey, can't you sleep?" I ask softly, turning his face to mine.

"No, must be the jet-lag." He pulls up the duvet around me.

"Do you want some warm milk?"

He laughs out loud. "Warm milk, what am I five years old?"

"No. I just thought it might help you sleep."

He kisses my forehead. "No, I'm good. Go back to sleep."

I sit up and snuggle into his rippling chest, stroking the soft down with my warm fingers. "I'm awake now. Let's talk." I know he's been doing some serious thinking. Is it work? Is it me? "What have you been thinking about?"

"Us."

With the grace of a sloth I lift my head until it's level with his. "Oh?" I don't want to press him.

"I was just thinking how long we've known each other and how far we've come in such a short time, that's all."

I try to hold off on a wide eyed stare. "And do you want to take it slower, is that what you want? It has been a little intense." I fake a smile.

He turns and I see apprehension behind those misty spheres. "Why, do you?"

Sensing his anxiety, I brush his lips with mine. "No. I've loved every minute of it."

He holds my face in his hands and stares, simply stares; there's an ocean of memories hidden behind those captivating eyes, deep and wide and, swimming in that ocean is a translucent reflection of me.

"Tonight felt like the first time, Beth, how you gave yourself to me. I know that wasn't easy for you."

He's right. "You made it easy for me. You were so patient and so gentle. You made love to me and it *was* the first time." He wraps his arms around me like a protective shawl.

"It felt that way. You've made me realise what I've been missing all these years."

I want to ease his pensive mood. "Hey, that's my line." I laugh softly. "You're the playboy and *I'm* the prude, remember?"

He sniggers at the thought. "There's nothing prudish about you, Elizabeth Parker!" He kisses my nose, and I feel him easing out of his melancholy. "But there's a reason I can't sleep and it's not jet lag." He considers his words carefully. "I need to know if this is real." He looks down at me with so much helplessness I want to kiss away all his fears.

"I think it's real. It's real for me." I look away. "I know I'm not what you're used to and I don't wear the right clothes or choose the right wine but ..."

He lifts me so my body is weighing down on his. "Why would you say a thing like that? I don't give a fuck about the clothes or the wine, but I do give a fuck about you, but I'm ..." He falters. "... I'm not sure you'll feel the same about me once we leave these four walls."

I don't get it. "What do you mean?"

"I ... I don't like to lose and there are things I've done that I'm not proud of."

"Ayden, nothing will change."

"You don't know me, Beth, not really. Not the person I've become."

He's worrying me with his serious face. "If you're trying to scare me off, you're doing a fucking good job." I sit up and run my fingers through my dishevelled hair. "I'm not blind. I know what you're like with other people, that's you, Mr. P., Mr. Powerful." From the look on his face, I realise what I've said means nothing to him. "Just go with it, it's a long story..."

I start over. "You're like a Minstrel or a Smartie, all hard shell on the outside and soft in the middle, I get that. You have to be tough and unbreakable. '*Everyone sees what you appear to be, few experience what you really are.*' Even your Renaissance man knew that." He smiles, surprised I should be quoting Machiavelli. "Your life has made you that way, but that's not the person I know. That's not you."

I reach up to him, tears welling in my eyes. "But I'm the lucky one, I don't have to break through your armour plating, I get the best of you; the you who's smart and generous and funny and sexy. I don't care about the rest." I kiss him for all I'm worth and his lips kiss away my tears.

"How have I got through a single day without you, Beth?" I assume I'm not expected to reply and let him wipe away what's left of my glistening tears. "Tonight, we'll leave these four walls and I'll take you somewhere. I want to show you off."

I manage a happy smile. "You may as well, you've bought the dress," I remind him, sniggering.

He rolls me over onto my back. "Less of your cheek, missy."

"I don't know what you mean, Mr. Stone."

Brushing my hair back he smiles broadly. "I think I want Elizabeth back."

"Don't you worry about Elizabeth, she's around and she'll get you to fuck her if you don't behave." I can't help but giggle.

"I think I might enjoy that." He's laughing and pretending to hold me down.

"I might enjoy that too." I can't stop giggling for some reason.

"Something tells me I've let this genie out of the bottle." His tongue is in my ear.

I'm wriggling and laughing. "Yes you have, and I'm *never* going back." With that, the excitement fades and, in a tangled bundle of arms and legs, we drift into a deep sleep.

Sunday morning comes in a blaze of sunshine. Last night's antics have left me stiff and sore. As usual, I've been abandoned and Ayden is hard at work - or so he'll tell me. I can hear him talking, spitting out orders between expletives; sparks flying off consonants.

When I trundle into the lounge, he barely notices me. He's focused on his iPad and having a face to face with someone probably thousands of miles away but, as he's using earphones, I can't hear them.

"Do I look happy? Does this look like a happy face to you? Yeah, yeah. Fuck that. I've heard all the excuses but this is time sensitive. Get it sorted! Back at you Jake." He spots me. "Later ..." He places his iPad down and ushers me over. "Come over here sleepy head."

I stumble over to him, pushing back messy hair from my face.

"Look at you with your, 'I've been fucked' hair." He smiles broadly and sits me down on his lap, cradling me in his arms. For a minute I think he might actually rock me.

"What do you want to do today?" I ask, rubbing my eyelids with the back of my hands.

He laughs and pats my head as if I'm a sickly child. "Poor sleepy, baby. There, there."

I'm enjoying the attention and nuzzle into him. "You smell sweaty ..." I sniff his moist chest, noticing he's wearing a white vest top, and black shorts.

"I went for a run at 8 o'clock."

"Why?"

"I wanted to. It gave me time to think."

Our early morning conversation comes flooding back. "Oh dear, you don't want to do that." I try to suppress a yawn.

He lifts my chin so I am facing him. "It's how I make my money; thinking and planning, that's my thing."

"I know." Actually, I don't. "What is it you do exactly?"

"As little as possible. I make sure smart people do what they're supposed to in record time."

"And that is?"

"Research, develop, market and supply high tech communication devices around the world, using satellite technology and ..."

I yawn.

"Am I boring you, Miss Parker?"

"No, but it is a little technical for 9.30a.m. on a Sunday morning." I kiss his nose and make my leave.

"Hurry back, I've got a surprise for you."

I walk away and raise my hand in acknowledgement.

I love surprises.

Twenty minutes later, I emerge, fresh faced and communicative. "I'm making omelettes, okay?"

"Only the whites," he calls out from behind the screen.

"No can do. I've only got six eggs. If I only use the whites, I'll have to serve it on a saucer."

"Whatever, surprise me."

I crack open the eggs and throw in some grated cheese and pieces of ham. Not sure if that counts as a surprise, but it's the best I can do. Whilst it cooks, I open the French doors, allowing the light to flood in, and lay the breakfast table. It's the beginning of another new day with my special guest.

Ayden sits himself down and makes small talk. I know he's purposely making me wait to hear about my surprise. In a battle of wills, I feign disinterest for a long, drawn out fifteen minutes.

"Aren't you going to ask?" he enquires with an arched brow. "You know you want to."

"You'll tell me when you're ready." I occupy myself with the clearing of plates.

He gives an exasperated tut. "Alright, I'm ready. I thought we'd have a picnic in Hyde Park today, the weather forecast is good and tonight I have to attend a book launch for an author one of my PR companies is handling. I thought we might go together."

I smile broadly, showing my pleasure at his thoughtfulness. "You have been busy, haven't you? We'll have to go and buy provisions though. I hadn't planned on a picnic." My synapses are firing at the speed of light.

Where the hell will I get picnic food from?

"No worries, I've got it covered." He looks very pleased with himself. "Lester will be here in just over an hour with a blanket and a hamper from Fortnum & Mason."

"Great. I won't be defrosting any cocktail sausages then?"

There's a trace of a smile. "Not today."

***

Sunday morning dawn patrol gets underway at 0600hrs. Dan is itching to get started and welcomes the day with a restored sense of purpose; the gloves are off and he's found himself a new sparring partner.

From the way Stone was manhandling his girl, he is in no doubt he'll find him at her apartment. That's where he'll be, or maybe he's taken her back to his place in Belgravia. Either way, he'll find them. It's just a matter of good reconnaissance.

He tosses the large flask of tea and the two breakfast baguettes he bought from the supermarket yesterday into his rucksack and hits the road. He puts his foot down and takes the exit onto the A10. He makes good time and is sat hunched down in his car watching and waiting by 0900hrs.

There is little sign of life, except for the dark haired runner approaching wearing black shorts and a white vest top; he seems to be sprinting towards one of the apartments. Knowing more about male physiology than most, Dan assesses his physique. He's reminded of the man he used to be before *she* entered his life. She changed everything, not least of all, his gruelling fitness regime. He used to run ten miles a day in his prime.

Through his rear view mirror Dan watches the runner as he approaches and comes into focus. "Hey! I know this guy: it's Stone."

For no more than three seconds, he contemplates swinging open his door. 'That'll put a dint in that perfect fucking face of yours,' he muses, wrestling with his need to inflict actual bodily harm. He slides his hand onto the door handle. 'I could take you out right here, right now and that would be the end of you, pretty boy, but no.' His fingers return to his thigh and stay there until the runner has passed, looking hot and sweating like he's run a marathon.

'No, that would be too easy, a sucker punch; you wouldn't even see me coming and that's not my style. I'm going to get up close and personal, close enough to see the whites of your eyes and then I'm going to launch a killer blow that'll leave you gasping for air.' Just the thought of it causes a current of sexual fervour to surge through him; he licks his lips to catch the escaping saliva.

The security door of apartment 53 clicks open and he watches Stone disappear inside. His arousal has morphed into something much more primitive: it's hot, smouldering rage. His heavy hands contort into white knuckled fists and, falling back on his boxer training, he has to take deep, energising breaths to centre himself.

Recalling something his former group commander used to say to him, he tells himself. "Stand down, Danny boy, discretion is the better part of valour."

With a twist of his wrist, his car roars into life and he pulls out into the empty road, gazing up at the third floor apartment which will be his new, temporary residence as from tomorrow. The radio hisses and finds its station. Before he is even a mile down the road, he's smiling and whistling along to rock music, allowing its throbbing beat to reverberate around the car, feeling more self-satisfied than he has for a very, long time.

***

It's 12.20 p.m., I'm laying out a blanket on a patch of green in Hyde Park and Ayden Stone is opening up a picnic hamper full of chilled delicacies.

Someone pinch me.

It feels good to be out of the apartment, out in the real world and, from where I'm sitting, it looks pretty civilised: family members throwing balls to each other, couples walking dogs and Sunday strollers. It's very calming.

Thirty minutes later, having consumed the contents of the hamper, he positions himself across my lap; he has his iPad to hold his attention, but keeps breaking off to caress my face or squeeze my hand. When I catch his eye, I swear he looks at least five years younger. He's truly at ease, but I'm finding it hard to concentrate on my Kindle, words are mingling; I'm reread line after line.

I put down his iPad and his returning smile is so soft it touches my heart. No man has ever looked at me that way, with so much tenderness. I bend down and slot my lips onto his; we're a perfect fit.

"This was a great idea." My voice is a breathless whisper, there are people nearby and what I have to say is not for their ears. Through hot breath I confess, "I love being around you, Ayden Stone."

"I love that you love being around me, Beth Parker." He pulls me onto his mouth and deepens his kiss as I slide my fingers into his hair.

"This is the best surprise." I touch the platinum kiss at my throat. "And I'll treasure this." In that outstanding moment of intimacy, we are inextricably linked. Nothing else exists, time stands still.

Out of the blue, he asks, "Does this count as a Titanic moment?"

I'm moved to tears. "Only if you want it to," I whisper, circling my right hand around his handsome face.

He spots the glistening wetness. "Then that's what we'll call it - our Titanic moment."

When I cannot bear to look a moment longer into those penetrating orbs of light that have become turquoise in the autumn sunshine, I blink and look into the distance.

"Beth?"

I return my gaze, hoping I'm communicating some of the powerful emotions I'm feeling.

"We're good, right?"

I lift up his palm and plant a kiss in its centre. "We're better than good, Ayden." I don't expect to see a grateful smile but, when it appears, I feel blessed.

After a moment or silent intimacy, I speak. "My mum used to take me picnicking." I want to share a little of my life history with him, spurred on by the family gatherings around us. "Yeah, she died of breast cancer and being here just made me think of her. I don't know why."

He kisses my palm. "That must have been hard to deal with?"

I nod slowly, harnessing my sadness.

"It was different for me. I didn't miss what I'd never had." He's holding my palm to his face and closing his eyes. I watch him refocus, take hold of my hand firmly and press it to his lips. "But I'd miss this."

His declaration touches my soul. I can do no more than lower myself onto him and pull his head to my breasts, feeling my body enveloped in his arms. I feel strangely paternal and pick-up on his need to be held: it's a silent surrender. It lasts until the emotion dissipates and we can bring ourselves to face each other.

I want him to know everything there is to know about me. "I'm an only child and my dad passed away just before my twentieth birthday. So, you see, we both know what it's like to be orphans." I run my fingers through his hair. "I know what it's like to be alone."

"But not anymore?"

I meet his eyes. "No. Not anymore."

He jumps up suddenly and startles me. "Let's go!"

I leap to his command and in a flash the caviar, crackers, champagne and strawberries are packed away. While I fold the blanket, he contacts Lester.

Away from the crowds it's easier to rediscover the intimacy we'd experienced earlier. In the car, we kiss briefly but it isn't enough to extinguish the smouldering embers in my stomach, threatening to catch alight. I fidget, the leather seat squeaks and creaks beneath my short dress. I try to distract myself by looking out of the window, but my thumbnail insists on finding my mouth.

"Don't!" he orders. "If you do that then I'm not going to be responsible for my actions."

Like a scolded child, I place my hands neatly on my lap and he keeps them in place with his firm left hand. "Try and keep still, for God's sake."

With my hands out of service, held in place, I turn and lean into him, but he withdraws. Seeing him so flustered does something to me. I whisper sweetly, "But, Ayden ..."

"Stop, Beth! I know what you're doing so cut it out." His eyes are darting from side to side, he can't look at me.

"But I'm so hot for you right now."

"Deal with it. We'll be back at your place in twenty minutes." He's trying to be so masterful but I've heard him give orders and this is more of a request. I'm impervious to his requests.

"Put your hand on the seat, palm up." I reposition his hand on his knees and raise myself up, ever so slightly.

"You've got to be fucking joking. No."

I'm getting off on the shock in his voice. "Yes." I slide his left hand under my dress. "Do as I tell you, Ayden." When I sit on his hand, I know he can feel the wetness through my lacy underwear. "Mmm ... that's better," I purr, gripping his left knee.

"Fuck!"

I turn to face him and, even though I know I've taken him by surprise, the size of his dilated pupils tells me he's getting off on this too. I feel him folding back his middle finger to pierce my panties, so I rock forward to ease his entry. The material tears and I can't help but voice an involuntary whimper.

But, he's Ayden Stone, he's keeping up appearances; he has no intentions of being caught in a compromising situation in the back of a Royce. So, as we move through the crowds and wait patiently at the traffic lights, he looks out of the window and uses his middle finger to penetrate me. I push down into the seat and his finger folds into the wetness, making me cry out and grip the seat with both my hands. Lester looks up and I cough to disguise my outburst and smile sweetly, pretending to focus on the road ahead.

A clammy layer of perspiration is forming on my body and the skin above my lip is becoming sticky. I pat it with my forefinger and concentrate on my breathing. I can see his chest rising and falling at the side of me and, despite his visible indifference, the knuckles of his right hand are white and taut as he grips the door handle.

Five minutes from home the car picks up speed and the crowds disperse. Ayden times his intervention perfectly. He breathes into my right ear, "You have been a very, very bad girl and now I'm going to finger fuck you until you come, right here in this *fucking* car."

His words work like a charm. My lower body convulses forward onto his two saturated fingers and, as I push down onto them he makes deep, burrowing circles inside me. When I climax, my mouth gapes and I hold my head down to conceal my rapture, gripping his left knee in an attempt to contain my cries.

As we turn the corner to park outside my apartment I lean forward and he pulls out of me. I glance at Lester. Did he have any idea what was happening? Oh, I hope not. I feel myself blushing at the thought. I pass him a tissue and he wipes his fingers.

"I'll keep this as a souvenir," he says with a mischievous grin.

We make our way to the front door. My hands are trembling and, for some reason, I'm a little unstable, weak at the knees. Ayden is at my rear. Is he strategically positioning himself to catch me or, is the erection I feel pressing into my derrière, his way of saying, "now it's my turn?"

I hope so.

"I think I should take it from here, my poor little genie doesn't look like she has the strength to turn the key."

I throw my keys in the air, he catches them and, with his arm wrapped around my waist, we make our way inside.

9

H ow can a woman be expected to be ready in only two hours. I've never been to a book launch before. After our post picnic tryst, Ayden left me to get ready and has arranged to pick me up at 7.30 p.m., but he was no help when I called him asking for advice.

"Wear whatever you feel comfortable in," he said. "We won't be there for long."

It's easy for him, he throws on his signature Armani suit and he's good to go; his hardest decision is choosing a tie. How difficult is that?

I opt for a classic dress from DKNY. It's one of my most expensive purchases and not something I would have picked for myself, it was only on Celine's recommendation that I tried it and - who knew! It looks spectacular on, if I say so myself. It's in midnight blue satin and the bustier makes me look and feel a million dollars, and the fact that it's strapless will allow my platinum kiss pendant to take pride of place on my décolleté. I even have matching, killer heels in dark blue and a silver clutch to complete the look.

When the buzzer sounds, I'm ready. I take a deep breath and prepare for my debut; I've never felt or looked better. "Hi Lester," I call out, offering him a friendly smile and slamming the door behind me. He opens the car door for me and I step inside.

Ayden's gasp is audible. "My God, you look absolutely stunning, Beth." I actually think his mouth is gaping.

"Thank you, I wasn't sure about the dress at first, but Celine chose it for me." I'm fussing over the folds, afraid to sit down in case it creases.

"Killer heels too, I like those." He runs his hand up my leg until he reaches the stocking tops and pulls his hand away quickly. I think I know why.

"Yes, I love the shoes, but you do know I won't be doing any dancing tonight, don't you?"

"I do now." He grins and I see a twinkle in his eye; it looks a lot like pride.

Once I've settled myself, I turn to look at him. He looks as if he's stepped out of a film set, so polished, so majestic. My mouth falls open. "Ayden, you look so handsome. You look like James Bond, only younger and better looking." I run the fingers of my right hand down his tie.

He sees a look in my eyes that spells trouble. "Keep breathing, Beth, you'll get over it."

"I don't think deep breathing will help." I edge closer to him and the magnetism between us creates invisible sparks. I take hold of his face and kiss him passionately.

"What's going on with you ... Oh fuck!"

Are the last words I hear before I launch myself onto his knee. As I straddle him, he presses a button in the door.

"Take the long route, Lester."

I don't hear any response because he's raised the privacy glass and we are in our own private bubble, concealed behind tinted glass.

"You're acting like an oversexed teenager."

"I can't help it; you look so hot in your James Bond suit." I wriggle around on his crotch.

"It's just a suit, get a grip!"

I look helplessly at him. "Do you want me to stop?" I manufacture a sad face and slide away from him to my side of the seat.

"Not so fast, let's think this through." He holds me in position. "You really have been a bad girl once already today, Miss Parker. I may need to take you in hand and discipline you."

What does he mean?

Just the timbre of his voice causes a rush of pure excitement to circulate my body, and he knows it.

"What is it with you and moving vehicles?"

"It's not the vehicle, Ayden, it's you." I place my quivering hand on his firm chest. "What have you done to me?" I brush my lips against his open mouth and watch him lick his lips, tasting my lip-gloss. "I feel like a ticking time bomb, permanently charged and ready to explode." I mean every word.

I feel the back of his right hand against my cheek. "Me too, Beth." He takes a long, penetrating look at my face. "It's taking every ounce of strength I have not to spread you wide and take you right here. The only reason I'm not is because you look so beautiful, I don't want to mess you up."

His hand brushes against my bare arm and I visibly shiver under his soft caress. He seems tense and off balance, just talking about sex is making him sweat; it's making *me* sweat. I can see the skin on his nose reflecting in the half light. He likes to think he's always in control, yet all it takes is one little request and he's stunned and overawed. I live for that look.

He's fumbling through the expensive material gathered on my lap. Through the layers he finds my lacy panties. "To start with." He rips them off in a single tear. "These have to go."

"Argh!" My gasp is audible.

In a smoky voice he states, "Today you had me do something in this car I've never done before and I'm going to repay the gesture: it's simple cause and effect. You cause me to lose control and I will, in effect, have you do something *you're* not entirely comfortable with."

He shows me my shredded panties, sniffs them, and slips them into the inside pocket of his Armani jacket. "I'll hold onto these."

I feel a crackle of sexual craving between us, it's electric. I have absolutely no idea what he's going to do next and that excites me, so much so I forget to inhale.

"Breathe, Beth," he commands. "Now I'm not going to kiss you or touch you, and I'm not going to fuck you and that's your punishment." I start to speak, but the look he gives me makes me think again. He takes my right hand and feeds my fingers into his mouth, sucking each one tenderly.

"You're going to put *this* hand under *this* magnificent dress and get yourself off, and I'm going to watch."

Feeling so needy and desperate to climax, I begin rummaging through the dress. With my fingers on my clitoris, I turn away. He takes hold of my chin and locks his eyes onto mine, causing me to gulp noisily. "I don't think I can do this with you watching."

"You don't have a choice, missy, besides, you know it turns me on to watch. That's the game, right?"

"What game?"

"Your game. The 'let's take Ayden out of his comfort zone game ... let's pull Ayden apart, piece by piece until he doesn't know which way is up, game.'"

I don't have an answer to that. I simply shrug.

Surely that's not what I'm doing? Maybe it is ...

"So ... let's get started." He tips down his chin and nods for me to begin.

I can't believe what I'm doing. I nestle myself onto his lap and set about my task.

I'll show him ...

I stroke my moist opening, it's swollen and warm to the touch; my clitoris is almost pulsating with need. I slide my left hand under his tie and try to unbutton his shirt; he said he wasn't going to touch me, but didn't say anything about not touching him. He lets me. The buttons are small and fiddly but I create an opening wide enough to slip my nimble hand inside. I feel soft hair, a pounding heart and pectoral muscles contracting beneath my palm. It's enough to cause my breathing to hitch. I give into the feeling of flames licking at my core, opening my mouth to suck in oxygen, looking into the dark sapphire eyes of the man I love. I'm holding back, trying to silence my ecstatic cries.

"All it takes is a little spark."

I gasp involuntarily.

" ... And there it is."

I'm aware of his hands moving towards my own hand, steadily climbing up my thighs, gripping tightly, holding me in place. He said he wouldn't touch me, but he has. He's folding already.

"That's it. You're trying so hard to be a good girl, and so quiet too. But your body is speaking to me, loud and clear."

I cannot escape his stare.

"I have my thumbs on your femoral artery and I can feel your heart beating faster and faster. I'm watching your breasts rise and fall, and now, my poor little genie is starting to pant. You see, I can play this game too." His mouth forms into a wicked smile. "And I *always* win."

He may think he is winning, but from the bulging mass forcing its way out of his pants and, from the way his abdomen is flexing and rolling, I would say it's more like a tie.

"So, before your heart explodes, let's hear it." He leans forward and whispers softly. "No-one is going to hear."

I inhale his delicious scent.

"Only me."

"Ay-den." As the two syllables gush from my mouth, I give myself to bubbling rapture and bury my orgasmic cries in his chest.

"There you go, that's my girl."

I keep my head bowed and fix my stare on my ruffled dress, feeling bashful. I've never done anything like this before.

His hand is tipping up my chin. The softest of kisses transforms into a victorious smile. "You really are such a bad girl, but you're *my* bad girl." He hands me back my torn panties to wipe myself and buttons up his shirt.

"Feel better?"

I nod modestly.

My panties find their way back into his inside pocket. He raises my right hand and lifts it to his nose before closing his eyes as a growling sound leaves his throat. "Remember to wash your hands when we arrive or you'll have me fucking you in public if I get a whiff of you in there."

The thought of that makes me smile, without embarrassment.

Still sitting astride him, he pulls my chin so our noses are touching. "I knew from the moment we met you were going to be trouble." He kisses me gently. "But nothing I can't handle."

With that, our sexual encounter ends; we rearrange our clothes and I fix my make-up, grateful for the fact that he has not messed me up, not physically, but mentally I may be dealing with the implications of what just happened for the next couple of days.

"Lester," he calls, lowering the privacy glass. "Go straight to the book launch as planned."

We continue the rest of the journey in silence, his thumb is stroking the knuckles of my pungent right hand, and we both know where it's been. I lean my head against his arm, enjoying the sensation of his lips briefly on my hair.

Feeling relaxed and playful, I remind him. "You owe me a pair of panties."

He rests his chin on my head. "You owe me an orgasm."

I smile, glowing with post orgasmic bliss. "I'm looking forward to watching that." I don't need to see his smile to know it's there.

"Me too."

***

Ordinarily, Sunday is Dan's least favourite day and usually his least favourite evening. Not because he's at a loose end but because it signals the beginning of a new week, another week spent trawling the internet and the newspapers for some kind of sign. All that's changed, thanks to a chance encounter with the one person in the world he thought he might never find.

The prospect of a reunion has raised his spirits to the point he's walking on air, every step he takes elevates his mood. His life has meaning; days that would otherwise be filled with dreary routine have begun and ended with one, all-consuming thought. That thought makes his skin itch and his hands twitch: the prospect of consummating his relationship with Frances Parker, the only girl he has ever loved and ever desired to the point of obsession.

Having had a premonition of Biblical proportions, he is filling up empty boxes collected from his local Off Licence. On the outside the label reads, Gordon's Gin, although the contents are definitely non-alcoholic but no less potent in the way they communicate intent. Plates, bowls, mugs and cutlery nestle together, two by two; a breadknife, a spatula and a bottle opener are wrapped in a washed-out tea towel.

A box formerly the home to 12 bottles of Bell's Whiskey houses a crumpled pillow, folded down the middle, a double sheet and an off-white bath towel. Like himself, every item he owns has seen better days; edges are frayed and colours have faded, everything has become soiled and tarnished over time.

He looks beyond the kitchen window into the dark space beyond. There was a time when he thought about tidying up the yard, pointing up the flagstones, adding some pots and a water feature but that was a long time ago. Since then, he's managed to occupy his time with more important things like work and tracking down his special girl. The yard has become a jungle of overgrown weeds; a neglected space fit for nothing, populated by misshapen bags of foetid waste.

For what he is hoping will be the last time, he returns to his much loved spot in the lounge, stepping over an obstacle course of bags and boxes.

"Here you are, princess. How you've changed, you've grown-up but you're still *my* girl. You've dyed your hair." He stabs at one of the photographs with a broad finger. "That's okay, we can always change it back." There is tenderness in his voice, a longing that would be endearing if it was not for the fact he has his hand down his jeans and is roughly stroking himself.

***

The first thing that hits me when we arrive at the venue is the lights and the banner: '*Loss of Innocence: no hope, no proof, no way ...*'

He is eager to get inside and has no time for photographers. I hold him back; his tie isn't quite right, so I straighten it and reposition the knot. Whilst doing so, he talks quietly to me.

"Just another reminder, but you will pay a visit to the little girls' room, won't you?" He looks down at me and I'm treated to a playboy smile that turns into a naughty, naughty grin.

"I may conveniently forget and have to straighten your tie a couple of times, just to see what happens." I floor him with a wide-eyed stare.

"Bad girl," he admonishes, before kissing my nose and dragging me inside. "We're most definitely going to talk about this later."

When we get into our stride I'm smiling from ear to ear and he's finding it impossible to contain his amusement. That's when I feel the blinding flash of the camera and it's enough to wipe the smile off my face in record time. I tip my head down and cover my face with my clutch.

"Who's taking photographs?" I ask, sounding much too anxious.

"Who knows? Fucking press probably. They follow me round like flies on shit. What is it with these guys?"

I give him a stern look, disapproving of the simile.

"Let's get inside."

The moment we enter, people are turning and acknowledging him: he's become the focal point of the room. Seeming jet propelled, he soars above his peers and I am caught in his jet stream, carried along at a pace. He accosts a passing waiter carrying an empty tray. "Two glasses of champagne." No please. No thank you.

He moves through the crowd with effortless grace and authority, shaking hands and introducing me as his friend. I'm not entirely comfortable with that but I'll save it for our talk later. It brings a crooked smile to my face when he refers to me by my full name: Elizabeth. That could get him in all kinds of trouble, but I don't doubt for one minute he's done that on purpose, knowing Elizabeth's preoccupation with boldness. Unfortunately, there's the paradox: I have no opportunity to be bold or even to speak. I don't like this kind of role play. I'm wasted as an accessory, doing no more than standing, nodding and smiling.

After twenty minutes of silent listening, I've had enough. My feet are aching and now I'm rocking from left to right: I'm bored senseless. "I'm going to the little girls' room and then I'm going to speak with Max Bradley," I inform Ayden, loosening my grip on his hand.

"Who?" He hasn't a clue who he is.

I'm shocked. "You know? The author? It's his book launch?" I tut and shake my head. "I won't be long."

I think he is advising me against it as I walk away and trying to keep hold of my hand but he quickly relinquishes his grip, realising I won't be contained a moment longer.

I wander across the room and pay a quick visit to the powder room. It's very stark and marbelesque, even the toilet seats look like pieces of sliced granite. It's a quick in and out and I'm ready to begin my adventure into the world of popular fiction. I collect a fresh glass of bubbly and scan the venue; there are quotes from the book plastered everywhere, even the music has a mysterious quality about it. Before me is a table covered in a cardinal red cloth, stacked high with copies of the book. Strangely, no-one is bothering to flick through the pages; no-one is even pretending to be remotely interested in it. How rude. I pick up a copy and read it, back cover first and then the opening chapter. Ten pages in, someone appears at the side of me. I'm conscious of their proximity, but I continue to read.

"It's a bit of a clichéd opening, don't you think?"

I shift my attention from the page and offer a rather distinguished looking gentleman to my right an amiable smile. "I suppose so, but in this genre it's important to establish characters and context quickly. The author's achieved that." I return to the book.

"What about the writing style?" He presses me further.

"I'm no expert, although it is engaging and using the omniscient narrator is probably the best narrative style for revealing multiple characters' motivations, and to move the story forward. I know Grisham favours it." I put the book down. "I'm sure it's a very entertaining read."

I take a closer look at my inquisitor; he has the darkest brown eyes I have ever seen and they are holding my attention. I break away. "Do you know the writer?"

He nods his head. "I do. And what about you, you're not the usual sort to attend these little soirees."

"I'm here with someone." Someone who is looking *for* me and *at* me, at this precise moment.

"Who?" He turns and looks around the room for a likely escort.

"Ayden Stone." I smile. "Do you know him?"

He gives me a knowing look. "Do I *know* him? That's an interesting question." His eyes flick to the side as if he's really thinking through his answer. "This is my third book and his marketing company Stonebridge handles all my PR, distribution etcetera, so *no*, I don't know him."

He picks up the book I was reading and it's then I realise he's the man of the hour, the writer himself. I feel very foolish. "Will you sign a copy of your book for me, Mr. Bradley?"

"It would be my pleasure, Miss ...?"

"Parker, Elizabeth Parker."

To Elizabeth, thanks for the critique. Let's discuss it over dinner. Regards Max. 07983200881. He signs it and hands me the book.

"Thank you, you're very charming, Max."

"Not at all, the pleasure's all mine, but if I may be so bold. What the hell is a beautiful, intelligent woman like you doing with a bastard like Ayden Stone?"

I'm struck dumb by his directness. "I'm sorry!"

"No, I'm the one who's sorry. Sorry no-one steered you away from him. Stone by name, Stone by nature." He reaches out to shake my hand and I position the book under my left arm. "Enjoy the rest of your evening." He scans the room and spots Ayden, who is burning him to the ground with a razor-sharp stare; it cuts through him with the intensity of a high powered laser beam. "Something tells me your evening just took a turn for the worse, Miss Parker."

I look over at Ayden and he's adopted an unfamiliar pose, leaning up against a pillar; not exactly in public view but not concealed either. He has his arms folded; his right foot is crossed over his left ankle. He's either sulking or seething or both. If it wasn't for the scowl, I'd describe it as a model pose.

"On a scale of one to ten, how would you describe *that* look?" I ask Max, as one lover of popular fiction to another.

"Oh, trust me it's off the scale. I'd have to draw on some superlatives and perhaps throw in some hyperbole to do it justice."

"Then that's my cue I think ... bye, Max." I walk directly over to Ayden, I do not stop, I do not pass go, I stay on a straight line until I'm stood in front of him. He has managed to unfold his arms from his chest and has slipped them into his pockets. If that's not classic anger management, I don't know what is. I face him square on and, with my heels I'm closer than usual to his face. You don't have to be a mind reader to know how incensed he is: he can't even speak.

"Do you think I've been too bold, Mr. Stone?" I ask quietly, strategically placing my hands over his trouser pockets to immobilize his hands. "Ayden, don't speak, just listen."

He is looking anywhere but my face.

"I was discussing the literary merits of the book we have come here tonight to launch with the author." He tries to take his hands out of his pockets but I hold his wrists in place. I have to employ all my upper body strength just to contain him. "Look at me."

His eyes are flashing a wild, fiery indigo and the green flecks are like sparks circling a Catherine wheel.

"I would never do anything to hurt you or to embarrass you. You're getting worked up because you're jealous and you're not used to feeling this way. But, you have nothing to be jealous about. I only want your hands on me, Ayden. Remember the car?"

He's becoming visibly calmer, his breathing is easing and even those flickering embers of rage are petering out. I release my white knuckled grip on his hands and he takes them out of his pockets. Before I can get another word out, he spins me around so my back is against the pillar; his palms either side of my head on the upright surface, framing my face, anchoring me in place.

What the hell ...

His formidable stance causes me to roll my eyes. "Now you have the use of your hands, maybe you should put them back in your pockets."

"I don't need my fucking hands. I've got this."

He pins me to the pillar with his hips and I can't help but feel his erection pressing into my stomach. My God, I'm so shocked and turned-on, I can barely speak. The fact I'm not wearing any underwear only adds to my arousal. I'm at my maximum height in stacked heels and still I'm looking up at him in awe. I'm holding my signed book and my clutch to my chest like a bullet proof vest, as if they will offer me some kind of protection against his overpowering sexual magnetism. They don't.

"Should I give your panties to your new friend as a souvenir?"

"No."

"Or maybe I should take you back to the little girls' room and fuck you, because that's all I can think of doing right now."

He would too.

"No." I anchor his eyes to mine. "You are behaving irrationally. I've done nothing wrong. In fact you're causing a scene. We have an audience and all I can hear is, 'Get a room!'"

He eases off me a centimetre at a time, finding some semblance of self-awareness before snatching the book from my grasp. He is actually holding it out of my reach so I can't retrieve it. Why do I feel like I'm being reprimanded? Probably because I am.

"Do you want this?" I know he isn't referring to the book.

"Yes," I answer sharply. "I do. I want a copy of the book but not *that* copy of the book. I'll go swap it for another."

I take hold of the book but he keeps a firm grip on it.

"Oh for goodness sake, Ayden, you can trust me to go walkabout without a leash. I'll come back to you."

In one split second he's cupping my face. "I've never felt so fucking incensed before in my life. I wanted to hit that bastard."

"I know." I caress his face and it's as if we are alone in an empty room. "I didn't do it to make you jealous. I was bored hanging on your every word. I'm sorry, but I don't make a very good accessory."

He sniggers. "Oh you'll never be that, Beth." The gentlest of kisses grazes my mouth and I see my lip- gloss shining on his lips for the second time tonight. As I begin to wipe it away with the forefinger of my right hand, he pushes it into his mouth and sucks hard. It's such a small thing but it's intimate and so erotic: my insides clench.

"Be good, Ayden. Remember the effect you have on me, you're the one who's let *this* genie out of the bottle."

He gives me back my finger. "I don't want you making anyone else's wishes come true the way you have for me, that's all."

I choose my words carefully. "There's no chance of that, you are my one and only master." He likes the idea of being masterful. The smile that follows forms slowly and is so provocative, it causes a longing in me that has me swooning. He sees that in me.

"Do you want to leave? We can go now and be at your apartment in twenty."

I shake my head, appreciating the offer but decide against it. It's a big night for him, he needs to circulate and I need to get my wear out of this ludicrously expensive dress. "No, I want to stay. This is a new experience for me." I arch backwards and pretend to straighten his tie. "Poor, baby, you're alright now. Go, do your thing. I'll amuse myself somehow."

I receive a wide eyed stare. "How?"

"I'll go talk to people and eat canapés, sip champagne, watch you work the room and show off this fabulous frock."

He ogles me from top to toe and back again. "You look good enough to eat."

I decide not to dignify that comment with a response. Instead I present him with a flat smile.

"But no more discussions about literature with aging authors, okay?" He takes hold of my signed copy of Loss of Innocence and reads the note. Thankfully he has enough self-control to let it go. "The only thing this book has going for it is the title," he comments, signifying something but saying nothing.

I pretend not to pick up on his intimation and give him a gentle push backwards. He doesn't move.

"No touching, Miss Parker, remember."

"It's a little late for that, don't you think?" I leave my hand where it is. "You're going to go and be my Mr. P. I'll watch and learn. Do you understand?" He cracks a smile, acknowledging Elizabeth's timely arrival.

I tut and stride away towards the book display and swap my signed book for a plain old paperback. I make a point of holding the new book aloft so he can see how obedient I've been. He does the, I'm watching you double finger point, laughs, turns and seeks out his minions.

Before embarking on my solo venture I head over to the ladies' powder room, it seems like a safe haven away from prying eyes and flirtatious writers. I take a moment to freshen up and to reapply some tinted lip-gloss. Before heading for the door a six foot, straight off the catwalk, auburn haired siren almost tramples me underfoot. I say sorry but she's the one who should learn some manners or drink less.

I'm stopped in my tracks when she strikes up an impromptu conversation. "You must be Elizabeth?"

I spin around to face her. "I suppose I must," I answer coolly. I think she actually sniggers but I can't be sure, after all, I'm looking at her through a mirror. "Have we met?"

"God no, he wouldn't allow that. I'm Alenka." She offers me her manicured hand in a kind of mock introduction. When that's coupled with her perfect teeth and Eastern European accent, I feel an uncomfortable flutter of something: jealously, maybe?

"How do you know my name?" I'm happy to play along.

"You're Ayden's latest play thing. You're the one he's been fucking for the past week."

I manage to conceal my astonishment quite well, under the circumstances. "I think Ayden's a little old for toys." I position myself next to her. I might be six inches shorter, but what I lack in height I make up for in intellect, or at least I thought I did until I realise the implications of the word 'toys.'

Shit! Why did I say that?

She's on it in a flash. "He will never grow out of his *toys*. He's a player and players like to play, that's what they do. You see, it is never a game of chance, he plays to win. He holds all the cards."

What the hell is she going on about?

Toys, games, cards ...

Now she's reshaping her already perfect brows: she's the one playing for time. Why is she so eager to have this conversation with me? It occurs to me ... she's seen the way Ayden listens to me, the way he looks at me, our sexual chemistry and she's seething with jealousy. Oh, this might be more fun than I first thought: actually, I'm the one holding all the cards, Alenka. I let her continue.

"You see, at first it's the attraction and then it's the chase: that's what he loves." She keeps stalling. "And, oh the romance, the flowers and the poetry, it's like a dream."

I'm feeling a little less sure of myself, suddenly.

"Then comes the gifts, and what lovely gifts." Dreamily, she circles her head and sways.

I don't like what I'm hearing. I'm starting to perspire; glossy beads are forming on the back of my neck and between my breasts.

"But you know this, Elizabeth?" She turns her head and observes me shrewdly.

I fear my expression may give me away. Too shaken to engage in witty banter, I turn to fix my dress. But she hasn't done with me, there's more. I watch her watching me and our eyes meet. I look away but out of the corner of my eye I see her smiling.

"And let us not forget the clothes."

I know she means my dress and I wish the ground would open and swallow me up. I'm not equipped to deal with this: she's eating me alive. Thank God, she's had her fill and begins to wash her beautiful hands. She pats them dry on the towel.

"It's all part of the game, Elizabeth, a game you can't win."

I've heard enough. "I think this conversation is over. I'm sorry, I don't remember your name." I pretend to check myself in the mirror. "You must be confusing me with someone else." I turn to leave.

"Goodbye sweet, Frances. I think it is too late for you, I can see he has your heart. He has already won."

With that, she wafts past me in all her catwalk glory and I feel as if I've just been run over by a freight train. I wobble on my high heels and grip the marble counter for support. What the hell was all that about? Why did she call me Frances? I haven't been Frances for over six years.

I manage to settle myself through a combination of deep breathing and by applying a cold water compress to the back of my neck. I'm nauseated and flushed. I practise a happy smile, but I can't do it; it's not me. All I see is a secondary school teacher in a midnight blue dress with a sad face. What was I thinking? Reinventing myself? I feel like an impostor.

Now might be a good time to leave, I can't stay in here forever. God knows what she's up to out there with Ayden. After what I've heard, do I care?

Who am I kidding, of course I care; that's the problem. He's made me care with his flowers and his poetry, his gifts, his soft words, and his fucking sexiness.

"That's what players do, they play." Those were her exact words.

I charge out of the bathroom, leaving my book behind and prepare to seek out Ayden.

He's chatting to a group of executive types. I'm fit to burst, but manage to position myself next to him: he kisses my cheek affectionately and introduces me as his girlfriend. I give him a surprised stare and his mouth twitches with amusement. When did that happen? How long was I gone?

Momentarily distracted by his announcement, my anger subsides. I start to pay attention. He's got so much to say, they're hanging on his every word: he's confident and Mr. Powerful. I feel him reaching for my right hand and, while he's talking and laughing, he's stroking my knuckles. He may not be including me in the conversation but it's his way of telling me he knows I'm here, we are together. I'm not an accessory.

With almost all of my senses triggered, I feel my heart starting to race. Is it the sexual tension between us, or is it fear? Am I the unwitting participant in a cruel game: is he the puppet master, pulling all the invisible strings that bind me to him? A kind of clammy sweat claims my body. I'm becoming moist all over. I feel his hand slipping in mine and he turns and pins me to the spot with a piercing stare of such ferocity, I think I might be punctured by it.

"Excuse us." He smiles and pulls me to one side. "What the fuck are you doing?" he asks in a strained whisper.

I can't think straight. "I'm ..." I feel helpless and exposed and nervously place my thumb nail in my mouth. I look up at him through mascared lashes.

"Stop! Fucking stop it, Beth. I know what you're doing. We're not in the car now. Don't make me want you here."

"I'm not doing anything, Ayden," I confess, and it's the truth. What I'm experiencing isn't sexual frustration, it's an anxiety attack and it's making me tremble.

"You drive me crazy with your antics." He grabs my hand firmly. "We're leaving."

I stand my ground. "No we're not." I centre myself.

"What!" His eyes are burning like molten lava. How quickly his mood has shifted from attentive to oppressive, in the space of two minutes.

"I'm not doing anything, Ayden. I'm a little over-heated, that's all."

He touches my forehead with the back of his right hand and is instantly concerned. "You're warm. We'd better get you home." He reaches for my hand, a lot less forcefully now but I have no intentions of leaving, not until he's answered a couple of questions.

"Ayden, who's that woman over there?" I look in the direction of Alenka. She's the only one surrounded by a flotilla of admirers, bobbing and weaving, vying for her attention.

From his expression, he recognises her. "Which woman?"

"Don't treat me like a fool, Ayden. You know which woman. Alenka. Who is she to you?"

His unconscious 'tell' gives the game away; he reaches for the back of his neck with his right hand and attempts to massage a tender spot. "She's someone I've taken out a couple of times."

"Where?"

"I don't remember."

"Try." My staccato delivery helps me to pin him down.

"To some award thing, probably, dinner maybe. Why?"

"Just answer my questions." I tip my head to one side and pause for a second. I want his full attention. "Did you send her flowers?"

"I suppose so ..."

"Did you send her a poem?"

"I guess I ..."

"Did you have Celine take her clothes shopping with one of your *special* Visa cards?"

"Only because ..."

"That's all I need to know." I feel a thousand daggers piercing my heart. Actual physical pain lances through me, but I refuse to let him see me cry. I release myself from his grip. Alenka was right to warn me. He *is* a player.

"I'll make my own way home." Fighting off an impulse to bolt, I walk in the direction of the exit, trying to offer polite goodbyes on the way. I see Max, stood by his pile of books and he gives me a sympathetic nod. That only makes me feel worse. I don't want his pity. I just want to get out of this fucking building without weeping.

Once outside, the cool evening air hits me and I look left and right for a taxi. At that very moment the Rolls Royce appears, its brakes screeching as it comes to a grand prix halt.

Ayden must have phoned Lester from inside. He jumps out of the Rolls Royce, looking agitated. Sprinting around the car he opens the door for me. I take one step back but, before I can walk away, Ayden scoops me up and forcibly marches me into the car. It all happens so quickly I have no time to protest as he bundles me onto the back seat. I try to slap his hands away while flopping down onto the leather upholstery with a thud. I'm not going anywhere. He'll make sure of that. God forbid I should cause a scene.

He slams his door shut. "Get us the fuck out of here!" he yells, trying to regulate his breathing.

I arch my body away from him, focusing on the changing scenery. Out of the corner of my eye, I see his reflection in the privacy glass Lester has raised without being instructed to do so. He knows Ayden so well, which is more than can be said for me.

My world is in turmoil, even the passing crowds and the flashing lights are no more than a psychedelic blur. I can't bring myself to look at him. The sound of his uneven breaths make my chest feel tight and constricted and I shiver, not because I'm cold but because I'm wounded and shocked to find out he's not the man I thought he was. I want to scream and shout and say I hate you for making me feel so special, when really, what I hate most is myself for falling for it; falling for him.

In a measured tone he speaks. "I know why you're upset, but you need to think back to everything that's happened between us; how I've treated you, even put you before my business. I've done everything to please you, so don't fuck around, Beth, and don't confuse kindness with weakness."

What! I don't recognise his acerbic tone. Is this the man who has been sleeping in my bed? Is he the one I gave myself to?

Who the hell is he?

When Lester pulls up outside my apartment, I make a point of reaching around my neck and unfastening my treasured kiss necklace. Before stepping out of the car I turn to him, open up his left hand, that same hand that touched me so intimately less than an hour ago, and let the necklace cascade into it. Without thinking I wrap my hands around his so it forms a fist around the platinum chain: now it's his to keep. I have to give it back. Of all the feelings I have, this simple act is the most distressing; it takes me back to the moment we met and it's ironic that such a delicate piece of jewellery should bring us full circle.

He grabs my wrist and I recoil. A single tear rolls down my cheek but I won't look at him, I can't.

"Let me go, Ayden," I plead in a broken whisper.

"Please ..." Slowly, a millimetre at a time, he releases me.

I step out of the car alone and make my way towards the security lamp outside my apartment block; it shines like a homing beacon. I don't stop walking until I reach my front door.

10

S tumbling, I make my way inside and put my back to the door, creating a human barricade. I feel as if my legs are too weak to hold the weight of my extravagant dress and slide to the floor. The silk material falls into disorganised creases, there's no discernible shape: how quickly its beauty fades. It's just a dark blue dress, fancy wrapping for something very ordinary: for me.

Like sad Cinderella, I pull off my uncomfortable shoes and throw them across the room, hoping that ridding myself of them will make me feel better. It doesn't. I need to cry it out, but I can't. I'm still too raw.

There's a buzzing sound. I can see my mobile phone dancing across the breakfast table; it's on vibrate. I stagger over to see who is calling: it's Ayden, Mr. P. himself but this time he has no potential, he's not perfect or powerful and most certainly not Prince Charming. He's a fucking *Player* and he's played me for a fool.

The phone keeps dancing and stopping and dancing again. If I hear his voice, I'll lose it. I take up what was Ayden's place at my breakfast table and open up my laptop. It takes a minute to boot up. When it's ready to go, I compose an email:

From:	songbirdBP@hotmail.co.uk
To:	a.s.mediainternational1@global.com
Date:	21st October 21.50
Subject:	NOTHING TO SAY

I can't bear to speak to you. I'll let the song do the talking.

I attach *Jar of Hearts* by Christina Perri. Welcome to my world Mr. Stone. You said we should add some new songs to my eclectic collection, and here's the first and last of them: enjoy.

Flat footed, I walk into my bedroom and barely recognise myself in my full length mirror; my hair has fallen over my face and the dress reaches my shins. I look like a broken doll, and that's exactly how I feel: misused and broken.

The dress doesn't put up much of a struggle and it's happy to drape itself over the chair by the wall while I climb beneath my duvet in an attempt to rid myself of the frigid air that seems to be enveloping my body. What sound does a heart make when it breaks; is it like glass shattering or the roll of thunder across an empty sky. I don't know. In my ears is the swishing of a heartbeat. I'm alive, but dying inside with every breath.

The realisation of what might have been settles in my consciousness like oil on water: a shifting slick of blackness, dragging me under with no hope of rescue. I am alone.

It's only 10.00 o'clock but it feels like four in the morning. My eyelids want to close, but my brain won't let them; instead it has them flickering and twitching frantically. I need to sleep. I need to forget.

I drop off to sleep, but the sound coming from my laptop wakes me. Ping. I have an email. I know it's Ayden, he'll have something to say in response to my musical message but I can't deal with it now. It pings again. A minute later it pings again.

I'm yelling at the top of my voice. "Stop! You're driving me crazy!"

I jump out of bed and before I can get to the laptop it pings again. I have four emails from him. It's the same message re-sent with an attachment.

I disconnect the charger and take the laptop to bed with me. At least I won't be sleeping entirely alone. I click open:

From:	a.s.mediainternational1@global.com
To:	songbirdBP@hotmail.co.uk
Date:	22nd October 00.35
Subject:	LISTEN!

Who am I?

There's no text, just a musical attachment. I recognise it. It's from my iTunes library. I climb into bed and place my laptop beside me, opening the track from Will Young's album. This musical message is unexpected but the only way Ayden can reach me, through a medium he knows I will welcome into my home and, more importantly, listen to. It begins. The lyrics that follow speak of love. It's a beautiful song.

When I wake up, it's 5 a.m. My laptop is still sleeping so I wake it up too. I have a song in mind. It will be my way of explaining how I feel. I let it play and the words have me sobbing into my pillow. I email:

From:	songbirdBP@hotmail.co.uk
To:	a.s.mediainternational1@global.com
Date:	22nd October 05.05

Subject: LISTEN!

What Hurts the Most

It's a country music song by Rascal Flatts and he won't know it, but the words echo what I feel. I settle myself down and try to sleep, knowing my alarm will start screaming in less than two hours.

Ping. I sit up, hoping it's another song from him. I check my emails:

From: a.s.mediainternational1@global.com
To: songbirdBP@hotmail.co.uk
Date: 22nd October 05.30
Subject: LISTEN!

All Over Again

I know this song by Justin Timberlake, it's a desperate plea. I play it and find myself pacing and weeping uncontrollably; every line is overflowing with meaning. It takes all my willpower not to pick up the phone. Instead, I head for the shower and allow the steaming spray to scatter my tears. It's only when I see my reflection that I'm reminded of what he's done to me.

The skin around my eyes is red and swollen, even my lips are twice their normal size. My face is the colour of sour milk and I look like a ghostly imitation of my former self. I'm drowning in my own sadness, tears welling, deep enough to swamp every hope, every wish.

This time yesterday we were in this very apartment together, making love. How will I survive a day at work looking and feeling so fucking wretched? I tear off wet underwear and wrap myself in my bathrobe. With dripping wet hair, I climb back into bed.

When the alarm sounds, for a couple of mindless seconds I feel okay, then I remember. My head aches, my pillow is damp, and I have no desire to ever leave this bed. The alarm repeats, and I want to throw it across the room but I need the toilet. I turn it off and drag myself from the sheets. Outside there's daylight, and I can hear traffic; life goes on, for the rest of the world at least.

I wash and clean my teeth before attempting to do anything with my hair; it's such a mess and I don't have the time, energy or inclination to style it. I twist it into a clip and fold over the ends. What the hell. I reach for my body spray and my hand accidentally touches Ayden's toiletries bag. Without a second thought, I gather up his things and bundle them together. His overnight bag is by the door, so I start to pack it. I resist the urge to inhale his T-shirt or to fold his jeans. Instead I gather them up like dirty washing and stuff them in. There is one other thing I need to do. I take the 'special' Visa card out of my purse and slip it into the side pocket of his bag. I won't be using that again.

On my way to the kitchen I give last night's dress a passing glance and snigger: 'Sorry, you did your best.' I wonder what happened to the killer heels but I see them abandoned and on their sides where they landed, and that's where they can stay. I throw back a couple of gulps of orange juice but even they threaten to erupt from my mouth. I can't face eating anything.

Arriving at school, I see the same old faces: students, colleagues and flustered office staff. I'd forgotten it was presentation evening. Thank God I did my planning last week. I won't be undertaking anything that requires any mental effort today.

The morning's lessons go well, considering. I take my foot off the gas and allow my students to entertain themselves with some private reading, I'm happy to baby-sit. Actual teaching is out of the question.

I work through lunch, unable to face my colleagues. I can't endure the simplest of questions today. "Did you have a nice weekend, Beth?" Could open up a whole can of nasty, little worms.

I'm grateful for my free period at the end of the day and occupy my mind with thoughts of contemporary poetry and examination preparation. I decide to stay at work and to get a head start on tomorrow's lessons. I have nothing to go home to. Besides, curtain up is at 6.30 p.m.

I've purposely avoided turning on my laptop all day. With time to myself, I boot up and it greets me with another ping.

From:	a.s.mediainternational1@global.com
To:	songbirdBP@hotmail.co.uk
Date:	22nd October 09.50
Subject:	LISTEN: IT'S THE LAST ONE!

The Reason.

I don't know the song or the group Hoobastank but, when I play it back, I realise it's his final assault; another despairing attempt to bombard me with a message, seeking forgiveness.

It starts off with a driving beat and I don't know what to think. When it begins, I know this is Ayden speaking to me directly. It's such a meaningful song. Maybe he does care, and he's not *playing* with me?

I pull up the lyrics off YouTube, play it through again, and I'm touched to think he's gone to the trouble of finding such a profoundly moving song. I'm torn.

Without a rational thought of my own I find solace in Jane Austen; *"You pierce my soul. I am half agony, half hope ... I have loved none but you."*

Some early-bird parents arrive before the arranged time, hoping to get a seat at the front of the theatre. I take a couple of minutes to assess my appearance; my hair is still clipped back, my knee length skirt and white blouse are clean and tidy and, best of all, I can hide behind my glasses: they'll go some way towards hiding my sadness.

I take my position near the front of the auditorium, seating former students in alphabetical order as planned. My back is to the stage and I'm doing my best to offer welcoming smiles and the occasional hug to my most dedicated protégées. I'm still getting them seated when the lights go down and the Head Teacher begins her speech.

"Good Evening, ladies and gentlemen, Governors, students, staff and special guest, Mr. Ayden Stone, who has very graciously offered to hand out our awards this evening."

Now I'm hearing things: I could swear I just heard her say, *"Ayden Stone."* I turn to face the stage and there he sits, every inch the mercurial MD.

He's so smart in his signature suit and I examine him from the knees up, terrified of what I might see the minute our eyes meet. I lower my nose to look over my glasses and we lock onto each other. He launches a missile of a stare my way and I lower my head and look away. I have no defence against an assault of that magnitude.

I walk to the back of the theatre and hide in the shadows. I can see him, he can't see me but he knows I'm here. Unlike his last visit, he doesn't seem quite so self-assured; he appears lost in thought and tired around the eyes. Maybe he didn't sleep at all.

For forty minutes he stands, smiles and shakes hands with students receiving their awards. With infinite patience, he poses with each one for a photograph and I know how he hates to do that. By student number 70, his smile is fading: he's running on empty, or am I just projecting?

Knowing it's customary for the guest of honour to give a speech, my hands are starting to sweat on his behalf - I'm nervous for him. Why should I be, he's done this kind of thing a hundred times before but, he's had little if any sleep and no time to prepare. My hands sweat a little more, and I remove my glasses and prepare myself. What is he going to say?

He begins, *"Good evening everyone, Governors, Head Teacher, teachers, students, parents and guests. I was very pleased to be invited back to your school after a very rewarding visit only a week ago."*

He looks calm but over-rehearsed somehow. His words waft over me.

"For those of you collecting your well-earned awards this evening, this is a time for celebration and for recognising achievement. In this vein, I'd like to share my observations with you about success, in the hope that you'll gain an insight into what it means to find fulfilment."

Oh great, the Ayden Stone story, the students will be riveted.

"When I was your age, I had one driving force: building a media centred business. I dedicated myself to it, to the exclusion of everything and everyone. And there's nothing wrong with that. The payoff has been immense and I have been very fortunate and surrounded myself with some very talented people and lots of beautiful things."

This is something new: the personal touch?

"So, what has that to do with you, you ask? In actual fact, quite a lot. Believe it or not, our destinies are inextricably connected: every time you listen to music, watch a movie, make a call, email, tweet or text, our worlds are colliding."

Colliding? I could be mistaken, but is he actually talking about us?

"My world is nothing without you. In fact, it is you who give it meaning."

Is the 'you' in this speech, *me?*

"This has been a hard lesson for me to learn. So I'm letting you in on a secret; pretending to be someone you're not is a worthless exercise. It has taken me some time to decide what I want, where my future lies and to be prepared to give everything I have to find professional and personal fulfilment. Now, it's your turn. Here, tonight we stand on the threshold of greatness; but greatness does not come from running away or seeing complications as insurmountable obstacles, it comes from here, from inside. It's what makes you the person you are. You want more. You deserve more. Each and every one of you has it within you to decide your fate... only you know what is right for you.

My God! This is a full blown apology.

"So learn from me. Be bold, take a chance, but never give up. If you have a dream, tell someone about it, someone who will listen; someone who sees in you what you dare not see in yourself, but make it happen. You have the power to change the world, one day at a time. Thank you for listening and good luck to you all, in everything you do."

There is applause and he appears grateful, but he's not hearing it. His mind is elsewhere. Only I know the depth of meaning in each and every, over-rehearsed word. He's just bared his soul to me. Do I really have the power to change the world, to change *his* world?

I return to my classroom and switch on my mobile. I have five unread voicemails, four from last night and one from this morning. I listen to them in the order they were sent:

10.15 pm:
I'm sorry Beth. Please forgive me ... I'm such a fucking arse hole! Please call me.

10.30pm:
I got your message. Good song choice ... Jar of hearts!
He is annoyed but I think more with himself than with me.
Please don't end it like this. I need to talk to you, to explain.

12.30pm:
I'm out of my mind thinking about you, Beth, answer your phone. I need to explain, please ...
I hear his tired appeal and I'm saddened to think of him in so much pain, pleading.
Listen to the song I've emailed to you. I'm not good at this, but just listen.
Will Young's words resurface and hold my attention.

5.30am:
I can't sleep ... I miss you, baby. Like your song said, I know you're hurting, and you have no idea how much I hate myself for being the one to make you feel that way.
There's a bottomless sigh.
For what it's worth, I sent you another song. It's not one I save for occasions like this because there's never been an occasion like this - so don't go thinking that. It's for you, every word.
I recall Justin Timberlake's profound lyrics and sniff back tears, wishing I'd been brave enough to answer my phone last night. But what if I had? Would he have gone all out to profess his love for me? This has been our moment of truth: no more games.

10.00am
I can't do this. You have to let me apologise. We have to work this out ... I feel like shit. I'm such a fucking bastard, Beth ... I'm sorry. I've given it my best shot. I can't find any more songs. I'm all out.
He sounds so despondent and I have to swallow deeply to contain my sobs. He saved the best for last: I had become The Reason for his proclamation.

With each voicemail the depth of his regret, and need for forgiveness became more tangible. I should have listened to them earlier, the fact I didn't has made it necessary for him to deliver his apology to a packed theatre full of strangers, still keeping every word relevant to them and to me. I hurt inside, and it's not because of my own suffering, but out of compassion for him.

In spite of the womanising, the mock courtship and the lies, he is my wish come to life. He's the one I have been waiting for, and the thought of ending what we have, even before it's begun, is unimaginable.

I shut everything down and make my way to the refectory where parents and guests are being served refreshments. That's where he'll be.

Before entering, I brush back my unruly hair, straighten my skirt, and project ordinariness. Within a minute of mingling with students and parents, I feel his eyes on me; he's watching my every move. It's like a sixth sense. We are connected. It's not just sexual chemistry, it's emotional and, when he touches me, that connection become visceral.

I position myself next to him so I don't have to look into those watery pools of cerulean light; his face is full of anguish and if I allow myself to look upon it, I will cry.

For once he holds off on the clever repartee, but simply holds my left hand behind my back with his right hand, out of sight; he's being discreet or holding me fast, I'm not sure which.

"I listened to your speech."

"You were meant to. It was all about us." His grip tightens on my fingers.

"I don't know what to say, Ayden. I don't have the energy to argue with you." I glance around the room, there are congratulatory pats on backs and proud smiles, no-one would guess for a minute we are hand in hand.

"I've not come here to argue." I sense his eyes upon me, burning through my cheekbones all the way to my tormented soul.

"You look beautiful in your disguise. But I *see* you, Beth. I see you now for who you are. I fucked up. I said I would. I don't know any better. I'm sorry. Please look at me. It cuts me to the bone, thinking you can't even bear to look at me." I feel an anguished squeeze.

"I can't, Ayden, I have to work here and standing here sobbing will do nothing for my reputation." I try to smile, but nothing happens. For some reason, facial muscles don't respond to signals originating in my brain. I can't manufacture a smile out of misery.

He seems suddenly animated. "But haven't you seen the photographs of us? They're everywhere: magazines, newspapers on the Internet. You and me together - the word's out. You've never looked lovelier and I've never looked happier."

I try to release my hand, but he won't let me go.

"I can't do this anymore without you."

I'm not hearing anything. All I'm thinking is *photographs* of me out in the public domain? The thought fills me with dread.

"What photographs?" I turn to face him squarely. "What fucking photographs?" It's no more than an undignified hiss expelled through clenched teeth.

"The ones of us in Hyde Park and then last night at the book launch. You look stunning." His face cracks into a proud smile.

I shake free of his hand. "I have to go, Ayden."

Gripped by the thought I'm walking away from him, he grabs me by the shoulders. God knows what we must look like.

"Go where? Go where, Beth?" There's a kind of controlled panic in his voice.

"I want to go home right now. Is Lester outside?"

He nods.

"Tell him to start the car. I'll be out front in two minutes."

"I don't get it, what the fuck's going on?" He grips me by the shoulders tighter, prompting me to answer.

"I can't tell you here. I'll meet you in the front car park. Just say your good byes and go!" With that I twist away and run to get my laptop, coat and bag. I can see my world falling apart and losing Ayden isn't the half of it.

Two minutes later, I dive into the car and Ayden is already there waiting.

"Miss Parker's apartment."

"Yes, Mr. Stone." The car eases out through the school gates.

I throw my glasses in my bag, roughly pull my hair loose from the clip and shake it free in the hope these straightforward acts of reveal will ease my anxiety somehow.

"So are you going to tell me what the hell's going on?"

I want to tell him but I struggle to find the words: where to begin? "I can't, not at the moment."

"I know we've got a lot to talk about but this is something else, isn't it?" He places his left hand on my face and I lean into it. God! How I've missed his touch. I close my eyes and I'm falling, safe in the knowledge he'll catch me.

"Tell me, Beth, what's got you so upset?"

I look down. "I didn't tell you the entire story, you know about the night when I was attacked at uni?"

He nods and lifts my chin so he can watch how the words form and leave my mouth.

"After the incident, the guy, he started to stalk me. I don't know, but I just got this feeling he was watching me and I even thought someone was getting into our apartment - things went missing or were moved. I thought I was going crazy."

He strokes my hair softly, thoughtful and patient. "Go on."

"It got so bad I couldn't face going out or going home at night, I expected him to be there, you know, waiting for me. So that's when Charlie and I changed our names. Back then, I was called

Frances Parker. She was known as Charlotte Miller and changed it to Charlie, said it would help her career if people thought she was a guy." I force a smile. "That's why I've tried so hard to remain anonymous. So, when the press tried to take our photos last night, I turned away." My thumbnail hits my teeth. "What if he recognises my face and comes after me?"

"He won't, baby, you'll be fine. It's just a couple of lousy photos. I'll make sure it doesn't happen again."

"But what if ..."

"I won't let anyone hurt you, Beth." He instinctively pulls me close and wraps his arms around me, sensing my need for protection. I take refuge in his warm embrace. I feel safe here; this is where I belong.

As we are approaching my apartment, Ayden spots half a dozen or so press photographers outside the security door, mingling around in the cool night air. "Stop and reverse out, Lester. Just drive for half an hour and then we'll come back."

"Yes, Mr. Stone." With the skill of a racing car driver, Lester reverses the car back down the street and we speed off in the opposite direction.

Ayden takes out his phone, scrolls down his contacts and makes a call. "Bridgette, Ayden Stone. Yes, yes good evening. I want you to set up a decoy for me. Yes. The press are hounding me again and I need some privacy, set something up." He listens. "Yes, make it good. Yeah, that'll do, The Ivy, down on one knee. That should do the trick. Put it out there. Thanks."

"Who's getting engaged?" I ask curiously, lifting my head to watch him explain.

"I am," he sniggers and pulls me to him.

When we arrive back at my apartment, the coast is clear. The decoy was successfully deployed. I can't wait to get inside. I've felt cold all day but now I'm shaking with an icy chill, dreading what the future might bring. I attempt to pour out two glasses of wine but my hands are trembling and Ayden urges me to sit down.

"I've got to make some calls. I'll set up round the clock protection and have someone come take a look at the security in this place. Are you okay?"

I nod and wrap my hands around the wine glass; its contents are warming me from the inside. I can't catch every word, but there's something about "24/7 and shifts ... locksmith, alarm ..." I feel much safer knowing he has everything under control.

Out of nowhere the doorbell rings and keeps ringing. I place down my glass and look to Ayden who comes bounding into the lounge. "Who the fuck's that?"

"I don't know, but be careful."

Off he strides with me trotting behind. "Don't worry about me, I've been fitness boxing since I was thirteen, I can handle myself." He opens the door and I can hear raised voices. Charlie?

In blows the whirlwind in one almighty gust. "Oh, Beth, I just got home and started looking through today's newspaper and I saw you there, with *him*." She gives *'him'* the kind of stare that would dissolve lesser men. "You were in Hyde Park, picnicking?"

I find her tone amusing. "Charlie, this is Ayden." I look from one to the other, assuming they'll shake hands, but Charlie is in no mood to make his acquaintance.

"Ayden, this is Charlie."

He's assessing the situation but makes no move towards her either. I sense a stand-off.

Her words leave her mouth like poison arrows. "Oh, you're here are you, you bastard! Do you have any idea what you've done?" My protective, older sister is venting like an overheated radiator.

"Charlie ..." I try to calm her but she's been building up to this on the drive over.

"Has she told you why she's been hiding out for six years, what happened to her?"

He looks horrified and shakes his head.

"Charlie no," I implore.

"You've come along and swept her off her feet with your fuck me face and fancy clothes, and now look what's happened."

"Charlie," I call out. "That's enough!"

She's becoming emotional. "But he didn't see you, Beth." Tearful, she turns to Ayden. "Do you know she never left the apartment for a month, she couldn't sleep alone, she wouldn't eat. It really threw her off balance." She turns to me and takes hold of my hands. "I don't want you to have to go through that again, hon."

"I know, Char, but Ayden had no idea. I only told him half the story, I ..."

"... Did you happen to mention the stalking?"

"No but I'm ..."

He is visibly shocked. " ... I've organised round the clock security starting tomorrow morning, so nothing's going to happen to you, Beth. I'll make sure you're safe." He pulls me to him and kisses my hair: a truce is established.

Charlie flops down on the sofa and addresses Ayden. "I'm sorry for being such a drama queen, but she's my baby sister, you know?"

I move to sit beside her and we hug tightly. "Don't worry. Ayden will look after me." Affectionately, I brush away a strand of hair. "Do you want a glass of wine? It'll take the edge off."

"No thanks, I've got to drive back, besides I've got a date." She shifts in her seat like she's sitting on wet sand; who would guess such a vibrant, beautiful woman could be so easily shaken. That's how special she is: no smoke, all fire.

"But I'll stay here with you tonight if you want me to?"

"No, I'm fine. You go and knock him dead."

"Well alright. If you're sure you're okay." She gives my arm a sisterly squeeze.

"I'm sure."

Ayden's 'excuse me' cough takes my attention away from Charlie.

"I'm going. I'll leave you two, to, you know ..." He heads out of the room much too quickly. By the time I catch him, he's standing by the security door with his overnight bag in his hand.

The events of the past twenty four hours have dinted my usually acute powers of observation, I've become desensitized and I'm finding it difficult to read his body language. Does he want to leave? Am I more trouble than I'm worth? Or is he waiting for me to ask him to stay? I don't know.

"Ayden ..." I want to say something meaningful, but I can't find the words. I'm too tense to even smile.

"I'd better go. You've got your Rottweiler to keep you company." He nods in Charlie's direction and forces a weak smile.

"Her bark is worse than her bite." I force a half smile too. "But thank you."

"For what, lying, making you feel like you're nothing to me and for putting you in danger?"

"You weren't to know about the photographs, you meant well."

"And the rest of it?"

"That's something different. You knew exactly what you were doing then."

The air becomes chilled between us, so much so I expect to see my breath crystallise and fall to the ground in a shower of ice.

"I suppose I had that coming." He shrugs, accepting my rebuke.

He caresses my cheek, and I feel the heat coming from his palm; I'm falling into it, it's instinctive, but I catch myself, open my eyes and refocus.

"You can't just assume that normal service will be resumed, Ayden. You've hurt me."

My words cause a twinge of pain. "I know. Are we over, Beth?"

"I don't know, I'm still too raw, too tired to think straight." He reclaims his hand, leaving my cheek warm and the flesh tingling.

"Okay." His heavy footsteps echo on the path and his hot breath plumes around him in the cold night air like a sail. He spins around, visibly troubled, looking as if he's aged overnight.

"I say that, but it's not okay that I haven't had a chance to explain. It's not okay that some psycho might be dreaming up a fucking plan to get to you. None of this is okay." A twitchy hand tugs at his hair and grips his neck. "I'm not okay, Beth."

My words rush out. "I know, but I need time."

"How long?"

"I'm not sure."

He's becoming more perturbed. "Speculate: an hour, a day, a week! How long?"

I hear myself shouting. "I don't know, Ayden, I don't know!"

"I'm out on a limb here ..." His voice is a whisper.

"I can see that." I place my trembling hand over my mouth.

He seeks out my eyes. "Tell me what I have to do to win you back, Beth. Just tell me."

His choice of words offends my sense of worth. Why is it always about winning? "I don't want to be *won,* Ayden. I'm not a trophy you can show off to your business friends, and I'm not a promising acquisition you have to put in a bid for."

"It's only a fucking word, Beth ... you know what I mean." He's reaching for his neck.

"Yes I do and that's the problem, it's the word you live your life by. But, as far as us, as far as we're concerned, you don't have the winning formula, not yet."

He laughs sardonically and takes a step back. "Touché - you win."

What!

"I'm not competing. It's never been a battle of wills for me." I shake my head from side to side to reinforce the point and inch towards him.

"No, but you can still bring me to my knees with a fucking smile," he roars.

That single declaration has me reeling. I'm stunned, but not into silence. "I'm sorry you feel that way. So ... so defeated."

"I don't, I mean I do, but I don't want to." His hands reach into his pockets and, out of frustration, he rocks back and forth. "Look, I don't know what I'm saying, I've got to go." With heavy lids, he takes a lingering look at me, as if committing my image to memory. He turns and marches off in the direction of his waiting car. Even though I know it's coming, the sound of the door slamming makes me flinch and I watch him speed away.

Wearily, I close the security door, leaning my hand against the glass for a couple of seconds to regain my composure. What the hell just happened? Dispirited, I return to my apartment.

"Beth?" Charlie calls from the lounge. Caught up in the commotion, I'd forgotten she was there. She must have heard everything.

"Here." She hands me my glass of wine. "I heard. What's that guy's problem?"

I have a simple answer. "He has to win."

"What the hell does that mean?"

"It means that unless he accepts that it's an irrational way of approaching everything, we're not going to make it." I shrug my shoulders and turn to face her.

"Oh, Beth." She takes hold of my hand, but sympathy is the last thing I need.

"In a way, it's a good thing." I'm having a positive thought for the first time in 24 hours: it's a revelation, so powerful it reshapes my face.

Puzzled, Charlie asks, "How's that?"

"We've got to the bottom of his problem. That's been his motivation! All these years he's been driven by nothing else, why didn't I realise? We could have avoided all this heartache."

"I'll take your word for it, even though I've not got a friggin' clue what you're talking about."

I throw my arms around her neck and kiss her affectionately on the cheek. "It doesn't matter. You don't have to, but thanks for listening." Feeling energised, I wipe the dampness from my cheeks. "I know what I have to do now."

Out of the blue, the external buzzer sounds and we look at each other. "Did you hear that?" Surely Ayden hasn't come back? What would motivate him to do such a thing?

Charlie jumps up. "I'll get it and, if it's him, I'll make myself scarce."

I can hear an unfamiliar male voice, *"Are you Beth?"*

"No, who are you?" Charlie answers in her 'don't mess with me' voice.

"I'm Jake Harrison, I work with Ayden Stone. Is Beth here?"

"I don't know, I'll ask her. Wait there." She returns to the lounge. "There's sex on legs at the door and he wants to speak to you, says he works with your Mr. P. Should I let him in?" She holds her hands together in a kind of mock prayer.

"Alright, ask him to come in. Just give me a minute to make myself presentable."

She dashes off and I do the same, in the direction of the bathroom. I don't want one of Ayden's colleagues to see me looking like this. My mascara is smudged and I'm ghostly pale through lack of food and sleep, but it's nothing a little blusher and a touch of lip-gloss can't improve.

I hear Charlie giving her all; her best flirtatious laugh is bouncing off the walls. It almost seems a shame to interrupt, but he's come here to speak to me and the least I can do is show my face.

"Hello, Mr. Harrison, I'm Beth Parker." I stretch out my hand and notice how quickly he reviews me. I wonder what he's thinking. "I'm pleased to see Charlie has been keeping you entertained."

"Yes, she has." He launches a beaming smile in her direction and I swear I can hear her heart skip a beat from the other side of the room. I know why, of course, he's ruggedly handsome and nicely turned out in his black suit and silver tie: he's just her type.

"Can I offer you anything, wine, water?"

"No thanks, I'm good."

Oh, you're American, I detect a west coast inflection.

"I wanted to speak with you about Ayden and it's a kinda delicate matter." Is he suggesting Charlie leave?

She picks up on it immediately, reaches for her bag and offers him her hand. "Of course, I'll get out of your hair. It's been very nice meeting you, Jake. I hope we meet again soon." She's all teeth and sparkling eyes.

"Sure thing."

Following a farewell hug and a kiss, she heads for the door. With Jake's back to her she holds up an imaginary phone, meaning get his number, but I look away quickly in case he catches my wandering eye. From his serious expression, I think he has more important things on his mind than arranging a date with my best friend.

I make a point of giving him my full attention. "So, Jake, what's on your mind?"

"Well, Ayden and I have been buddies for, well since we were kids. I went to the U.S. to college and he stayed here building his empire, but we always kept in touch. These past five years, we've been working together on projects. I'm his CCO, right hand man and his sparring partner in and out of the boardroom: he's the ideas guy and I figure out how to make things happen, sort out the logistics, kinda ..."

"I see, so you're telling me you're close?"

"Yeah, we're close I guess, or as close as you can get to ..." He nods his head knowingly and I resist the temptation to do the same. When he starts to fiddle with his tie, I sense something more pressing is about to be discussed. "I don't know how to put this politely but ..." He's trying to find the right words.

"Don't bother sugar coating it for me. What's up?"

He laughs softly. "He said you were sharp."

I acknowledge the compliment.

"I think he's lost his fucking mind over you!"

As hard as I try, I can't conceal my astonishment. "Really? Why do you say that?"

"Well." He runs his right hand over his close cropped hair. "It started last week. He bailed on two major meetings in New York last Friday and the one he did attend, he was totally distracted. Can you believe it? He had two video conferences on the plane. That's unprecedented."

I'm sitting back, wishing Ayden back in my arms with every new insight. Keeping my amusement under wraps isn't easy. Clearly Jake is in need of some answers.

"Not only that but he's only been available through email and video conferencing this weekend; it's like he's gone off radar. On Sunday morning, he even blew me off and he doesn't do that."

"Sunday morning?" I have a recollection of a very happy man organising a picnic and commenting on my 'I've been fucked hair.' The memory lingers, making me smile.

"Yeah, was he here?"

"Yes. I heard him talking to you and he ended the call when I walked in the room." I point over to the kitchen table. "He was sitting right there."

"And why did he end our face to face, we had some important business to discuss?" He's gripped, impatient to hear more.

"So he could put me on his knee."

His mouth opens and stays that way. "And do what exactly?"

"Stroke my hair, cuddle me." Knowing exactly what I'm doing, I smile sweetly.

His hand is in his hair again; for Ayden it's his neck that's his tell, for Jake it's his hair. Like a wide toothed comb, his fingers move from front to back, forming a wide circle that finishes on his chin.

"Look, I don't think we're talking about the same guy." He tips his head back to stress the point and blows out hot air.

"Oh, I think we are." I reach for the kiss pendant but find only a vacant space. "Have you spoken to him today?"

"Have I! Oh yeah, we had a real early start. At 3a.m. this morning, he calls me asking about love songs, songs that say sorry. I mean, what the hell do I know about songs?"

Obviously he's finding the whole affair difficult to comprehend, so I encourage him to continue.

"Anyway, I went round to Stone Heath this morning when his secretary reported him AWOL."

"Stone Heath?"

"You know, his place in Belgravia?"

I don't, but I nod as if I do.

"And he's there in yesterday's clothes writing some God damn speech to give to a bunch of school kids. I mean, what's all that about?"

I know perfectly well what that's all about, but simply smile.

"So, I ask him, what the fuck's going on? You're supposed to be in LA in two days giving the opening speech at a conference attended by some of the leading players in global communications, and you're here downloading songs and attending kids' parties and ..." He holds my attention with a wide stare. "... d'you know what he said?"

"No."

"Fuck off!"

I know I shouldn't but I start to laugh. "That sounds like Ayden." I'm trying to under-react, but peals of rippling laughter are erupting from my mouth. My poor Mr. P.

Jake reaches down and takes a couple of gulps of the unclaimed half glass of red wine sitting on the table; he really is feeling very stressed.

"Hey, that's not the reaction I was hoping for lady. You wanna tell me what's going on? Because, I tell you, if he doesn't get his shit together and come up with a monumental opening speech, we'll be fucked. Six months of planning right out the window and A.S.M.I. along with it."

"There's nothing wrong with him, not really." I know but I'm hesitant.

Should I tell him?

"If you're messing around, then you're gonna have to stop. There's a lot at stake and I don't just mean his reputation."

He finishes off the wine and I feel a sudden chill in the air. His once hazel eyes are now a penetrating charcoal colour. I sense an approaching battle of wills. Here it comes

"How much will it take to get you off his back?"

As hard as I try, I cannot conceal my disgust. "What! How dare you come here to my home, and offer me money to stop seeing him. Don't you realise what this is all about?"

His piercing stare doesn't leave my face; it tunnels through my eye-balls like a truth seeking missile.

"He's in love with me," I announce, waiting for his reaction before elaborating further.

"He's what?"

"You heard me." I allow him a couple of seconds to mentally digest my revelation. "He won't admit it because it would feel like he'd lost the battle but, once he realises he can win the war, if he just stops fighting, he'll be fine." I smile, feeling proud of myself for solving the puzzle.

He's standing, pacing, running his hand across his hair again. "I don't get it. You're as fucked up as he is."

I nod in agreement. "Yes, I am. Please sit down."

He exhales and faces me.

"Now, tell me, when should Ayden go to LA?"

He runs his now sweaty palms over his thighs. "He's scheduled to fly out of Heathrow tomorrow around midday, stay over, run through his speech and face the music Wednesday morning 10 a.m., local time. But I can't see it happening, not now when ..."

"He'll be there."

He gives me a knowing smile. "I sure hope you know what you're doing?"

"I think I do now." I stand, brush down my skirt; I'm ready to give him his marching orders.

He's a smart guy, he reads my signals. "OK. I'm outta here. I can see you've got things to do."

He leans into me and kisses my cheek. "Just so you know, Ayden likes to operate out of sight, in the shadows, but this is big, he has to be seen to be engaging in the social debate about corporate communications: he *is* A.S Media International. If you're serious about him, you'll get him to L.A." He offers his hand to me. "No hard feelings about the pay-off? I had to give it a shot."

I reach out to shake his hand. "No hard feelings. Just don't ever try to insult me by offering me money again, or I'll make sure that long standing friendship you and Ayden have, the one you value so much, comes to a very swift end."

"You bet." He lets go of my hand first. "It's been good to finally meet you. I've heard a lot about you."

"Not all good, I hope."

"Mostly." He grins, cheekily.

"Oh you shouldn't believe everything you hear." I think we actually have an understanding, finally. "Ayden is a very talented businessman, but you already know that."

He nods.

"What you don't know is that he's so much more than that to me." I purposely hold off on the smile, to make my point.

He winks and gives me a knowing look. "I think you'll be good for him, once he sorts his head out."

"I think so too. Thank you for coming to see me." I usher him to the front door.

He spins around, forcing me to take a step back. His right hand is in his hair again. "Look, I'd kinda appreciate it if you didn't mention me coming here, Ayden can be ..."

I beat him to it, "Difficult."

"Yeah, difficult." Smiling, he turns away from me and strolls towards his waiting car. I wave him off, feeling so much clearer about what I have to do. I rush inside, pick up my phone and press Speed-dial 1. Ayden picks up on the third ring.

"Hi, it's me."

"I know."

That's a curt reply.

"You asked how long and, what's it been, an hour?"

"More or less." He's unsure about my line of questioning but is willing to go with it.

"I've had all the time I need. Will you get over here?" I picture him smiling, if only for a second.

"Only if you ask nicely."

My God, even now after all that's happened, he's still fixated on winning; if it's not bloody buttons it's bloody please. I find my best girlie voice. "*Please* will you come round because I want to talk to you, and I'm stood here in your T-shirt feeling as horny as hell." I switch back. "Will that do?" The line goes dead.

***

A silver BMW way past its prime, is chewing up the tarmac on the A1, only 12 miles from ground zero. The weight of equipment and basic provisions is playing havoc with the suspension, forcing its impatient driver to curse and swear.

Thankfully the route is quiet for 1500hrs on a Monday and Dan is able to reserve his spot in the inside lane, refusing to give the budget saloons a second glance as they flash past him doing 70. As far as he's concerned, they are mindless drivers on the road to nowhere, whereas *he's* a man on a mission. He knows better than to rush when embarking on an operation of this scale.

'I've waited seven years for this, another couple of hours won't kill me.' His mood lightens. He readjusts his seat and takes in the scenery.

He loaded up the car at 0400hrs, drove the 17 miles to work to make the early shift at 0600hrs and looked busy until his shift ended at two. From there he headed straight to the estate agents to hand over his Landlady's signed reference, which he typed out for her, and the email address of his Line Manager Mr. Crowther. It was all done and dusted in thirty minutes.

Now, with almost sixty miles behind him, he's running on pure adrenaline; the route to Elm Gardens is engraved permanently into his psyche and the registration of Stone's car is engraved permanently on his skin like a pink tattoo.

Discarded on the passenger seat is yesterday's Daily Mirror, folded back on the page he read during his tea break. As hard as he tries to distract himself checking out drivers and passengers as they overtake him, his eyes are drawn to the photograph taking up almost a quarter of the page. He snatches it up and flattens it out across the steering wheel; his impatient hands fold the outer edges around it, allowing him to hold it firmly in place.

Out of sheer wilfulness he proceeds to inspect the photograph at close quarters whilst steering. But, doing two things at the same time is proving to be more of a challenge than he first thought, not because he is actually driving, but because the words on the page keep merging. Ayden Stone and Elizabeth Parker are side by side in the picture and in print, as if they are meant to be together. He smiles inwardly. 'Elizabeth Parker, right. What happened to Frances?' His thoughts are his own and they are coming thick and fast, triggering a disturbing response.

Dan Rizler is gripped by rage, it has him by the throat and he can barely swallow. Momentarily, he has a lapse in concentration and the car veers onto the hard shoulder, making a loud, rumbling sound that jolts him back into consciousness.

"Fuck!" He swerves back into position and holds firm, checking his mirror for an unwelcome observer or, worse still, a police car. The last thing he wants is for the cops to pull him over and to start asking questions, even though he knows he has nothing to worry about. He doesn't have a police record and they would be hard pushed to find anything in his car worth investigating. No worries, he's just an ordinary guy, moving his stuff from A to B. Why would they think otherwise?

Back on track, he allows his eyes to settle on the road and briefly on the black and white photograph of the 'happy' couple. There's something about a book launch and some writer's new crime thriller but it's of little consequence. All he can see is Stone holding her hand, turning on the charm.

"Fucking poser!" He hisses between his teeth, slamming his hand over his image, almost puncturing the paper. Only Elizabeth Parker remains intact. His jealousy fades and it's just the two of them again, the way he likes it, the way it's meant to be. Her beauty transcends everything else, he cannot look away. Even dressed in black she's an angel, his angel. He stretches out his thumb and caresses her image, up, down, left and right nonstop for the next eight miles.

When he reaches the Pinner turn-off, feeling pacified by the proximity of her image, he glances down once and then again, preparing to say farewell, but she has vanished. All he can see is her escort, standing there next to a blurred and faded ghost. He takes a look at his thumb. It's black and the ink has found its way around the entire nail and into the cuticle. Without noticing, he has erased her from the page. She no longer exists. Surprised at his own clumsiness, he chuckles, holds up his thumb and inspects it. "How's that for a prediction, princess? I've got you under my thumb already and I haven't laid a finger on you yet."

A couple of roundabouts later, he finds himself at his destination. It's 1600hrs. He's wearing his new check shirt and feeling uncharacteristically buoyant. With the gait of a man excited at the prospect of moving into a new home, he steps out of the car and leans in to pull out a box of second hand crockery and cutlery. He bounds over to the security door, letting the contents rattle and jangle beneath his arm. Without looking at his Tenancy Agreement, he punches in 1479 and, to his satisfaction, it clicks open.

Assuming the occupant of 53a is not at home, he begins carrying in his meagre possessions up two flights of stairs, leaving some of the bags and boxes at the bottom. The move-in takes no more than half an hour.

There's the rattling of a door lock behind 53b and, for a second, he is frozen to the spot. What if the labels had been wrong on the front door and his girl steps out onto the landing, bringing them face to face? 'What to do? Nothing's in place. It's too soon.'

To prevent a possible cockup, he climbs the stairs, two at a time and drops his last item on the floor with an echoing thud. The mattress slides down the wall and comes to rest in a sitting position in the living room. It's queen sized and second hand, he picked it up on the way over for twenty quid. He won't be needing anything fancy for what he has in mind.

11

Feeling as if I have a new lease of life, I speed walk into my bedroom, throw off my stale work clothes, shower, and put on Ayden's T-shirt and the prettiest panties I can find. I just have time to brush my hair and clean my teeth before the doorbell rings.

I take my time. It rings again. When I open it, I swear he's out of breath: has he run all the way here? I'm floored by a vertical stare and want him to take me right there on the doorstep, but we have to talk first.

He enters cautiously, throws down his overnight bag and kicks the door shut behind him. "I like the T-shirt," he states, following me into the lounge.

"Then you'll love what's underneath it." I grin over my shoulder. "Come in and sit down." Rather than settling for the sofa, I switch off the lamps and make straight for the bedroom. It will only be a matter of time before we're in here anyway. "Take a seat."

"Where?"

Does he think I'm being Elizabeth?

"Anywhere, on the bed, the chair." I fold my arms and the T-shirt rises a little up my thighs. I catch him looking and like that he's being so attentive.

"I don't know what's going on, Beth, but ..."

"Ayden, just be quiet and listen. I don't want you to say anything, alright?"

He nods. "I'm all ears."

He leans back onto the bed, allowing his strong forearms to take his weight. Now it's my turn to visually undress him. I notice he's discarded his tie and the top two buttons on his shirt are undone, revealing a few strands of protruding chest hair; his fitted shirt isn't tucked in, but it's lying across his fly, creased.

He looks so hot.

I clear my throat and begin. "I've had time to think, and I know what's been driving you for most of your life and throughout our relationship: your need to win. That's been your motivation. It's impacted on your business in a positive way - you said so yourself in your speech tonight - but it's had a negative impact on your love life, on us."

He's clearly surprised by my candour, but not shaken by it. "Should I be writing this down?" He has to throw me off, doesn't he? He's settling back onto the bed, looking like the main course at a buffet. That's not good, especially as I haven't eaten all day.

He cocks his head to the right and signals for me to carry on. I swallow noisily and try to tear myself away from his intense scrutiny. I wish I'd opted for a pair of jeans and an overcoat now. When he looks at me that way, I feel as if I'm being stripped bare. I pull his T-shirt down over my thighs as far as it will go, but that only makes it cling to my hardening nipples. He's enjoying the view, I can tell.

Regardless, I press on with my deliberation. "You've regarded every woman you've ever dated as a challenge, one you've set yourself: to woo her, to win her heart, to fuck her and then to move on. And, that's worked for you until now: until you met me."

I stop to breathe, get into my stride and give him a second to take it all in. "You followed established protocol: flowers, poems, gifts, clothes and it worked like a charm. You even threw in the sub idea to clinch the deal, but things have not gone exactly to plan, have they?" The question is purely rhetorical and I don't give him time to answer, even though I can see words forming on his lips.

"Come the time to move on, you found yourself wanting to stay and that's not something you do. God forbid you should let anyone, a woman at that, monopolize your time and steal your affection right from under your nose."

I take a breath and draw out the shape of a TV screen, as if I'm playing charades. "I've got a newsflash for you. You're in love with me, and it scares you to death because it feels like you've surrendered and I've won."

He's silent now, so absorbed in thought I simply continue with my commentary. "You said yourself that guys think with their dicks and you were one of them; going all out to be the alpha male, having your choice of prime partners. But now, your heart speaks to you. It tells you to send me songs declaring your love for me and, for the first time in your life, you feel as if you've lost control, you're not in the driving seat anymore but merely a passenger who's enjoying the ride. That's an alien concept for you."

I break off, distracted by his smile. Even though it's more of a twitch, it reaches his eyes and I hear him speaking to me through silent words.

"You've found someone you truly can't live without - me!" I arch my brows and offer an overly animated shrug. There, I said it.

He considers my revelation and tips his head over to the other side, like an adorable puppy hearing his name for the first time. I'm rooted to the spot.

"You think you're very smart, Miss Parker."

I grin. "That's because I am, Mr. Stone."

"Yes you are." He reaches out to me and I fall onto him, squeezing his face in my hands. "But, I've not finished ..."

"Oh! Dear God. Not more revelations?" He covers his face with his hands.

"Hush." I kneel up at the side of him on the bed, feeling exhilarated and proud of myself. "Business has always come first, it's your raison d'etre, or it was until now. And, do you know when I knew?"

He shakes his head and brushes a strand of hair from my face.

"When you cancelled meetings to fly home to me, turned off your phone and organised a picnic, stayed up all night trawling the internet for forgive me songs and then bared your soul to five hundred strangers, in the hope I would realise you were talking directly to me. That's love Ayden. The only reason you've not been able to diagnose the symptoms is because you've never felt like this before: you're not losing your grip, you're love sick."

Even though he's lying down and I'm kneeling over him, he's comfortable and relaxed and I wonder if this is active submission.

"I'm just as guilty, I didn't recognise it - I've never been in love before either."

Why does he look so surprised? "You're in love with *me*!"

"Of course I am. I became Elizabeth for you. I cut my hair for you. I stayed up all night sobbing at the thought of not holding you ever again. Don't you see, we're destined to be together. I've been waiting for you to find me my whole life and you have." I caress his cheek with my palm and fall into him.

"Yes, at last, I have. And you've found me, Beth."

It's been at least 24 hours since we've kissed and, right now, it's the only thing I can think of doing. I allow myself to be smothered in mouth-watering kisses and lose my hands in his hair.

"I love you, Ayden."

Like a tumbling wave, he rolls me over until I feel his full weight on my body. "I love you more, Beth. I was awake all last night thinking about you. That was when I wasn't looking for 'I love you' songs. Have you any idea how hard it is to find songs that sum up what you're feeling?"

"Yes, I have, that's why I loved the music you sent me. Doing what you did was out of character." I undo one of the buttons on his shirt. "Not everything in life can be solved by barking out orders or fucking. That may have been the way you've dealt with things in the past, but that was then and this is now."

He starts to laugh. "I love it when you talk dirty."

"I wasn't, I'm being serious." I mean it, but his laughter is contagious and I'm folding by the second.

He's suddenly very serious, stopping the frivolity, pulling my face to his. "The prospect of living my life without you made me want to throw myself under a fucking train."

"Please don't say that. Now the truth is out we can start to enjoy each other." I solidify our bond with an equally serious stare. "I feel safe with you."

"You are," he states, as the subtle glow from the lamp reflects in a glistening stare. "And you feel like home, Beth, and that's something I thought I'd never hear myself say." His eyes continue to verify his revelation. "I want to keep saying the words. 'I love you,' even though it feels like I'm speaking a foreign language." He's smiling at me in such a way I can imagine angels watching and crying with the sheer beauty of his devotion. It's a Titanic moment.

"You see through all my faults, Beth, and in spite of them, you still love me. Your innocence allows you to see the world through a child's eyes; in your world, there's no deception, only truth and trust. I love you for that if nothing else."

So intense is his stare, I'm self-conscious all of a sudden. "Stop staring."

"Why? You're a beautiful woman, inside and out. For as long as I've known you, I've wanted to fix my eyes on you like a heat seeking missile, but I've stopped myself, scared you might read my thoughts."

A broad smile takes shape. "I can. I know exactly what you're thinking."

"That's not difficult, seeing as I've got the biggest hard on waiting for you."

"See, I knew that."

He traces the shape of my nose with his forefinger and gives it a gentle tap at the end. "You have special powers, Miss Parker,"

He teases further, kissing every inch of my neck, my jaw and edging me backwards across the bed. I tip my head back in a kind of helpless joy. This is what I need, my daily dose of Ayden Stone.

"I love this spot," he whispers, kissing the tender skin beneath my right ear. "Because, when I kiss it, you make this noise."

He kisses it again and, one cue, I moan in response.

He laughs seductively. "There's another part of your body which quite takes my fancy." He rolls up my T-shirt and it gathers around my stomach. "Ah, here it is." He allows the tip of his tongue to tickle the area around my navel and then my pubic bone: the promise of what is to follow has me stretching and writhing. "Let's see what we have here."

I feel his hands skimming my calves, my knees, my thighs, leaving my legs dangling over the bed, waiting. My breathing is irregular and I feel the heat of passion starting to sear through me.

"I think I've found what I'm looking for," he announces, lifting his head to nail me with a look of such intensity it makes me gasp. "The thought of never doing this again with you made me crazy."

I feel his hands taking down my panties and parting my thighs. My God this man has amazing hands, what he can do to me. The instant his tongue touches my clitoris I start to move and groan; I'm defenceless. Breath rushes from my mouth, fingers clutch at bedding, perspiration coats my skin. A soft cry leaves my lips, and I instinctively press myself into him.

"Oh yes ..."

My body temperature is rising, so I shut out the light to allow my senses to focus on that central apex where my clawing need originates. To call this sexual delight would be an understatement: it's raw, unadulterated ecstasy.

"Make me come, Ayden, make me forget last night." My back bends and bows and I'm panting, begging. "Please."

He does exactly that and I'm forgetting everything that has happened, living only in the moment. His fingers find me, and their steady, relentless thrusting push me to the edge of orgasm. When he leaves me saturated and needy, I think I've been abandoned, but his salty tongue pushes into my mouth and the pad of his right hand picks up where his tongue left off. His sinful mouth is on mine and I suck and taste myself.

With a breathless whisper he commands me. "Look at me, Beth." I open my eyes to see his beautiful, vulnerable face. He's stripped bare. "You speak to my heart, you always have, you know me and you love me, in spite of everything. I don't deserve you."

"Don't say that, please don't say that." I cannot hold back; his words and his hands are tipping me over, everything is tightening and building. My tender orgasm sweeps through my body and my sob-like cries are kissed away. I grip his shoulders and hold him to me.

With a softness I had not expected, he wipes the tears from my cheeks and allows my heart rate to slow.

"I want to feel you inside me," I hiss, moulding his mouth to mine.

In the blink of an eye, my lips are disregarded and my T-shirt is lifted over my head and flung across the room. He's standing upright. With frenzied hands, he's pulling off his shirt, unbuttoning his trousers.

I lean up on my elbows, without shyness and look at his muscular torso for as long as he will allow. "Ayden, you're perfect, inside and out. You just don't realise it yet."

He pushes down his Calvin Klein boxers and presents himself to me. "Do you want this?"

Isn't the fire in my eyes and the wetness of my crotch proof enough?

"Yes, I want that, in me, right now and, if you ask me to beg, I will ask you to leave." I hold up my right hand to him and spread my legs a little wider, without shame or embarrassment. Why conceal what is his?

He stretches out his hand and our fingers weave together, we hold on tight, locked together by animal magnetism. He smiles with dark thoughts etched on his face. "I wouldn't dare. I can't wait to be inside you."

I watch as he slides the condom down the length of his stiff cock; merely watching makes me clench and ache inside. Just for the hell of it, he rolls me over so I am lying on my stomach, waiting. In a smoky voice that I barely recognise, he states, "I want to take you like this."

I'm not sure what to expect, but when I'm treated to the sensation of his sizzling body on mine, I know I'm in for something special. There's no rush; he's massaging my neck, palming my shoulder blades, gripping my waist with both hands, cupping my behind and it all feels like veneration. When I feel the prod of his erection and the hairs on his outer thighs against my inner thighs I brace myself, in spite of the preparatory massage.

Patient fingers inch inside me, spreading the wetness from front to back; over my clitoris, within my folds, between my cheeks. He's touching me so tenderly, I can feel myself drifting, giving in to the sensation.

He pulls me to the edge of the bed and leans in, whilst his other hand slides under my body to my stomach, anchoring me in place. His arousal is unsurpassed: ragged breathing, fervent ardour. "I love you, Beth," he utters in my ear, placing his hand over my mouth.

I open my eyes wide and have the oddest feeling. Is something strangely unfamiliar about to happen? What is he doing? I don't react, even though I can't move and can't call out. Not until I feel the tip of his penis against my anus do I stiffen. I inhale deeply, becoming aware of the smell of sex on skin, on my lips. It's intoxicating. Do I want this, does he? Is this his way of winning?

His weight shifts. "I want to be inside you here, to have you possess me, to own me, but not yet." I feel him sliding downwards, finding my slick entrance.

"Don't speak, don't move."

With that, his left hand raises me up off the mattress, while his other hand covers my mouth. I'm not sure why, but it's so fucking erotic.

As his erection brushes against my folds I want to position myself onto him but, instead, I give him the satisfaction of finding me, taking me. I like feeling bound to him, unable to free myself from his overpowering grip.

He slides into me, causing a moan to escape from my mouth and bury itself in his hand. It's an extraordinary feeling having my cries contained, but surprising in the way it forces me to absorb sensations, to centre myself and listen to him calling out and groaning with wild desire.

His primal need to come causes him to speed up; circling, moving to a relentless rhythm, he stretches me and fills every centimetre, urging me to move to meet his thrusts, burning, building towards orgasm. His tongue finds my right ear, licking, nuzzling, biting and whispering. "I belong inside you, Beth, this is my home now."

But I can't answer. I'm not meant to answer, just feel. I feel him igniting my over-heated core, I feel him pounding into me. I feel...

"That's it, feel the burn." His command forces my body to quiver beneath him. With every penetrating thrust, a surge of ecstatic energy radiates out and explodes and keeps exploding again and again, making me jerk into him.

His breathing is becoming frantic and his cries are a guttural roar. His climax is brutal and ferocious, grasping hands clutch my hips and pull me onto him, bruising soft flesh, until I'm almost at my limit. It's deeper than before, forcing me to call out, even though I know he cannot hear me. He's in a nameless place, a place where wild, carnal needs dictate actions, not rational thought. He starts to tremble, withdraws then collapses at the side of me, utterly spent. We rest for ten minutes or more.

With the earthquake over, I reflect on the night's events. Thank God he revealed enough about himself to allow me to see through all that pretence. Just imagining life without him makes my entire body stiffen.

When I turn to face him, he's gazing up at the ceiling. I position my head next to his and adopt the same position. "What are we looking at?"

"Nothing, I'm thinking." His left arm wraps around me and I snuggle into his clammy chest, flattening hairs under my nose.

"Oh? Good thoughts?"

He turns to face me. "Yes, very good thoughts, thoughts of you and me, together." I see a sensual smile. "I enjoyed the make-up sex."

"Me too." I feel his hand brushing hair off my forehead. He's examining my face so carefully it causes a wave of emotion to flood through me. "Tell me, what's on your mind?"

"I was just thinking how I'd like to spend tomorrow with you."

I smile and stroke his face, but I'm remembering the promise I made to Jake about his crucial trip to L.A. *"He'll be there,"* I said confidently. Maybe I shouldn't have been so quick to flaunt my powers of persuasion? Here's Ayden talking about spending the day in bed, as if he has nothing better to do.

"I can't take the day off, Ayden, we break-up for half term in two days and I have lots to do before then." I plant a chaste kiss on his lips. "But it's a lovely idea though."

"Fine, I'll take a rain check. But I just thought, after our misunderstanding, we should spend more time together, so I could make it up to you."

He looks a little too repentant for my liking. "I thought you just did?" I sit up and rest my hand on his heart. "I know what's in here, I see it in the way you look at me, I feel it in the way you make love to me. So, we're good. Stop apologising. You're forgiven."

Two simple words fall from his mouth like the ticking of a clock: he has perfect timing. "Thank you."

"You're welcome."

"You have such a sweet nature, you didn't have to forgive me. You're soft on the outside *and* on the inside: a gentle genie wrapped in velvet." I feel his chest rumbling beneath my hand as he laughs at the absurdity of his description. "I'm no different than everyone else. I'm drawn to your gentleness like the sea to the shore. I couldn't stop myself even if I wanted to."

"That's a very romantic thing to say."

He tips his head. "I have my moments."

"Yes you do." I stretch across his body to caress his lips with my own. "But, along with the tides, the world keeps revolving, Ayden. The last thing I want is to turn you into a love-sick puppy." I shrug my shoulders and arch my brows, leaving him silent and bewildered.

"Imagine that, *me* a love-sick puppy?" He's shaking his head in disbelief, stifling laughter.

"I want you to be the media mogul you are and do what comes naturally, to be yourself."

"I am myself when I'm with you, more so than at any other time," he states with total conviction.

"Then stop apologising, go and be masterful and order some Thai food. I need to shower." I leap from the bed and scoot off into the bathroom, leaving him to ponder and hopefully reconsider going to L.A.

I'm in the shower, making the most of precious time to myself. I'm considering the state of play, doubting there is little I can say or do to persuade him to change his mind: he's not a man to be easily swayed. When it comes to business, he means what he says and he says what he means, 100% of the time. What was I thinking, making assurances to a stranger about a man who already feels the need to demonstrate his commitment to me?

Just when I'm about to reach for a towel, the door of the shower cubicle opens and I feel a gloriously naked torso against my back. Hot hands are slithering around my foam covered body, smothering my breasts in bubbles and easing their way down to my stomach. He pulls me tightly to him with his outstretched left hand while the other follows the flow of water to my thighs. I rest my hand on his and follow the flow.

"Don't *you* smell nice." His nose delves into my wet hair and finds a resting place beneath my ear.

"Don't you *feel* nice?" I lean forward slightly, enjoying the sensation of his growing erection against the base of my back.

He's insatiable!

"As commanded, I've ordered Thai food. Is there anything else I can do for you?"

Don't tempt me ...

"Nothing comes to mind at the moment."

His fingers deftly find my clitoris and rouse it into responsiveness, zeroing in on sensitive nerve endings with the accuracy of an Exocet missile. "Are you sure?"

"You're very skilled at changing my mind, Mr. Stone."

"This is true, Miss Parker." He sucks on my ear lobe, sending such a delicious shudder of delight through my body that has me folding onto his hand. He whispers softly. "Put both hands on the wall."

"Why?"

"Just do as you're told, missy, you'll see."

I obey. The tiles are slippery to touch and it's difficult to find purchase, but I can duck away from the shower and enjoy the feel of the steaming cascade as it caresses my shoulders. This is turning into a very erotic experience and we've only just begun. "What are you planning to do?"

A steaming whisper tickles my ear. "Number one, to give you an orgasm. Number two, to take you from behind and number three ..."

"Yes?" What's happening to my voice?

"Three. To eat Thai food."

The steam catches in my throat. "That sounds like a plan."

"Yes it does. I love it when a plan comes together ... you're close."

How does he know that?

"Yes."

"Sit down."

What?

He senses my surprise. "Sit down onto me ..."

I slowly lower myself, feeling the prod of his erection against my steaming folds, my skin tingling at his touch. I'm drowning in ecstasy.

A primitive groan leaves his throat and vibrates around the cubicle. I'm tipping back my head and the spray is finding my cheeks, making them prickle and burn. I'm on fire, inside and out. How can he take the weight of us both and balance me with one hand, while the other teases me into an orgasmic surrender? This man has skills.

He edges nearer to my neck, I want to lift my hands off the wall and touch him, to participate in this steamy, fucking event but I daren't. I have my orders.

"You still want me to go to L.A?"

Oh no. Now he isn't playing fair...

I can't speak. Every time I'm about to, he doubles his efforts and shatters my resolve with inexorable pounding. My knees are buckling, I'm folding, letting go, allowing the ripples of molten lava to ignite me. My hands fall from the wall and I drop onto him, calling out his name. "Ayden."

"I'm here." He responds to my cry and finds his noisy release; he comes inside me, straining to keep his balance. At that moment, the cubicle door flies open and he tumbles backwards onto the bathroom floor in a most undignified fashion.

When I turn to check he's okay, I am met with an unmistakably, shocked expression that touches a nerve and causes me to laugh out loud. Without a stitch on and royally fucked, I can't control myself. As hard as I try, I simply cannot contain my amusement. The fact of the matter is, I have an Adonis of a man lying flat on his back on my bathroom floor, wearing nothing but a used condom and an embarrassed smile. That look is priceless.

My fingers are trying, unsuccessfully, to hold back laughter. "Are you alright?" The floor is slippery and he stumbles to get up, making me laugh even more.

Oh dear!

I think he's having trouble seeing the funny side. Losing his balance in flagrante delicto is clearly not something he has experienced before.

"So how was it for you," I enquire, leaning against the cubicle frame naked and folding my arms.

"Fucking embarrassing!" He's still trying to get to his feet but now, he looks less than amused.

"Oh, you can't be serious? Here, take my hand." I reach out, but he pulls me on top of him. Now we are both rolling on the saturated floor. I'm laughing and trying to push him off, while he's edging closer to my face. With every decreasing centimetre, the sparkle is returning to his eyes.

"Miss Parker, I'm not accustomed to being laughed at by naked, hysterical women."

"Then stop *making* me laugh."

"If you continue to laugh at me, I will take you across my knee and spank you."

Maybe, accidentally on purpose, I keep laughing. "You wouldn't dare."

"That's it, I warned you." In a move worthy of a professional wrestler, he flips me over his left shoulder, finds his feet somehow and carts me off into the bedroom, still laughing. I feel the sting of his hand on my right cheek and I scream out in happy surprise. He smacks my left cheek with the same force, sending a ripple of something unexpected through my body.

Just when I think he has taught me a lesson, I find myself across his lap; the damp skin on his thighs has attached itself to my stomach and his left hand is keeping my upper body in place on the bed. This is turning into a very sexy game.

"Now, are you going to say sorry for laughing at me, or must I seek atonement for your sins?"

I turn my face to his. "That depends on whether you can maintain your balance long enough to keep me on your knee," I state playfully, seeing eyes filled with love and lips curling into the kind of smile that literally takes your breath away.

The air leaves my body in a wheeze. He really is enjoying this, but what is *this?*

"How can someone so beautiful be so naughty?" he asks, stroking my moist cheeks with his hot palm.

"You tell me. I was a saint until you came along."

"And now?"

"And now you've spoilt me for anyone else."

That single statement has him rethinking his game plan. The sexual tension between us is morphing into something else, something more profound; less physical more metaphysical. He lifts me off the bed and sits me across his lap. "Is that true?"

"Yes, but in a good way."

"Is there ever a *good* way to spoil someone?" he asks, his damp face shrouded in uncertainty.

"You spoil me all the time with your kindness and your gifts and your body and your love. You overwhelm me." I take his face in my hands and plant a chaste kiss on his lips.

"And what about my ability to maintain my balance and equanimity in flagrante delicto?" Here comes the 'spoil' me part I love the most: funny Ayden.

"Especially that." He pushes back my matted hair with both hands and stares at me. He keeps staring, sensing a cosmic shift in the space between us as an air of total serenity envelopes the room.

I feel it too. "What?"

"It just hit me."

I tip up my chin, eager to hear more.

"How much I love you, Beth. I've always loved you, or the promise of you."

I want to respond with something equally as sincere, but words escape me. I hug him and flatten my breasts against his clammy chest, hoping the gesture is enough. Then the words come to me. "Thank you." I place my fingers over his mouth, preventing him from speaking.

"I love you more."

Leaving the bathroom tidy, I throw on a camisole top, a pair of pyjama shorts, and re-join him in the lounge.

"The food's arrived, you must be hungry?"

He's right. I can't remember when I last ate. I'm famished. "Great! What time is it?"

"Eleven thirty, time for bed."

I give him a pre-emptive look and he starts to laugh in such a way my chest aches: he's radiant. Before this moment I would have sworn he could not look any more handsome, but here he is wearing suit trousers and a smile and he's awe-inspiring.

He turns and reads my thoughts. "Assessing?"

"Enjoying," I answer, feeling caught in the act.

"Well stop and enjoy your food. If you're good, I'll tell you a bedtime story."

I clap my hands together and tighten the towel around my head.

"Just eat."

The food is delicious. He may not be able to boil an egg but he certainly knows how to order the best food.

Twenty minutes later, we stroll hand in hand into the bedroom. I tug on his hand but he's reluctant to let go of me. "I need to dry my hair or I'll look like the Wicked Witch of the West in the morning if I let it dry naturally."

"Sit down. I'll dry it for you." He loves to give orders and, this time, I'm happy to oblige.

I position myself on the bathroom stool and let him finger dry my hair; it's a small thing but it's so intimate for all kinds of reasons. Mainly because I suspect he's never been close enough to anyone before to do it. "Have you done this before?" I enquire casually.

"No."

Details please...

"You're *very* good!"

"You're my first customer."

I knew it.

"A new skill to practise."

"Practice makes perfect," he states, clearly enjoying the experience.

"Yes it does."

"All done. Can I get anything else for Madam?" He lifts my chin so I can observe his role play.

I act out my own wide eyed stare. "Only a bedtime story, you did promise."

"Yes I did, didn't I? Get into bed."

The sheets are cold to the touch but soon warm once I settle myself under Ayden's right arm.

"Are you sitting comfortably?"

I nod into his chest.

"Then I shall begin ..."

There once was a boy called Ayden who travelled the world looking for things to possess. At first, he bought precious gems, equipment and patents, then manufacturing companies and distribution networks, before setting his sights on satellite technologies. He thought he had everything he wanted in life: fast cars, houses, fancy clothes, money and all the take-away food he could eat, but he still felt as if there was something missing in his life.

So, one day he left his ivory tower and wandered into a school, and this was a very special school full of special children and very special teachers. He was lucky enough to meet one of those special teachers and, do you know what she did?"

He taps my shoulder.

"No, what did she do?"

"She lifted a spell off Ayden, such a powerful spell that he thought he would never break free of it. At that very moment, he realised he had found the one person he had been searching for. He promised to love that special teacher because she made him feel special, she transformed him into a better man and he knew, even if he searched far and wide, he would never be able to find the words to thank her for showing him what life could be like. He would never tell her, but she had probably saved him from a sad and lonely life by loving him unconditionally. Ayden and his special teacher lived happily ... ever ... after.

The end."

I turn my face into his chest, sobbing quietly while he kisses my hair and pulls up the duvet around my neck.

"I know it wasn't very good, but it wasn't *that* bad," he chides. "Poor baby." He strokes my hair until I fall asleep.

***

The sound of a car pulling up outside, alerts Dan to the arrival of the 'object of his desire.' He stands by the window in the darkness like a giant spectre, watching and taking in every detail.

It's the chauffeur driven silver Rolls Royce. He doesn't bother checking the registration, he's way past that. His nose inches towards the glass. It's the closest he has been to her in almost seven years. From up high she seems diminutive and flustered; the quickness of her step and her fearful expression only amplifies her vulnerability. He likes that.

At the sight of her handsome escort, he shakes his head disapprovingly and mutters under his breath, "Fucking, Stone, I might have known."

In an instant, she's out of sight but not out of mind. He draws the curtains and switches on the light. It's just a bulb, no need for window dressing. He won't be supplying roses or arranging candle lit dinners for two, that's not his style. With or without the lights on, his dishonourable intentions will be the same: to claim what is his and to take what he wants.

Ten minutes later, the sound of a car coming to a screeching halt has him flicking off the light and bounding towards his look-out post. A red Audi mounts the curb and almost collides with the Rolls. He cannot believe his eyes.

"Fuck me if it isn't Charlotte. This is turning into a fucking reunion." If he had the energy, he'd punch the air, but he's expended so much today already and wants to conserve a little for the early hours. He has a 55 mile drive to work in the morning and, if he's going to make his 6 – 2 shift, will have to be on the road by 0430hrs.

Chancing his luck, he slips out of his apartment and tiptoes, as well as he can for a man of his size, down twelve stairs and sits on the landing outside apartment 53b. Mrs. Knowles won't mind if he takes a seat and listens into what their neighbour is saying one floor below.

He's fast approaching that point when he thinks it's a wasted effort when there are raised voices. Five minutes later Stone comes out of the apartment, looking like a man fleeing the scene of a crime. *She's* not far behind him. They are face to face at the front door, talking, arguing. Most of their words are lost on the night air but Dan learns something revealing about Stone. He calls out, "*You can bring me to my knees with a fucking smile.*" Dan is dumbfounded, but relishing the 'show.' His mouth curls into a knowing smile. "You and me both, Stone."

His words trigger a distant memory. From the moment he saw her that day in the refectory, eating a simple salad and giggling with her fellow undergrads, he knew she was the one. The time it had taken him to trace her, to work out where she was staying and with who turned into mission impossible. But, what he did find out was how often she visited the College Bar and, from that, had numerous opportunities to observe her covertly; to follow her home, to take pictures and to worship her from afar.

Using the bannister he pulls himself up and turns, only to be rooted to the spot again when the outside buzzer sounds. He knows it's not for him; the old lady will probably be in bed with her hot chocolate so ... he resumes the position and listens hard.

Charlotte's voice carries the length and breadth of the hallway and, for once, he's grateful for that. "*No. Who are you? Wait there.*"

Dan holds back on a smirk. 'Way to go Charlotte, you always were a charmer.' Doors slam. The new guy joins the party.

Back at base, standing in the darkness, Dan checks out the new vehicle. "Another chauffeur driven Rolls? What is it with these posers, can't any of them drive?" He can't make out the registration, but doesn't have to. His instincts tell him this guy is a lightweight compared to Stone.

He sees Charlotte leave, followed by guy number two. What a night! "There's more drama here than the West End," he announces, throwing a used tea bag into the sink. "People would pay good money to get a load of this."

With a chocolate digestive in one hand and a mug of tea in the other, he saunters into the bedroom. Everything he bought has been installed and is ready. If it were possible, he'd give himself a pat on the back.

Finishing his tea, he puts down the empty cup by the mattress and reaches into the box of latex gloves. They are sticky like toffee paper and have to be peeled apart so he can wriggle his fat fingers into them; they're snug and need some adjusting before becoming a comfortable fit. He looks down at them, feeling a wave of something uncontrollable rippling around his groin. The thought of removing her from her safe little world stirs him into arousal. He grabs his hardening cock through his jeans and instinctively closes his eyes. She's no longer a ghost but a living, breathing, seductive little girl: his girl.

Hearing the security door shut with a bang downstairs, he dashes to his observation post. No sooner does one Rolls leave than another arrives. It looks familiar. His chest inflates and bile fills his mouth, "Stone! You just can't keep your fucking hands off her, can you?"

Gloved fingers, the colour of stale yogurt, appear on the glass in the shape of an elongated strangle hold. Dan stomps off into the bedroom and rips off the gloves in a frenzied display of brutish rage; they lay by the mattress shredded.

His plan of attack is on hold and Stone's intervention has put a spanner in the works: it's a non-starter. He checks his watch, picks up his rucksack, and prepares to leave.

There's always tomorrow ...

12

T he tap, tap, tap of busy fingers on laptop keys stirs me into wakefulness. What's he doing at five thirty in the morning? I throw on his T-shirt and stumble into the kitchen, but he's so engrossed in his composition that I have to cough to get his attention.

By the light of a small lamp he's typing away furiously. I walk over and stand behind him, draping my arms around his shoulders.

"Whatcha doing there?" I glance at his lengthy email. Shit! I rub my eyelids and fear the worse.

"I'm composing an email, excusing myself from the Conference in L.A. tomorrow. I won't be attending." He continues typing.

"Why?"

"Because I have other commitments, like being here with you," he answers, planting a kiss on the upturned palm of my right hand.

This is not good!

Trying to conceal my panic, I remind him: "But I won't be here." Thank God he can't see my face.

"You will tonight. I'll plan something special, take you out to dinner. I know a romantic restaurant in Chelsea."

Before he can finish I interject, desperate times call for desperate measures. "But, like I said, I won't be here. I've made other plans." I hate lying.

"When?" he asks, pulling me around to sit across his knee.

"Ages ago."

Think of something, think of something.

"It's Charlie's birthday next week and I said I would help her organise her party."

"On a school night?"

A chuckle escapes my mouth. "Yes, on a school night."

"Okay. Then what time will you get back?" He presses me further.

For added effect I gesticulate with my hands. "I'll probably stop over and go to work from there. There'll be wine."

"Right." He looks disappointed but, thankfully, he's stopped typing and is considering his options. The moment his forefinger finds his lower lip, I know he's halfway there. I go in for the kill.

"Wednesday night's likely to be a write-off too. I'll probably stay on at school to finish off my marking and sort out photocopying for next term. I doubt I'll be good company after all that." I run my fingers through his hair and offer a smile of resignation. "I'm really sorry. Anyway, what's happening in L.A?"

"It's the annual meeting for CEO's and MD's: leading players in global communications."

I present my widest stare. "Isn't that you?"

He nods, but his eyes remain glued to the screen.

"Then you're taking yourself out of the game because of me?" I launch a loaded question and let it fly.

"Not exactly."

"Yes, exactly. If you're writing an apology then you're expected to attend?"

"Yes, I'm supposed to be giving the opening speech."

"What! And, because of me, you're throwing away an opportunity like that?"

"No. It's not like that."

"It looks like that from where I'm sitting." My attention moves from the screen to him. Taking his face in my hands, I prepare for my final assault. "Ayden, you had a life before me, remember. Your company is everything to you. I don't want you to look back on this and blame me for a missed opportunity."

He rests his hand on my thigh. "I wouldn't do that."

"No, but I would. You have to go."

"I don't *have* to do anything, Beth." I detect an inflection.

"You *have* to do this, besides, I've got Charlie's party to help plan and books to mark before half term; I want to tidy up the apartment ..."

His neck takes the brunt of my attack and his hand massages it roughly. "I don't know."

"Yes you do. Nothing will change. I'll still love you when you get back. I may even love you more. They do say absence makes the heart grow fonder."

He's thinking.

How long must I keep this up?

"I suppose it wouldn't kill me to give you some time to yourself." He's folding.

"It'll hurt a little, but you're right, it won't kill either of us."

"Maybe I should?"

He's going.

Stretching, I slither off his knee and go for broke. "It's your decision but hurry up, decide and come back to bed. My alarm will be going off in an hour and a half." I take a quick look at the screen and watch him press '*discard.*'

Thank God!

Tuesday morning comes much too soon. I hit the alarm with such force it bounces off the bedside cabinet, and it insists on torturing me with its muffled cries from the floor. Leaning across Ayden's vacant space, my hand finds it and turns it off. There's the aroma of coffee; it's drifting through the apartment urging me to rise and shine. The familiar sound of typing holds my attention. Surely, he's not redrafting his apology? I don't have the strength to talk him round, not again.

I make myself presentable and slip on a school blouse and a skirt, before tying back my hair in preparation for another working day spent stressing the importance of accurate spelling and punctuation to a generation of texting fanatics.

With a spring in my step, I enter the kitchen. "Good morning."

"Hey, you decided to get up then?" A cheeky smile appears from round the screen.

"I had no choice, what with the alarm, the smell of coffee and your incessant typing." Why do I sound so grouchy?

"I've only been up half an hour. I wanted to make a start on my speech."

My spirits leap but I suppress a triumphant smile. "Do you want to read it back to me, I'm pretty good with words."

"Of that I have no doubt." He offers a knowing smile. "It's still in the early stages."

"OK but if you need to, you can ask for help. That's what I'm here for, amongst other things." I blow him a kiss: he sends one back. "Don't think of it as a power struggle Ayden. We're combining forces. That's all."

"I know, no need to call the therapist, Beth, I get it."

I munch on cereal. "Good. Have you got a theme in mind?"

"I did, but I've changed it due to recent events." He's winking at me.

What does that mean?

I look at my watch. "Look, I'd love to chat, but I've got to go." I punch my arm into my black Mango jacket. "What time's your flight?"

"Midday. I'll call you when I land, but I'll be seven hours back, so I won't leave it too late."

I nod, grateful for his explanation.

"By the way, I've organised something for us on Thursday."

"Another picnic?"

"No, I'm taking you to Rome for a couple of days."

I can't conceal my excitement. He remembered our first date. "To check out intercity parking?"

A smile of remembrance plays on his lips. "Not quite."

"That's a wonderful idea. It's called the Eternal City, you know?"

"No I didn't know that." He pulls me onto his knee, inching in towards my face with every word. "I'll pick you up at eleven Thursday morning. I'll have slept on the flight back."

"And showered?"

"And showered." We laugh and share the joke.

I trace the shape of his face with my right hand and enjoy the feel of overnight stubble. This is the first time I've caught him unshaven and I love the look.

"You see, everything's working out. Now you won't get under my feet while I'm packing and planning for our trip, and you'll be out there being my Mr. P."

"Your what?"

"My Mr. P., for Powerful."

"We'll have to see about that." He can't conceal his amusement; the way his mouth twitches and his eyes sparkle is a tell-tale sign.

I taste his lips and inhale the coffee on his breath one last time. "Have a safe flight, Ayden. I'll miss you."

His hands frame my face. "I'll miss you more." Our kiss has to last over three days so we savour it. With immeasurable tenderness he kisses me good bye, making me regret ever having promised to get him on that damn plane.

"By the way, don't be surprised to see a silver Audi behind you. I've organised some security to and from work and through the night, until we can get you fixed up with some security in this place."

I wrap my arms around his neck. "Thank you, what would I do without you?"

He has no answer to that and can only shrug. "Go, you'll be late."

"Bye." He releases me.

"Bye, baby. Be good."

I blow him a kiss over my shoulder and make my way to my car, giving my escort a wave as I pass. First order of the day is to speak with Charlie; she's my alibi and must be able to corroborate my story. En route I call her mobile and put her on speakerphone.

"Hey honey, I've been waiting for your call. How's things?" She sounds bright and breezy.

"Oh, how long have you got?"

"Not long."

"Then, you'd better take a rain check. I'm calling because I need a favour." I know I only have to ask, but it's only polite not to assume.

"Fire away."

"I had to get Ayden to go to an important meeting in L.A. so I told him we had plans tonight."

"Okay?" She sounds unsure.

"We're meeting up so I can help arrange your birthday party, alright?"

"Sounds plausible enough. And are we?"

"Sure, if you don't have plans. I had to think on my feet and you were my best alibi."

"Happy to help, and are you stopping over?"

"I said I might."

"Then why don't you? It seems like ages since we had a girlie night." In the background I can hear the sound of car horns. *"And the same to you mister!"* she calls out.

"So I'll see you later then? Say around 6 o'clock?"

"Sounds good. Bring wine, I plan on getting you very drunk." She laughs loudly.

I'm smiling. "I *bet* you are. Anyway, I've got school tomorrow, it's my last day and then I'm off for a fortnight."

"You lucky sod. I wish I worked part time." I refuse to take the bait. "Look, I've got to park up. See you later, honey. Have a nice day."

"I plan to, same to you, Char."

"See ya."

"Bye."

I give a little sigh of relief, having sorted out my cover story. If Ayden rings her, for whatever reason, I know I won't be caught out. I hate being devious but it's done with the best of intentions. Besides, it's a magnanimous gesture on my part, I'd much rather be spending time with him than trying to shake myself free from Charlie's thumb screws.

Morning lessons come and go and break is enjoyed by one and all; the Head of Music is celebrating her birthday and there is a selection of cakes and biscuits laid out in the staffroom. I take myself to a quiet corner to text Ayden a safe flight and send him my love. His reply is instantaneous, as is the promise of *more* love.

Still energised by my sugar fix, I skip lunch and settle for an apple and a bottle of water. My new wardrobe is full of snug fitting clothes. The last thing I want to do is stack on the pounds, risking burst seams and uncomfortable waistbands.

By the end of the day I'm exhausted, but I make an effort to check the duration of Ayden's flight: it's eleven hours. I don't expect to hear from him until midnight. That gives him ample time to fine-tune his speech.

Before heading over to Canary Wharf to see Charlie, I decide to call home to change and pick up a bottle of Charlie's favourite Carsi Vineyard Chardonnay. Just as I'm about to exit my bedroom, I notice something on my pillow; it's my platinum kiss necklace. I grasp it tightly in my right hand until my fingertips glow. He's so thoughtful. It feels good to have it around my neck, simply wearing it sends a warm, fuzzy feeling through my body, much like the one I felt the day we met. I miss you already, Ayden.

***

After a morning spent unblocking drains and repairing a leaking roof, Dan is ready for some rest and recuperation. Unfortunately, neither activity features on his mental 'to do' list. Getting to his new apartment before *she* arrives home from work is his number one priority, and that is why he is pushing his dilapidated BMW to its limit in the outside lane. The finger on the speedometer is twitching between seventy and eighty and still he's being pushed to go faster by impatient motorists.

"I can see you, I'm not fucking blind!" he calls out when the glow from the flashing headlights in his rear view mirror pierces his eyes. Reluctantly, he pulls into the middle lane and stays there, allowing his car to take a well-earned breather.

By 1600hrs, he's pulling up outside Elm Gardens, checking the parking area for a black Ford Fiesta, he assumes that's her car. He gives himself the 'all clear' and makes a run for it; in through the door, straight up the stairs and into his apartment. A little breathless, he leans against the front door. His eyes are darting from left to right. He has his thinking face on. Last night's events were a setback, that's for sure, but he won't be deterred. He's ready to take it on the chin and move on.

He strategically places a folding chair by the window; standing, waiting and watching plays havoc with his back. He learned that seven years ago and ended up having to take painkillers around the clock but it was a small price to pay. Some of his best photographs were taken as a result of dedicated surveillance.

Earlier than he had anticipated, a black Fiesta parks up at the end of the cul-de-sac and out she steps looking all business-like and lovely. The tripod holds the camera steady and the zoom lens captures her, unguarded and alone. Dan cannot conceal his joy, he rubs his hands together with tenacious swipes: there's no stopping him now. In his eagerness to get to her, he kicks the lightweight chair away and a half empty cup of tea spills over the carpet.

"Shit!" he calls out, seeing the mocha coloured stain forming on the plush fibres. Cursing all the way, he by-passes the bedroom and heads for the bathroom. He tugs at the toilet roll and wraps waves and waves of it around his hand.

The paper absorbs the seeping liquid and quickly turns into a sickly, brown mush. His feeble attempt at clearing up his mess has flustered him. He had not planned for that and a little detail he could not have anticipated has become a costly distraction.

He takes a minute to calm down and to mentally prepare for what he has to do. Once again, he slips on the latex gloves; he's done it before and this time he has no trouble sliding in his fingers. They fit like a second skin. He checks his watch: 1700hrs.

Time to face the music.

With no more than his physical strength and the element of surprise on his side, he prepares to move onto the next stage of 'Operation Snatch Back.' He slips his keys into his back pocket and heads out of the apartment, but halts on pulling the door to. There are voices on the stairs.

"I'm off to see a friend in Canary Wharf."

"Oh that's nice. You won't have met the new tenant upstairs then?"

Not yet, but you will ...

"No, I've been busy."

Busy fighting off that fucking poser Stone ...

"He's called Daniel, I think."

"Really? I'm sure we'll meet at some point."

You can count on it, princess ...

"Bye, Pat."

"Bye, Beth, have fun."

Beth?

The sound of the security door closing hits him hard. Quickly, before the lady downstairs gets to her apartment, he nips inside and pulls his door shut with the softest of clicks. He sprints over to the window only to witness the Fiesta disappearing out of sight.

Crushing disappointment is etched on his face. Once again, the gloves are shredded and discarded. He takes his frustration out on an innocent chair now lying on its back on the sodden carpet, tearing at the candy striped material until it is no more than a tattered selection of colourful strips. They dangle from the aluminium frame like pieces of bunting, seeming to celebrate his failure, mocking him. Seething, he folds it up and leans it against the wall. Now it's like a Hawaiian skirt beneath a square frame. It looks ridiculous, he feels ridiculous. He's had enough.

Like a petulant child, he throws the tea soaked paper into the toilet and storms off home, not relishing the 75 mile drive back to Ely. Getting her back is proving harder than he thought.

Feeling an overwhelming sense of failure, he flicks in a CD, hoping the booming sound of heavy rock will improve his mood. It does. The famous words of one of his movie heroes comes to mind: "I'll be back."

***

I take the North Circular Road and head over to Canary Wharf. Charlie's new apartment is an ultra-modern, million pound, eighth floor investment which could easily be described as a party pad, except for the fact she's not much of a party planner. She prefers to be out and about and, when she's not socialising, she's networking; sometimes she manages to do both at the same time. She's everything I'm not. We're like opposite sides of the same coin, inseparable. As much as I love her, I couldn't live *with* her, and that's why I plan on leaving no later than 10.30pm. It will take me an hour to get home and then I intend to spend the rest of my evening devoting myself to Ayden. I have a plan.

Considering her birthday party will be taking place in just over a week, Charlie is pretty laid-back about everything. If it was me, I'd be counting down the days and dusting off wine glasses.

Following on from an hour of less than serious planning, she makes a decision about the theme. It comes as no surprise: it's Film Heroes. Charlie is obsessed with film and music, believing she has missed her calling and should have been a screen siren. Throughout the nine years of our friendship, there have been times when I might have agreed: she can be a drama queen.

She is itching to know about my love life, so I broach the subject and save her the hassle. "Ayden's in L.A. on business. He wasn't going to go, but after some subtle persuading I got him to fly out this afternoon. After our chat last night, I realised what was going on with him and asked him to come back to my apartment."

She's quick to get involved. "I hope he apologised, for whatever he did!"

I'm not in the mood to elaborate. "Yes, he did. Anyway, it was a misunderstanding. It's all sorted now."

"I'm pleased to hear it. And does he know how lucky he is?" She throws me an exaggerated smile.

"Yes, he does, but I feel lucky too. He's the only guy who really sees me, you know?"

"Yes, I get that, hon, but you've made *yourself* invisible; locked yourself away for years, and now you're falling for the first guy who comes along."

She means well but she can't appreciate the depth of our love. How could she? "I feel safe with him Char. Now we've opened up to each other, I know he won't hurt me. I need to know that."

She pats my hand. "I'm pissed and if you keep talking like that, I'm going to start crying and make a fool of myself. You make it sound so beautiful. Is he that perfect?" Forever sceptical, that's her style.

"He's as near to it as I'll ever find," I confess. "If we last until Christmas it will be worth it, but I'm sort of expecting we'll last a lot longer than that." I lean over and give her a hug. "Thanks for being such a good friend to me all these years. I know I've been a miserable bitch most of the time, but I'm happy now, so be happy for me. OK?" I can see tears welling in her eyes.

"Sure. But if he as much as steps a foot out of line, you've got to be strong. Don't take any crap off him. Even if he is one of the sexiest guys I've ever had the pleasure of insulting." She throws back the last drops of wine settling in the bottom of her glass.

"Hey, Beth, be honest with me now, does he fuck as good as he looks?"

I know it's the wine talking. "He's good at everything, Charlie, and that's all I'm saying." I give her a knowing look, which, thankfully, she recognises as my final word on the subject.

"Good to know. I'm happy for you, hon. You deserve to be happy after what you've been through."

With that she snatches the empty bottle, from which she has drunk two thirds, and staggers off into the kitchen. I walk over to the enormous floor to ceiling windows and take-in the spectacular view of the O2 Arena and the London Skyline, illuminated against the cloudy night sky. I wonder what Ayden is doing now? It's 10.30pm. In half an hour he'll be landing, reliving the last seven hours again, five and a half thousand miles away. Is he missing me? I hope so.

Coming home to an empty apartment is not as much fun as it used to be. It's so quiet. I'd even welcome the tap, tap, tap of laptop keys right now. I switch on mine, hoping for a message but expecting nothing, it's almost midnight. Just as I'm pouring boiling water over a tea bag, I hear the familiar ping, signalling the arrival of an email. Quickly I open up the message. It's a long one.

From:	a.s.mediainternational1@global.com
To:	songbirdBP@hotmail.co.uk
Date	23rd October 16.50
Subject:	SWEET DREAMS!

The Promise: Tracy Chapman

I've just arrived at the hotel. It's late afternoon here, but you'll be off to bed soon. I've been thinking, and I want to say thank you for taking the time to figure me out. I know I'm a head case, but I still haven't explained ... I'd like to try.

What you said was right, but I think my behaviour was a reflex response. For as long as I can remember, losing has not been an option, misjudging anything has seemed like failure and feeling has been something I've avoided. Because, if you let yourself feel then you can be hurt and there have been times when I could have been seriously hurt, emotionally and physically. Winning has been my coping mechanism, you've made me see that now.

So, what happens next? I still need to win or be seen to be winning. Everything I've achieved has come from that single impulse; it's made me self-reliant and I'd be an idiot to lose sight of that. But ... right now I feel as if my armour has been stripped from me, yet I'm still expected to go into battle and win. Knowing what makes me tick has left me feeling exposed. Maybe I'm not your Mr. P. after all?

I've still got to fine-tune the speech I thought I wouldn't have to write, thanks to some clever man-handling this morning. I'll have to watch out for that!! You were right though, there was no power sharing - I didn't stand a chance! You should come and work for me - with me - I can always use a good negotiator!

During the flight, I had time to find a song for you. I can't kiss you goodnight, but imagine these words leaving my lips and finding their way to your heart. It's late, get to bed. Don't email back, I've got work to do!

Sweet dreams, Beth.

All my love.
A. x

After reading his email, I'm left with a terrible sense of foreboding. What have I done? Perhaps I shouldn't have been so brutally honest, telling him things he's not ready to hear, not now, not on the eve of one of the biggest corporate events he will ever have to open. I don't care what he said, I have to email him.

From:	songbirdBP@hotmail.co.uk
To:	a.s.mediainternational1@global.com
Date:	24th October 00.05
Subject:	ARMOUR PLATING

Shine: Take That

Thanks for your lovely song - there's tears - it's become one of my all-time favourites. I know you're busy, but I have three points to make:

What I said wasn't an exercise in subjugation, it was my amateurish attempt to help you deal with feelings you couldn't get your head around: I was desperate! I knew, if I couldn't make you understand, then you'd move on and we'd be over. I don't want that and now I know you don't want that either.

Your fixation with winning has seriously fucked up your 'love' life, but I'm selfish enough to be glad that you were such a Playboy. As ridiculous as it sounds, being a player has brought you to me.

As far as you and your company are concerned, nothing has changed. You should feel empowered not disarmed: now you can begin to channel your motivation. Not only that, you have someone in your camp 24/7.

So ... stop feeling sorry for yourself and finish that speech so you can blow their socks off tomorrow and get yourself on a plane back to me!

Have a pleasant evening, Ayden.
All my love
B. x
P.S. Enjoy the song x

Before I have time to turn out the lights, I receive a reply. I thought I might.

From: a.s.mediainternational1@global.com
To: songbirdBP@hotmail.co.uk
Date: October 23rd 17.12
Subject: WHAT HAPPENED TO ROMANCE?

Thank you for the précis...
I send you my heart in a song and you send me a fucking sing-a-long - THANKS!
DON'T email me! If I don't finish this speech I'll be too busy SHITTING myself to SHINE!

Get to bed!
All my love

A. x

Oh, he's such a romantic ...

From: songbirdBP@hotmail.co.uk
To: a.s.mediainternational1@global.com
Date: 24th October 00.17
Subject: GOING TO BED HAPPY

That's more like it! Welcome back!
I'm going to bed now, with a smile on my face ;-)

I love you.

B. x

He's found his voice and his armour plating too by the sound of it. There's an instant reply.

From:	a.s.mediainternational1@global.com
To:	songbirdBP@hotmail.co.uk
Date:	23rd October 17.19
Subject:	SWEET DREAMS!

I've got a smile on my face too. ☺ You have such a good heart Beth. To have your love is such a special gift. I treasure it.
Thanks for the wake-up call. I know why you sent the song. I'm good.

I love you more
A. x

I shut down the laptop and make my way to my lonely bed, safe in the knowledge that Mr. P. is back. One more day to get through and then our romantic city break to the Eternal City. The thought of it makes me want to jump up and down on my bed. Instead, I throw on Ayden's cotton T-shirt and slip between the sheets. The drama of the last few days seems to be catching up with me. In the blink of a very tired eye, I feel myself falling into a deep sleep.

13

After last night's disappointment, Dan is finding it difficult to conceal his frustration. He feels nothing but contempt for the students and the staff at the University and, anyone taking the time to look him in the eye would see that. Ernie's good natured attempts to initiate friendly banter are met with lacklustre, single syllable responses and disinterest. Why? The big man is consumed by thoughts of 'Beth' Parker, to the point of distraction. He's had to abort two attempts at extraction and is beginning to feel that, in spite of all the planning, the expense and his best efforts, it's never going to happen.

Worst of all, he cannot tell a soul; hope and fear are eating away at him like cancerous growths. No amount of medical attention will cure him of his ailment. There's no cure for lust. Twice during his shift he's had to pay a visit to his locker to see her, to find release from carnal cravings that threaten to erupt from him like paint from an aerosol.

Knowing how close he came has only intensified his craving for sexual communion. Not only can he visualize her with her cute blond hair, he can smell her, hear her voice, feel her breath on his skin. She's become too close for comfort: she's real, tangible, a temptress.

For the first time in his life, he can't face lunch. The free meal sits on the tray in the crowded dining hall, untouched. Ernie assumes he's unwell.

"You must be sickening for something."

He's not wrong.

"Got no appetite."

"You want to get yourself off to the doctors. P'raps you've got a bug."

"Yeah, must have. Been doing too much."

Too much planning and driving and wanking...

"Not too chatty either."

"No."

"Tell Crowther, see if he'll let you leave early."

"No. I'll finish the shift and deal with it later."

"OK. Just take it easy champ."

"I intend to."

"That's the spirit." Ernie slides over his dessert. "Can I tempt you with a blackberry muffin?"

"No thanks, I'll pass. Got to watch my figure."

"It's a bit late for that! Better keep your strength up. Don't want you wasting away. Who's going to lug all that furniture around if you turn into a ten stone weakling?"

"Some other dumb fucker."

"Exactly. Eat your muffin and stop moping about. Looking at your miserable mush is giving me a bloody headache."

Dan forces a contrite smile.

"That's better." Ernie licks his thumb and flicks over the page to the football results.

By 1415hrs Dan's mood has improved and he is southbound. His BMW has never been so mechanically challenged; a distressed sound is coming from somewhere under the bonnet. He turns down the CD player and listens, checking dashboard gauges for signs of mechanical failure. Under sufferance, he pulls over onto the hard shoulder and clicks open the bonnet.

Even before he opens it, he can smell the dreaded odour of burning rubber. When he tries to open the bonnet, he flinches; it's hot, too hot to handle.

"Fuck!"

He pulls down the cuffs of his jacket over his palms and lifts it tentatively, keeping the scorching metal away from his skin. Settling over the engine is a cloud of steam and sizzling droplets of water. He's no mechanic, but even he recognizes an over-heated radiator. He checks his watch, time is against him. It's 1500hrs. He's over forty miles from home and less than thirty miles from Elm Gardens. His hands are tied. If he chances the drive to Elm Gardens, he may not be able to get back. If he heads home, then he'll have to go another night without her. That thought hits him like a body blow.

"Shit! Shit! Shit!" He roars to the heavens, but no words can convey the tormented nature of his ferocious anger. So profound is his misery that he slams down the bonnet of the car again and again, ignoring the scorching pain in his hands as the hot metal sears his flesh.

Like a man drunk on despair, he staggers along the hard shoulder, heavy boots on gravel, eyes smarting in the autumn wind. There are no bars but, to the passing motorists, he looks like a caged animal, unable to escape, unwilling to accept his fate.

'Operation Snatch Back' will have to be put back another night.

***

Every half term ends the same way: excited teenagers wearing their own clothes, lesson plans being filed, films being projected onto whiteboards; the perfect reward for seven weeks of hard labour.

By 4.15 pm the natives are off school premises, leaving me to focus on marking and planning. First stop the photocopier. As the worksheets mount, my thoughts shift to Ayden's emails last night. I haven't needed to worry all day, the time difference has meant he's been preoccupied with speech writing or sleeping. Now, 45 minutes before his conference opens, I'm anxious.

Margaret from the office bounds into the staff room, "Oh great, you're still here, Beth. I've just had an urgent phone call for you."

My pulse starts to race and I clutch my chest. What's happened, is it Charlie? Is it Ayden? Oh dear God no!

"A gentleman rang and insisted I find you. Apparently your phone is turned off and he needs to speak with you urgently." She searches the note for a name. "He said his name was Mr. P." She gives me a capricious look and I take the note from her.

"Thank you, Margaret."

I snatch my pile of photocopying from the machine and dash off to my classroom for some privacy. I turn on my phone, silently scolding myself for turning it off on such an important day. What was I thinking? I press Speed-dial 1. He picks up immediately.

"Elizabeth?" I'm about to speak but the fact he's addressing me as Elizabeth stops me in my tracks. "Elizabeth?"

"Yes, Ayden, I'm here." I want to speak softly but I sense he needs more than that. "What's wrong?"

"It's ... it's this fucking speech, I don't think I can pull it off."

What!

"You can't be serious!"

"I can't seem to get my shit together." I barely recognise his voice, it's a nervous whisper.

"Where are you?" I boot up my laptop and access the CNN website. They're bound to be covering the conference. "Can you talk?"

"Yes, but ..."

"... Be quiet and listen." I nibble my thumb nail and contemplate my words very carefully. "You can do this blindfolded with your hands tied behind your back, I should know." I think I can hear a snigger of sorts at the other end of the phone. "Are you listening to me?"

"Yes, Elizabeth."

I need his full attention. "Take out your final draft." I hear paper rustling. "How does it begin?"

"Good morning ..." He starts to read it out; it's disjointed, rushed.

"It's a good speech, Ayden," I lie. "You need to read it through and centre yourself."

"How?"

"Do you have the lock of hair I gave you?" Please let him have it.

"Yes, it's in my pocket."

"Well it's no good in there, is it! Take it out and wrap it around the fingers of your left hand." I swear I can hear him breathing, his chest sounds tight and that's not good. "Wrap it really tight and close your eyes." I give him a couple of seconds.

"It's done."

"Tell me what the lock represents, breathe slowly and tell me."

He breathes in, out, in, out. "It's you next to me, holding me, keeping me safe. It's tight and it's like being inside you."

"And how do you feel when you're inside me?"

"I feel safe, invincible and powerful." There's a noticeable change in his voice, the timbre has altered: he's becoming more assertive, more imposing. He's becoming my Mr. P.

"Read the next paragraph. At the end of each sentence feel the lock, see how it centres you and makes you focus? The words will come to you." I nibble my thumbnail and wait for his reply with trepidation.

He starts to read. "Yes. You're right."

Thank God! "Now you're ready. You only have to read the speech through, slowly, breathe and feel the lock tight on your hand. Do you understand?"

"Yes." There's the exhaling of breath down the line. "I'm good." He pauses.

"So, what are you waiting for?" I hold my hand to my mouth, preventing an emotional gasp from escaping. "Go be Mr. P."

"I will." Now that's the man I love. "Watch the speech. The wink will be for you."

I sense a grateful smile. I've accessed CNN coverage of his press conference, which must have taken place earlier this morning.

"I'm watching you at the press conference earlier. Straighten your tie and take that 'fuck-me' look off your face. This isn't the Playboy channel, Ayden: it's business. Now go out there and shine, like the star you are." My voice is not my own.

"Yes, Elizabeth."

"Are we done?"

"We're done."

I end the call and leave him hanging. He's ready.

I sink into my chair visibly shaking, sweating: what just happened? I keep watching the coverage. It's live. An overweight counterpart with a skin-tight waistcoat has introduced Mr. Stone and is inviting him to the podium. He's approaching, shaking hands, checking his tie, looking confident and serious: he means business.

Oh dear God, please let him be brilliant.

Quickly the distinguished members of the audience settle and he positions himself, back straight, hands either side of the lectern, head held high. I wipe my hands on my skirt. I'm perspiring and having to make a conscious effort to breathe.

Ayden thanks them for their kind introduction and launches into a cohesive dialogue, pausing only to acknowledge applause. He speaks of a *'defining moment.'* and stresses the importance of *'global integration.'* Every new sentence is shaped; *'commercial innovation'* is juxtaposed with *'consumer application.'* He concludes with a directive, *'If we are to expand our geographic reach we'll need to work smarter, creating new pathways through expansive leadership and by offering transparency, reliability and affordability. Let us not forget this is a small planet, we are all connected.'*

Applause reverberates around the auditorium. The camera moves in for a close-up, I watch him discreetly slip the lock of hair into his jacket pocket. Looking directly into the lens he winks. I smile. We connect.

I want to call him but I can see he's surrounded by his peers. I let him be, let him have his moment in the spotlight. He's had his chance to shine and so dazzling is his brilliance, it hurts my eyes. A glossy tear streams down my cheek. I do love this man.

Driving home is an exercise in patience and good grace. I know Ayden will not call until I get home, but every traffic light is against me and I want to speak to him before he boards his return flight. He'll be exhausted, having added an extra seven hours to his day and sleep is the only thing he should be thinking about at 40,000 feet above the Atlantic.

I'm listening to classic Fleetwood Mac on my iPod and I'm singing, wishing I could be with him *Everywhere,* and never a truer word has been spoken. I break, envisage what tomorrow will bring, accelerate and picture him coming to whisk me off to the Eternal City. When I park up, my excitement is discernible; the skip in my step is a dead giveaway.

After snacking on a tuna salad, I set about the unenviable task of packing, but not before I flick through my post. All my bills are paid via direct debit so I know I'm debt free and most of the junk mail goes straight into the bin. I take hold of a small parcel, give its contents a gentle rattle and fondle it. I think I've seen this discreet wrapping before.

With eager fingers, I tear off the brown paper and open the black box. Something tells me it's not a bracelet. I lift the lid and sneak a peek. It's a kind of silicone ring with an attachment at the top. Oh!

This is one toy I won't be using in the privacy of my own home, not alone anyway. Does this actually count as a gift for me? Shouldn't this have been sent to Stone Heath? It has Ayden Stone written all over it.

Usually, I hate packing but tonight there's nothing I would rather do. Thankfully Celine has simplified the task by matching clothes and accessories; getting a collection together to take account of the weather is *my* problem.

I'm planning on throwing my faded suitcase away, but not before I have inspected its contents. It's collecting dust under my bed and my dad's small treasure chest is keeping it company. I must move one to get at the other. The case weighs as much as I do and I soon realise why. It's full of books. When I flip open the lid, I'm reminded of a former, solo pursuit and I lift up a couple of paperbacks, realising instantly what drew me to them: escapism, pure escapism.

Carrying half a dozen at a time, I pile them up against the wall beneath my window. There they sit, having promised so much but actually having given me nothing more than a sanctuary and a place to dream. Now, I have no need of dreams, I have a trip to pack for. I have Ayden.

The one thing I cannot relegate to the other side of the room is the small, battered wooden chest: it's a treasure trove of memories, a visual record of my childhood loves and losses, laid bare for all to see. I don't have the heart to disregard its contents, to hide them away as if my life before Ayden didn't exist. It did. I did. I've got time to take a look.

I take hold of two stark, white envelopes; they bring to mind a cold, harsh reality. I don't have x ray vision but I know the words written on my mother's and my father's Death Certificates and I have no desire to be reminded of them. Softly I place the two envelopes side by side on the bed. They'd like that.

Before me is a scattering of photographs, the most recent on top. Two young women in their early twenties holidaying in Rhodes framed by an emerald sea and fishing boats; a beaming Charlie and a bemused Beth, self-consciously posing for the camera in a bikini which, in retrospect, doesn't look that bad.

Turnover, move on: my graduation photograph. An orphan girl dressed in black, wearing a silly hat. The feelings I had on that memorable day resurface: the loneliness, the disappointment, the despair. I remember going home alone and downing a half bottle of Bacardi, just so I could get through the day. I cried myself to sleep and woke up the next day with a monumental hangover and my parents' wedding photograph on my pillow. God knows how it got there.

Turnover, move on: I glance and flick through school holiday snaps, me as Hermia in a school production, holding a netball trophy, eating ice-cream with my dad on Brighton Pier; a petite girl of around fourteen with wayward brown hair, looking like Medusa caught in a backdraft. What was I thinking? I smile at my dad, noticing the absence of sparkle in his eyes. He'd lost that three years earlier, the day my mum died; buried it with her with no prospect of ever finding it again.

Now this next group of photographs require a double dose of endurance. My eleventh birthday, the last recorded image of my mum; a floral dress two sizes too big, hair in a plain pink scarf the colour of ripe peaches against her cream complexion. Dark circles like Saturn's rings around her eyes, a weak smile. She was always beautiful, even ravaged by cancer and more so only two days away from saying goodbye, forever.

I daren't look, yet can't bring myself to tear my un-focusing eyes away. I must. I lay her to rest next to the two envelopes, close to my dad, knowing wherever she is he will have found her and will be taking good care of her. I have to believe that.

I rummage around, in search of happier times, hoping to find images to neutralize this numbing sense of loss. They come in droves: the whole family sitting around a dining table wearing Christmas hats, a holiday in Cornwall, an unsteady tent, dad with a mallet and mum off-loading a car, me stroking a stray dog that hated the rain but loved cheese. It's all coming back to me, making me choke back tears.

I'm done. There's nothing left to see, it's all so far back I can barely remember, but I try when I see my dad standing tall and proud in his white overalls, leaning against a second-hand van. 'Parker's Painting and Decorating Services,' such a fancy title for a one-man-band. I was his five year old apprentice, passer of brushes, stirrer of paint extraordinaire. There we are: a proud father and a daughter who worships him and would not leave his side.

I remember that summer, hiding under billowing dust covers and climbing ladders, playing king of the castle and pretending to be a princess perched on a tower, out of reach of a monster or a wicked witch who had cast a spell on her. I was Sleeping Beauty wrapped in white, waiting to be rescued by a prince. I remember.

I splay out the photos from that summer in my hand like a fan, trying to put a name to faces and places, but it was twenty two years ago, and every recollection is wrapped in memories that have become no more than shapes in smoke. I hold onto the final photo and take a long sip of warm rose, with it emerges a memory, forgotten.

In the background is a large Victorian house with three children haphazardly arranged in front of it. A dark haired boy has his arms around two small girls, the smallest, on the right is me, I think. I have my thumbnail in my mouth, as was my way even then, and a pink bow in my unruly hair which I've allowed to blow across my face to mask my shyness. To one side is my dad's van which he just *happened* to get in the picture.

For the first time in an hour, I smile. Sometimes it's the simplest of things that mean the most; realising what a wonderful childhood I've had lifts my spirits, leaving me with a warm glow that circles my heart. I have been loved and I am loved. I can ask for no more than that.

I return the contents of the chest to their rightful place and close the lid on my past. The precious container slides back into position under my bed, right where I place my head to sleep, close enough to be a comfort when the dark shapes buried in my dreams awaken and take hold of me, again.

By 9.30p.m. it's done, everything bar the proverbial kitchen sink is wedged, crammed and crushed into 32 inches of luggage space. I haven't weighed it, I daren't. I pour myself another congratulatory glass of rose, take my phone off charge and hit Speed-dial 1.

Ayden answers, "Hey, I was just about to call you. I'm on my way to the airport." He sounds cheerful but tired and relieved.

"Good, you managed to get away from your adoring fans then?"

"Just about, thanks to you they wouldn't let me go." He pauses and I'm not sure why.

"I was just the monkey, you're the organ grinder," I reassure him.

"Well, you're a very clever monkey. I couldn't have done it without you," he sniggers. "There's something I never thought I'd hear myself say."

"Well you have and you won't have to say it again. Like I said last night, we're a team." I love saying that.

"Seems that way."

"Are you okay? Are we good?" I throw back one of his perfunctory questions.

"Yes, just tired. I'm looking forward to showing you just *how* good we are, together." He purposely inserts a dramatic pause and waits.

I smile into the phone. "I'm looking forward to that too. Can you see me smiling?"

"*All* I can see is you, Beth."

There's a gentle hum in his voice and it touches me. "You've been in my thoughts the whole time you've been away." I find myself gazing into space, just the sound of his voice and the way he says my name is enough to send a shiver through me. "Access your emails before you go to sleep and don't email me back, I'll be sleeping too or maybe not … I've got gift number two."

"And?"

"And I feel like I'm taking in deliveries for you."

He's laughing down the phone. "I love it when you talk dirty."

"I know." I'm laughing too.

"Did you know what it was?"

"No but I do now."

"Then you must know that it's a *joint* gift?"

"I've yet to be convinced," I tease.

"Then I'll be happy to convince you when I get back."

"I can't wait. I already feel like a kid getting excited the night before Christmas. I won't sleep." Why am I telling him this?

"I love your honesty. You're my favourite naughty girl, especially when you're sat on my lap in the back of my Rolls."

Oh that's so unfair, bringing up that memory now. It feels like play time all over again. "But I like sitting on your lap, especially when you have the biggest hard on for me."

"Whoa!" I hear him clearing his throat. "Any more mischief from you and I'll put you across my knee again, missy." He's smiling down the phone, but that doesn't stop it being a very sensual threat.

"Is that a threat or a promise?" That warning has sparked a visceral response. I'm finding it difficult to keep still on the kitchen chair. The idea of his hand leaving marks on my skin has me writhing.

"That's up to you."

"Then we'll call it a promise," I answer boldly and wait for his reply.

"But you do know I always keep my promises, don't you?"

I do.

"I'm counting on it." I can play this game too.

His breathing falters, he exhales noisily. "Beth … if I'm going to get a wink of sleep on this long haul flight, we're going to have to end this conversation *right* now."

I hear the yearning in his voice and want to soften it with some words of reassurance. "I understand. Sleep well, Ayden. Arrivederci mio caro."

I hear him laughing softly. "Sleep well, baby."

The instant he leaves, something unexpected finds its way into my home; maybe it's the promise of his unbridled love. Whatever it is, it enfolds me, wraps me up tightly to the extent I can barely breathe. But, it's not desire. It's fear.

The way this man makes me feel is frightening. All this time spent analysing his irrational behaviour has caused me to ignore my own. I realise I've given so much of myself, perhaps too much, too soon to someone who already has his life mapped out. My intervention nearly ruined him, nearly brought two decades of hard work crashing down around his ears. What if he hadn't been able to speak to me and I hadn't been able to get him back on track? It doesn't bear thinking about.

What if we aren't meant to be together? He'll be able to cope, he has the survival gene. Of course he'll miss me but his life will go on. I can't say the same for mine.

I unwind my hands from around my arms and take a swig of wine. Nothing's going to go wrong, I tell myself.

I reach back in time and hold onto words Charlie said all those years ago. "Stop thinking you caused what happened to you. It wasn't your fault. You deserve to be loved, you're not soiled goods."

Right now, that's exactly how I feel. My fear stems from the horrifying idea Ayden will stop loving me when he knows what happened to me. I won't be his little genie or his clever monkey any more. I'll be back to being ordinary me. That thought scares the hell out of me.

Remembering my insistence that he check his email, I compose a goodnight message and prepare a musical attachment. He is still sending me love songs even though we have resolved our differences and we're closer than ever. Here I am, a self-confessed media junkie, keeping some of the best love songs ever written to myself. He said we should create our own soundtrack and that has to begin with the songs we fell in love to. I have just the song to ease him into a gentle repose.

From:	songbirdBP@hotmail.co.uk
To:	a.s.mediainternational1@global.com
Date:	25th October 10.20
Subject:	DREAMING OF YOU

What Means the Most: Colbie Caillat

Having had your chance to shine, and shone sooooo brightly, I'd like to put the romance that you missed so badly last night, back into our long distance relationship. This song spells out EXACTLY how I feel about you: these words from my lips, to your heart.

I love you, Ayden

B x

Having endured a restless night spent mentally preparing for my first holiday without Charlie, and with one of the most eligible bachelors in the western hemisphere, I'm sitting in my travelling clothes: black silk blouse with silver poker dots, black fitted trousers, black boots and silver scarf, all courtesy of Emporio Armani, by way of Ayden Stone. I also have a black military coat to throw over my arm, just in case.

It's 10.50a.m., Katy Perry sings *Wide Awake* on the radio and the song reminds me that, for the first time in my life, I truly am. Ayden has opened my eyes to the possibility of real happiness, a far cry from the mundane existence I called a life before he came along. My wish has become my reality; I'm being swept away, carried along on a tide of immeasurable joy, embarking on a sensual adventure with the best of guides.

When I hear his car pulling up outside, an involuntary scream leaves my mouth. Thrown off balance by the butterflies in my stomach, I stumble over my handbag in my eagerness to get my hands on him before he reaches my door. Taking a moment to compose myself, I stop and take a breath and pull open my front door and then the external security door.

As he steps from the car I'm enraptured by the sight of male perfection. He looks too good: black jeans, grey sweater and a zip-up, designer jacket that accentuates his broad shoulders. Forgetting every rational thought in my head, I run down the path to greet him, spurred on by his easy, heart stopping smile; the one he saves for me. With the speed of an Olympic sprinter, I reach him and wrap my arms around his neck.

His hands are gripping my waist, and he's lifting and spinning me around. "That's what I call a welcome." He grins affectionately, obviously taken aback by my impulsive behaviour.

"I've missed you," I admit much too readily. Feeling his soft lips against mine, I dissolve into him.

He holds my face in his hands. "Hello. You're a sight for sore eyes, Beth. I've missed you too. Are you ready?"

"As ready as I'll ever be." I'm nodding my head and shrugging my shoulders, unashamedly excited.

"Then let's go." He turns towards the car.

"What about my cases?"

"Lester will collect them. Give him your passport." I look up and he's already on his way over to my apartment.

"Can't you get them?" I ask.

"I can, but I won't because if I take one step inside with you, we'll miss the flight." He's tipping his head to one side, coupling it with a suggestive smile. Is it any wonder I'm feeling light-headed? When am I going to stop feeling this way? We're fully dressed, it's before midday and already I'm imagining this gorgeous man doing all kinds of naughty things to me. Be still my beating heart.

I follow Lester inside, collect my handbag and coat and thank him for his help. "Here's my passport and the tickets. I'll lock the door behind you."

"Thank you, Miss Parker."

Without so much as a flicker, he slips the documents into his inside pocket, lifts up both cases and secures them in the boot. We're all set.

It's much warmer in the car and I can hear music playing. It's not classical or jazz, it's commercial radio. I can't hide my surprise.

"You have the radio on?"

"Yes, it's a local radio station. I'm carrying out market research, you never know when that perfect song might come along." He winks and turns away.

I laugh quietly. "Are you a convert, Mr. Stone?" I wait for a humorous reply.

"A guy's got to believe in something, it might as well be the regenerative power of music. It works for you."

I present a flat smile and I'm treated to a whisper of a kiss on my right hand. "You look lovely."

"Thanks. You don't look too shabby yourself."

I bump into his shoulder and he bumps me back. I smile aimlessly at the world outside as it passes by, happy to enjoy the connection. When I turn to face him, I catch him looking at me. So fierce is his scorching stare I cannot look away. I feel naked, stripped of any pretence, ensnared. My pulse starts to race. He knows what he's doing. Silent seduction, it's what he does best. Can he see the depth of my love for him, I wonder? Am I that transparent?

"Stop it!" I admonish. "I know what you're doing with your fuck-me eyes. Just don't"

He throws his head back in raucous laughter and treats me to the sexiest grin. "Oh Beth, you're adorable. I can't wait to be inside you."

Why does he say things like that?

I feel his left arm around my shoulders and a wet kiss beneath my ear. Now he has me squirming in my seat, but I have a rebuttal. It's my turn to fight back

"I've a good mind to sit on your lap and wriggle around until you come in your pants."

He's calling my bluff, opening his jacket and outstretching his arms along the length of the headrest. "Be my guest."

Oh I want him so badly when he's like this, carefree and playful. As hard as I try, I can't stop smiling. "No. I don't want to crease these trousers. You paid a lot of money for them." It's the only answer I can think of and, regardless of what I say I know I'll be out-manoeuvred.

"Then I'll buy you another pair in Rome."

I knew it. He's like a chess player, always one step ahead. With a soft voice I make my final move. I whisper in his ear, "The only time I want you to crease these expensive trousers, is when you take them off, lay me across your knee and spank me. After all, you did promise."

He lowers his arms and sits quietly, licking his lips and loosening the collar on his sweater. "I'll wait."

I hold back on a triumphant smile. Is this what winning feels like? No wonder Ayden regards it as his mission statement.

To my surprise, we are whisked through security and passport control via a side entrance. He takes my hand and rushes me along a glass panelled corridor.

"Where are we going?" I ask between breathless gasps.

"To catch our flight, it leaves in thirty minutes."

"What about the luggage?" I turn, looking for Lester but we're moving too fast and I trip.

"For Christ's sake, try and stay on your feet."

"I am. You try slowing down. If you were planning on sprinting to the plane you should have told me. I'd have worn trainers." I'm becoming breathless and he's laughing at me.

"The luggage has been taken care of. Don't worry, your Jimmy Choos are in good hands."

A professional looking brunette in her early thirties, dressed in a black suit and sensible shoes, approaches us. She recognises Ayden. "Mr. Stone, Miss Parker, good morning. Can I take your passports please?"

He dismisses her, he is much too self-possessed. We keep moving. "They're with my chauffeur," he calls out.

She looks down the corridor, offers a polite smile but it's wasted on us. It's obvious Ayden knows where he's going, and he has neither the time or inclination for polite conversation.

"Why are we going this way?"

"I don't stand in line for anything, Beth, we're not flying commercial. We're taking the company jet." He notices my surprise. "It's the only way to fly."

"Of course it is," I muse, finding his hand around my waist.

"Jump in."

He points to a black limousine parked outside the exterior door. The cold air hits me. I shudder before quickly settling myself on the black leather seat next to him.

"The Challenger, Mr. Stone?" asks the immaculately dressed chauffeur.

"Yes, it should be fuelled and ready for take-off."

With that we wind our way across the airfield, coming to rest beside a sleek and glossy private jet in white and navy blue. Etched on the side of it is Challenger 300 and underneath that: A.S. Media International. I step out of the limousine, wrapping my coat around my shoulders. It's cold and it's noisy but so exciting.

"Let's get on board," Ayden calls out above the vibrating sound of the turbines, stretching out his hand for me to ascend first.

I take the six steps up and I'm on board, turning my head from left to right. Wow! "Oh, Ayden, it's spectacular." I turn and kiss him. "This is a wonderful surprise. Will you show me round?"

"Sure, welcome aboard." He begins the tour. "This is the galley." He rejects it and moves on. "This is the seating area, as you can see there are four leather seats, and that's our lunch."

I nod in approval at the antipasto selection of cold meats, cheese, olives and champagne.

"Obviously we have TV, WiFi and an iPod station etcetera." He leads me to the back of the aircraft. "Back here there are two more chairs and a couch which, incidentally, opens out into a bed."

There's that knockout fusion of a sexy smile and arched brows: a winning combination. It's a well-considered body blow that leaves me tingling all over.

"Very convenient."

"Yes it is." He turns about. "So that's it. I'll leave you to discover the wash room and the shower for yourself. Take a seat."

I look around. "Where?"

"Anywhere," he smiles. "We're the only passengers, take your pick."

I settle myself into a forward facing, white, leather chair. "I'll sit here, although I'd much prefer your lap," I tease, feeling way too giddy for a woman of my age.

He lifts his chin feigning arrogance. "Oh don't worry, you'll be spending a lot of time on my lap in the next couple of days." He positions himself opposite me. "I think it's time for us to make a toast." He pours out two tall glasses of champagne. "Cheers."

I watch the bubbles as they dance and pop excitedly in the glass. I know how they feel. "Cheers, let's drink to memorable days and unforgettable nights."

He smiles broadly. "Why not?"

There's the sound of someone boarding the aircraft. Ayden turns and the smile fades.

"Mr. Stone, here are your passports. Can we store the luggage for you?"

He moves aside and a male, uniformed employee passes me with our cases then proceeds to arrange them in the storage area.

"Thank you." I smile and get a polite one in return.

"Have a good flight." The brunette leaves, giving me an envious smile.

"Do you want to keep these?" Ayden asks, handing me the passports.

"I can do." I take hold of our passports and walk to the rear of the plane to secure them in my handbag. Leaving him to chat with the pilot, I take a peek at his passport photograph.

His passport is eight years old, he was 24 when this picture was taken. He looks stunning and so young, so ardent. I reflect on what I was doing at 19. Not much. There he was building an empire and there I was working my way through an English Degree at Cambridge. My mother had been dead for eight years, and my father was still finding it hard to come to terms with the loss of the only woman he had ever loved. Little did I know, before my 20th birthday I would be an orphan.

It's amazing how a photograph can bring back so many memories. My passport photograph tells a very different story. It's only five years old: what a sombre individual I was.

One look at Ayden and I'm brought back to the present with a jolt. From the doorway I watch him conversing with the co-pilot. He's charming, captivating and so handsome.

Realising I've been gone too long, he calls out. "Everything alright?"

With the documents and my life history safely stowed I jump out, making a dramatic entrance. "I'm still here, I haven't bailed out."

He moves over to me and kisses my forehead. "Buckle up. The pilot says we have clearance for take-off."

"Great." I sidle over to my seat of choice. Little does he know, but I'm a nervous flier. I try to pacify myself by looking out of the window but without any direction from me, my thumb nail finds its way to my mouth.

"Are you alright?" He asks. "Or are you trying to see just how quickly you can get me hard with your little girl antics?"

"No, I'm not. I don't like take-offs and landings." I take my thumb nail from my teeth and force a smile.

"Now she tells me." He leans forward in his chair. "Do you want to hold my hand?" He stretches out his hand and I do the same, but the seat belts are too tight and it's uncomfortable.

"Shit! I can't sit like this. Come on."

He unbuckles his belt, then mine and leads me to the couch. Leaning over, he secures my belt, sits beside me and buckles himself in too. He grabs my left hand and sandwiches it between his. "Better?"

"Much. Thank you."

I kiss his right cheek and mentally prepare myself for take-off. I'm quaking with fear, but there's no place I would rather be than holding the hand of the man I love, on our way to one of the most beautiful cities in the world.

Buon viaggio.

After a smooth take-off, we're soaring through the clouds up to a flight ceiling of 45,000 feet. The food is great and the company is even greater. Ayden is the perfect host, treating me to humorous anecdotes and tales of Far Eastern adventures. It's refreshing to see him so relaxed.

I told him after his trip to L.A. I may love him more, and I was right. I do. But feeling this way and showing him are two very different things. I know I push him too hard. I tease and bend him to my will, disarm him for my own pleasure, taking no account of his feelings. When I look at him now, so refined, so special and yet so vulnerable, I'm reminded of his fragility. Less than a fortnight ago I made him a promise to take care of him, in whatever way I could. Like him, I always keep my promises.

Forty minutes in, he suggests we retire to the couch and I'm pleased to oblige. He disappears into the storage area and returns with an 'I have a secret' smile, which heightens my excitement.

"I wanted to say thank you for your help with the speech and I wasn't sure how. This is for you." He hands me a navy blue box about the size of a large egg.

"A simple thank you would have sufficed. What is it?"

"Open it and see." He looks very pleased with himself.

I peel the lid open and look up to him and gasp. Inside is a platinum bracelet with a kiss charm to match my necklace. It isn't until I lift out the bracelet I notice the extra special addition; a skilfully cut, midnight blue stone in the shape of a heart. It's exquisite.

"Oh, Ayden, you didn't have to buy me this," I gush. "It's beautiful."

I reach up to him and caress his face with my hand. He leans into it and a warm glow finds its way to my heart, radiates out and envelops him like a cloak. "Will you put it on for me?" He fastens it around my wrist and I hold it up to the light and shake my hand. "I'll treasure it."

He moves towards the single chairs and strokes my hair on the way. "I have to check a couple of things, can you amuse yourself for a while?"

"Of course. I've got my kindle." I reach into my bag and lift it out.

"You can put music on if you want. Something off our iPods." He winks, knowing we have exactly the same music stored on them.

"I'll see what I can find." I run through my albums and put Colbie Collait on shuffle. I make a conscious decision to make myself useful and venture over to the galley area. There's a coffee percolator and a stocked fridge. Surely the pilot and co-pilot would appreciate a coffee and a snack? I knock on the cockpit door and pop my head inside.

My God, it's like mission control in here: knobs, dials, levers, buttons and, best of all, clear blue sky. They're surprised to see me. It would appear neither Ayden, or any of his passengers have ever ventured into their private space.

"I'm making coffee, can I get you anything?" They look at each other with puzzled expressions.

The pilot speaks for them both. "That would be very nice, Miss Parker. Thank you. No sugars, please."

"Yes Captain." I smile, glad to be of service.

The coffee is brewing nicely, giving me time to organise some biscuits. I glance over to Ayden; he's out of his seat and pacing. I can't quite catch what he's saying but the volume and the inflections tell me he's not offering words of praise. I decide against asking and prepare his coffee just the way he likes it: strong and black. I pour the steaming brew into two more cups and deliver it to our deserving pilots.

"Thank you, Miss Parker. You might want to buckle up, we're going to try and fly above it, but it's likely we'll run into some turbulence."

"OK. I'll let Mr. Stone know." I force a grateful smile.

The door clicks shut behind me and I rest my back against it. I may need to throw back another travel sickness tablet. I take one look at Ayden and I'm disinclined to break the news, he's so preoccupied with something. So much so his hand is resting on his neck for far too long. I want to help but I'm afraid to intervene. I'll wait. If he needs my help, he'll ask for it.

I place down his coffee cup but he doesn't notice. This trip is turning out to be a real eye-opener. I'm being given an insight into his working practice and, seeing him in action reminds me there's more than meets the eye when it comes to this wonderful man. I think I've been blinded by physical perfection: the come-to-bed eyes, coming to get you smile and what he can do with those hands ... this might be a voyage of discovery after all?

I listen to him putting the world to rights, he's authoritative and in total command. I can't take my eyes off him. He throws his phone down onto the chair and picks up the coffee cup, still deep in thought. I've become invisible, I'm not even acknowledged as the waitress.

"Did you make this?" I believe he is addressing me.

"Yes, there's more if you want another cup but be quick because the Captain says we're about to fly into some turbulence." I smile and return to my edition of *Gabriel's Inferno*; things are hotting up ...

"Did he tell you that?"

I nod.

"When?"

"When I took in their coffee and you were on the phone."

"You served them coffee?" He's astonished and shaking his head in disbelief.

"Yes, so drink yours and buckle up." To stress the point I click my own into place, watching him seat himself opposite me. "Have you sorted out your problem?"

He turns his head clockwise in a wide circle, in an attempt to ease the tension settling in his neck. "More or less. But it's nothing for you to worry about."

I take that as a thanks but no thanks to any offer of help. "Great. I'm sure you have everything under control."

Before I can continue, the sudden loss of altitude hits my stomach and every rational thought evaporates. The engines struggle to maintain altitude and the clear air turbulence has us bobbing and swaying like we're on an out of control rollercoaster: it's terrifying.

I scream, "Shit!" When I look at Ayden, he isn't exactly scared but he isn't smiling either. He's a seasoned flyer and has experienced this before, but *not* with me.

"Is this normal?" I ask, holding onto the arms of my chair with knuckles the colour of melted snow.

"We're okay, Beth. It'll take a minute or two but we'll get through it. This is one of the safest aircrafts there is."

He holds out his hand to me but I can't release my grip on the chair. "Perhaps I should have mentioned it before, but it's not just the take-offs and landings I hate. I'm not too fond of the middle bit either, especially when it's like this."

I feel the colour draining from my face. With every abnormal fall I scream.

"Look at me, Beth."

I lift my eyes from the floor.

"Just look at me and tell me about Rome. What are we going to do when we get there? I know you must have something planned."

Nice distraction Ayden...

"I've found us a little ... Ah! ... restaurant that has great ... Ah! ... reviews ... it's in the centre so we can stroll ... Ah!" I give up trying to speak. I can't think straight. I'm dizzy. I'm going to be sick.

"Beth! Beth!"

I hear him calling my name but I feel too out of it to answer. His expression turns suddenly very solemn. In a flash he's out of his seat cursing, swaying, struggling to keep his balance. He's unbuckling my seatbelt. What is he doing? He's lifting, carrying me to the rear of the plane.

We land heavily on the couch, and he wedges his feet against the opposite seat and holds me on his lap, rocking me like an injured child. I close my eyes, wrap my arms around his neck and whimper. His reassuring words and soft kisses make the ordeal bearable and, for the first time in the longest thirty minutes in my life, I feel safe.

The plane levels out, I release my grip and frame his face with my sweating palms; it's warm to the touch, an angelic visage. I find his mouth with mine and deliver a grateful kiss. His protective arms release me and adopt a very different role. No longer is he my saviour, he's my lover.

There's nothing like a near death experience to get the adrenaline pumping and pumping it is, making every muscle tighten and contract with an all-consuming need for sexual contact. I lift my leg over so I can straddle him, I'm so turned-on I'm losing control, forgetting where we are, willing him to take me.

"Beth, stop, we can't," he states in a less than convincing voice. "We can't."

"I need this, I need you, Ayden." I barely recognise myself.

"Not here. We can't. Not here."

Breathless with need, I hear myself pleading. "Stop saying that. Please, Ayden. You must have done it before?"

"No. Never." His startled look tells me he's being totally truthful.

Knowing that drives me on. His kisses intensify and find my throat, he brushes his lips beneath my ear and I make that sound he loves so much. "Ah."

It's enough to stimulate him to the point from which there is no return. He stands me upright and snatches my hand. "Come with me."

He escorts me to the rear of the plane like I'm under arrest for a crime of passion, and pushes me into the washroom. It's hardly spacious but there's room enough to do what he intends to do. He switches places and sits on the toilet seat, locking the door behind me. I reach down, fondle his erection through his jeans and revel at the sight of him leaning back, defenceless. The thought of doing this has been rattling around in my head all morning.

I take his tongue in my mouth and suck, deepening our kiss. Our moans echo around the small compartment.

"Jesus, Beth, you're killing me," he purrs.

I will hear none of it. "I'm not killing you. I'm loving you." Unable to hold back, I start rubbing myself against him. "Can't you tell?"

I want to feel his skin on mine, flesh on flesh. In a dramatic pull, I lift off his sweater, arms up, hair all over the place and then proceed to pin him down with my craving for forbidden sex. My hands are resting on pectoral muscles wrapped in scented hair and the fusion of the two is driving me wild.

I begin unbuttoning his black jeans, all fingers and thumbs. When I take hold of him in both hands, he utters a deep groan and tilts his head back. His noises ignite my steaming passion, my breathing hitches and my insides start to quiver. The aircraft is beginning to fight its way through clear air again, but I don't care, I'm too focused on Ayden's impressive hard on as it stands to attention, unsupported by my hands.

His hands are everywhere, gripping my thighs, devilish thumbs heading north, testing the durability of the seams as they progress towards my saturated crotch. He pulls down my trousers and lacy black panties in a most ungentlemanly fashion, but that's okay, we don't have time for lengthy foreplay. The sensation of his right hand sliding beneath me is unspeakably good. When the fingers of that hand make their way through wet flesh and insert me, my God I have to call out his name. "Ayden."

He's coming undone. "Forty six thousand feet and I'm here fucking you in the toilet. What the hell am I doing?"

With his free hand he grabs the back of my head and pulls my mouth forcefully onto his, so he can wrap his tongue around mine to the same rhythm as his invasive fingers. I keep time with my two handed grip on his pulsating cock whilst rocking into him and clenching forcefully around his fingers. I'm so close.

"Make me come." I plead into his mouth, yielding to my appetite for an orgasm. His left hand fists my hair while his thumb curves into position, massaging my clitoris in slow rhythmic circles. He has me right where he wants me, on the edge of an abyss.

Gasping for air I tighten and rock into him, scorching spears of fire burning me from the inside out. I come, screaming with ecstatic joy and ease back down to earth trembling.

Ayden has watched me up close and the beads of sweat forming on his nose and the darkness of his pupils confess his arousal. I lean into him and wipe his nose with my fingers.

"Do you have a condom?" I ask impetuously.

He gives me a reproving look and shakes his head.

"What do you want?"

His breath quickens at the prospect of ... something. In fractured breaths, he makes his request. "I want you to get on your knees and blow me."

Well that's unequivocal. I respond with an indignant stare; he mirrors my indignation. The man who was so masterful earlier, clearly has not left the 'building', he's very much alive and kicking right here in this confined space.

He senses my hesitation. "What's the problem?"

"Nothing." I try to ease my way onto the floor, but there's just something about kneeling on a toilet floor that troubles my sensibilities. No matter which way I move, I can't seem to position myself comfortably.

"You'll have to stand," I state, clambering up over his thighs, "There isn't enough room."

He rises and lifts me up briskly into a standing position, turning us around so we are facing in the opposite direction: now *his* back is against the door.

"Are you sure you've not done this before?" I ask, bright eyed. "You seem to have come up with a solution pretty quickly."

He rolls his eyes and starts to button up his jeans.

"Hey, not so fast, now we've sorted out the choreography, I want to dance." I unbutton my blouse and open it up. "See? You have me undoing *all* the buttons."

We share the memory and his mouth forms into a sexy smile. "You're very disarming, Miss Parker and very naughty."

"I'm also good at BJ's, apparently." I tip my head to the side and move in to him, allowing my mouth to caress his lips very, very gently. I make my way south whilst being manoeuvred backwards onto the toilet seat.

Once seated, I find myself perfectly positioned to carry out his request. I pull down both his jeans and his boxers and take a lecherous look; he stands before me, a glistening example of male, physical perfection. Taut skin stretched over sculptured abs and hips. How lucky am I?

His semi-erect penis falls into my right hand and I begin moving up and down, up and down, rubbing my thumb around the tip, coaxing him to harden. My new platinum bracelet tinkles and rattles as I move, a reminder of his love for me.

I gaze up at him through dark eyelashes, monitoring his arousal. He's open mouthed, his breathing is ragged, leaving his lungs in hot waves. "Why do I let you do this ... to me?" he asks, struggling to complete the sentence.

"Because you want me to. Because I want to," I declare confidently.

Within seconds he hardens, gently takes my head in both hands and puts me to work. I draw my tongue across my lips in preparation and boldly begin by licking the moist crown while both hands hold him in place. I mouth him, taking the rigid mass deeper and deeper into my throat, feeling his body folding over me and his knees starting to buckle. He outstretches his arms and presses his hands against the panelling to make the shape of a giant T. This is his Titanic moment and he doesn't even realise. I press on.

Each long, drawn out suck causes him to hiss with pure pleasure and causes me to squirm, wishing this rod of pure muscle was inside me.

"My God, Beth... suck me, deeper."

His wish is my command. I take him to the back of my throat and gaze up at him. I want to watch him fight for breath at that moment when I consume him with my gluttonous mouth.

"You're making me come so hard," he growls, watching me watching him.

The intensity of the connection is not wasted on either of us. In a spectacular display of masculine virility, he spurts into my mouth and I have to work hard to suppress a gag reflex. His body shudders and pulsates around me, until his groaning sounds subside and I release him.

He falls backwards onto the locked door, out of breath and spent. For some reason, he doesn't pull me close or offer me one of his grateful smiles. He looks dejected. Why?

Feeling downcast, I rearrange my clothes and take a hard look at myself in the mirror. I'm flushed, my lips are swollen, the water-proof mascara I applied this morning is intact but my hair is a tangled mess. I turn to Ayden, he's fixing the buttons on his jeans. I pass him his sweater, a little fearful of meeting his eyes. "Have I done something wrong?"

He wriggles into his sweater in the confined space, causing me to move left then right to avoid his outstretched arms. "No. Of course not." His head appears above the neckline. "You were ..." He considers his words. "The best."

I smile. "So were you, but then you always are." He pulls me close and I wrap my arms around him, feeling my ears popping. "We're descending. We'd better get seated." I pull away.

With the force of a tornado, he hauls me to him, spins me round so I'm pinned against the door by his flexing hips, and arches himself into me; he takes my face in his hands, then proceeds to consume me with feverish passion, kissing me until I am close to suffocation.

Scraping back my hair he leans backward and prepares to speak but ... Thoughts take shape, I see them forming behind his eyes, but he is unable to translate them into words. I wait. His face erupts into a broad smile and I see he's come to terms with whatever it was that was troubling him. But what the hell was it?

"Let's get ready to land."

With a single click the door opens and we tumble out, he breaks my fall and we begin giggling, even our eyes are laughing. I run my fingers through his hair, trying to rid him of that post orgasmic look, but it's hopeless. Even wearing a hat he'd still look the same: utterly fuckable.

Whilst I salvage what I can from my make-up and tame my hair with serum, I notice two extra coffee cups and saucers on the galley shelf: that makes all four, present and correct. The co-pilot must have returned them mid-flight. He will have seen the empty cabin and put two and two together. I don't have the heart to break the news to Ayden, but there is no doubting the fact, we have become honorary members of the Mile High Club.

14

Thankfully, our landing into Fiumincino airport is uneventful. Ayden takes my hand and we walk at a pace through empty hallways, catching sight of queuing tourists as we go. By the exit door, a well turned out gentleman with slicked back hair and a twinkle in his eye holds up a sign: **Stone**. I don't doubt it's meant for us. Ayden makes that assumption too and allows him to lead the way, leaving an airport employee behind us struggling with our bags on a trolley that refuses to stay pointed in the right direction.

Quickly, the bags are loaded and we ease into the traffic. The experienced driver weaves the limousine through parked cars and scooters. Sounding his horn for no apparent reason seems to be an unwritten rule.

It's a stop-go, thirty minute journey, to our destination: Hotel De Russie. From the outside it's not very grand; from the inside it's a revelation. Two eager doormen dressed in morning coats tip their tall hats to us and open the door to the ultra-modern reception which is captured in light cast by an impressive chandelier. Neither of the two female receptionists recognise him, but they are quick to recognise him as a man who does not suffer fools easily.

"We're booked into the Nijinsky suite for two nights, the name's Stone." With that, we are led to the lift. There's no check-in, no handing over of passports or form filling; apparently we can do that in our room.

A distinguished looking gentleman in a well cut, black suit and shiny shoes escorts us to the elevator and presses the button to the sixth floor. He leads the way into the suite, opening doors and pulling back full length drapes to reveal an enormous roof top terrace with panoramic views over Rome. There's a hilltop castle to the left and church spires to the right: it's spectacular. I turn to catch Ayden's eye and mouth: 'Wow!" but he simply rolls his eyes and directs the maid to the bedroom, where she's about to hang up our clothes.

He comes out onto the terrace to join me. I saunter over to him and take his right hand in mine. "It's lovely, Ayden." I plant a soft kiss on his cheek.

"You haven't even seen the suite yet," he replies, taking in the afternoon air.

"I know, but it's all wonderful."

The distinguished looking gentleman coughs by the door. "Excuse me, Mr. Stone, will there be anything else, Sir?"

"No, thank you ... Oh, is there Champagne in the fridge?"

"Yes Sir. But if you would prefer a particular brand or vintage, it can be arranged."

"Then send up three bottles of Krug Grande Cuvée, with some cheese and fruit."

"Of course. Mr. Stone, I'll get that now for you, Sir."

With that, he's off and we are left to appreciate Rome from a great height. "Shall we take a look at the suite?" I ask excitedly.

"Yes let's," he mimics with exaggerated enthusiasm.

I give him a dig in his arm. "Are you making fun of me, because if you are I'm going to have to get Elizabeth to sort you out." His raises a single brow and grins. "Stop that now. Be good."

Once inside I see the suite in all its glory; the larger of the two lounges is painted white, plush leather furniture in cream is accented with cushions in dark red and purple. Out of one doorway to the right, there's an enormous dining table, big enough to seat ten people. Off that, there's a kitchen and a library leading onto a spacious bedroom which is dominated by a king-sized bed, laden with gold coloured cushions and pillows.

The piece de resistance is the bathroom: it's stunning. Apart from the fact that it's as big as my apartment, it's a spa retreat embellished with mosaic tiling and marble tops. It's in a kind of Art Deco design, worthy of a photograph. Everything about this suite is exquisite. It's the perfect choice for us.

After losing myself in the countless rooms, I find Ayden in the study. I stand behind him, gazing over his shoulder at his laptop. "Have you seen how big this place is?" I ask, my voice raising half an octave. "You'll have to drag me out of here kicking and screaming." I smile into his hair.

"I'm glad you like it." He carries on reading and holds a conversation with me at the same time. "Do you want to do anything in particular? It's only four o'clock."

"I'd like to make up for the time you've been away and show you just *how* much I've missed you. Does that count as anything in particular?"

"I'd say so." His mouth begins to twitch.

"Or we could sit out on the terrace and relax for a couple of hours, drink fancy champagne and nibble on fruit before we get ready for dinner." I brush his hair; the soft black flicks are soft to the touch and smell of something delicious. "I'll let you decide."

"Thank you."

I think he's smiling but I can't tell from where I'm standing.

"As much as I like the sound of option number one, I think I may need a couple of hours to regroup. It's been a busy week. Option two sounds good."

I plant a soft kiss on his hair. "Alright then, champagne on the terrace it is."

I shift position so I'm perched on his desk. I want to see his handsome face and invite him to watch my appreciative words form and fall from my lips. "It's like a dream, you know, all this." I turn my head from left to right and then back to him. "Thank you for arranging it."

He dismisses what he's doing and faces me head on. His eyes are a soft diopside green, captivating. "It's my pleasure. I want you to be happy and this is just the start."

I reach out and caress his cheek. "You don't have to, you know. I don't expect it."

"I know and that's why I'm doing it. Besides, it's not an entirely altruistic gesture. I get to spend time away from the office with you."

"Well, when you put it like that, I suppose you should be thanking me." I kiss him softly. "You can thank me later." I squeeze his shoulder and head out towards the private terrace.

The sun is settling in the west and the terracotta rooftops are starting to take on a different dimension in the late afternoon light; shadows are forming and windows are becoming opaque. Families are gathering around kitchen tables and small children are getting ready for fathers returning home from work. Beyond this terrace, life goes on much the same as it did yesterday and the day before, but here time stands still. On this private terrace only the two of us exist and that's a very evocative thought.

Ayden directs both waiters to the table by the comfortable chairs to the left of the terrace and follows them out. He allows the more senior of the two to pop the champagne cork and pour.

"Cheers," Ayden whispers. "... To memorable days and unforgettable nights."

I smile broadly. "I've heard that before somewhere."

"And that's why I've repeated it, it was apt then and it's apt now."

I sit beside him, sipping the creamy, gold coloured champagne. The minute it touches my tongue, there's an explosion of flavour: it's delicious. We chat about my final day at school before breaking up for half term; having to throw myself across my case to close it and other incidentals. Being around each other is easy. It feels like a weight has been lifted from us, freeing our hearts and minds to explore the nature of our love, giving us time to foster our fledgling affair, to nurture it and watch it grow into ... I don't know what. Not yet.

They say it takes a storm to clear the air and we've weathered our storm and come out the other side better for it. Sitting on this terrace, with the world at my feet, I feel so blessed. Being here with this sexy, smart guy is beyond wonderful. He has no idea what he's done: he's come along and rescued me from a life of utter misery. He has never had or will ever have a white charger, that's not his style, but he has me and my heart: it sits in the palm of his hand like a pocket watch.

I'm going to ring reception and ask them to book us a table at Ad Hoc on Via di Ripetta. It's a quaint and romantic restaurant that is renowned for its typically Mediterranean cuisine. I found it on the internet and reviews were good. I know it's not what Ayden would choose, but I like the look of it.

**

Still vexed by the idea he has wasted a day, Dan is taking no chances. He's given his car a health check: oil, water, petrol. He's even topped up the windscreen wash bottles and that's something he never does. Having received some attention, his radiator is suffering in silence after its blow-out on the A1 yesterday; two hours wasted, waiting for the steam and heat to disperse from the metal casing and from his brain.

The journey home was mind-numbingly slow and he didn't arrive home until 1800hrs, with a sore head and sore hands. With every agonizing mile, the skin on his palms was becoming puffy and pink. He dug out some antiseptic cream from the bathroom cabinet, 18 months past its 'use before' date but it was better than nothing. He massaged it into his palms and flinched, watching the flesh deepen in colour from rose pink to the colour of over ripe raspberries.

Now, he holds them out in front of him, catches sight of himself in the mirror and laughs sardonically; he looks like a waiter without a tray or a saint, seeking divine intervention. Just the thought of it makes him smile. "I may be down, but I'm not out," he tells his reflection, not waiting for a reply. That thought is enough to lift his spirits. That combined with a medicinal dose of lager.

Being unable to eat yesterday was down to loss of appetite; not eating it today is not the result of psychosomatic tension, but physical impairment. Even lifting up a spoon is painful.

"What kind of daft sod grabs a bloody car bonnet when there's steam coming off it?" Ernie's shaking his head in disbelief.

"That stupid sod would be me."

"Didn't you think you'd get burned? It must have hurt like hell?" His face pulls into a grimace.

"Not at the time, but now ..." Dan overturns his hands and blows onto his glowing palms.

"It pains me to say it, but you're not much use around here if you can't pick stuff up."

Dan knows what's coming and starts to shake his head, annoyed with himself, with his stupidity. "Yeah, I know."

"We'll have to find something else for you to do or Crowther will be giving you your marching orders. Thank God it's Thursday, come Monday morning and we'll be up to our eye-balls in it."

"You're not wrong." Ernie's right. Unless he can be seen to be working, he'll be out on his ear.

Thinking out loud, Ernie comes to the rescue. "What about some painting? The gates could do with a touch-up. Can you hold a paintbrush?" It's a serious look for a serious question.

"Sure! I'm not a fucking invalid. I'll be as right as rain tomorrow."

"Don't count on it. I once over-filled a flask and it bubbled over onto my feet. Even though I had my socks on, it hurt like hell. Took the bloody skin off and blistered. Not a pretty sight, I can tell you." He glances over to his feet and circles his ankles. "Alright now though."

"It's not that bad. I've had worse sunburn than this and lived to tell the tale."

"Maybe, but I'll get you a pair of gloves and a couple of pads."

"Cheers." Dan throws down the last drops of his tea, holding onto the handle with the tips of his fingers like a Dickensian aunt.

They stand. Ernie pats Dan on his back. "No problem champ. We'll soon have you fighting fit."

"It'll take more than a pair of gloves and a couple of pads for that." Dan grins. "More like a fucking miracle."

By lunchtime, Dan is ready to punch the wall, so bad is the pain seeping from his hands. He cannot think to eat or to speak. Instead he takes himself off to his locker in search of two items: pain relief and light relief in the shape of Elizabeth Parker. He swallows two painkillers in one heavy gulp and checks for unwelcome bystanders. There are some habits that are hard to kick: one is smoking and two is jerking off to her image. He needs a couple of minutes alone with her to help him feel better.

He disappears into the cubicle and puts her picture on top of the cistern while he fiddles with his belt and his zip. It takes longer than usual and, before he can finish off what he's started, he has unwelcome guests. A couple of familiar voices start up a conversation only a couple of feet from him about football matches and transfer fees, making it impossible for him to concentrate.

Looking at her and having to listen to them ... it just isn't happening. He closes his eyes and tries again, but the minute she comes into view he's forced to break off. Their laughter is too loud and their proximity is too distracting. He gives up. He dresses himself as quickly as he can and looks up the moment he hears his name being called. It's Ernie.

"Are you in here champ? I've brought a sandwich over, in case you get peckish later. Dan?"

"Thanks. I'll be right out." For effect, he flushes the toilet and flicks back the lock.

"They only had ham salad, but it's better than nothing." Ernie places it on the bench. "Everything okay?"

Dan is close to breaking point. "Yeah, just fucking peachy." He snatches the sandwich and heads towards the exit door, pushing past his twin interrupters and catching a shoulder on the way. There is no denying that he is feeling two sets of discomfort, one from his hands and the other from a perverse need to hit or fuck someone, preferably Elizabeth Parker and not necessarily in that order.

As usual, his shift ends at 1400hrs and he manages to slip into his own clothes with as little help as possible from Ernie. Before placing his clothes inside his locker, he lifts up the prospectus to say a sarcastic, "see you later" to Ms. Parker but, when he reaches in to grab the photograph, it's not there. In wild panic, he drags out the contents of his locker: old wage slips, letters, memos and his clothes fall onto the floor in an untidy pile. His thoughts leave his mouth in an involuntary yell. "Where the fuck are you?"

Ernie stands back and folds his arms. "Lost something, champ?"

Dan doesn't hear him. Instead, he's rummaging around on the tiled floor, using his fingertips to sift through the heap.

"Looking for this?" A guy wearing dark blue jeans holds the missing photograph so low down, it almost touches Dan's nose.

He's torn: does he say no and carry on looking for something, anything? Or does he say thank you and put her back where she belongs? He decides to play safe and carries on looking. He's got plenty of other photos but ... not that one. Not of her wearing that tight, black sweater.

"No, I had a lottery ticket and I think I had a tenner on it to collect. Put it in my locker this morning but, what with my fucking hands, I must have lost it."

"Oh, this isn't yours then?" Blue Jeans takes a look at the photo and instinctively both of Dan's hands form into stony fists, making him wince with pain. He says nothing, but rises from the floor, holding the contents of his locker, unable to bear the thought of anyone looking at her, not that way.

"She's a sweet little thing."

Dan turns away and wrinkles his eyes, as if doing that will shut out the words and the image of him salivating over his girl. Yeah, that's what she is, *his* girl. She'll always be *his* girl. "Where did you find *her*?" He cannot bring himself to look at him.

"She was sitting pretty on the cistern in there." Blue Jeans points to the cubicle from where Dan emerged. "I expect she was keeping someone company, if you know what I mean …?" He gives Dan a wink, turns and makes his way out of the changing room. "I think I'll take her home with me. I've got a bit of a sweet tooth myself."

No fucking way!

The thought of his hands on her, him forcing her to do all kinds of things to him is simply too much to bear. Dan calls out after him, "That ain't happening … give me the fucking picture."

Blue Jeans stops dead in his tracks. Dan has not touched him, but the tenor of his voice resonates across the walls like the aftermath of a roar: it hits him like a body blow. Slowly, as if initiating a duel, he turns to face him. "I thought you said she wasn't yours?"

Dan recognises a rival when he sees one. "Take a dive mate. She sure as fuck ain't yours." He watches him squirm

"And she's not yours either *mate*, is she?"

"Yes. She is." He approaches him and reaches out one inflamed hand for the photo. He'll do anything to get it back and, from the menacing look on his face and the way his lips are welded together, there's no doubting it.

"And what if I don't, what if I want her to suck my dick? What will you do then, bust-up your fucking hands even more?" He takes hold of the photo and pretends to tear it in two, provoking Dan, goading him on; playing with fire.

Dan takes a menacing step forward.

"Here, take her." He throws the photo onto the floor. "I prefer blondes anyway." He shrugs his shoulders and leaves the room. Dan can hear him whistling nonchalantly as he disappears down the corridor.

Ernie has been a silent onlooker. He stretches out a hand and places it on Dan's arm, but Dan flinches and he pulls it back and slips it into his trouser pocket. "Let it go, champ. You got your photo back, no harm done. Best leave it for another day, eh?"

Dan is too enraged to speak; his heart is thumping out of his chest and flaming breath is leaving his body in waves. He retrieves the photo, blows on it, wipes it clean against his shirt and slips it back into his locker. He slams the door shut and locks it. Says nothing.

Sensing his need for silence, Ernie escorts him to the car park and they go their separate ways. Dan sits in his car, gripping the steering wheel with smouldering palms and catches sight of himself in the passenger window. "Nearly lost you, princess, but you know I won't let anyone take you away from me, don't you?" He flinches and turns the ignition key, his face contorted with agonizing pain and indecent thoughts.

"Yes!" His heart leaps when he sees her black Fiesta parked up in its space on the cul-de-sac, and then he realizes the implications. She may come out at any moment and blow his cover, jeopardizing the whole operation. He needs to think it through.

His watch says 1600hrs. The late afternoon clouds are grouping and wrapping themselves around the insipid sun. Soon it will be dark. Feeling the need for reassurance, he takes out his wallet; tucked behind two five pound notes and a twenty is a battered, old photograph. He holds *Beth* Parker between his forefinger and thumb. Images of their time together begin to tilt his mind, inclining him towards dark and lecherous recollections.

The photograph slips easily into its hiding place but something in front of it holds his attention: it's Elise Richard's business card. That too fits nicely between his finger and thumb. He taps his chin with the edge, feeling it catch against his stubble. He had intended to give her a call but hadn't got round to it. 'Now's as good a time as any,' he reminds himself. 'Besides, I've got nothing better to do.'

Miss. Richards answers the office phone on the third ring. "Hello, Taylor & Main, Elise speaking. Can I help you?"

"I hope so, Miss Richards. It's Dan Rizler from Elm Gardens."

"Ah yes, Mr. Rizler. How are you settling into the apartment?"

"I'm getting there. It's Dan by the way."

"That's good to know ... Dan. What can I help you with?"

"Well, I was wondering if I could buy you a thank you drink. You really pushed the boat out, getting me into the place in a couple of days." He listens for her reply.

"Well, that's very nice of you, but it isn't necessary."

"I know that, but I thought it might be nice to get together and have a chat. I don't know anyone this side of the city and you seemed like such a lovely lady." He rubs his aching hand across his mouth, holding back on a smirk.

"Oh, thank you."

As he suspected, she's not used to receiving compliments. "So what do you say?" He knows it would be unwise to rush her. She has to decide for herself. That's all part of the game.

"Well ... I suppose I could meet you for a drink after work."

"Great. I know where your office is. I'll meet you there in an hour at 6 o'clock. OK? Don't want you walking around the city centre on your own at night, do we?"

"That's very considerate of you ... Dan."

I'm a considerate guy.

"I look forward to seeing you then."

"See you in an hour."

"Bye, Miss Richards." The card slips snugly back into his wallet. He pulls down the sun visor to check himself out.

"And there you were, thinking you'd lost your touch." He's tipping his head from left to right checking his profile, feeling the bristles on his chin with his fingertips. "A bit of spit and polish and you'll be as good as new."

He takes a lingering look at the three story apartment block. She's in there; she's within his reach and ... who the fuck are the two guys in blue overalls walking in and out of the building? It's then he notices the white transit van; it's open at the rear and inside are shelves organised one on top of the other, rows and rows of electronic equipment.

With his rucksack over his shoulder and his clothes and toiletries stuffed into a shopping bag, he saunters over. A young guy is up a small ladder fixing a box to the wall. Another, older man is inside 53a by the window, pulling wires and cables through.

One word comes to mind. 'Alarm!' He seizes the moment. "Hey, what you putting in, satellite TV?"

The younger of the two men looks across to him dismissively. "No, it's an alarm system. Or it will be if we can get these bloody wires through."

"Oh right. You can never be too careful these days." Casually, he slips his hand into the pocket of his jeans. "I'm upstairs in 53c."

Knowing that puts the young man at ease. "Oh right, sorry for the noise. We're under strict orders to get it done pronto; had to put everything else on the back burner to sort this out."

"No pressure then?"

"Not much. It's got to be installed today and that means we'll be here until the job's done." He shakes his head despairingly.

"I'm going to put the kettle on, do you want a brew?"

"Wouldn't say no."

"What about your mate?" Dan pokes his head through the front door of 53a. "Cup of tea?" In the time it takes for the distracted technician to answer, he's given the apartment the once over.

It's just the way he expected it to be, tidy and inviting; cushions are strewn over a comfortable cream sofa and a marble fireplace is decorated with crystal candle holders and expensive ornaments. Above the fire is an enormous mirror in a gilded frame into which her world is reflected. For a couple of seconds, he's dumbstruck.

"That would be great, thanks. No sugar."

"No problem." He turns to leave but is rooted to the spot. In a tray by the door is a set of keys. Noticing that both men are engrossed in their work, he snatches them from the tray, makes for the stairs and keeps walking. The cold, hard metal digs into his pulsating palm, but that's okay. It's a small price to pay for having access to her private world.

Just as he's about to turn and take a step towards his apartment, he becomes aware of the presence of someone behind him. Does he turn or keep on walking?

"Good evening, Dan, I saw you park up."

He decides to throw her a bone. "Sorry, can't stop to chat, got a phone call from an old girlfriend, meeting her at six for a drink." He smiles over his shoulder, hoping that morsel of gossip will give her something to gnaw on.

"That's nice. Everyone seems to be meeting friends and going places at the moment." She laughs.

Everyone?

"How's that?"

"Well, you're having a drink with a lady friend and Beth downstairs has gone off to Rome with her handsome gentleman friend. Oh, what it is to be young. You're a very lucky man, Dan."

"Yes I am," he answers sarcastically.

Who the fuck goes to Rome on a Thursday afternoon?

Fearing she may have picked up on the sarcasm, he softens it. "Although, I've never been to Rome either."

"Haven't you?"

He shakes his head.

"Well she's only gone for a couple of days, she'll be back on Saturday. Maybe you can meet her then?"

"I hope so." He isn't lying. "Night, Pat."

"Night, Dan."

He can barely bring himself to open the front door. The place is costing him £600 a month and four days in, he's got nothing to show for his investment other than a broken chair and two fucked-up hands. Inside the sparsely furnished apartment, there's the smell of emptiness; no-one home to throw out the welcome mat, not even Honey to meet and greet him by the door. Exhausted from emotional torment and physical pain, he checks his watch. It's 1650hrs. Just time to make a brew, freshen up and hit the road, but not before he's got the name and address of a key cutting shop in town.

While the kettle boils, he flicks through the Yellow Pages left on the floor by the front door. 'Keys ... locksmiths ... cutting.' Quickly he makes a note of the telephone number and address and prepares two mugs of tea. The sensation of hot water on his prickly palms is excruciating but he's way past caring about something as insignificant as that. Meeting his reflection, he smiles through it. 'Got her keys, got a date. You're boxing clever, Danny boy.'

He slams his door behind him and descends two flights. "Here we are, two teas. I've got to shoot out for a couple of hours. Looks like you'll be here for a while. Do you want a sandwich or anything?" He's role playing the kindly neighbour.

"No thanks, mate. The lady upstairs made us a sandwich a couple of hours ago, so we're alright for now." They sip on the tea and glance around the apartment. "Cosy, isn't it?"

Yes, it's just how you'd expect my girl to live ...

"If you like that sort of thing," Dan replies, turning up his nose. He leaves them to their beverages. "See you later."

The drive into the city centre takes twenty minutes with the traffic. Dan parks adjacent to the small shop on St. Anne's Road. While dodging cars he's turning the keys over and over in his hand; he's become desensitized to the pain and is riding on a wave of adrenalin and opportunism.

The keys to the front door and the French doors are cut in less than twenty minutes, leaving him ample time to get across town to meet Elise Richards.

The minute the fingers on his watch stretch out into a vertical line, Dan takes the key from the ignition and prepares to climb out of his car. The Taylor and Main office is only four doors down from the lay-by, making it possible for him to see Ms. Richards in his rear view mirror. He hopes she's not late, of the many things that tick him off, tardiness comes top of the list: that, and a smart mouth.

Right on time, she appears, carrying an oversized bag, looking as if she's about to spend a weekend away at a spa resort. Her blonde hair is swept back behind her ears, her jeans are a tight fit and she's made an effort to look her best. The light from the window display illuminates her face. Dan hadn't paid her much attention before but, from this distance she's quite pretty, but limp wristed. Dan to the rescue.

"Miss Richards, let me help you, you look like you have your hands full."

She's flustered but happy to let him pull the door to and struggle with the lock. "Hello, Mr. Rizler. Thank you."

He hands her back the keys. "No problem. It's Dan remember? Where do you want to go for a drink?"

"There's a wine bar around the corner?"

Wine? I had you as more of a lager girl.

"Great."

She looks at him from under her fringe. "I need to put this bag in my car first." Her car alarm flashes next to his recovering BMW.

"Nice car." Dan nods towards the black Golf GTI, less than a year old. "Jeez. You must have sold a lot of houses?"

She seems a little embarrassed and flushes the colour of a sugar coated pear drop. "Not really, it was a birthday present from a friend."

"I wish I had a friend like that," Dan declares, expecting to hear more. He waits in vain

She slams down the boot and turns to him. "I'm ready for that drink now."

"Then lead the way." He stretches out his hand and allows it to remain behind her, not touching, just making it clear to anyone watching, they are together.

The wine bar is only 100 yards away, past the row of shops. It's the kind of establishment he would go out of his way to avoid, normally; all canvases, candles and cushions. The pretty barmaid looks scarcely old enough to be serving drinks and the young man opening up a bottle of Pinot Grigio has barely the muscular strength to extract the cork. Dan is a fish out of water.

They settle themselves on a curved red, tapestry seat to the left of the doorway; far enough away to avoid the autumn chill but close enough to the bar to suggest a lack of romantic involvement.

"What do you want to drink?"

"Do they serve lager?"

I knew it!

"I hope so." Dan whips up an agreeable smile.

"Then that's what I'll have."

A couple of minutes later, he returns with two tall, decorative glasses of lager that are golden and iridescent against the flickering tea light on the mosaic table. He wants to say, *"Do you know how much they charged me for these?"* Instead all he says is, "Cheers."

"Cheers."

An observer would easily pick-up on the newness of their relationship. They are virtually strangers and that's exactly how they look: awkward and uncomfortable, neither of them wanting to prompt conversation for fear they may say they wrong thing.

Dan bites the bullet. "I didn't think you'd say yes when I invited you for a drink."

Sensing an approaching compliment, Elise responds by putting down her heavy glass and turning to him. "Why not?"

"You must get hit on all the time and I'm not what you'd call dating material."

"I'm flattered you think that, but you're wrong, on both counts." She reaches into her bag and checks her phone. He's surprised by her directness. He'd under-estimated her, she's not a woman to be messed with. He likes that.

"Thanks. I'm not much of a socialiser, you might have guessed that?"

"Socialising is over-rated. I don't get out much either. I used to, but not anymore." Her words take her attention away from the conversation to another dimension. Her devil-may-care past, perhaps.

"How long have you worked at the estate agents?" He focuses on his lager, taking a long, refreshing gulp and enjoying the coolness of the glass against his right palm.

"For almost eight years, I'm hoping to have my own branch soon. I've attended lots of courses and they say I have a great future ahead of me." She seems genuinely excited at the prospect and then, realising how animated she had become, looks down and settles her hands on her lap.

"That doesn't surprise me. You sorted me out quick enough." Dan lifts up his glass. "Thanks." She does the same and gives him a 'you're welcome' smile.

"What about you? You must have had an interesting life?"

What the fuck does that mean?

"If you mean as a boxer, then yes. I s'pose I have."

"Yes, that's what I mean." She focuses on his features, at a nose that has been broken and mended four times and the small scars around his eye-brows. "Were you any good?"

Well yeah ...

"I had my moments ... fought at Wembley stadium and sparred with Mike Tyson once." He throws her a wink and picks up his half empty glass. "Didn't make enough money to retire on, but I don't complain."

"At least you had a go." Her mouth curves into a half smile. "Most people accept their lot without so much as a whimper. You stepped into the ring and fought back." She smiles quickly and returns to her drink.

You're right about that ...

He accepts the compliment. "I s'pose."

She checks her phone again and, visibly disappointed, throws it into her bag.

"Expecting a call?" Dan enquires casually.

"Not exactly. I texted a friend and haven't heard back from them yet." Realising her rudeness, she pulls down her blouse and angles her body in his direction. "Ever had a friend who let you down?"

What the fuck?

"Sure ... that's why I keep myself to myself, I roll with the punches." He does a kind of sparring move, fists close to his chest.

She sniggers and shakes her head from left to right, finding him comical in a friendly sort of way. "I'll leave you to your memories. I'm going to powder my nose."

He follows her with his eyes all the way to the end of the bar, sees her squeeze between four young men, throwing back shots and laughing out loud. Left alone with his thoughts, he's replaying their conversation; he's good at that, remembering words and faces.

As a rule, Dan Rizler doesn't rile easily, not as far as fighting is concerned; his 'weapons of mass destruction' could cause serious damage if he let them fly. Better to keep them under wraps, under-control. Usually, his size is deterrent enough, but these fuckers by the bar are seriously pushing his buttons. He's come for a quiet drink. If he'd wanted rowdy, he'd have gone to a bar with big screens and a karaoke machine.

When Elise returns from the bathroom, the noisy foursome are ready for her; they block her path and ensnare her with their crude suggestions. Dan gives them time to back-off and to see how she handles herself. She eyes them with disdain and tries to push her way through, but one of them takes hold of her arm. That's it!

Dan steps from his seat, knocking a chair over in his wake and approaches the boisterous crowd. Without a word, he takes hold of the hand on Elise's arm, removes it and slowly crushes it in his oversized paw. "I don't think the lady wants to play, boys."

Crouching, his victim calls out in agony.

"Now is there anything you'd like to say to this lovely lady before you leave?" The timbre of his voice is chilling and, when it's coupled with a flat smile that doesn't even touch his eyes, they have no misgivings about his malevolence: he's capable of anything.

Not surprisingly, they apologise, drink up and make a speedy exit. One of them nursing a hand which will probably be useless for several days.

Elise sits herself down, unruffled by the incident. "I didn't need rescuing, you know. I was perfectly capable of handling them myself."

Dan didn't doubt that for a minute. "I could see that, but I was getting lonely over here and they were taking up too much of your time."

"Then you should learn to be more patient Dan – it's a virtue, you know?"

Tell me about it!

"I'll bear that in mind next time, Elise."

"Next time?" She feigns surprise.

"Yeah, Saturday, you eat lunch don't you?"

"Was that an invitation?"

He nods and empties his glass. "Don't you shut-up shop at 2 o'clock? I'll pick you up and take you for something to eat, be your bodyguard."

She cannot hide her amusement. "I don't need a bodyguard."

"Well, you've got one anyway."

Elise places her hand on his arm, feeling the hard sinews beneath her fingers. "Thank you."

"No problem. Come on, I need a smoke. I'll walk you back to your fancy car." Once again, he holds the door open for her, detecting a grateful smile.

It's a short walk to the lay-by where their cars are parked and Dan edges away from her, not wanting to shake hands. He's managed to keep his infirmity under-wraps but his palms are super-sensitive. As soft as her hands may be, even the slightest touch will cause him to grimace and the last thing he wants is to be the wounded bodyguard. That just wouldn't do. He watches her shoot off into the night, brakes squealing, wheels blazing.

When Dan returns to Elm Gardens, the two technicians are at the bottom of the stairs chatting with Pat. He's less than surprised to see her there. She must have been itching to strike up a conversation. He greets the bunch with a friendly smile.

"All done?"

The younger of the two lifts his mug of tea. "Just stopping for a tea break, still got loads to do. Expect we'll be here 'till bloody midnight at this rate."

"Whatever it takes, eh? Did you manage to pull the wires through?"

"Eventually. Got to leave it tidy though, orders from the top." The experienced technician raises his head to the heavens. "Looks good though." He wanders into the apartment, proud of his handy work.

Nonchalantly, Dan follows him, hands in pockets, yawning. He looks up at the neatly positioned box to the right hand side of the window frame, tucked away behind the curtain. "What's happened to the window?" Dan asks, watching as the guy nearly chokes on his tea.

"Shit! I've not cracked the glass?"

As he walks over to the window, Dan slips the keys into the tray by the door and steps backwards laughing. "Just messing around."

"You had me going there, had visions of having to fit a bloody window as well as an alarm. Would have meant pulling an all-nighter." He exhales long and hard and scratches his head. "Back to work."

"I've leave you to it. Give me a knock if you want a brew." He collects the two empty mugs and trots off upstairs. From the back, it's impossible to see the width of his smile and the roguish sparkle that has returned to his eyes, but it's there.

***

It's seven o'clock, I've taken too long showering and getting ready, but I'm pleased with the result. I've selected a little black dress by Donna Karan, it's a lovely fit and the off the shoulder design helps to create a flattering silhouette with my hair up. Black Jimmy Choos, black clutch and I'm done. My new platinum jewellery completes the ensemble. I'm a little light-headed after the champagne but in a happy way. Once I've eaten I'll feel fine.

Ayden showered quickly, probably so he could get some work done before I appeared. I'm getting attuned to his little ways; he likes to give the illusion of care-free leadership but I've never known a more committed individual.

My instincts were right; he's back in the study having a heated conversation with someone. *"For fuck's sake Jake. Get on it, what do you mean where am I? I'm in Rome with Beth ... so just take care of it. OK? No, I won't be taking calls, we're going out to dinner. Text me when you have news."*

Rather than disturb him I tiptoe onto the terrace, wrapping my shawl around my shoulders to keep the evening chill from my skin. The sky is Ayden's signature colour. Unlike his suits and my sapphire charm, it's peppered with pin pricks of light. There's too much light pollution to pick out any constellations but I know they're up there somewhere. I hear music and turn to see where it's coming from.

Ayden is carrying his iPad, playing is Michael Bublé singing *Feeling Good*. I have a choking sensation in my throat, I'm fighting back emotion. I inspect my beau from head to toe. He looks princely in his slate grey suit, black shirt and silver grey tie; right hand in his pocket, left hand holding the iPad. He sets it down on the table and approaches me. I feel my chest inflating and my bosoms heaving at the sight of him.

"May I have this dance?" He takes my hand, slots my hand in his and spins me around and around before pulling me in close and sweeping me across the terrace. He whispers in my ear. "You don't have to say what this is, Beth, I know." He reads my thoughts: this is another Titanic moment, the best so far.

He steps back and studies my face, my hair, even my dress before smiling proudly. "I'm a very lucky man. You look amazing. I'm looking forward to getting you out of that dress."

Those seductive words cause my breath to catch. "Then you'll have to wait." I smile shyly. "You look so handsome. I'm a lucky lady too." I mirror his playful smile and stroke his face with the back of my hand.

"If you say so, Miss Parker, then it must be true. Are you ready to go?"

"Yes."

"Then, let's go eat."

The limousine is waiting for us outside reception. As we manoeuvre ourselves onto the back seat, I offer our driver a greeting, "Buona sera." He does the same and makes his way through the one way system to the restaurant.

He pulls up outside an innocuous looking building on a narrow street just over five minutes later. "Dov'e il ristorante?" I ask him.

"L'aggiu," he answers, pointing.

I reply with "Grazie tanto," and we step out of the car and make our way inside.

Ayden takes my arm and leans in to me. "You speak French *and* Italian?"

"Only when I have to," is my reply. "That's what becomes of having too much time on your hands and keeping your head down for six years: you attend lots of night school classes. You should see my flower arranging."

He offers me a down-turned smile, a solitary nod and I assume that means he's impressed, but who knows?

When we enter I scrutinize his face, knowing the venue is a little rustic for his taste but, when in Rome...

We receive a warm welcome and are quickly seated in a private booth. Two minutes in and it's a feast for the senses: wine bottles are arranged along the walls and inside cabinets, they're everywhere. Crimson red cloths are drape across intimate table covered with pungent food being eaten by contented diners. It all looks very civilised, but it's not the Ritz.

The menu is in English, thank God. My night school Italian will only get me so far. Even before Ayden utters a word I know he'll be trouble. Why is it he never orders straight off a menu? The waiter arrives, pad and pencil in hand. I should have suggested he sharpen it first. He'll be taking copious notes.

With little fuss, I order the beef fillet carpaccio, followed by sea bass with honey and mushrooms. Then, it's Ayden's turn; he opts for the house speciality and the title of the dish should be a clue as to its quality, but no. He wants the pan fried pumpkin flowers with asparagus and black truffle without the asparagus, but he will have any other green vegetable. Then it's the Fillet of Tuscany beef and fondue cheese served with Italian salad and toasted pine nuts. It sounds delicious, but no, the cheese must be low fat, the beef well done on the outside, very pink in the middle and he doesn't want the pine nuts. Five minutes later with the order placed, he starts to peruse the wine list.

Before he even speaks my face splits into two with a ludicrously broad smile. He looks up completely oblivious of how amusing he is and actually looks around, wondering what is making me smile. Still reading through the list, he speaks softly. "Something has put you in a very good mood."

I try to pull myself together but I can't help it, away from our four walls he's a different person. Right now, he's a waiter's worse nightmare with his flippant attitude and pretentious manner, but I know it's all part of the façade he has created for himself. It's all part and parcel of being Mr. P. and tonight he looks gorgeous framed in candle light on this, our first diner date.

"Have you seen anything that meets with your high standards, Mr. Stone?" I enquire, rearranging my cutlery.

"No, but I'm still looking."

I get the message, so refrain from saying another word. Instead I snap a breadstick and nibble on that.

"Do you like Chianti?"

"I'm not sure if I've had it before." I carry on nibbling.

"Then we'll try it." He lifts up his hand and signals the waiter. "Can we have a bottle of this?" He points to the dearest bottle available and hands back the wine list to the attentive waiter. "And bring some water to the table, please."

With the food and wine out of the way, he focuses his attention on me. "You've regained your composure, I'm pleased to see." His mouth twitches slightly at one side but he cannot mask an amused smile.

"I have, I don't want to be accused of being a naughty girl." I smile cheekily, putting the breadstick a little too far into my mouth so I can suck on it as it leaves my lips.

He smiles gleefully, charmed by my innocent attempt at seduction and looks away, shaking his head from left to right. "Something tells me this is going to be one of those nights."

When he turns and his eyes find their target there is a dark, carnal longing within them that makes every muscle in my torso contract. I'm squirming in my seat, hoping he hasn't noticed. I no longer have the urge to giggle, more the need to look away for the sake of my sanity. He's eye-fucking me.

"Are you feeling alright, Beth?" he asks, as if he doesn't know. "You look a little ... flushed."

Bastard!

"Yes. I'm fine, it's a little warm in here, where's the bloody water?" I scrape back an invisible strand of hair and bite my thumb nail.

He actually starts to waft me with his napkin. "There, is that better?"

No it isn't!

"Yes, I'm fine now, thank you!"

His smug expression is both annoying and arousing at the same time. Why do I let him do this to me? The point is, I don't *let* him. I simply have no defence against stares of that velocity when they are directed straight at me. And he knows it.

The waiter comes to my rescue. I'm pouring water while Ayden is wine tasting. By the time he's approved the Chianti and the waiter has poured, I've thrown back two full glasses of iced water.

Feeling internally chilled I confront him. "Why do you do that to me?"

"Do what?" He tries for a secondary volley and reinforces it with a sexy grin.

"You know what." I glare at him.

"Because I can." Nonchalantly, he reaches for a breadstick. "I like to play games too, Beth, you know that. The difference is, I always win"

He has the audacity to claim a victory.

"Besides, I like making you *moist* all over." He liquefies my insides with one word.

Oh dear God!

I fashion a look of mild indignation. "I'm not *moist* all over."

"Shall we pay a visit to the ladies and check?"

What kind of question is that?

"Or maybe we should check right here?"

Oh no ...

I roll my eyes but that really is not the appropriate thing to do. Now he sees this as a challenge. "There's no need for that."

"Oh, it's more of a want than a need, Beth." He's tipping his head to the vacant space at the back of the booth. "Come over here."

Inch by inch he's moving around to the other side of the table, out of public view. "Hurry up, or I'll have to scoot over to your side." The wink tells me it's not an idle threat.

With each passing second, I'm becoming more physically aware of him; the thrill of anticipation is rippling through me like an unstoppable tide. I follow orders and move to my right until our elbows are touching. I really hope no-one has noticed.

"Now what?" I sound a little put out, but the way my hands are pulling at the material on my dress covering my knees, blows the whistle on my excitement.

"Lift up your dress at the back."

How can he sip wine and tell me to do something like that? "What?"

"You heard me."

"No, this is a £3,000 dress, it will crease." I've made a valid point.

"I'll buy you another. Lift it up at the back or I'll do it for you and I'll be a lot less discreet."

I tut and roll my eyes. "Why?"

"You'll see. Reach for a breadstick"

"I don't want another breadstick."

He's blowing out air in exasperation. "Just do it, Beth, for once in your life will you just do as you're told?"

As I reach over to the other side of the table, he places his hand on the seat. When I sit down, I'm startled to find his fingers moving around underneath me. "Ah!"

I feel his hot breath in my right ear. "Does this bring back memories?"

I'm looking anywhere but at him; across at other couples, at pictures on the walls. "You've got to stop, Ayden."

What if someone sees us?

"Why, what will I find? Creamy, white lies?"

His words make me ache inside. Of course I'm slick and ready for him; I'm always ready for him. But, I keep up the pretence.

"Don't be ridiculous."

Voluntarily I lean forward, allowing him to trace the lace on my panties, to edge towards my moist opening. He pushes into me with two fingers.

"Oh."

"Hush, or you'll get us thrown out of this quaint little restaurant."

When I find the courage to face him, he's smiling in such a way I feel drawn to his eyes like metal filings to a magnet. I want to kiss his mouth. I lean towards him.

He pulls away. "Now, now we'll have none of that. This is a public place. Behave!"

Feeling like a schoolgirl who's been reprimanded, I look away. He drives me crazy with his games: crazy mad, crazy in love.

The waiter arrives, carrying our first course. Initially, he's surprised to see we have moved and is unsure of exactly where to place the food. Assuming we will return to our original places, facing each other, he puts the plates down, smiles and walks away. He must know what we're up to, surely?

I lift both plates over to us and rearrange the cutlery. "Do you want me to cut up your food for you?" I ask, worked-up and damp around my hairline.

"Why not?" Ayden begins picking at his colourful starter with his fork in his right hand.

Just as I'm about to do so, he intensifies his fondling, the delicate material of my panties giving way to his insistent fingers. It tears and he has me right where he wants me, right where I want him: circling inside me.

"Ah!" I cry out, my breath hitching and my eyes widening.

"Eat your meal," he urges, seeming oblivious of my arousal.

I pick up my knife and fork and try to eat but my hands are trembling too much.

"Oh dear." Now his smile has become a sexy grin. "I'd cut up your food for you, but unfortunately my hand is otherwise engaged."

He places a morsel of food in his mouth off his perfectly balanced fork then repeats the act, only this time he's holding the fork in front of my mouth. "Eat up."

It's not easy chewing when you're smiling. He plays the best games.

"More?"

"Please." I sit patiently, panting, waiting to be fed. There's something very erotic about this. I can't put my finger on it, but Ayden seems to have everything under control, my dietary requirements included.

"Reach for another breadstick."

Highly aroused and agitated I protest. "I don't want another breadstick. I want to be able to eat my meal."

"You know what will happen if you don't. I'll bend you *over* your lovely meal. Reach!"

He is so infuriating. I reach over and grab a breadstick and wave it in front of his nose. In that split second, he pulls out his hand. I watch as he wraps it in his napkin, lifts it to his nose and closes his eyes. I'm mesmerised.

A groan leaves his throat and finds its way to my thighs that are now sticky with perspiration. With his right hand he pulls my face to him so we are eye to eye; green and blue flecks, flickering in the candle light. "That's the sexy smell I get when I go down on you." I feel his lips on mine. "Is it any wonder I want to spread you out and fuck you right here on this table?"

After only a second, he frees me and I look away, barely able to contain myself. From the corner of my eye I watch him tip water into a spare napkin and wash off his hand with the moist cloth. He begins cutting up his food, as if he's done nothing, said nothing.

I pat my upper lip with my napkin. "Mr. Stone, really, you're so naughty." I'm swallowing hard and focusing on my meal. "You're turning me into a very naughty girl."

He's grinning from ear to ear. "Yes I am. *My* naughty girl."

I stand corrected ...

I continue to cut up my food and place my fork in my left hand. Now it's my turn to play. I slide my right hand under his clean napkin and settle it on his semi erect penis.

"Let's see if *you* can eat with shaky hands."

He sniggers. "My hands won't be doing any shaking tonight, Beth."

Oh we'll see about that...

He carries on eating, seeming unaffected, which is surprising considering the impressive hard on which is taking shape under my fingers.

I claim back my hand, disappointed in my inability to make a discernible impact on his concentration. I stop eating, turn and wait for him to do the same and face me. When he looks into my eyes, I smile. Facing me are the deepest, darkest pools of indigo I have ever seen.

"Your hands may not be shaking but your eyes are telling a different story, Ayden."

"Oh, I don't think so." He turns back to his meal, unwilling to admit defeat.

I set about my delicious meal, feeling exhilarated and victorious. "There's two, big, black lies right there."

He stops eating long enough to give my right knee a squeeze. "Touché. Eat your meal, keep your strength up. You'll need it for later."

Smiling between mouthfuls I devour the scrumptious food, leaving my plate spotlessly clean. He passes me my wine and our glasses chink. From only a foot away, he tries but cannot hold back on a secret smile, I return that smile with interest; for every loving thought he invests in me, I can multiply it to the power of ten and then some.

"Drink up. That is, of course, if your bladder has any room left for wine after your gallon of water."

We laugh unselfconsciously and don't stop laughing until the waiter arrives with our main course. Even then, I glance at him through mascara coated lashes and giggle, intoxicated, high on pheromones and humour. He touches me on so many levels. I can't begin to count the ways. I love him. How could I not?

By 9 o'clock, we are merrily drunk on what turned out to be a very pleasing bottle of Chianti.

"Do you want coffee or should we head back?" he asks, stroking the knuckles of my right hand with his thumb.

I pretend to be thinking when really I'm admiring the view. He has loosened his tie slightly and is rubbing his chin with his finger and thumb, that way he does when he's strategizing. I remember where that finger has been and what he can do with those hands, and the coffee idea becomes redundant.

"I think we should leave."

He pays the bill with his card. We offer our thanks and make for the exit. Ayden waves over the limousine and we slide onto the back seat.

"I had a great time tonight," I confess, hoping the act of constructing a sentence will make me feel less fuelled by wine and desire.

"Yes, so did I." He wraps his left arm around my shoulders. I rest my head in the crook of his neck. He feels so warm and firm against my cheek.

"You smell divine." I exhale a little too loudly, trying to rid myself of the hot air gathering in my lungs. I feel him smiling into my hair.

Without a word from me he opens the window halfway. "My poor little genie; so responsive yet so little self-control."

I lift up my head and look into his devilish eyes, a little taken aback. "What does that mean?"

"It means, in terms of nocturnal activities, you're still learning."

I tip my head to the side and continue to focus on his bemused expression. "Where the hell did that come from?"

"It's just an observation." He taps my nose with the tip of his forefinger before turning to look out of the window, as if he hasn't spoken.

Feeling a rush of the kind of self-assurance that comes with two glasses of full bodied wine, I stand my ground. "Well, I might be a novice but I haven't had any complaints from you."

"This is true. But you should always keep an open mind about these things. For all your *so-called* dominance, vanilla *is* still your favourite flavour."

I'm aghast. I've read about *that* ... "Something tells me we're not talking about ice-cream here?"

He kisses my forehead. "No, we most certainly are not."

"Then you shouldn't make assumptions about my favourite flavour then. If I'm still so ... plain, then maybe that has something to do with the tuition I'm receiving?" I've made a valid point and it's back in your court Mr. P.

"I can't argue with that."

"Good." I think?

"We'll see."

That's not fair. You can't end a conversation with 'we'll see.' I'm not a two year old. We pull up outside the hotel and his cryptic conversation ends. He turns to help me out.

"I don't need any help. I've already *learned* how to walk."

I hear a deep throated chuckle behind me. Once I'm out of the car, I take a look around; the hotel gardens are lit and there are tiny lights dotted around on the steps and by the flower beds. It's enchanting.

Ayden acknowledges the young man on reception with a perfunctory nod, letting me lead the way to the elevator. The key card opens the door to our suite and we step inside but the lights have been turned off; one side of the room is bathed in moonlight, the other wrapped in shadows.

Unsure of where the switch is, I call out melodramatically, "Lights!" But, when I turn to face him I'm caught off guard. There's barely a trace of a smile. I know that look. I take a step back, I'm not sure why.

In response he takes hold of my left wrist. At first I think it's to steady me but his grip is a little too tight for that.

"Let's go to bed," I whisper, turning on my heels.

"No!"

I swivel back to face him and our eyes lock hypnotically. There's something very arousing about a man who is seriously contemplating how he's going to fuck you, especially when he looks this hot.

"You said you wanted to gift yourself to me."

I nod, slowly.

"Then it's time for me to collect my welcome home present."

I swallow hard, unsure of exactly what he means. I'm just about to speak but feel his hand over my mouth.

"I'm not used to people answering me back, so tonight I'm taking away your power of speech. Just for tonight."

I give him a curious stare.

"Now listen carefully. You're going to go into the bedroom and stand in the pool of light by the window and wait for me. Go."

This is so unexpected. Just thinking about what he is going to do to me, has my heart racing.

I'm standing silently with my back to the window in our extravagant bedroom; outside I can hear crickets and the distant rumble of traffic. Inside, there's only my expectant breathing and the sound of Ayden approaching out of the darkness.

He sits, fully clothed on the edge of the enormous bed, removes his tie and gives me another command. "Undress, slowly."

I falter.

"Stop thinking about it, Beth, I'm not asking I'm telling. Just do it."

He's totally serious and I obey, slowly removing my dress, letting it come to rest on the nearby chair. I'm wearing my black lacy bra, panties and my black Jimmy Choos, standing before him while he directs the most intense of stares my way. In the half-light, I see flames flickering, dancing around depthless pools of blackness. Has he ever been more turned-on? Simply looking at him in this primal state affects my breathing, so much so I'm forgetting to exhale and have to keep reminding myself to do so. I reach my hands around my back to unclip my bra.

"Did I say move?" He calls out.

I launch an indignant stare in his direction. "There's no need to ..."

"... Be quiet, Beth, or I'll have to gag you."

What? Is he threatening me? I drag an imaginary zip across my mouth and stick my hands by my sides, signalling obedience.

Happy now?

Deliberately spelling out each word, he addresses me. "Gifting yourself to me, means you have to submit to my will. So stop with the fucking attitude."

Now there's a thing: he's totally serious.

I've met this man before, only once, on the way home after the book launch. I didn't recognise him then and I don't recognise him now, but that doesn't stop me wanting him.

"Kneel down. Get on all fours."

I tip my head to one side in disbelief, asking why but saying nothing. Feeling very awkward, I do as he asks, settling my hands and knees on the plush carpet.

"Come to me," he instructs without emotion, making me feel very intimidated.

I crawl towards him slowly, keeping my head down so he cannot see my unease. The wine is rushing to my head, making me feel a little giddy and light-headed but I keep moving. When my hair reaches his crotch I stop, waiting for my next instruction. What does he intend to do to me?

He reaches for my chin. "Look at me."

I do, resting my chin on the forefinger and thumb of his right hand. Our eyes meet; his are alight with raw desire, mine, I expect, convey more trepidation than submission.

In a broken whisper, he explains. "You drive me fucking crazy. I can't sleep, I can't eat, I can't even think straight when we're apart and it's all because of you."

In his confession, there's a vulnerability which moves me, but it's tinged with something else: suppressed anger. Has he been bottling this up the whole time we've been together? I try to shake my chin free, but he tightens his grip. It's firm but not painful. Seeing me wince a little he releases it and strokes the reddened area softly with his thumb.

"Have you any idea how hard it is for me to operate when I feel as if I've lost all self-control?"

I can't move and I don't need to, his confession has me riveted to the spot.

"What happened in L.A. can't ever happen again. It's too high a price to pay for loving you."

I try to sit up, pulling on his knees in an attempt to find a comfortable kneeling position. He removes my hands and places them by my side. Why won't he let me touch him?

"The flight home gave me the time I needed to think, and it's been eating away at me ever since."

I have no idea what's coming next so remain static, focusing only on his despairing face, offering my silent submission.

"I can't let you speak because I know you'll tell me everything is fine and you'll bewitch me with your gentle assurances. But things are far from fine." He pauses, looks away for some reason and turns to face me head-on. "I'm not the man you think I am."

My face must show my astonishment. That single statement literally rocks me and I sway to the right. I go to speak but stop, my lips forming into that rounded O.

His fingertips brush against my lips. "You even had *me* believing I was this 'Smartie' guy." He stifles a smug smile. "I wanted to be soft and yielding for you and I've tried so hard to suppress every urge I have to be dominant, but pretending to be that person nearly fucked up 16 years of seriously hard work."

He takes my face in his hands. "I am a dominant man, Beth, there's no denying it. When I think of you, I imagine doing ... well, let's not get into that now, other than saying we're not talking about vanilla sex, even though I know it is the only flavour you're comfortable with."

His attention wavers as he considers the implications of what he is saying; his focus settles in a distant dark corner of the room where he can be alone with his thoughts.

Maybe I should be, but I'm not shocked. As inexperienced as I am, I've had my suspicions. But, now I'm fearful this could be an unforgettable night for all the *wrong* reasons.

He clears his throat and starts again. "I have certain needs, Beth, and pretending I don't is not good for my mental health."

I find my voice. "So all this time it's been a game, nothing about our relationship has been genuine?" He looks mortified and takes hold of my arms. I start to tingle, feeling his trembling grip.

"No, it's been real and I suppose it has been a kind of game at times, but it just got real for me."

"Lucky you," I retort sarcastically.

"Yeah, lucky me. I am lucky, lucky to have found you. If I didn't care so much, do you think I would have tried so hard to be the man you want?" He looks so despairing, I want to hold him, but I fear his rebuke.

I risk rejection and frame his face with my hands. "You are the only man I want, Ayden." Here we are eyeball to eyeball, holding onto each other as if our lives depend on it.

"I've tried so many times to tell you but I'm afraid I might not be *that* guy. How many times have I said I don't deserve you? How many fucking times!"

"I don't know." My eyes glaze over with tears.

"I need more," he asserts, his voice overflowing with emotion. "I just need more."

"I don't understand." I pull back, helplessly confused.

He lowers his hands from my face and I do the same, watching him pinch the top of his nose and wipe his nostrils with the back of his hand. "I've trusted you. I've given my body to you. I need you to trust me enough to give your body to me."

"I said I would gift myself to you, I said that," I implore.

"But that was you teasing, Beth, you playing innocent games with me. The difference is, I'm being serious."

What he said in the car was absolutely true. I'm such a novice. To think I could satisfy a man like Ayden Stone? What was I thinking?

"How can you expect me to sacrifice all I am to be with you, then go out and rule the fucking world? I can't do it."

My knees are throbbing and there's a cramping sensation in my toes, but I'm not moving. I daren't. "Is this what you wanted all along, to dominate me, to demean me, to hurt me?" I can't hold back the tide of tears that has been threatening to burst from my woeful eyes; they cascade down my cheeks like a melting glacier.

He pulls me to him. "Oh, Beth, It's not like that. I love you so much. I want to give you everything, I always have. I want you to experience everything, with me. Baby, I would never hurt you."

I sob into his neck. "I'm way out of my depth with you. I don't know how to play these games." I try to stand but he keeps a firm grip on my arms, he won't release me.

"I know you're hurting, it kills me to think I'm the one inflicting this kind of pain on you, but look at me, Beth."

I struggle to focus.

"This is the face of the man who loves you. I have always loved you, the promise of you; no more so than the moment I saw you in your prim and proper disguise. I knew if I was myself, if I behaved the way I always do, you would reject me outright, and I couldn't risk that because I knew, thirty minutes in, you were the one. I would have said and done anything to keep you, and I did." He looks down shamefully at the carpet.

"I know, I'm a deceitful bastard who has to win, but it's never been about the winning with you, not really. It's been about not losing, not losing you. I won big time when you said you loved me: you're the prize, Beth. I *can't* lose you." He wipes away my tears with his tie and tips his head, trying to meet my eyes.

"Every day I thank God for you, you've taught me so much about myself, but I can't keep up the pretence any longer. I just can't." He lifts up my face and I sense he is preparing to say the words that will end this heart-to-heart. "I need to know how far you are prepared to go to make this relationship work."

Even though I'm still tearful, I can speak. "I don't think I get to decide, do I? It's all about you. It's about *your* needs, *your* expectations."

"No, that's not true. It's not in my nature to please, but I want nothing more than to please you – not only in the bedroom but in everything; now, tomorrow and every day after that. But, Beth, I have to know you feel the same about me or ... or I'm fucked!" He pauses to take an invigorating breath. "The question is whether *you* want to please me?"

And there it is, the truth is out. It hits me like a bolt out of the blue. That one salient question, that's what this is really about: a promise, submission, trust. I ask myself, do I want to please you?

He's searching my face for clues, but I give nothing away. I begin to speak but stop before a single utterance can be heard and reconsider, while he strokes my hair with so much adoration I feel he may weep.

"What's going on in that beautiful head of yours? This time you *have* to tell me."

I wipe my eyes, inhale deeply and, speaking slowly, prepare to put the world to rights. "I want to please you too, Ayden. I've never wanted anything more." I manage a confident smile and watch him visibly deflate; he's been holding his breath for so long, letting it out causes his body to sag like a punctured balloon. He's so relieved.

With sparkling eyes that glitter and light up the darkness, he announces: "Thank God."

We wrap our weary arms around each other as if it is our last embrace. When we break apart after several minutes, I reach for his face, feeling the moisture on his skin. "Oh Ayden, what am I going to do with you?"

He nuzzles his tear stained face into the palm of my hand and closes his eyes.

15

After fixing my face, I return to our bedroom, wearing my new baby doll nightie in white with matching thong. Filled with unease, I enter slowly, sensing a mood change in the room. It's bathed in the warm glow created by two decorative wall lights above the bed, right and left above Ayden's head. He's used the guest bathroom, I can tell; his face has that just scrubbed look and he has a youthful glow. Even the way he smells from across the room is inebriating: this is the man I love.

He glances up from his iPad once, then again, noticing my seductive attire. I have purposely left my hair up, I want to look elegant, refined, untouched.

"Hey! I like the outfit," he smiles softly.

I feel my breasts responding to his constant gaze; my hardening nipples begin protruding through the silk material. He can't help but notice.

"Come to bed," he instructs softly, pulling back the sheets to reveal the right side of his naked body.

How can I refuse? He's beyond beautiful. Everything about him is virile and intoxicating. His jet black hair is damp and messy; his pectoral muscles keep flexing and moving as if he's carved out of a flexible material, soft to the touch but as hard as granite. And those eyes, those penetrating sea green eyes, how they set my insides quivering.

I position myself next to him, we're both sitting upright. I'm preoccupied with the aching sensation between my thighs, so powerful is the sexual pull between us.

He speaks first. "The effect you have on me is unnatural." He runs the forefinger of his right hand the length of my arm and it's such an unassuming act, but even this has me squirming around on the velvety soft sheets. Not touching him is actually painful. I close my eyes, lost in my own private thoughts.

Without even facing me, his seduction gets underway. "I'm going to make love to you, because it's all I've been thinking about from the moment you stepped into the car this morning and every morning before that." He turns my face to his, eyes blazing, chest heaving. "Do you want me?"

"Are you giving me back the power of speech?" I ask, taking in his dreamy visage.

"I'll give you anything, you know that." His emasculation is humbling. What kind of dominance is this?

"Then, it's only fair I should do the same." I pull his mouth to mine; at first his kiss is soft, exploratory, but there's a growing urgency. I feel it in his breath, the sounds he makes and in his steel like erection pressing into my hip.

With grasping hands, he fists my hair urging me to respond to his impassioned kisses while his tongue licks and penetrates me: he's unstoppable.

Using his free hand he lowers me beneath his Herculean body so I can feel the full weight of him flattening me to the mattress. It's all bump and grind: silk material against hard muscle, nails on bare skin, my saturated flesh up against his hard cock. Every nerve in my body is tingling, every breath a fight for survival. I want him so badly.

In fractured syllables he speaks. "You ... you need a safe word, Beth, choose one. Not stop or enough or no. You decide."

It's impossible to think with him nibbling my ear and rubbing himself up against me like this. One word comes to mind. "Romeo."

"What?"

"That's my safe word, Romeo." I feel him smiling into my neck.

"Romeo it is." He leans into my ear. "I'm going to make you feel so fucking hot you'll never have to say it." So confident is he in his assertion that I believe him. A smouldering look of pure, unadulterated desire pins me to the bed: I am his for the taking.

From under the pillow he slides out my silver scarf. "I'm going to fasten your hands to the bed frame."

It's an erotic threat that has me writhing in anticipation beneath him.

" ... I'm going to lick every inch of you until you come. And then slide inside you." He leans over me, our noses are almost touching. "Do you understand?"

I can barely speak, I'm so needy. "Yes."

"Yes what?"

"Yes, I understand."

"Good girl."

With eyes that have morphed into his signature colour, he reaches above my head and ties my hands to the bedframe to create a wide V shape, all the time pressing his steely cock into my thighs and then my stomach. It's more than I can take. I'll willingly submit to anything this man wants: my body is his.

"Now I have you where I want you, let's begin your first lesson." He eases off me and slides down the bed, leaving my stomach and panties exposed below my crumpled nightie.

I try to lie still, but it's impossible. Catching sight of his predatory stare does something to me, I can't look away. He slips his hands underneath my arms, why?

"Let's sit you up so you can see how I'm pleasuring you."

What?

He raises me up until I'm almost sitting upright; two fluffy pillows are stacked behind my head. He slides off the bed, reaches for the iPod remote and music starts to play. I know the song, I recognise the guitar intro; he's found it on my collection of 80's hits. It's *Lullaby* by the Cure. What a strange choice.

It isn't until he begins his performance that I realise: it's a stroke of genius. With every beat, he crawls onto the bed, positioning himself between my legs, running his hands up my shins, across my knees and along my thighs.

His eyes never leave mine.

The beat picks up, he's licking his lips and my already breathless body is starting to quiver, longing for the touch of his lips on mine. He begins his assent, climbing my torso like a prowling cat. I forget about the scarf, and it isn't until I try to touch him I am reminded I'm being restrained. But, my beautiful Ayden is so engaging, and so stunningly gorgeous in this primal state that I'm happy to forget.

I watch him lift my nightie higher with his teeth and have to accept this stunning man is taking me to a place I've never visited before. I can't contain a gasp. This is beyond erotic. He follows through with his hands, causing me to arch my back slightly, wanting, needing more.

As he covers my mouth with his, he begins to tear away the front of my nightie with both hands.

Oh my God!

Every one of my senses is being stimulated: taste, touch, smell, sight and now the sound of my nightie being ripped off me. As he reveals my navel, my rib cage and then my breasts, he blows softly and every hair on my body stands to attention.

"We don't need this, do we?" With his powerful hands he tears the front of my nightie in half, revealing my bare breasts and hardening flesh.

Oh Christ!

I have to look away, this is too much.

"Look at me, Beth."

And I do.

"Your breasts are perfect. These hands are made to fit every part of your body. See?"

I look down and watch him fondle, squeeze and suckle on my breasts. I almost convulse and tug again on my restraint but I'm not really trying to free myself, it just looks that way.

"Stop, Ayden. This is too much," I plead. He doesn't stop. I keep watching. Inside, muscles are clinching, my clitoris is throbbing, begging to be stroked. "Stop." I can't take any more. Giving in to the sensation is my only option.

Is this what it's like to be dominated?

The music fades and, as far as he's concerned it's mission accomplished. He has me well and truly saturated from head to toe and in all those aching places in between.

With blazing eyes that cause my insides to incinerate, he presses into me. "Are you ready to submit?" he whispers softly, allowing his tongue to linger on the soft, sensitive skin beneath my ear.

"Yes. God yes," I answer, finding it hard to speak, overwhelmed by an aching desire to feel him inside me.

He takes hold of the clip fastening my hair and snaps it open, dragging his fingers through the ringlets so they frame my face and tumble around my shoulders.

"You've grown into a beautiful woman, Beth. You're home to me. I have to be inside you."

Yes, yes ...

He moulds his mouth over mine and kisses me so passionately, I think I might faint. There's no escaping that seductive tongue.

"Give yourself to me, Beth," he urges, descending my body, not waiting for a reply. My flexing hips and groans of pleasure are reply enough. I watch him as he advances southwards and I hear myself panting: it's the most erotic moment of my life.

"I'm going to use my hands on you until you come. Watch me!"

Watch you!

With that, his right hand slides between my abdomen and my panties and it keeps going until two fingers are buried inside me. We both gasp.

"Jesus, you're tight." The in, out movements have me lifting and writhing, making me squeeze my thighs against the palm of his left hand as he struggles to keep me still.

"I said I was going to kiss you all over and I will, but you have to come for me first. Can you do that?"

I try to close my mouth to speak but can only manage a nod.

"Say it."

I groan much too loudly. "Yes ... yes."

"Good." He seeks out my clitoris with his thumb and an involuntary whimper leave my lips.

"I can feel you flexing inside, squeeze me."

I do.

"Again."

I do.

"Again."

I do, until I'm at the point where I have to come against his fingers, but he stills ... bringing me back from the edge of orgasm.

He picks up the pace again and I come close. He stills.

"Don't do this, Ayden." I plead, tears stinging my eyes.

"Beg me."

"Please."

"Again."

"Ayden, why are you doing this?"

"Because I can. I'm teaching you a lesson, remember?"

I meet his stare but see a stranger with soulless eyes starved of light, reflecting domination. Nothing more. Fear grips me by the throat.

"You tease and seduce me with your words and disarm me with your gentleness, I have no defence and I love you for it. But, right now I want you to know how it feels to be powerless, because that's how you make me feel."

"Ayden."

I don't like this game. Where is he going with this?

"Romeo," I whisper, just loud enough for him to hear. "This isn't you pleasing me. This is you punishing me for loving you." I turn my head to the side and feel him pulling out of me. Here I am, tied up, turned on and being punished for ... what?

"I'm trying really hard to submit. You have no idea how hard it is for me to do this, you don't know." I look into his eyes and, thank God he's back; the disturbing hues of blackness have morphed into the colour of kindness. A cerulean sea of sadness ripples and glistens before me. This dominant man is forlorn, lost and contrite.

My naked Adonis reaches for his neck and then for the scarf tying my hands to the bed head. He unties me and rubs my grazed wrists with his thumbs. The silence is suffocating.

"Come here." I reach out my arms and he falls into me.

"I'm sorry." he mutters, holding me tight.

"I had no idea you felt like this. When I'm teasing, it's because I assume we're close enough to be like that with each other. I don't do it to emasculate you, quite the opposite. I do it knowing you'll win." I kiss his hair over and over. "You break down all my defences too."

His grip tightens around me; he's listening to every word.

"Think back, Ayden, I made you a promise. I said I would take care of you in whatever way you wanted me to and, even if the sub thing was a ploy, it was a promise made and one I intend to keep." I kiss his hair one last time and wait for his response.

Five minutes later, I'm still waiting.

In one swift movement, he sits upright, eyes flickering, mouth twitching: he has a plan. "Go and get dressed."

"What?"

"You heard me, go and get dressed." He brushes the hair from my face and points to the bathroom.

"Where are we going?"

"Don't question me, Beth, go and get some fucking clothes on." He's swearing but his eyes are bright and alert.

Is this a game?

I do as I'm bid and sidle off to the bathroom, throwing my shredded nightie in his face as I go. I decide to take a quick shower, before brushing my hair and applying a little lip-gloss and tinted moisturiser. The clothes I travelled in are hanging over the towel rail and, as they are the only clothes I have close to hand, I put them on. Fully dressed and utterly confused, I re-enter the bedroom.

To my horror, I find Ayden is also fully dressed. We're going home. He's sitting in darkness on the edge of the bed, exactly as he was earlier in the evening before our disastrous sexual liaison.

"Go and stand in the pool of light and take off your clothes," he commands.

Pardon me?

Ah ... I see where he's going with this, he has us on replay. Only this time we're going to do it right. I stride over to my spot and start removing my boots. I throw them in his direction and, even though his face is only a silhouette, I know he's smiling.

Next I unbutton my blouse, recalling the fun we have had with buttons. Now *I'm* smiling. I place it on the nearby chair. My trousers slide to the floor and I'm left standing in my black underwear, waiting for my next instruction. There's the rustle of clothing and I just make out his iPhone in front of his face. Realising he's about to take a photograph, I turn side on, buckle my knees and pull my hand to my mouth coyly. A blinding flash illuminates the darkness and my modesty is forever compromised.

"For my eyes only," he states. "Come to me."

Slowly I approach him, feeling sexual tension fizzing between us. When I reach him, his face is next to my breasts and I want to pull him into me, to wrap my arms around him, to say I get it. But I don't.

He lifts his eyes to mine and I catch a glimpse of melancholy behind those cloudy, cerulean spheres. It pains me to see it.

"I made a terrible mistake before. You're much too delicate to be subjected to the glare of bright light and exposure. I'm sorry. Forgive me."

This is unexpected. I lift my hand and brush back his hair, losing my fingers in his curls; he's dressed quickly and it's wonderfully messy. My fingertips float across his cheek and I caress his handsome silhouette in the darkness. I don't need to see him to know his eyes are closed and he's falling into my embrace. The heat is radiating from his clothes. I want him.

"Don't apologise, there's no need."

"I can't keep fucking this up. It's too important." Desperation oozes from every syllable.

"It is, but nothing's changed."

He bows his head in disgrace. "How long can you keep saving me from myself?"

"Oh, Ayden, I'm not. You're the one who's saving me." I search his face for signs of relief.

"There was a time when I thought that. Thought I'd be your knight in shining armour, but I'm not. You're a purifying force, Beth, and God knows I need purifying. I'm not a good man, in spite of you believing otherwise. I've never been worthy of you. We are the sum of our deeds and, for my sins I amount to nothing compared to you." He folds a wayward strand of hair behind my ear. "I've been pushing you too hard, forcing you to step out of your comfort zone."

I won't have that. "You're wrong! There was no comfort in *my* zone. Not until you came along," I scoff, offering wordplay as a kind of rebuttal. "Before you, I was a mess. I was cursed with bad luck or bad karma or something. I couldn't have imagined a life like this, a life with someone like you. When we met and your lips touched mine, it was as if the curse was lifted. I was free, free to love, free to *be* loved, by you." I'm shaking my head, stressing the point, watching gratitude flicker in doleful eyes. "You've been very gentle with me, I know that, Ayden, but now it's time ..."

Our eyes lock. A powerful connection binds us to one another: it's intense.

"You said you wanted to do things to me, with me? What kind of things?" As hard as he tries, he cannot conceal a startled look. That look will stay with me forever.

He turns away, unwilling to elaborate. "You're not ready to hear."

Gently I cup his face, seeking out his stare, witnessing the faint glimmer of something, maybe the embers of a glowing fire. "Now you're making assumptions about vanilla being my favourite flavour again. I don't expect that from my naughty boy, not when I'm enjoying being your very naughty girl."

His eyes are alight with expectancy. "What are you saying?"

I place my hands by my sides, signalling my compliance. "I'm saying, stop pretending. Show me."

"Are you sure? I want you to experience *everything*, with me."

"I'm sure. I trust you to take care of me." I feel his hands stroking mine, thumbs over knuckles, a tightening grip. "So what are you waiting for, permission?"

"Yes."

I glance around the room. "Where do I sign?"

"Right here." He places my hand over his heart and smiles triumphantly, and that's okay. He's showered me with the most expensive gift of all, his love, and paid for this victory tenfold.

He stands abruptly and unfastens his belt. Flatfooted, I glance up at him, trying to decipher his expression. It's one I've not seen before: potent and persuasive. To my surprise, he pulls the leather belt out from his jeans and stretches it out in front of my face.

"Do you know what I want to do with this?"

I shake my head, wondering if it's something that will sting or leave a mark. That thought causes me to moan unconsciously.

He picks up on my reaction and scrutinises my face for clues. "You want this?" he asks, watching me purse my lips together, preventing another moan from escaping. He tips his head to the right and an infectious smile finds its way to his lips.

What a turn-on!

He places the belt around my neck and pulls my mouth onto his, teasing me with his mischievous tongue. The sensation of leather on my skin and his hot breath on my lips does something to me. I'm not sure why.

Moving to my rear, he unclips my bra and slides his hands underneath it, cupping me from behind, fondling, rolling my nipples between his forefingers and thumbs until they are hard and erect. The straps slip and he lets them fall somewhere near my feet into a black puddle of lace. His warm hands sweep my hair into a make-shift pony tail and hold me in place. I let another gentle moan escape from my mouth.

"You want this?"

To make his point, he pushes his erection into my derrière; even through his jeans I feel the twitching mass of hard muscle. Knowing he could take me at a moment's notice excites me further. I reach behind to pull him into me, wanting more.

His hands release my hair and splay across my shoulders, wrap around my arms and come to rest at my hands. He's looping the belt around my wrists. "You want this?"

I do.

It's like he has a sixth sense. We are so connected, he can perceive my arousal.

"Kneel down."

I fall, slowly, resting my knees on the plush carpet. I feel him straddling my body from behind; legs spread wide, knees against my shoulders, I'm held fast. I like this, so much my heart is racing but not as fast as my imagination.

He finds my ear and explains. "You've been very naughty, Beth. You've been teasing me and had me thinking about doing this to you at the most inconvenient of times. I've jerked myself off more in the last week than I've done in the last year, and I think I deserve some recompense for my troubles, don't you?"

"Yes." That sensual thought makes me smile.

"Yes, *Mr* Stone." He says with his breath steaming into my ear.

Now this is a game I *do* like. "Yes, Mr. Stone. What can I do for you ... Sir?" I say softly, surprising him with my willingness to improvise.

"To begin with, you don't have to call me that."

"You want me to, don't you?"

There's a weighty pause: he's thinking. "Yes." That breathless word floats around my head like a satellite.

"Then I want to say it. What can I do for you, Sir?"

"Baby, you can trust me. That's all I ask. Lean over the bed."

With my hands tied, getting up is a struggle. I feel him lifting, easing me onto the sheets, head first. He's a moving shadow, towering over me, enveloping me. I feel incredibly aroused and, for some reason, relaxed at the same time. His clever idea to replay the scene has worked. We have discovered a way to satisfy both our desires.

"Now we're going to begin a game I *know* you'll want to play." The sound of the drawer opening causes my eyes to widen: I know what's in there.

He turns the device on. "You know what this is?"

Of course I do, it's mine.

"Yes."

"I want to use it on you. I want you to find your voice and I want you to come calling my name. Do you want to play?"

"Yes. I want to play."

"Good." He whispers into my ear. "Me too."

Under his skilful direction, the smooth egg shaped toy vibrates against my shoulder blades and my spine, causing my skin to tingle. He skates over my anus and inside my panties and I flex involuntarily, willing him to continue. My breathing is ragged and whimpers are leaking from my mouth. I want to straighten out my legs but I cannot. I want to free my hands but I cannot. I push into his vibrating palm, trying to contain the throbbing wave of heat building in my overheated core.

Fuck!

I bury my face into the bed to smother my cries. The vibrating object touches the lips of my sex and I clinch and pull in my stomach muscles, craving more. The intensity of the vibration causes electrifying impulses to fire like static energy through my groin, making the hairs stand up on the back of my neck. I rock into him, lift up my head and open my mouth. "Oh."

His other hand caresses my throbbing cheeks, playing with the lace on my panties, sliding in his thumb and testing the tension in the elastic around my thighs.

"You want this, but you know what I want ... to pleasure you like this but to get you off with words. It's my voice that has you creaming, isn't it?"

How does he know that?

I have to set myself, to control my breathing to answer. "Yes, it's your voice."

For a second, he stops and I soon realise why. He's turned up the intensity of the vibrator and now it's humming, making my whole body sing. "Oh God."

"That's it." Using skilled hands he settles the soft toy against my clitoris and eases his thumb into me, bending it slightly to stroke the front wall of my vagina, finding that illusive G-spot.

Yes!

Inside I'm clenching and igniting; outside I'm melting. My hair is sticking to my forehead; my mouth is dry from sucking in too much air. The vibrations are beginning to spread outwards like ripples on a pond: I'm flying, soaring to the edge of infinity.

"That's more like it ... find your voice. Come for me."

Just as he said they would, his words spear their way to my core. In need of no further instruction I keen until the loud, gasping cry of relief transposes into his name. "... Ay-den ..."

I'm sagging into the sheets, boneless and exhausted with barely enough energy to smile. The leather belt is holding my hands fast behind my back, but both his hands are free and the sound of his zip being lowered excites me further; to the extent my body is quivering with lust. I need him inside me, now.

But ... I feel the sudden sting of his hand on my bottom. He has spanked me! I cry out, not in pain but because the sensation has left me feverish with need. I made him promise to do it and this is what I get for teasing.

"Now I *know* you want this because you made me promise to do it." His words linger in the air like a prayer. He spanks me again, hard, making me call out. "This is for the three occasions when you have brought me to my knees, in your bedroom, in my car and in my fucking jet."

A third and final slap has me gasping for air. Behind me, fervent fingers are pulling down my panties; strong hands are between my thighs, bending my legs at the knees, parting me. Leaning into me, he utters the words he knows will tip me over.

"I'm going to take you now."

His sweater lands on the nearby chair and immediately I hear the sound of the condom packet being torn. Oh, how I have missed that sound. He's over me. I smell cologne and manliness mingling on his skin. I feel the thickness of his erection against my cheeks.

"It has been three days, eleven hours and 45 minutes since I fucked you and I don't intend to ever wait that long again."

With that, he takes hold of my hips and nudges the tip of his rigid cock against my saturated folds and doesn't stop until he's buried deep inside me. I utter a high pitched cry and feel a delectable tightness as he thrusts, powering his way towards ejaculation.

At first his movements are controlled, but thirty seconds in and he's lunging and clawing at my skin, undulating his hips to penetrate me further, pounding frantically on. Possessing me.

Enraptured, he growls, "Feel me."

I can and it feels too good. Just when I think he might tear me in two, a deep throated roar echoes around the room, followed by uncontrollable hisses.

"Holy fuck!"

He falls onto me like a hot, steaming blanket. For several minutes we are fused together; a smelted mass of human flesh and bone.

Once I'm unbuckled and we're naked, we crawl beneath the sheets without feeling the need for conversation. We are well and truly expended. I snuggle beneath his arm.

A goodnight kiss presses into my hair and a firm right hand squeezes my shoulder possessively. "Sleep well, baby."

The steady beating of his heart lulls me into a restful slumber. Sleep comes easy.

It's four thirty in the morning when I wake, needing the bathroom and something to drink. I tiptoe out of the bedroom in the direction of the kitchen. There's an array of beverages in the fridge and I settle for a small bottle of fresh orange: I'm in the mood for something sweet. I can hear a strange pipping sound coming from the study. Gaining my bearings, I head in that direction to investigate.

Ayden's phone is flashing. When I click it on, there are six missed calls and three messages. It would appear Jake has some news for him and, by the number of calls, it's unlikely to be good. I'm tempted to read one of the texts but decide against it. I turn away feeling very curious and place the phone back in the same position.

He's in a deep sleep; his breathing is shallow and even. Sipping the orange juice from the bottle, I sit on the chair facing the bed, pull my knees to my chest and gaze at him lying there.

I see his leather belt discarded on the floor. The buckle catches the moonlight and draws my eye. The memory of it rekindles my craving for physical contact and I quickly settle my gaze on something else, something less evocative. But, everything in the room has significance, nothing more so than my silver scarf carelessly tossed onto the bed. I close my eyes and visualise myself splayed out, laid bare and I feel my cheeks burning. Even now it embarrasses me to think of myself that exposed. Perhaps that's why his replay worked so well; it was dark, I could retain a little of my modesty. Even though I was bound and pinned, I had something of myself left in reserve. Maybe I *am* too delicate for bright light?

And what of the toy, sitting unhatched by the bed. I'm not sure what I feel about that. It's amazing how, in the right hands, something so small can induce so much pleasure: that and Ayden's words, of course. Who would have thought in less than a fortnight, I'd be playing these kind of games. Ayden's games.

I don't doubt my feelings for him and I truly believe he loves me, in his way. I recall him saying he could be brutal and I thought nothing of it at the time, but I can clearly remember him using *that* word. After last night and the way he denied me my orgasm, having gone to so much trouble to get me to that point, I believe him.

What I cannot believe or reconcile myself with, is the idea he feigned submission. In my bedroom and on the jet ... he was turned on, I was turned on. I have to put my theory to the test. If he can switch between domination and submission, then so can I. And I will.

I drain the bottle of orange juice and return to bed. It will take lots of stamina and a good pair of walking shoes to cover all the sights tomorrow. Rome wasn't built in a day, but a day is all we have to behold its magnificence.

***

In view of recent events, the hours between dawn and dusk have passed quickly. All the ducking and diving has left Dan feeling punch drunk. The palms of his hands are a lighter shade of red, more ruby that claret; the skin is stretched tight over fatty muscle and rough to the touch, but the pain has eased. The drive home was uncomfortable, turning left or right caused the steering wheel to scuff a little. His eyes were on the road, but his mind was elsewhere; the prospect of riffling through her things just stimulated the hell out of him, so much so that now he cannot entertain the idea of sleep.

The hours tick by, they seem elongated somehow, forbidding. Even though his isolation is self-imposed, he is beginning to feel perhaps the time has comes to free himself, to let go. But that thought is no more than a flicker. In the blink of an eye, it's smothered out by time-honoured images of a more carnal nature.

In washed out boxers, he stands by the microwave, watching the turntable wobble and shake the molecules of his meal into a steaming heap of nothingness. He pictures her barefoot, wearing no more than a cotton dress, cooking.

"What would you like to eat, Dan?" she'd ask him.

"Only you, princess," he'd reply, lifting her off her feet and plonking her down beneath him. She'd laugh out loud. He'd pull up her dress and settle his eyes on her wet crotch. He'd finger her until she begged him to fuck her. And he'd do just that, making her scream in sweet agony.

The turntable stops revolving and the four pings sound, stealing Dan away from his erotic daydream. Dinner is served.

16

I hear unrecognisable voices. Rubbing my eyes I glance at the bedside clock, it's 8.30a.m.. As usual Ayden's side of the bed is cold. He appears in the doorway.

"Hey, you're awake. I was just coming to get you." He sits by me on the bed and brushes my hair from my cheek. "I've had them put breakfast out on the terrace. You'll need your bathrobe." I feel his soft lips next to mine; he tastes of toothpaste and smells divine.

"You should have woken me earlier." I smile, sit up and stretch.

"Why, you need your beauty sleep." From the arched brows and cheeky wink I know he is joking. "After last night's activity, I thought you'd be glad of the extra hour."

I make my way to the bathroom naked. "Are you suggesting I can't keep up, Mr. Stone?"

"I wouldn't dare, Miss. Parker." He's leaning on the door frame with his arms folded watching me pass, looking much too hot for this time of the morning. "Do you want me to come in and sponge you down?"

I close the bathroom door. "No thank you, I can manage, besides you need to recharge your own batteries for tonight."

"Rest assured, Miss Parker, my batteries will be fully charged by this evening," he calls, walking away.

This is the best way to start the day: playful banter is my favourite morning pursuit.

Fully dressed and with finger dried hair, I stroll out onto the terrace. A feast of all things delicious is arranged on the table: pastries, fruit, yoghurt and so forth. Ayden is reading the paper. He offers me a flat smile when I appear.

"See anything you like?"

I rest my eyes on him. "Oh, just one."

I'm rewarded with a cheeky grin. He's sitting comfortably on the patio chair; his right leg is off the floor, resting on his left knee. I don't know what he's done with his hair but it's all over the place, and I want to run my fingers through it, not to smooth it out but for the sheer hell of it. My God, it's nine o'clock in the morning. Get a grip woman!

I tip my head to the side, inspecting what he's wearing; pale blue jeans and a fitted white, cotton shirt with epaulets and covered buttons, very understated but very Ayden. I feel rather plain by comparison. I'm playing it safe with a black mini skirt, black tights, heeled boots and a simple baby blue sweater. As usual, he doesn't miss a thing.

"And does madam approve of what Sir is wearing?"

"She does." I blush, knowing by saying 'Sir' he is alluding to last night's love-making. Quickly I busy myself with the task of choosing what to eat.

"Oh, I'm *so* glad." I can't see his face behind the newspaper but I know he's grinning. "I like the mini skirt. It's very provocative."

I look up and meet his eyes above the newspaper with a wide stare.

Please don't give me the look...

"It's just a skirt," I muse, remembering how he said the exact same thing when I was so taken with his James Bond suit. I look away and begin spooning yoghurt into my mouth.

He folds up the newspaper and stands. "This hotel has a very good gym and a spa if you want to visit it later for a swim, a facial or a massage, whatever." His hands are on my shoulders; firm thumbs are easing the tension out of my shoulder blades and it feels very sensual.

"Good to know. I might pay it a visit later. Have you been?"

"I went to the gym and had a swim earlier, it felt good to exercise."

I'm saying nothing. I keep eating and enjoy the attention I'm receiving from his skilled hands.

He rests his chin on my head. "Are you happy, Beth?"

What a strange question. I swivel around in my chair to face him. "Of course, why do you ask?"

"I've been thinking about last night and things did get a little ... out of hand. You did safe-word me." He seems less self-assured than usual. He's recalling the orgasm 'thing.'

"I did. I realise now, it was your way of showing me how you were feeling. I had no idea I was affecting you like that." I place my hand on his and leave it there on my shoulder. "Now I know."

"And the thing with my belt?" Just the mention of that forces me to take an extra breath. "Did I misread your reaction? You did like it, right?"

My God, I have to turn away. I look down to hide my embarrassment. "Yes ... I liked it."

"And the toy ..."

"Oh, I especially liked that." I can't disguise my enthusiasm.

"And would you be happy to try some *other* toys?" He asks tentatively.

I nod, yes.

"But the scarf, that's out of the question ..."

"For now." I still can't face him, but all this talk of low level bondage is causing me to heat-up; my palms are becoming a little sticky to the touch, just like every other part of my body.

"Why?" He continues to massage my neck but now his fingers are moving under my hair, around my throat and, even though I've only just showered, I feel a fine layer of perspiration coating my skin.

"I ..." I know what I want to say but can't seem to find the words. "I think it has something to do with that thing I told you about, you know at uni?"

"I thought it might." He ends the massage, bends into me and kisses my neck from behind. It tickles and I giggle, he nips my right ear lobe and I pretend to wriggle away. "And how about feeling my hand on your delectable ass?"

"It was very ..." I'm having some difficulty forming a coherent sentence. "It was very ... arousing."

"Yes it was. Did I hurt you?" His words leave his lips like bubbles from a steaming bath.

"No, don't worry, you didn't hurt me. Nothing you said or did last night hurt me, quite the reverse."

"Good. And I plan on keeping it that way." He kisses my hair softly and returns to his seat opposite. I lower my eyes from his face and become aware of his almighty hard on. His pale blue jeans are bursting at the seam. I struggle to shift my gaze, but can't take my eyes off it. I swear I can see it stirring.

After what seems like an age, I shift my attention and our eyes meet. He knows I know and I swallow deeply, ensnared by his hunger for me. I feel myself flushing, betrayed by my lascivious thoughts.

"You see the effect you have on me?"

I observe the way his chest is heaving and how tightly his hands are gripping the arms of the wrought iron chair. He's experiencing a kind of sensual agony, it's painful to watch.

"This is how it's been for me since we met. I have withdrawal symptoms when I'm away from you. That's what I was trying to explain last night. I feel out of control and it's not something I'm used to."

I smile softly but leave him to spell out exactly what he's feeling.

"When I'm with you and this happens it's fine, I can deal with it. But in meetings, in the car, on flights, it's a whole different ball game. No pun intended." He stops to snigger at himself and I offer a sympathetic smile. "Is this how it's going to be, Beth?"

"You're asking me?" My voice is a little higher than usual and that only amplifies my nativity. "And ... when you get like ... like this, what are you thinking about?"

"What do you think?" He's becoming agitated and fidgeting like a fisherman sitting on hot rocks. He reels me in.

"I don't know." I shrug my shoulders. "Tell me."

"This, I'm thinking about this."

I look around the spacious terrace. "Eating breakfast on a terrace?"

"No, not eating breakfast on a terrace, being with you. Being anywhere with *you*." He glances out over the rooftops exasperated.

"Then don't." I say simply. "Don't think of me. Think of something else."

He shakes his head from side to side and his raucous laughter reverberates out across the terrace. "Only you, Beth. Only you would tell me *not* to think about you. Every other woman on the planet would say the complete opposite." He tries to settle himself in his uncomfortable jeans.

"It's just a thought." I look away, trying to look offended when we both know I'm not.

"You see, every time you say something like that, it makes me want you more because I'm reminded of just how willing you are to put me first, even if it means you being denied something you want yourself."

"I think you're reading too much into it, Ayden."

He leans over and takes hold of my right hand and sandwiches it between his. "Don't you think I know what you've done?"

I answer with a shrug.

"With no questions asked you welcomed me into your world. Saturday night curled up on your sofa; breakfast, watching you eat cereal with the sunlight behind you, rocking you to sleep while you sobbed into my chest over a silly fairy-tale and this ..."

I'm so overcome with emotion I can barely speak. "These are simple things, Ayden."

"They are to you. But they're priceless to me." He pauses to consider his next statement and looks deep into my eyes, watching me closely. "You've humanised me, Beth, and there's no going back."

"Oh, Ayden." I jump up from my seat and position myself across his knees, wrapping my arms around his neck. "You've done so much more for me." I pull back and take his face in my hands. "You have no idea."

"Neither do you, you're too busy seducing me with your soft ways to even notice that I have fallen so hard for you."

His impatient lips find mine and devour me with such passion, it's almost painful. "I could give up everything right here, right now. Liquidate the whole fucking lot and not batter an eye-lid and you know why? Because I have something more important in my life. I have you."

I lean back, placing my hands on his shoulders for support and also to keep him at bay. "Ayden ... hearing these words from your lips makes me so happy." I brush my hand against his mouth to emphasise the point. "But please don't rush into anything. I'm not perfect."

"No one's perfect, Beth, especially not me, but we're perfect for each other, perfect together and that's all that matters."

It's the right answer, and I fall softly into him. He lifts me up from the chair and slides his hand underneath my thighs and carries me like a weightless bride into the bedroom. "I make no apologies for what I'm about to do, but I *have* to have you. Right now."

The sexual longing between us crackles in the air like static; it cannot be harnessed only channelled into rough, hot sex. I feel the soft duvet beneath me and scoot backwards, watching him crawl onto the bed to reach me.

"I want your Spiderman music," I murmur. "Pass me my iPod."

While he samples the soft skin under my chin and nibbles on my ear, I press play and reach over to slot it into the deck by the bed. With every beat I'm arching my back and responding to his wet caresses. The bristles on his chin are tickling my stomach, making me giggle and so he does it all the more. His hands are lifting my skirt and strong fingers are squeezing my thighs. It's an exercise in self-control and I'm losing, losing myself in the music, in him.

He times his movements to perfection and when his hand slides between my legs, I writhe and push into his palm. I feel him pulling down my tights, my panties and I lift up to ease the process. I couldn't be any more saturated and ready.

Dear God just take me...

I reach for his face and sink my tongue into his mouth, urging him to do the same. He leaves me bereft. I hear the sound of him tearing the condom wrapper and watch as he lifts my knees.

"Wrap your legs around me."

I pin him into position, eyes locked, lips parted. He presses into me with a rigid cock, in need of no instruction. He knows what he's doing, he's making me wait, and so I rock into him until it presses against me.

"Say it, Beth..." I clear my thoughts of all things except two little words. The words he needs to hear. The words I want to say.

"I submit," I whisper.

His face explodes into a thousand megawatt smile for one split second, before he utters another impassioned command: "Pull."

I tighten my grip and drag him forward, my ankles locking and crushing him before he lunges into me with such force I think I might be pushed off the bed. My back is bowing under the strain and every muscle is tightening in my groin, as a kind of orgasmic wave drags me under, down, down to the point of no return. What started out as a game is now a serious case of unbridled, unstoppable fucking. This delectable man *has* to have me. That thought has me unravelling, throwing my head back in wild abandon, forgetting myself, forgetting everything; caught up in the overwhelming need to come over and over.

He lures me to the edge of oblivion with his relentless thrusting, coaxing me to clench and hold him deep inside. My quickening breaths echo his and our eyes fix on each other.

Through gritted teeth he stakes his claim. "You belong to me, now." He rolls his hips and I cry out, feeling him sinking further into my core. "Say it."

"I ... I belong to you."

With that I come loud and hard, gripping every inch of him until he explodes in a savage cry of liberation, pumping into me again and again.

Any doubt about this man's love for me evaporates, along with my fear he would love me any less, knowing the truth about my past. Today, I've seen him out of control, powerless, coming undone. And he thinks I'm the submissive one in this relationship?

As Ayden would say ... we'll see.

Getting ready takes less time than anticipated, it's just a case of redressing and freshening up. With time to spare, I text Charlie:
Having a great time in Rome, hotel suite is as big as our apartments put together and the view is amazing. We're off 2 C sights now. Wish you were here. Beth X

Her reply is instantaneous:

I hate you! Suite, Rome, sights, next thing you'll be telling me the bloody weather is fantastic and the men are gorgeous! Seriously, hon have fun. How's Mr. P shaping up? Is he keeping you well serviced? ;) C. X

I smile at her reply but decide not to play into her hands by responding. I throw my phone into my bag. I have an idea. Quickly I scroll through my iPod and find the one song that sets the record straight and place it back into the dock.

Ayden is sitting in the lounge waiting patiently, it's ten o'clock.

"Sorry I took so long." I grab my black Armani jacket and plonk myself down on the arm of the sofa next to him.

"I'll get my sweater." He squeezes my knee affectionately as he passes.

"You might want to press play," I call out. Immediately I hear the song. The words are very poignant. Will Young sings '*Happy Now*,' and sums up exactly how I feel. I lean back to assess his reaction; he has his back to me, his right hand clutching his sweater, the other in his pocket. He's listening.

The music stops and he returns to the lounge. "You did it again. You touched my heart with one of your songs." He threads his free hand under my collar, through my hair and plants a delicious kiss on my mouth. "Thank you." He rubs noses. "Let's go."

Hand in hand, we take the lift and descend to the ground floor, giving me time to fix my hat.

"Very cute," is all he says and it's all I need to hear.

We stroll through reception into the exclusive Stravinskij Bar for our rendezvous with Signorina Magnani. She's our private Tour Guide.

I scan the atmospheric space and take in its easy sophistication: mauve furnishings, mood lighting and abstract wall art. I feel under-dressed, again. Seated on the soft chairs are an array of people; guests waiting for flights, businessmen on laptops, middle-aged film star types wearing dark glasses and a lone woman sipping espresso from a fine china cup. Even from behind I estimate she's borderline model material. When she turns, sensing our arrival, I am in no doubt. She's stunning. I shift my attention to Ayden, he's noticed her too.

As we approach, I see she has a small netbook open and just visible is our book launch photograph and news story. She's checking Ayden out. My animosity towards this woman peaks; every nerve in my body is super-charged. She has brains and beauty *and* ambition. What a very challenging set of attributes to be faced with.

Up close I assess her. She must be around five nine, hazelnut hair and matching eyes, framed by long dark lashes. When she stands, she has legs which are disproportionately long for her height. Her jeans must be made to measure and her coffee coloured T-shirt, well, it's indecently clingy. I take an instant dislike to her and it's not surprising: her middle name is Temptation.

He reaches out for her hand, "Signorina Magnani, I assume?"

"Ah yes, Mr. Stone, what a pleasure to meet you, I'm Cara." By the way she greets him, I realise something: I'm about to meet my second adversary. With seductive eyes, she assesses him at the speed of light. I break her concentration by offering her *my* hand.

"Signorina Magnani, I'm Miss Parker, Beth. I believe you will be conducting our tour today?"

"Of course. Good morning. Are you ready?"

Don't I look ready? I'm wearing a hat and a jacket. Surely that's a big enough clue?

"I think we are," Ayden interjects, fixing me with an inquisitive stare.

"Sure, why not?" I turn and lead the way towards the reception. Cara raises her hand and wafts an instruction to the doorman to bring the car around.

"It is over three kilometres to the Colosseo, so we will take the car. Please ..." She holds out her perfectly manicured hand to Ayden. "Your limousine is outside Mr. Stone."

Yes, we all know it's his car.

In a gentlemanly fashion, he allows me to enter the car first. I wonder if it's so he can sit between us but when she opens the other door and sits up front, I treat myself to a grateful smile. This is probably one of those rare occasions when I'm happy to sit back and let Ayden's condescension keep the congenial Cara in her place.

He leans across to me and takes my hand. "OK?"

"Sure, I'm looking forward to seeing the sights, aren't you?"

He gives my hand a squeeze. "I mean are you *okay?*"

From the way he's tipping down his chin, he must be referring to our post breakfast, fast and furious fuck.

I mirror his sensuous stare and slip my thumbnail between my teeth. "Why wouldn't I be? I Belong To You."

He takes my thumb from my mouth but cannot hold-off on a sexy smile. "Yes, *you* do."

Here I sit with a neat pile of hands on my lap, trying to suppress a giggle. This is going to be an interesting day.

The tour gets underway with the monumental Colosseum; the four storey structure is in the heart of piazza del Colosseo. It stands before us at the end of a wide road, surrounded by poplar trees. It's bigger than I imagined and the sunlight on the brickwork creating shadows and crevices, adds to its charm. Cara escorts us over to the entrance, by-passing the queue of impatient tourists. She shows the security man her pass and we make our way beneath the arches and take a step back in time.

"It was built in 80AD and could house over 50,000 people who came to watch the gladiators' battles. Sometimes beasts were introduced to ..."

And on she goes with more dates, statistics and smiles, when all I want to say is "arrivederci!" The best part is the photo opportunities; Ayden has his phone and I have my digital camera and we never stop clicking.

One kilometre down Via dei Fori Imperiali, sits the massive ruins of the Roman Forum, the once corporate heart of the city. The mighty pillars stand tall and imposing but make for stunning photographs. Thankfully, Cara has less to say and leaves us to wander, climb and imagine how it must have looked in its prime.

Twelve long minutes away is Capitoline Hill along the Piazza del Camidoglio, the headquarters of current day Italian Government. These three stunning buildings, dating back to the 16th century, were designed by Michelangelo, including the impressive Cordonata, the staircase leading from the bottom of the hill to the beautiful square. It is adorned with granite statues of Egyptian lions at the foot and two large classical statues of Castor and Pollux at the top: a perfect backdrop for more remarkable photographs.

With weary feet and only half way through our tour, we reach the Pantheon. It's a glorious temple to the Gods which goes back to 27BC. Sixteen pink granite columns welcome us into the vestibule, antique bronze doors try but can't hold back time or the hundreds of tourists flooding through to inspect the tombs of ancient kings and queens. The dome opens up and what a breath-taking sight. To think, over the past 2,000 years, countless feet have walked exactly where we're walking. The scent of the multitude clings to the ancient stones like lichen. The building is a feat of engineering and a memorable sight for us both.

Cara takes our photograph, and I sense she's wishing our roles were reversed. Thankfully, Ayden suggests a coffee break. I suspect his phone is vibrating in his pocket and he needs to attend to it but, whatever his reason, I welcome it. Cara knows just the place.

The Tempio Bar overlooks the Pantheon and could be considered our half way house. I order caffè con panna for Ayden and I before heading off to powder my nose. I want a couple of minutes to myself.

It's been a while since I've experienced the noise and fervour of a foreign city; our bolt-hole has been a wonderful sanctuary. Here there are so many distractions, not least of all Signorina Magnani. Ayden has absolutely no interest in her but, I have to confess, she does disturb the peace. It must be difficult for her too; she can't have met many multi-millionaire, *former* playboys who look like him. Having said that, this tour would be so much better without her. My challenge is coming up with a justifiable reason to send her packing, without appearing like a jealous bitch. Something will come to me.

The toilets are adequate, and I wash my hands and check myself. I look okay, just okay. Time to raise my game. A dash of mascara and lip-gloss is as much as I can do, without looking like I've made too much of an effort. I don't want her to think I feel threatened by her ample bosom and seductive smile. This really is something I will have to get used to. He is doing nothing wrong, other than looking utterly irresistible.

I weave my way through the cafe, stopping in my tracks when I see her leaning across the table, coveting another woman's lover. My lover. I can't see her face but her body language speaks volumes. I shift my gaze to Ayden. He's responding with his polite smile, deploying it with the precision of a guided missile, but she couldn't possibly know that. She's mistaking it for weakness or responsiveness: poor Cara, if only she knew. I stand and keep watch, he doesn't need rescuing; he's in his element. Women like Cara are his specialty.

He is pretending to read a map of Rome when I return. Immediately Cara's back straightens and she adheres it to the rear of her chair. Our coffees arrive and Ayden sticks his finger into the whipped cream and gives me *the* look, but I have no inclination to play. I need my wits about me. I launch a *'don't you dare'* stare and look away. He licks the foam off his finger slowly, while I roll my eyes reprovingly and watch him stifle an intimate smile.

I know what you're doing Mr. P.

Cara moves away to the right of us but not out of ear shot. "Please excuse me, I have to make a call. Enjoy your coffee." While Ayden checks his texts and emails on his phone, I listen in and what an entertaining piece of banter it is.

Even with my limited knowledge of the language, I get the gist: *"un magnifico milionario... (a magnificent millionaire) molto semplice (very plain) ... Mi piace (I like)... Io gli do il mio numero. (Giving him my number)*

I've heard enough and have all the ammunition I need. I take out my phone and turn to Ayden, "There's a lovely restaurant I'd like to visit, it has rave reviews and a great lunch menu. Shall we go?"

He looks a little puzzled. "Now?"

"No, it's near the Spanish Steps, where our tour ends. I have the number here, I found it on the internet before we came." I scroll down my contacts and find the number for Nero. I touch his knee and lean over to him. "Do you want to play?" I lift my brows.

"Does it involve the soon to be leaving Signorina Magnani?"

"It does. Watch her face."

"If I must." He grins cheekily, making me even more determined to go ahead with my devious plan.

She seats herself. "Mi scusi. Are you ready to see the wonderful Fontana Di Trevi?"

"Not quite, give me a moment. I have to make a call." I remain seated and punch in the local number." Ayden places his thumb and forefinger around his chin in quiet contemplation; he's taking great delight in watching me execute my plan.

An elderly gentleman answers on the fourth ring. "Ciao, Vorrei un tavolo per due per favore.(Hello, I would like a table for two please.) Per le due e mezza per favore. (For two thirty, please)

In nome di Parker. Grazie." (In the name of Parker. Thank you.)

I return my phone to my bag and focus on Cara. She cannot hide her embarrassment. She realises I understood her less than complimentary conversation with her friend. Game, set and match I think, Signorina Magnani.

Ayden stands unexpectedly and towers over me in my chair; he places his hands on the wrought iron arms and tips me back slightly. I can't help but look up at him. What the hell is he doing?

With his lips touching my left ear, he whispers. "I'm so fucking hot for you right now."

When he straightens up, my heart is fluttering and I'm blushing like a schoolgirl. He never makes public displays of affection, but what a perfect time to start.

So everyone can hear, including our ex-guide, he says, "Ti adoro." And kisses me so gently I think I may have imagined it. When I open my eyes he's gone. I straighten out my clothes and regain my senses.

I turn to Cara. I do believe her mouth is open. "You see Miss Magnani, you were wrong. He does like his women *plain.*"

She has no answer for that and quickly looks away.

Ayden returns, drains his caffe don panna and speaks directly to her. "Thank you for your services, Miss Magnani, we won't be needing your assistance further. I'm sure with Miss Parker's Italian and my map reading skills we will be able to complete the tour on our own." He turns to me and reaches out his hand. "You can contact my office via the hotel. Bill me." Dismissively, he turns his back to her and we walk away.

I turn and see her beauty fade, ever so slightly, and then she is lost forever in the crowd.

He wraps his right arm around my shoulders and prepares to speak. "That manoeuvre was a tour de force, Miss Parker, I couldn't have done it better myself. She made a serious error of judgement."

I nod and keep my triumphant thoughts to myself.

"She under-estimated my little genie." He kisses my cheek. "Where are we going, any idea?"

I reach into my bag and lift out a small leather case. "I have my Sat Nav, we can use this."

"Great." He stands and watches me fire it up and, following on from an extended session of screen pointing, lead us in what I assume is the right direction.

Considering the Trevi Fountain is only supposed to be five minutes away, 30 minutes later we find it, having had a *slight* detour. In the middle of a very small square, over-crowded with tourists, stands Neptune in his chariot, being led by the Titans and sea horses. The baroque ensemble is spectacular and such a remarkable piece of sculptural engineering. I love it, even more so as we get to experience it together.

Ayden has me posing for photographs, and I turn this way and that, tip my hat, take a bow; he stretches out his arm and pulls me in close and tickles me at the same time. I must look as if I've lost my mind, but I don't care. I turn the tables on him but he's way too cool to pose. Instead he simply looks in my direction, peeps over his Ray-Bans and steals the show. Just as I predicted, the camera loves him and so do I.

We conclude the tour with, what on the Sat Nav appears to be a short walk to the Piazza di Spagna, where the Spanish Steps are located: one of the most photographed tourist attractions in the city. The 138 steps leave me gasping for breath but Ayden doesn't even break a sweat. I hardly have the strength to hold up my camera but he clicks away and I rest on the wall for five minutes. He wanders off to take a look at the church, and I find my second wind before looking for him.

When I reach the top of the steps and look around, he's nowhere to be seen amidst the jostling crowds of people. I keep looking and happen to spot a swathe of black hair in the middle of a group of young Italian women.

From what I can deduce, they've asked him to take their photograph, thinking and assuming with his chiselled features, athletic build and engaging blue-green eyes that he's Italian. Now they have him cornered, surrounded on all sides unable to escape. I lean against the wall, fold my arms and watch him do what he does best: charm them, even though he doesn't speak a single word of Italian. He speaks the universal language and actual words are unnecessary when you have a smile like that. One of them, an outrageously good looking woman of around 22, with auburn hair and a husky voice is asking him to go with her for a coffee. She is insisting. Does he need rescuing? I think so.

I stroll over, feeling the need to prise my 'husband' away from her audacious grip. "Mi scusi se mi credete avete attesa di mio marito." She instantly lets go of his arm and apologises. As I take him by the arm and lead him away, one of his admirers calls out to me.

"Siete molto fortunati donna."

She's right. I am a very lucky woman.

Ayden is unruffled, but a little put-out. "God damn women, they were like a pack of wolves, couldn't get away from them and didn't have a clue what they were saying."

"Oh, my poor Mr. P. I think you know exactly what they were saying." I smile, focusing my attention on the steps as we descend.

He says nothing and doesn't have to; his smirk says it all.

One hundred and thirty eight steps later, we reach ground zero and turn to look back. The Spanish Steps really are quite striking, but more fun than historically significant. I, for one, had a lot of fun.

To the left of them is a famous Museum. "Look where we've ended up, Ayden, exactly where we started." The thought of it takes me back to our first meeting, making me feel suddenly very reflective: how far we've come.

I point over to the pink and white stripped building. "It's the Keats' Museum. Do you want to go in?"

"Have we time?"

"No, not really. Our meal is booked for two thirty and it's twenty past. What a pity, you being a Romantics man too."

"That's me." He pulls me to him by my collar and looks down at me for longer than is comfortable.

"What?"

"I just want to take a minute to look at you. *'Beauty is truth, truth beauty, - that is all you know on earth and all you need to know.'*"

"Hello Mr. Keats." I take his face in my hands and on tiptoe, kiss him softly. Never has a quote been so fitting to a time and place. I feel his hands grasping mine and my arms being outstretched into a flying position. Passers-by step aside, giving us space.

He doesn't have to say anything, but he prepares to. "You stir my soul, Miss Parker." He releases my arms and lifts me off my feet, so our faces are level. "Ti adoro."

"I adore you too, Ayden." Overwhelmed by his declaration of love, I fight back tears and match his passionate kiss with my own. The noise around us fades, time stands still, all we have is each other and it's everything. He lowers me onto my feet. Feeling a torrent of emotion, I look anywhere but at him.

I hand my camera to a trustworthy looking English tourist. She's plainly dressed in sensible shoes. The perfect candidate. "Just click away," I tell her as we turn this way and that, leaving her to capture our merriment in each frame. I give thanks and realise the time.

"We'd better head off to Nero, we've only got a couple of minutes." With tears gathering, I search his face and see nothing but undying love for me, forcing me to stifle a cough and lick my lips. I'm moved beyond words.

"Come on, I think I know where Via Borgognona is." He takes hold of my hand, kisses my knuckles and leads me in what I expect, for the first time since leaving the Pantheon, is the right direction.

Nero is everything it professed to be; behind the terracotta coloured frontage lies a family run restaurant which has played host to the likes of Tom Cruise and Brad Pitt, but that's not why we're here. The ambience is calm and old-worldly; walls panelled with dark wood, mellow yellow walls and champagne coloured tablecloths.

An elderly waiter dressed in a smart, white shirt and jacket beckons us to our table in a quiet corner, sensing our need for privacy and seclusion. I ask what he recommends and we go with that, why not? Everything is supposed to be good here. Besides, I don't think I can sit and watch Ayden dissect what is already a very simple, traditional menu. Instead, I hand him the wine list and he opts for a bottle of Barolo Acclive and, of course, water to keep me cool.

We agree to share our spicy, garlic flavoured starters: Roman artichokes and marinated aubergines with a portion of sauted porcini. The main course is a revelation: osso bucco with mashed potato for Ayden and cannelinni beans, tagliatelle bolognese for me. The combination of old world charm and a typically Tuscan cuisine makes for a lovely meal. We have barely enough room for dessert but the castagnaccioa, chestnut cake, is too good to ignore and we order one portion and request "due cucchiai." The two spoons arrive and we devour what is probably the best cake in the world.

"This is a great little restaurant, Beth," Ayden remarks, sitting back in his chair and finishing off the remains of the wine. "It's very you."

"How so?" I'm curious.

"Classy, understated and unforgettable."

"I can live with that." I smile broadly, taking hold of his left hand across the table. "This has been a very memorable day, Ayden, not one I'll forget in a hurry."

"Me neither." He takes hold of my other hand and we steal another precious moment of quiet devotion. The waiter shuffles over with two tiny glasses of grappa and our bond is broken, but only temporarily. It will take more than a casual interruption to break what we have. It's probably too soon to call, but what the hell, I adore this man.

***

Considering it's only seven weeks until Christmas, the weather is unseasonably mild. There's a nip in the air but the sun is shining and there are splatters of blue between the grey clouds. With his pride restored, Dan ends his shift, settles himself behind the wheel of his patched-up BMW and hits the accelerator. The roads are busy, white lines stretch out for miles as the storm clouds gather and swallow up the daylight; usually cats' eyes point in one direction, to Elm Gardens, but today they seem to be leading him nowhere. Without his girl in his sights he's lost, moving forward aimlessly without purpose.

The 54 mile journey from Cambridge to Harrow is a pleasant one, giving him time to think through his plan of action and to take in the scenery. He continues to push the car hard. Even though he's finished an hour earlier as it's Friday, he wants to get to Elm Gardens before nightfall. His reason being he won't have to switch on any lights and draw attention to the fact that there's someone in her apartment, when she's supposed to be away.

Just in case, he's brought supplies along: a small torch, his knife and, not forgetting the most important item, a set of her keys. He has every reason to believe that the technicians will not have set the alarm and so, this is his window of opportunity.

Knowing he's within touching distance of her stuff causes a familiar twinge to circulate his nether region. For days now, he's been out of sorts, not himself, but he's about to put all that behind him.

All fired-up, he enters the apartment block and makes his way upstairs, whistling and heavy-footed, knowing Pat will have seen him arrive. If anything goes awry, she'll be his alibi.

Once inside his apartment, he cautiously checks the front of the property for any new vehicles, or any unwelcome guests. There's no one and nothing out of the ordinary. Next, he slips on the latex gloves and fixes them in place over his hardened, boxer's hands and throws his rucksack over his shoulder. All set.

Having already worked out which stair creaks and where to step, he tip-toes down two flights of stairs and takes a moment to listen. The coast is clear, he makes his move and enters 53a, allowing the door to click softly behind him. He closes his eyes, savouring the moment, taking it all in: the delicate floral fragrance, the ticking of the clock, the silence. He breaks it.

"I could be happy here."

With his senses finely tuned, he scans the room with telescopic vision, wondering what to touch, taste and take. There are endless possibilities. Bypassing furniture he heads for the bedroom. It beckons him like a homing beacon, with promises of sweet surrender and sex. Even before he opens the first drawer he's hard and primed.

The large set of drawers near the door invite him to fondle their contents; to sample the sweet sensation of lace on skin. He removes the glove on his right hand and rummages through underwear, lifting, sniffing, kissing; he wipes the sweat from his brow and licks the crotch on a pair of delicate white panties.

"I usually take, princess, but I've left you a gift from me. It's only fair."

He dismisses one item after another. He'll know it when he finds it. Everything is new, he wants something worn and a little frayed around the edges. He slides the top drawer shut, still in search of that illusive item. His next stop, her wash basket.

The bathroom light flickers on, illuminating the many lotions and potions that have felt her fingers inside them; he envies them. He tips out her wash basket and rummages through the contents like a vagabond, smiling when he strikes gold. It's a simple blouse, the one she was wearing when he saw her on Monday night; beneath the arms are patches of sweat the size of tea bags. He smiles with satisfaction. The blouse fits easily in his rucksack.

Next stop, her bed. He pulls back the duvet, revealing clean, white sheets. "Very nice," he comments, approving of the simple bedding. His hand glides along the bottom sheet, it's cold to the touch but sensual nevertheless. With his eyes closed, he can picture her there, lying, waiting for him and reaching out. Better still tied and gagged, squirming on the sheet until it ripples beneath her like a wave of white foam. As he pictures the scene, an upwelling of something hot and powerful overcomes him. He cannot rid himself of it. In his mind's eye there is not a shred of self-doubt: he *will* have her.

For the time being, he settles for masturbation. He drags her blouse from the rucksack and crushes it between his fingers; with his other hand, he wrestles with his belt and his fly, eager to act out his fantasy. Being careful not to put his feet on her bed, he lies across it and manhandles himself until he climaxes with a guttural roar. His semen is smeared across his jeans, over the sheets and has over-spilled onto the carpet, so forceful was his release.

"Fuck me. You sure know how to show a guy a good time." He wipes himself off with the blouse. "That's my girl."

He arranges his clothes and flattens out the bedding, taking care to smooth out the duvet. "Looks as good as new," he commends himself, smiling with self-gratification.

In the kitchen, he checks the contents of her fridge. He tuts and nods his head. "Oh dear. What have we here?" He closes it and continues his exploration of 53a. He walks over to the French doors and doesn't bother to open them; he already has the key. Thinking ahead, he pulls down the top bolt, just in case.

Before leaving, he sits himself down and acquaints himself with the layout of the place. The sofa is the most appropriate vantage point to take it all in. Feeling at home, he lifts out a cigarette and lights up, taking great delight in his accomplishments. "We're going to have a lot of fun here, Beth, until we retire to your new home upstairs." He crushes out the cigarette between his fingertips and rubs the fallen ash into the carpet. Has a prolonged look at the cosy space and pulls the front door shut behind him.

With a happy heart he tiptoes upstairs, feeling like a real contender.

17

W hen we arrive back at the Nijinsky Suite, I'm thrilled to see flowers in the room. Two enormous bouquets overflowing with pure white calla lilies and giant chincherinchee and philodendron leaves, expertly tied with a phormium leaf to create an extravagant indulgence for the senses. I look over to Ayden and mouth *'thank you'* and he mouths back *'you're welcome'* and it's enough. I feel tears forming and I'm not entirely sure why. A moment alone, sitting on the bed and it hits me: it's attention overload. It's so much more than I'm used to. We've come so far in such a short time and yet it feels as if we've been together forever. You know when it feels right and this feels right. We're at the stage where it's almost too good to be true and now all I can do is wait for the bubble to burst. Tonight, there's every possibility it may happen and that's a very scary thought.

He bounds into the bedroom looking like a cat on a hot tin roof, all fired up about something. "Do you mind if I have a quick shower before dinner, I've got some calls to make?"

"No, of course not, you go straight ahead. I'll check my emails if that's okay and upload the photographs?"

"Fine." He disappears, unbuttoning his shirt on route.

His laptop patiently waits in the study for his return. Along the task bar is his email counter: he has sixty-seven emails waiting to be read, and something tells me at least fifty percent of them are urgent. By dedicating so much of his time to me, he has put himself under immeasurable pressure. I had no idea.

I check the thirty emails I have received over three days and dismiss ninety five percent of them. Charlie gets an update. I check my Twitter page and delete everything else. It takes five minutes. My finger hovers over Ayden's email counter, I really want to take a look, but I think he's out of the shower and I'm not about to be caught spying.

I occupy myself with the simple task of transferring photographs from his iPhone and from my camera onto his laptop, creating one long slideshow. I sit back and enjoy the visual memoir of our romantic holiday in Rome. I'm surprised at what I see: a catalogue of images, predominantly of me.

Some of the shots I remember, but most I don't. His eyes had been on me the entire day, even at those times when I was consumed with jealousy and more so when I was left alone with my thoughts. Unselfconscious shots merge into playful poses, all lovingly framed in Rome's eternal light but, more importantly, what the photographs have captured is our love. We are so undeniably into each other, of that there is no doubt.

Such is Ayden's imposing beauty that he elevates the attractiveness of those around him, me included, and that's something I hadn't bargained for. He has taken me out of the darkness and has shown me what life can be like out of the shadows and there's no going back.

I copy all the photographs onto my pen drive for safekeeping and pop it into my bag. These are treasured images I will want to view again and again.

The terrace beckons me, and I wander out to take my last breath of Rome's early evening air. This time tomorrow, I'll be back in my minuscule apartment sipping tea and loading a washing machine. Ayden will be preparing for his trip to Hong Kong, taking my love with him.

He appears behind me, hair dripping down my neck and Calvin Klein's Obsession filling my nostrils. What a titillating treat for the senses.

"Do you want to go and get ready, I have a table booked for seven and you might want to wear something special?"

I need no further encouragement and turn around to face him, tracing the grooves forming between his eyes with my forefinger. "If you have work to do, I can call room service later and we can eat here. I appreciate the time you've lavished on me, but life goes on for you outside these four walls." I glance around at the open space. "Metaphorically speaking."

He smiles and runs his hands through my hair. "I'm good. Give me an hour or so and I'll be all yours." He kisses my nose affectionately.

"It's a date. Right here in sixty minutes. Dry your hair though, I don't want you catching a chill." I head back inside and blow him a kiss.

"Yes, dear."

He watches me leave, and I swear I see the smile fade from his lips with every lengthening stride. What is he keeping from me? We've become so close but there are still so many secrets to be shared, not all of them pleasant and perhaps, not all of them worthy of forgiveness.

I select music from my iPod by the bed as a distraction. The familiar sound of Ellie Golding's *Starry Eyes* fills the room and I sing along, effortlessly. My favourite Alexander McQueen dove grey gown draws my eye; it fits me beautifully and the oversized bow is a stunning accent to the bustline. I lay it across the golden duvet, and it rests there like a dusting of snow on a rural landscape. I can't wait to pour myself into it.

Seventy minutes later and I'm dressed to impress: silver clutch and heels, simple platinum jewellery and I'm ready to face the world. When I stand before the full-length mirror, I barely recognise myself. I have been awoken from a great sleep and transformed into a vision of beauty, and it's all thanks to the man in the next room. He has liberated me and I am forever indebted to him.

Straightening my dress and taking a deep breath, I open the bedroom door and make the short dash over to the lounge. A man in a waiter's outfit moves across the corridor to my right and another appears out of the lounge. "Hello?" Ayden is nowhere to be seen until, that is, I walk out onto the terrace.

My jaw hits the floor.

The terrace has been turned into a wonderland; flickering tea-lights scented with jasmine frame the entire area and, centre stage is a table covered in a white table cloth, crystal wine glasses and tall white candles. It's picture perfect.

He turns to face me and, as if the whole romantic milieu wasn't enough, he's dressed in a black dinner suit, complete with bow tie. He makes my chest hurt and I reach for it with my right palm and try to take it all in. My tear filled eyes scan the area and I notice the string quartet, patiently waiting for their cue to start-up. Ayden clicks his fingers and they begin. I cannot speak. I cannot move. I am awe struck.

"You look so beautiful, Beth," he states, taking my hand and twirling me around so the tiny train wraps around my ankles.

My spell of silence is broken. "Wow! This is amazing, Ayden. I thought we were going out to dinner." I brush his hand against my cheek and feel the early evening breeze in my hair.

"Isn't this more romantic?" He captures me with a hopeful stare.

"Just a bit! How did you organise it in such a short time?" I pick up my dress and take his arm.

"I spoke to the Manager this morning and he sorted everything out. I did very little." He pulls back my chair and I seat myself.

"Don't make light of it. This is a grand gesture and I love it. Thank you."

I slip his hand into mine across the table for the second time today and reignite that spark of sensual longing between us. This wonderful man moves me in so many ways. "Ayden, you look insanely handsome." I make no excuses for gushing.

"*Insanely* handsome, I like that." He gives me a broad smile and I reciprocate with a playful pout.

Before beginning the meal, he ushers over a tall, blond haired gentleman of about 25 who is carrying an array of cameras around his neck.

"This is Josh. I've flown him in to take a couple of photographs." Ayden reaches for my hand and I stand, unsure of exactly what I'm supposed to do or where I supposed to stand.

Thankfully, Josh is a consummate professional. He drags over a powerful light, tilts it in our direction and positions us in such a way I know we'll look perfect together. Sensing my nervousness, Ayden touches my waist with his fingers, making me smile broadly and I gaze up at him. I must look like a lovesick teenager but, what the hell. I'm deliriously happy and I don't care who knows.

Twenty minutes later, he leaves us to our meal. We talk quietly until the waiter arrives with the first course and, even then, I find it difficult to stop smiling. Being crazy happy can do that to a person.

Our musicians leave at around 8.15p.m. and the plates and coffee cups are cleared by 8.30p.m. We take our glasses of champagne over to the sofa and sit back, gazing up at the heavens. The night sky has descended and turned into a rich, midnight blue; sharp, little stars are piercing the velvet clouds, twinkling above our head. Ayden has his bow tie undone, resting around his collar and hanging seductively around his open necked shirt. Casually coiffured and composed in his dinner suit, he strikes a princely pose. What more can I ask for?

"This has been a wonderful break, Ayden, I can't remember ever being this happy."

"It's not over yet." He knows something but isn't telling. The only clues I have are a knowing look and a coy smile.

"Oh no! What have you arranged a meteor shower, fireworks?"

"No but there's an idea, let me write that down." He pretends to pat his jacket, as if looking for a pen and paper.

"Oh stop. You can't top this, so don't even try." I take hold of his left bicep and wrap both my arms around it. "To think I ever doubted you." I begin to laugh at myself.

He's intrigued. "Whatever do you mean?"

"When we met, you said you were, I quote '*a Romantics man*' and I said '*I doubt that.*' Do you remember?"

"All I remember is wanting to take you in my arms there and then. And you saying I didn't win. That's what *I* remember." His tone is clipped but it's merely for effect.

"That's close enough," I concede. "Anyway, it's been a trip of a lifetime and I want to make one last toast to memorable days ..."

"... And unforgettable nights."

Oh yes, especially those.

The thought of his hands on me, makes me fizz all over. "Cheers."

Our glasses touch and the sound of them chinking echoes into the night. "Cheers."

Ayden inhales deeply. For some reason his chest feels a little tight and, even though his eyes are overflowing with green gorgeousness, he's preoccupied. I wonder why.

He gazes at the night sky and back down at me. "You know, Beth, of all the stars I have ever looked upon, you are by far the brightest and the most precious."

Wow!

"Listen to you waxing lyrical! We'll make a poet out of you yet," I tease. "That's a lovely thing to say."

But there's more. "I've not done my party piece yet."

Allowing him to see the depth of my love for him, I raise my head. Can he see it in my eyes?

> *"O first and fairest of the starry choir,*
> *O loveliest 'mid the daughters of the night,*
> *Must not the maid I love like thee inspire*
> *Pure joy and calm Delight?"*

I know this poem. "Samuel Taylor Coleridge?"

He nods. "It's a much longer poem but that's the part I like the best, that's the part that reminds me of you."

I snuggle up even tighter. "Thank you, it's beautiful. You're a romantic at heart, Ayden. Don't let anyone tell you otherwise."

Right here, right now, there's no place I would rather be. In a single heartbeat, I'd trade every night spent alone for this. My destiny has been decided for me and I'll willingly continue to follow my fateful star, wherever it leads me. I break the silence. "We packed a lot in today, don't you think? I had fun."

"Sure you did, once you calmed down and started to enjoy yourself."

I know where this is going. "I was calm, for most of the day anyway."

"Not when our delightful tour guide was around, you weren't." He's tilting his head down, waiting for my response.

"Can you blame me? She thought she had you in the bag." Now I have his attention.

"Really? That's interesting. What gave her that impression?" He raises me off his chest, positioning my face directly in front of his.

"You were giving her *the* look."

He's smiling boyishly. "What look?"

"The one you have perfected over the years, the one you use on unsuspecting females when you want them to fall at your feet. The one you use on me."

He starts to laugh but it's embarrassed laughter. He's been found out: his cover is blown. "And how do you feel when I give you *the look?*"

"Don't be coy, Ayden, you know." Affectionately, I push him away with my flat palm.

"Yes, I'm sorry, I do know." He kisses my forehead. "I do it on purpose with you, but no one else. I only have eyes for you, baby. You know that."

I don't say a word. I'm content to look upon my handsome suitor and quietly glow.

"Nothing I have done before could possibly compare to the fun we had, *I* had today, having *you* as my tour guide. Watching you and your Sat Nav leading us up every back alley in Rome was priceless."

"Are you ridiculing my orienteering skills?" I smile, feeling a little self-conscious but bemused at the same time.

"Skills!" His laughter is a roar and so forceful, he almost launches me off the sofa.

"I got us from A to B didn't I, eventually?"

"Eventually being the operative word."

I pretend to be offended. "You weren't exactly Marco Polo yourself, you know?"

"I chose not to be, it was *your* day."

I look into his eyes; they are filled with warmth and love. "What do you mean?"

"I've been around Rome several times."

"You didn't say."

"You didn't ask."

That's true. "So, all the time you knew where we were going?"

"More or less, or rather the Sat Nav on my iPhone did." He gives me a 'got ya' smile.

"But you didn't use it, why not?"

"Because it was more of an adventure for you. For us." As hard as he tries he cannot hold back on the laughter. "But when we were five metres away from the Trevi Fountain, could almost feel the spray on our faces, and you were pirouetting, trying to find your way, it was beyond funny then."

I burst into laughter. He does have a point. "It was that bloody arrow, it kept shifting and changing direction on me."

He cannot speak for the laughter, he's throwing his head back and tears are gathering in his eyes. "That's what happens when you've reached your destination." Still chuckling, he reaches for our glasses of champagne. "To memorable days." Still he finds it difficult to drink because of stifled laughter.

"I hate you," I muse playfully, climbing over him until he is lying beneath me, eyes full of laughter, heart full of love. "I'll get you back for this."

"Please feel free." He takes my head in his free hand and pulls me to him. "Happy days, Beth. Happy Days."

The laughter subsides and we snuggle together, basking in the afterglow; pheromones thick in the air, triggering my desire for sex. But what I have in mind is more of a sexual *fantasy* than physical intimacy.

I stand before him. "Give me a minute then go and sit on the chair in the bedroom, don't turn on the light, don't undress." He's curious and I'm resolute. I glance back at him, he looks so refined and in control, but not for long ...

He calls out, "I'll be waiting." and I picture a sexy smile.

When I appear from the bathroom, I know I look good. The black basque Celine suggested I buy gives me confidence and God knows I'll need it to pull this off. Victoria's Secret is not a secret any more.

I set myself, winding the supple cord I brought from home around my hands as I walk out of the bathroom. At first glance, I see he is sitting comfortably, resting his right leg across his left knee. When I appear, he leans back in the chair, tips back his head and widens his stare. "Wow! Look at you."

With the glow from the bathroom acting as a backlight I stand, legs splayed, black Louis Vuitton heels firmly planted on the carpet.

"You have been very bad, Ayden." I press the iPod remote and Mr. Timberlake sings *Future/Sex, Love/Sounds* and my alter ego strikes a pose.

"I have?" He tries to mask a smile, but the warmth radiating from his handsome visage tells me he's enjoying himself. "Can you find your way over here, or should I fetch your Sat Nav?"

I try to suppress a chuckle, feeling the effects of the champagne and the left over laughter from ten minutes ago. "No I have you in my sights." I approach him and feel his eyes burning through my half naked torso. I like the feeling.

"You seem to have gone out of your way to make me jealous today." I trace the shape of his face with the fingers of my right hand and slip behind him, building his anticipation and trying to contain mine. "I saw you, coveting the curvaceous Miss Magnani."

"... Coveting?"

He tries to speak, but I lean into him and place my fingertips over his lips. "Hush. I saw the way you smiled at her; I know that smile. I've been on the receiving end of it often enough." He's happy to play along. "Because of your fuck me eyes, you had her making all kinds of assumptions."

"Really?" He is genuinely surprised. "Tell me more."

"Oh, I intend to. Do you know what she said on the phone?"

"No, but I suspect you do." He's smirking.

I circle him, brushing his hair as I go, feeling the softness between my fingers. When I am in position behind him, I slide my hands from his shoulders, over his pectoral muscles and begin unbuttoning his dress shirt from behind; it's stuffed into his trousers and, after a couple of gentle tugs, frees itself from his warm body. I peel it back until it drops off his arms, leaving him deliciously naked from the waist up. At no point do his hands leave his thighs, he's letting me take the lead and I intend to keep it that way.

"I want to tie you up and fuck you," I mutter softly into his left ear.

He tips back his head and groans, raising his left hand to take a handful of my hair. "I was hoping you'd say that."

"Place your hands behind the chair." He obliges and I tie his hands together. "Is that too tight?"

"No."

I pull on the cord. "Is that tighter?"

"Yes."

I whisper in his left ear again. "Now I have you where I want you, I'll explain." In one languid movement I drag my left hand across his back and shoulders and then his chest, watching it rise and fall as I circle him like a skulking cat.

I position myself in front of him; legs spread wide, the moonlight at my back. "She said you were coming onto her and she was planning to slip you her phone number, but there was one *small* problem. What do you think that problem was?"

Without a moment's hesitation he answers, "That problem would be you, baby."

"Exactly. She considered me too ..." It pains me to say it. "Too *plain* to be a permanent fixture."

"Another serious miscalculation on her part," he points out, tipping his head to the side and setting my flesh alight with a vertical stare.

"Quite." I move closer to his face, close enough for him to look, to smell. I stretch out a blindfold. "Now tell me, do I look *plain* to you?"

He smirks sexily. "Oh, baby you could never be plain."

I descend onto my knees and look up into the dark pools forming in his eyes. "And what flavour would you say this is?"

"It ain't vanilla," he states without a second thought.

My insides clench in response. "No, it ain't and we're just getting started." I play with the blindfold. "I was going to blindfold you, but I've decided against it. Watch how I please you."

The searing look he lets fly causes me to arch my body towards him, he's just too fucking hot; he's tied up and still calling the shots. "Choose a safe word."

"I won't be needing a safe word," he states, holding my attention for far too long. "You think too much of this body to damage it."

How right he is...

"Oh I wouldn't be so sure, what I have in mind may surprise you."

"Then surprise away." He's actually calling my bluff. I hate and love it in equal measure.

"In that case, we'll say it's 'Romeo,'" I declare, confidently.

"Whatever."

I crawl up his knees and then his thighs before sitting astride him, rubbing myself against his swelling erection while my mouth lingers on his left ear, his neck and finally his mouth. "Do you want to call me Beth or Elizabeth?"

He takes no time to decide. "Elizabeth." He pushes his nose into my hair and even his breath excites me. For a second I forget who's supposed to be in charge, and he feels me giving into him.

"This isn't something Beth would do."

When I lean back he is so indecently sexy, he makes me want to sink myself onto him. "Okay, Elizabeth it is then." He constructs a semi-serious stare and I feel as if I have control, or the illusion of it.

I make my move and head south; his dress pants are welded to his perfect body by a soft, black leather belt. I slip it out of the loops, drag it through with my left hand and wear it around my neck like a scarf. He jerks slightly, feeling my hands squeezing his thighs on my way down to his feet.

"I'm going to take off your shoes and tie you up." From his expression, it is clear he is enjoying this game; he is passive, cooperative and utterly delectable.

I fling his handmade shoes across the room and massage his muscular calves. Making it up as I go, I slide the belt from my neck and loop it around the leg of the chair, securing his right leg and then his left leg. Stringing out this game will not be easy.

"Let's get started." Even though I'm not seeking permission, he nods. I scrape my fingernails down his bare chest, only stopping when my hands rest on his waistband. I make short work of his buttons and zip and, with my eyes on his, slip my hand inside his boxers, feeling through pubic hair until I reach firm flesh. I'm not sure whose breathing hitches first but I know mine is getting to the point where I'm having to open my mouth, to inhale extra oxygen.

"You're hard and ready for me, Mr. Stone," I gasp.

The look he gives me is hot enough to start a fire. "I'm always hard for you, Elizabeth."

"We'll see."

My words resonate and we have a shared recollection of the previous night's conversation. I'm unprepared for the increasing intensity of his libidinous look: it sets my insides alight, forcing me to squirm at the thought of him inside me.

In a spontaneous act of physical longing, I pull down his trousers and his boxers to his knees. He's tied, hands and feet, virtually naked and clearly aroused, and yet it is he who has the power over me. I want to ask for guidance but dismiss my need for direction. I can do this. I have to set him free.

I position myself in front of him and wriggle out of my black lacy panties, giving him time to take in the implication of my exhibitionism. This time, when I settle my sodden crotch on to his flexing cock, he is visibly overcome with carnal lust. His expression hardens and his top lip twitches unconsciously.

"You feel so wet," he mutters, dragging out the vowel for effect and tipping back his head, giving in to the sweet sensation of moist flesh rubbing up against moist flesh. My clitoris is aching for attention and my hand fulfils that need. I'm so wanton and allow him to watch as I please myself.

"Jesus, untie me." He's becoming agitated, pulling against his restraints as I edge closer to climaxing. I brush away his words with my other hand and he sucks ravenously on my fingers until I am able to fold my lips over his, moaning into his open mouth.

Words hiss from his lips. "That's it, let me hear you."

My gentle punishment gets underway: I'm denying him access to my sex and it's driving him crazy. He's frantic with lust. I begin to cry out, I'm so close.

"Fuck me, Elizabeth."

I ignore his plea, taking his chin in my right hand, turning him to the left, allowing access to the right side of his face and neck. I drag my tongue along his chin then taste his lips with the tip of it, as I come loudly against my hand. He sucks my tongue into his mouth, desperate for physical contact, tugging and pulling against the cord and the belt keeping his feet in place.

Still panting I reach for the condom, concealed in the top of my basque, tearing it apart with my teeth. He's lurching and rearing off the chair, his hard cock is pulsating underneath me, frantically seeking me out.

"You can't do this."

I look into his eyes, knowing this is fast becoming more than a game. "I can and I will. You're not giving yourself to me, Mr. Stone. All this time you have been pretending and that's a very naughty thing to do."

"Stop ... *Beth!*"

He just took himself out of the game.

"Stop pretending, Ayden." I stand over him, leaving his most treasured organ exposed. I slide the condom down it, causing him to throw back his head in ecstatic agony. I grip the rigid shaft and place the tip against the entrance to my vagina; it slides back and forth against my saturated skin

"Christ, Beth!"

"Now I want you to give yourself to me, say the words and make it real, Ayden."

"I love you, Beth, isn't that enough?"

"No. Accept your fate." I begin to rock my body back and forth whilst fisting his rigid cock, knowing he desperately wants to be inside me.

"Stop! Beth, I can't."

"Then use the safe word. Make me stop," I order him. "You have to say the words, Ayden, not for me, but for you." I lean into him and whisper in his ear. "Give it up for *me,* baby." Those words take him to breaking point.

He calls out. "Yes, yes I submit. Everything I am, you have me. I Belong To You." Between gritted teeth he commands. "Now, fucking ride me!"

It's what we both need to hear and, with those words echoing in my ears, I sit onto him, taking him deep inside, gripping his legs until it's almost painful; clinching and crushing him internally.

He growls, "Ride me."

I respond, picking up speed, moving to a turbulent rhythm, swerving and rocking until the heat in my groin reaches boiling point.

"I'm going to come so hard," he exclaims, arching his back off the chair. "You're so fucking hot, you're killing me, Beth."

His ejaculation ripples through me and triggers a chain reaction. I come and contract around him, and he pumps out into me again, jerking and groaning into the darkness.

I wait until he stills and rest my head on his shoulder; his skin is clammy and glazed with sweat, but it doesn't matter, he's still the sexiest guy in the known universe. I ease off him on unsteady legs, and edge behind him to untie his hands. When I release him, I see there are red rings cut into his skin. I kiss the red areas and he rests each hand against my face.

I straddle him, preparing to say ... what? 'I'm sorry I hurt you.' Tears sting my eyes.

He raises my face to his. "You didn't hurt me, Beth. You've saved me on so many levels. I adore you." He plants a soft kiss on my lips and strokes my hair with such veneration, I think I may weep. "Undo the belt so I can stretch out my legs."

I do so immediately, rubbing his ankles, fearing they too will be marked and sore.

Looking troubled, he takes the belt from me. "What have I done to my little genie?"

I smile adoringly and confess, "You've set her free," and fall into his arms.

It's three in the morning when I wake, with the sound of Ayden's words of submission still ringing in my ears. He's not beside me again and, I realise, it's his voice I can hear. The only difference is, he's not submitting now.

I trot into the bathroom and glance at myself. I'm weary from lack of sleep but behind my fluttering eye-lids, there's a brightness that wasn't there a fortnight ago; my eyes are glistening with love. I tip-toe into the lounge and the volume increases.

"It's three in the morning ... I've told you not to call me. It's over. I didn't say that, I didn't promise you anything ... you need to move on. No, you can't come round, I'm out of the country. It's none of your fucking business who I'm with ... look it's late ..."

The floorboard creaks beneath my feet, making me grimace. I've been found out. "Ayden? Is everything okay?" I call out, seeming as if I've just woken.

"Go back to bed, Elise. I've nothing more to say to you. Don't call me again. Goodnight."

His impressive silhouette comes over to me, any trace of harshness gone. "Hey sleepyhead, what are you doing up?"

"I woke and wondered where you were, is everything alright? You were shouting."

"Sure, it's business as usual in Hong Kong. You know? The time difference?" He turns me around into the opposite direction.

"Oh yes, I forgot."

Elise?

"Let's get you back into bed." He slips his arm under my naked body, picks me up off my feet and carries me back to bed as if I weigh nothing at all.

The soft sheets are cold beneath me. Nuzzling into him, I feel how cold his body is and I wrap myself across him, sharing some of my warmth. "You must have been there for ages, you're so cold." I begin rubbing his left arm with my hand.

"I'm warming up, see?" He slides my hand onto his growing erection. "... and getting warmer by the minute."

"Mmm... and so you are." I smile into his chest and rub my hand up and down the hardening shaft.

He gives me back my hand. "I'm sorry I woke you. Let me give you something to help you sleep. Open your legs." I take his left hand and place it between my legs.

"You feel so moist."

I roll onto my back, allowing him to feel his way along soft flesh before sliding into me. His breathing hitches and so does mine.

"You're warm." He moves his fingers in and out to a rhythm that I synchronise with my rocking hips. He bends his fingers ever so slightly and finds that sensitive spot inside me. It feels divine.

"For someone who claims to have little experience of pleasuring women, you're a very fast learner," I state, breathless and needy.

"Long flight. Lots of research."

"Thank God for the Internet." Is my only response, even though I don't believe a word of it.

"Besides, you're a very responsive woman. Your body speaks to me."

I bet it does!

"And what is it saying to you now?" I pant.

He nestles his mouth against my left ear. "It's saying, make me come, Ayden." He's not wrong.

"Oh really?" I gasp and feel him slow slightly.

"I'm going to miss this. Just the thought of it will have me reaching for my cock."

Is he purposely talking dirty, because his words are bringing me closer and closer to a climax.

"Why don't you come with me to Hong Kong? We'll see the sights, take a cruise, sip cocktails at the Ritz Carlton and watch the sun go down. What do you say?"

The prospect of all that and the fact I'm a couple of strokes away from an orgasm make it almost impossible to say no, but I have to. My voice is hoarse and there's no way of concealing my arousal. "I can't."

He intensifies his penetration.

I'm starting to arch my back and groaning. "You shouldn't mix business with pleasure or the lines will become ... blurred." I just about get the words out.

"Oh. I'm way past that." The palm of his right hand begins to skim my stomach and I know what he's doing; he's using *both* hands to pleasure me. In the darkness, his face is just an outline; strong jaw, cheek bones carved out of marble, fierce eyes: a vision of masculine beauty.

"I want you to tell me something, Beth."

"Anything, just let me come."

"Not yet, tell me what you want, what I can give you. No holds barred, anything money can buy, whatever you've dreamed of. Tell me."

"Only you, Ayden. Let me come." I'm so close.

"No, you already have me. What can I give you?"

In my rapturous state, I begin to speak but hold back, focusing on my approaching orgasm. I reach out to his face and try to pull his mouth to mine, but he will have none of it.

"Tell me."

"A ... a..."

"Yes..."

"A ..." My insides explode and I lurch into his hands. "A ... baby." I come with such force, it leaves me trembling and gasping.

He's pulling out of me but still staring into my face. He is open mouthed and clearly shocked. "Did you say what I think you said?"

Dry mouthed I answer, "Yes, that's the only thing I want from you, after yourself. I want you to be the father of my children."

He falls onto his back, hands in his hair, gazing up at the ceiling. "I can't do that, Beth."

After several minutes of post orgasmic contemplation, I turn on my side to face him. "Can't or won't?"

"Both."

"Can't because of sperm count or won't because ...?"

He's shaking his head from side to side. "I'm not father material, believe me."

I rest my right hand on his heart. "Don't say that. You would be a wonderful father, any child would be so lucky to have you."

"You're right about so many things, Beth, but you're wrong about this. Like I said last night, I'm not *that* guy." He can barely look at me and it's painful to see him despairing over a single word.

I feel muscles settling beneath my navel; somewhere inside there's a part of me breaking into tiny little pieces. "You are *that* guy, Ayden, you just don't know it yet. I'm not talking about tomorrow, next week or next year. Just one day, that's all."

I fall back onto the mattress. What possessed me to scare him like that?

He rolls over, propping his head on his right palm. "Why is it you always find my Achilles heel? You push me to my limit with everything."

What a revealing thing to say.

My hand finds its way to his face. "Because I see you for the man you are and your potential for being so much more. You put it so beautifully yesterday." I blink away a tear. "We're not perfect, but we're perfect for each other. Is it so wrong to want a new life to come out of that perfection - the best of both of us?"

In an impulsive act of raw passion, he moulds his lips to mine and kisses me deeply, his tongue is licking and tasting me in a kind of frenzied eruption of pent up emotion. Where is this coming from?

"I don't think I could bear to share you, knowing someone else was inside you."

I try to speak. "But ... it would be you, for nine whole months, Ayden."

It's as if a light goes on somewhere in his fevered brain. He seems a little less fraught and slightly more sedate.

"Anyway, that's what you get for asking me what I want, ten seconds away from an orgasm. Ask me what I want tomorrow when my feet are on the ground and you might get a more favourable answer."

"I will." The sparkle returns to his eyes and I see the outline of a genial smile.

I pull his head into my neck and cuddle him like a small child needing my undivided attention and he responds, throwing his left leg over me until we are squashed together like two peas in a pod.

I stroke his hair softly. "Go to sleep, baby."

I feel his smile on my neck. "I love you."

"I love you more."

I concentrate on slowing my breathing and turn my head away from him, feeling salt water building in my eyes, bubbling over onto the pillow in a silent trickle. Even with my feet firmly on the ground, chances are, I would say exactly the same thing: a baby *is* all I want, after him, naturally.

***

With his BMW's capacity for speed and endurance already tested, Dan is about to give the chassis a road test. With time on his hands before his date with destiny, he's clearing away the numerous piles of newspapers and magazines he has accumulated over the years, in his hunt for *Beth* Parker. He's flinging pile upon pile of yellowing paper onto the back seats, having already filled the boot to capacity. The aging car looks as if it's been parked on an incline.

No one pays him any attention, he's a solitary figure in the darkness clearing his shit, maybe he's moving out. Who knows? Who cares? It's Friday night; everyone has something better to do.

When he returns to his apartment, it appears to have undergone a change for the better; he has room to move around, to cross from one side to the other without stumbling over yesterday's news. Best of all, he can stroll over to his cork noticeboard and speak with his girl, unhampered by stray inserts and junk mail. It's just the two of them and he plans to keep it that way.

"I visited your apartment tonight, princess, and enjoyed every minute of it. You weren't there but soon we'll be spending a lot of *quality* time together. You'll see."

He pulls out a cigarette and lights it leisurely, exhaling the smoke and watching it linger over her already fading image. With his free hand, he traces the outline of his erection through his jeans. "I hope Stone is treating you right, 'cause if he isn't, he'll have me to answer to. Fair's, fair, can't expect him to keep his hands off a pretty little thing like you." He pulls a speck of tobacco from his tongue. "I expect he's broken you in good and proper, got you used to feeling something hard inside you."

He's laughing and smoking at the same time, like a man intoxicated by his own grotesque fantasies. "We both remember how that feels, don't we, princess?" His hand never leaves his crotch, his eyes flicker from picture to picture.

"Not long now ..."

18

For some reason I wake, needing to visit the bathroom but take the opportunity to observe Ayden while he sleeps peacefully beside me. That's surprising, considering my revelation. Never has a man looked more captivating. I watch his finely honed chest rise and fall, the air leaves his mouth in whisper soft breaths and the skin around his eyelashes ripples slightly as he dreams. The pouting precision of his lips draws my eye; as if carved out of stone, his top lip forms that flawless V. I touch my mouth, remembering the taste of perfection.

His left hand rests on the pillow by his head, powerful but soft to the touch; the thick band of platinum on his middle finger, tempting me to weave my own between his to reaffirm our connection. How could he be so adamant about his lack of parenting skills, after everything he has done for me. He has such a good heart.

I edge silently into the bathroom and relieve myself. Shrugging on my bathrobe, I leave and tiptoe out onto the terrace. The sun rises at 7.40a.m. and I want to catch it as it welcomes a new day, a day that promises to be even better than yesterday, if that's possible.

The tea-lights have long since died but their fragrance lingers; the scent of jasmine pervades the open space and evokes memories of the night before: great food, great conversation and the greatest lover. What did I do to deserve all this?

The watery heat from the sun filters through the clouds, chasing away cool night air, casting a hazy film over the landscape: it's beautiful. From nowhere Ayden appears behind me, dressed in his bathrobe.

"Hey, what are you doing out here? You'll catch cold." He opens up his bathrobe and wraps it around me, folding my back into his naked body. "Couldn't you sleep?"

"I woke up to go to the toilet, but found myself out here watching the sun rise."

"Then we'll watch it together."

He kisses my neck and I lean back into him, my head resting just under his chin. There we stand cocooned in fluffy white robes, silently watching the shadows form on the tiled rooftops.

"This whole trip has been like a dream, Ayden, you've made it very special. Thank you." I take hold of his fists either side of my collarbone, where he grips onto his bathrobe. "I've downloaded the photographs, you should take a look."

"I intend to, there are a couple I'm especially looking forward to seeing."

I smile, recalling the one of me standing half naked in the bedroom and any one of a hundred or more he has taken of me. But, I'm haunted by a single sentence: *'untie me, Beth.'*

"You'd tell me if you felt uncomfortable about anything I've done, wouldn't you?" I ask.

"You'd be the first to know." As if he is reading my thoughts, he continues. "Last night, the submission thing, it started out as fun but giving up control, that wasn't easy for me. You were right though, I needed to say the words out loud; accepting that we are bound to each other makes things easier." He kisses my hair. "You've taught me that letting go isn't a sign of weakness: it's all about trust and that's the foundation of our love. It's taken me longer than you to figure it out. I get it now."

"Good, I don't want you to feel the way you did in L.A., so ... vulnerable." I pull his hand to my mouth. "It's the intimacy of it all that makes it so special; we don't have to give it a name. I'll always try to give you what you need to keep you strong, you know that?" I plant a soft kiss on his knuckles. "For all my games, I'm yours whichever way." I lean onto his warm hand and feel the heat of it on my cheek.

Gentle laughter rumbles through his chest and vibrates through my spine. "Baby, I was all yours last night." He whispers into my ear. "I would give the whole fucking lot up for you. You know that, right?"

"I do now."

"So, don't worry. I'm good." I feel his warm breath on my hair before his lips nibble my ear. "Anyway, all that's water under the bridge." He tightens his grip around me.

"I'm glad, being with you has made me realise just how lonely I was. I wasn't living. I was existing, getting through each day just waiting, waiting for you to find me."

"Thank you for waiting."

I start to laugh quietly.

"What's funny?"

"You thanking me, shouldn't it be the other way around?"

"That's where you've got it all wrong, Beth. I didn't know it at the time, but I was opening so many doors only to find they were leading me nowhere, when all the time I was searching for you. If you hadn't waited for me, then I would have spent my life never experiencing this." He nuzzles into my hair and breathes in my perfume. "And what a fucking tragedy that would have been."

I smile with a curious thought. "Good metaphor. How many *doors* did you open exactly?"

"Behave!" He grins.

That's as much as he is willing to say on the matter and I let it drop. I turn around to face him, his firm body radiating heat and desire, his eyes ardent and captivating. "I didn't mean to frighten you with the baby thing, but you made me confess. Under *normal* circumstances, I would keep thoughts like that to myself."

I witness the beginnings of a sexy grin. "You were under ... *duress.*"

"I was under *you*, or maybe that's the same thing?" I mirror his salacious smile and feel my mouth twitching as a result.

"There's an idea ..." Through my towelling robe I feel a frisky penis greeting the new day. "Now look what you've done."

He arches himself into me and I tip back my head in search of his lips. I can't conceive of a day when I will stop wanting this man. Even in the dimmest of light, his eyes enchant me. I can't pull away. I'll never pull away.

"You're insatiable."

"I'm yours," he confesses.

He releases my body; his arms rest by his side and the front of his robe remains open. He's standing there, exposed. "We'd better go inside. It's too cold out here for me."

Instinctively, we both look down, to check for adverse effects. From where I'm standing his impressive erection looks impervious to the drop in temperature. I start to giggle and wrap his robe around him. The last thing I want is to affect his performance capability.

"That's my second favourite sound," he smirks. We can both guess his number one. He takes my hand and leads me inside. "Come, I need to make love to you."

Our sumptuous bedroom is still in partial darkness; a small gap in the damask curtains provides just enough light to make out features but touch and taste are the primary senses being used for exploration. There's no denying his amorous intentions as I'm steadily reversed backward towards the bed, but there's something eating at my conscience: my confession. I have to tell him the truth about me, even though I know by doing so I'm risking everything.

"Ayden." I take hold of his face and hold him a couple of inches from mine, my neck still tingling from his moist caresses but, for me to say what I must, I will need all my faculties. "There's something I want to tell you."

He tries to remove my hands and inches in to continue devouring my supple flesh.

"No, I mean it. Listen. What would it take for you to stop loving me, to stop wanting me like this?"

He looks squarely at me, unable to comprehend my words. "Are you serious?"

I wish I wasn't but I am, totally. "Yes."

"You ask me that now?"

"Yes." My earnest expression settles him.

"Well, I don't know." He blows out a stream of hot hair. "If you were unfaithful which you're not; if you tried to interfere with my business, which you're not. What else is there?" He's at a loss.

"What if there was something in my past which was really bad and you found out? Would you still love me then?" I try to avoid being overly dramatic, but I'm failing miserably.

"Yes, I would still love you then." He tips his head to the right and begins making light of my conversation. "Why, what did you do? Rob a bank, cheat in an exam?" He laughs to himself and stops dead. "There is one other thing ..."

I nod yes, rapt.

"I suppose if you were a guy and you'd had a sex change, I might find that a little ... disconcerting."

"Oh, Ayden, it's nothing like that." I'm trying to be serious and all he can do is attach himself to my right earlobe. I push him away and rest my palms against his chest, like a mime artist traversing a sheet of glass.

"OK. What's got you so spooked?"

Now I have his undivided attention, the room starts to fold in on me, becoming a little claustrophobic: warm skin, intense scrutiny, heartbeats. I feel cornered. I begin: "Remember when I told you about being attacked at university? I didn't explain fully what happened and ..."

"You don't have to."

"Yes I do," I say, my voice rasping with grit and determination. I pull the cord tighter on my bathrobe, drawing it in and around my body. I prefer to wear it this way, like an invisibility cloak, something to hide behind.

He touches my troubled face and urges me to continue, sitting me beside him on the bed, his arm around my shoulder. He waits.

"This isn't easy for me, Ayden, but I don't want there to be any secrets between us, for you to be under any illusions about me. I've been afraid to tell you because I feared it would change the way you feel about me."

He's shaking his head. "Nothing you say could do that, Beth." He strokes my cheek with the back of his hand, not daring to actually caress it, offering only reassurance.

"Okay, then I'll give you the full story, instead of the edited highlights." I try to make light of it but, it's my nerves, they're jangling and making me say the silliest things; anything to fill the frigid air that is beginning to envelop me.

"Don't make light of it. It takes a lot to bare your soul. I should know. Now, take a big breath, and tell me what happened and then you'll be rid of it. And, if you don't want to, we'll never speak of it again."

Feeling my hand warming in his, I prepare to risk everything. "It was a Sunday night and a whole bunch of us headed out to the University Bar, it was an 80's theme night and I wasn't going to go because I had a 9a.m. lecture, but Charlie persuaded me. I was tired and decided to leave early."

"On your own?"

The intensity of his stare tells me he knows what's coming. "Yes, on my own. It seemed like a good idea at the time." I pause, reminded of my foolishness. "I caught a bus and then walked the rest of the way and had to cross a car park to get to our apartment but, out of nowhere, a car swerved in front of me, blocking my way. These three guys got out..."

Ayden's eyes are on stalks.

"Well ... they grabbed me and two of them held my arms and the one giving out the orders, he was this broad guy, over six foot. He put his hand over my mouth so I couldn't scream." My focus settles on a vacant spot somewhere by the window, as my mind replays the horrific scene. Like I always do, I pretend it's a scene in a movie. I turn to him. "He called me princess and kept making these lurid suggestions about what I secretly wanted to do to him - a real psycho."

Sensing what's coming next, he begins stroking my hair as if I'm a forlorn child or a Persian cat. I feel loved.

"He stunk of beer, I could smell it on his breath. I tried to fight but they held onto my arms and I couldn't break free. I was terrified."

"I bet."

"He said he had something for me and that's when ..." I swallow back bile. "That's when I felt the bottle ..."

Ayden's hand stills momentarily then finds its way from my hair to my shoulder; he pulls me into his chest and wraps me in his arms, cocooning me in love. But I've not finished. There's more. It gets worse.

"I thought he was going to kill me. Then a light came on and an old guy came out whistling his dog, taking it for a walk or something, I'm not sure. In the light, I got a good look at the guy's face; he was enjoying hurting me, I mean really getting off on it."

"The two guys holding my arms got scared and wanted to release me, but he didn't want to let me go. He pressed his face against mine, dragged his hand across my face and licked my cheek and said ... "This isn't over, princess, we'll finish this another time." I remember the words exactly because they were all I could hear for the next month or so."

"Beth, look at me." I meet his tender eyes. "It's all water under the bridge, remember. We've both had our share of experiences, good and bad."

I turn my head and look into his sympathetic face; in the half-light, I see his eyes glossy and kind. That look is more than I could have hoped for, more than I deserve.

"I've not told you everything ... I need to tell you."

"I'm listening." He leans back, giving me the time and the space I need to release myself from my affliction. He rests his hands over mine.

"I ... I heard them drive away laughing and managed to pull myself together somehow. I dragged myself home ..."

"... Did the guy with the dog call the police?" he asks, with a sombre expression.

"No, I told him not to, I pretended I was drunk and staggered off."

"And you didn't call the police?"

"No, I was too upset, I just wanted to dive into a hot bath ... I shouldn't have left on my own. It was a stupid thing to do."

"You weren't to know. Those fuckers should have been arrested or worse."

"I suppose." I bury my head in his chest. "When Charlie came back in the early hours, she found me in the bath. The water had gone cold and I was death white. She said she thought I was dead, I was the colour of alabaster." I try to smile. "She put me to bed and sat up all night with me. When I woke in the morning, she was still sitting there wearing last night's make-up and her 80's dress."

"And she called the police?"

"No, I wouldn't let her. I thought I could deal with it my own way, but I was wrong. It took longer to get over it than I expected."

"So the bastards got away with it?"

"Yes." I look up and find his eyes. We intensify our connection. "I'm sorry I lied to you, but it's so horrible and just telling you makes me feel soiled."

His hands wrap my face in warmth. "Never think that, Beth, you were very brave." A whisper of a kiss finds my lips. "I'm proud of you for being so strong. You came through it ..."

"No, I didn't, not really. He took things from me." He tips his head, inviting me to elaborate. "He took my bag, my phone and my purse, but those things are nothing compared to ..."

"Yes ..."

"When I looked at myself in the bathroom mirror, my face was smeared with blood, my blood..."

"He cut you!"

"No. He stole ... he stole my virginity and licked the blood off my face."

There is a deafening silence: it rings in my ears and stabs at my heart. He's lost for words.

"My poor baby." He wraps me up in his arms so tightly, I can barely breathe; crushing the pain and shame from me until it's too small to feel.

"So, you *were* a virgin when we met?"

"Not exactly ..."

"Yes you were! That doesn't count, baby ... you were and that's final. Don't explain. Don't tell me you weren't. I won't hear of it."

My sobs are smothered in his bathrobe. I'm warmed by his body heat. He's my comfort blanket.

He lifts my chin. "Tell me what Charlie meant when she mentioned the stalking."

He forgets nothing. "He kept my phone. People were sending me texts, so he knew my name. He even found out where I lived and called me on the communal phone."

"To say what?" He's wide eyed and patient.

"To tell me he would kill me if I told anyone, he knew how scared I was."

"So that's when you both changed your names and left Cambridge?"

"Yes, and the rest you know." I take a deep, cleansing breath; relief expels from my lips. I have told him. My secret is revealed and his to do with as he wishes.

He shakes his head from side to side. "You should have told me, Beth. I feel terrible, putting you in danger, putting you in the public eye after you'd been hiding for so long."

"You weren't to know, Ayden, media is your business and you have a high profile. I knew what I was letting myself in for with you." I brush back my dishevelled hair. "If you want, we can spend some time apart? You know, if you want to think about things ... about me."

He looks horrified. "Are you serious?"

I nod yes.

"Why would you think that? I need to be spending *more* time with you. Not less. I want to take care of you, I've done a poor job of it up to now, but that's going to be rectified. I can't let anything happen to you, Beth." He plants his face in front of mine, until there's only an inch of space between us. "With all my heart, Beth, I promise to take good care of you. None of that matters." He kisses me with so much tenderness and longing, I'm swept away.

"We've started over, we're creating our story, one chapter at a time. Our lives didn't begin 'til the moment we met, so let's stick to the story of us, okay? Nothing you say will ever make me want you any less than I do right now."

"I need you to make love to me, Ayden. To make me forget."

I stand before him and push my robe from my shoulders, leaving it to pool on the floor around me like a melted snowman. My body is my most precious gift and I want to give it to him. "Show me how much you want me, please."

"You don't want to invite Elizabeth along?" I'm floored by his generosity. He's willing to forgo his need for dominance for me, to submit, to capitulate without a fight.

How I love this man.

"No. She's taking the night off." I smile, feeling bashful as I stand, exposed. It occurs to me, here we are talking about me and my alter ego, in the third person. What a weird and wonderful relationship we have.

Bare footed and naked, I stand before him. There's something about the way he's looking at me; I feel treasured, sacrosanct. I'm still feeling a little self-conscious but not as much as I used to, knowing he loves me deeply makes it so much easier.

I reach over to the iPod deck to put on some music, but he takes my hand and kisses it. "No, no music. I'm going to make love to you and I need to hear your body when it speaks to me." He stands, reversing me gently until I feel bedding against my calves. "I'll never grow tired of looking at you. You took my breath away when you appeared on the terrace last night; you were like an angel who'd been heaven sent. You're beautiful. You move me, can't you tell?"

He places my right hand on his heart. It's racing, pumping blood at a rate of knots. He lifts his eyes from my torso and fixes me with the kind of stare that quite literally leaves me weak at the knees. I rock backward a little then try to regain my equilibrium.

"I know it's wrong but I like to think that I own it, your body belongs to me, every perfect inch of it." He runs the back of his right hand across my breasts, making my heart flutter, causing my nipples to harden and push outwards.

Slowly, he lowers his head to meet his hands while suckling like a child on each breast in turn. I raise my hands and my fingers disappear in his hair. This is gentle love making, exactly what I need: medicine for the soul. It truly feels as if this is something Ayden *needs* to do to rescue me. I think I need it too, but I *want* more.

"Harder," I utter, feeling an instant serge of pressure as his lips take hold of my erect nipple. I groan and lean into him. His fingers flutter southwards and, with tantalizing strokes, he caresses my thighs with the outside of his hands. A whimper leaves my mouth and my body sways. He catches me with the open palm of his right hand and steadies me.

"You're on fire, Beth," he states in a half whisper. "Let me chase away your demon."

"Do it," I hear myself moaning. "You say you want me to experience *everything*, with you." I pause to lick my lips. "I'm ready." I pull his mouth onto mine. "Please."

I feel a momentary lapse in his concentration. "Are you sure?"

I wrap my arms around his protective body, pulling him towards me with as much force as I can muster. It's time for us to face facts: even when I've been Elizabeth, he's been in complete control and that's the way I want it. There's a name for that: he knows it and so do I.

"Ayden, we both know you've been topping from the bottom from day one. Last night you flicked a switch and there's no going back." I take a deep breath, sensing his surprise at my awareness of the role play. "I'm yours, this body is yours. I Belong To You."

He is visibly moved. "I'll take such good care of you, Beth." The thumb of his right hand brushes against my cheek.

"I know you will." I tremble in response to his touch. When it comes again, I lurk slightly as his hands skim my back, pinning me to his chest; my heart beats to his hurried tempo, sending rippling vibrations through my expectant body. Our heartbeats are synchronised, our bodied are attuned: we are one.

His hands descend to the base of my spine and he takes my buttocks in both hands and squeezes and lifts ever so slightly, allowing his fingertips to stroke my moist folds. I call out. "Ah."

"You're allowing yourself to feel me, Beth, finally..." I see his exultant smile and I reciprocate with a grateful version of the same.

I push back his bathrobe, taking a moment to trace the shape of his collarbone with my fingers. He is a fine specimen, by anyone's reckoning. "Just looking at you makes me moist all over," I confess, sharing my most private of thoughts.

"And that's exactly how I want you, always." His tongue slips into my mouth and teases me to do the same, before it invades me further with ardent longing. "Do you remember our safe word?"

Our safe word? *The one he said he would never need? That safe word?*

"Yes. Romeo." We both smile. It sounds as if I'm addressing him. "Will I need it?"

"No, I'll make sure you don't, but it's good to know you can stop me at any time." He's pushing back my hair from my face and planning something, I just know it.

"Then I won't need it. I trust you to take care of me." I remember his words. "You think too much of this body to damage it."

He smiles broadly and rubs his nose against mine. "This is true." He leans to the right and opens the drawer by the bed. I know what's in the drawer and knowing causes a surge of excitement to sear through my body. He's holding the blindfold in his hands, purposely folding it over his knuckles for me to see.

"Last night, I *tried* to take away your power of speech, now I *will* take away your sight. It'll feel a little strange at first but give yourself time to adapt. Trust me."

I lean back, stopping him in his tracks. "You've done this before?"

"Yes, but I've never wanted to do it as much as I do now." He projects such sinful sexiness it makes me think I must have done something really good in a previous life to deserve this.

He slides the blindfold over my head but, before covering my eyes, he launches one of his high voltage stares, and that's the image I take with me as a black shroud envelops my world.

He's right, it does feel weird, but with the loss of vision comes the loss of embarrassment. What a revelation. If I can't see what he's doing to me, then he can do anything and it's alright. It becomes all about sensation not humiliation. That's why last night's sexual encounter was disastrous for me: I saw too much.

"Are you ready to surrender yourself to me?" He asks with such authority, it causes my chest to heave.

This is the man I want, My Mr. P. "Yes, I'm ready," I gasp, finding it hard to conceal my arousal.

His hand grips my chin softly, keeping me in place. "Yes what?" I feel muscles clenching in my groin.

"Yes, Sir."

"Good girl." He locks his lips onto mine and rocks his hips into me; it's bump and grind again and I give myself to the sensation. I hear him breathing into my ear.

"Does this feel good?"

"Yes." I pant. "I want more." I have libidinous thoughts and they all begin and end with him.

"Lay back on the bed. I'm going to make love to you." I shuffle onto the bed and lay modestly down, eyes closed, hands by my sides, knees together.

"I'm going to tie your hands to the bedframe. Give me your hands." I respond to his persuasive fingers as they lift my hands above my head. Every inch feels like a mile, every second an hour: it's a big ask.

"I know this is difficult for you, but it'll be worth it, trust me." His words comfort me, as he ties my hands to the frame with the soft cord from the drawer. I focus on my breathing and wait.

"It's time to let me love you, Beth."

I nod with a powerful, sexual awakening as he begins the colonisation of my body ...

Tentatively, he outlines my face with a finger and runs his thumb across my mouth, easing it between my parted lips. "Suck me." I wrap my tongue around his thumb and I swear I can hear a groan somewhere out there in the darkness. He runs his hand up my legs, starting at my shins, ending at my thigh. I picture him looking, coveting. I feel desired.

"I love this body, it's soft, it's perfect, it belongs to me." I picture his face, stunningly gorgeous and serious in his claim. I want to take it in my hands, to smother it in kisses but I can't. I feel him astride me, holding me fast between strong thighs. Hot palms find their way into my hair, fixing me in place. I'm pinioned beneath him: taken prisoner, without any means of escape. It's unsettling, disturbing even. I'm pulling on my restraints, he can't help but notice.

"Centre yourself, Beth."

I'm trying ... I want to.

"Stay with me."

My agitation is offset against his unstoppable kisses; the combination of pressure and wetness eases my anxiety and my body responds, rising to meet his.

"That's it ..."

The insatiable nature of his kiss is nothing compared to the hum of his growing arousal; with my eyes covered, each sound he makes is an aural expression of unparalleled adoration. Every muscle in my body responds. Making the most of each precious second he places his knees, one at a time, between my thighs and spreads me.

"Do you love me, Beth?" He asks, surely not needing more assurances. Before I can answer, he asks another question through clenched teeth, breath escaping his mouth in a hiss. "Do you want me, Beth?"

I find the words from somewhere. "Yes ... yes."

"Let me take care of you." I feel his hands pulling up my legs, inspecting what is his and I'm grateful for the blindfold: I am utterly exposed. His fingers pave the way and push into me, dipping into my saturated opening.

"Yes, yes." I call out, abandoning any bashful thoughts, simply rising and falling to the rhythm of his urgent fingers. My swollen clitoris cries out for his thumb. "I need to come," I plead. "Please don't torture me."

"I won't. I'm going to lick you until you beg me to stop." His words are like flames to my core; they ignite my passion and set my internal organs alight.

"Feel me." I jerk to the sensation of his tongue lapping against my clitoris. No amount of mental preparation could have readied me for this moment. Every thought is centred around that sensorial point of nerve endings. I'm losing all self-control, climbing to the sound of his breathing, reaching the point where I can take no more.

"Stop," I call out, pulling against my restraints, writhing into his mouth. He pauses and before I can regain my sanity, thrusts his hard cock into me in one long, forceful motion. I visualise him, his arms lifting my thighs, his body wedged against mine and him living inside me. It's so fucking erotic. I don't know which way to turn.

Through muffled groans he growls, "I want to give you everything, Beth." And I believe him. His movements become frantic, as if he's possessed by some primal need to fuck: hard, fast penetration, pushing me to my limit.

"Come with me." He leans over and snatches off the blindfold.

I blink to accustom my eyes to the light. I'm shocked by what I see. His body is glistening with sweat, his hair is flat against his forehead and his once sparkling eyes are the colour of the charm on my bracelet: dark, midnight blue.

"We're going to do this together." He doubles his efforts, all the time binding me to him with his fierce eyes. I'm watching him, watching me climax and it's such a powerful turn-on I start to pant, trying to hold off my orgasm, anticipating that monumental moment when our two worlds collide in a riotous explosion of pure passion.

"Let it go, burn for me, Beth," he calls out, making it impossible for me to contain my ecstasy. Responding to my involuntary clenching he comes with a raucous yell, loud enough to raise the dead, ejaculating what feels like hot lava into my core.

"Feel me, Beth, it's all for you!"

I throw back my head and gasp my way through an earth-shattering explosion of pure pleasure, calling out his name, surrendering my orgasm to him. "Ay-den!"

He fights to regain his composure and, still inside, leans up and kisses me hard. I can taste the salt in his perspiration and feel the heat coming off his skin; he's totally wasted.

Leaning over my head, he releases me from the cord. It feels good to stretch my arms. His gaze rests on my wrists which have been marked by the corded rope and I see he is unhappy about the tell-tale signs of my struggle. Me, I'm too overcome with post coital bliss to care.

Flat and motionless, he lays beside me. I turn onto my left side and take stock of him. He is absolutely knackered. All I can do is grin.

He can barely turn his head to look at me and I receive a side-ways glance. "That's a happy face," he remarks, with every ounce of stamina sucked from his body.

"I'm a happy person," I announce proudly. "You seem a little, what's the word ... exhausted?"

He sends a wide stare in my direction and silences me with it. "You don't say."

I lean over and kiss him softly, feeling him raise his right arm to hold me close. "Thank you for taking care of me, Ayden." I frame his left cheek with my hand.

"Thank you for letting me." His lips rest on my hair. "What time is it?" he asks, suddenly alert.

I glance at the bedside clock. "It's 9.15a.m.."

Straightaway, both hands are in his hair. "Shit!" Pushing me off his chest he slides out of bed. "I told Jake to call me at nine. I had no idea I'd be involved in a fucking marathon."

With that, he picks up his bathrobe and stomps off into the study.

Oh dear!

***

With no more than a half-eaten chicken carcass and a bloated cat for company, Dan flicks his way through this month's issue of Hustler magazine. Some men buy it for the pictures, others for the articles. He buys it for both. Across his lap, a blond bombshell bares her wares to the world and her nakedness causes sexual yearnings to stir in him. With all her brash exhibitionism, the girl in the photo is no match for *his* girl. He will not allow a stranger to corrupt his mind, to steal his affections. He's saving himself for Beth Parker, no-one else. But, with his hands hardened and fit for purpose, what to do?

He closes his eyes, abandons reality and waits, waits for her to arrive, to take her place in the well-rehearsed scene. When she makes her entrance, she floors him with a look of such magnitude his pants moisten with pre-cum. Some may see terror in those sky blue eyes, he sees only desire.

"Welcome home, princess. It's been a while, but you've come back to me." In his fevered brain, she twirls and dances over to him, when really she's turning away. On his command she stills and becomes a statue, a Grecian beauty. Most people fear him, give him a wide berth, but not her. She wants him, has to have him.

The leash around her neck keeps her to heel, all it takes is a gentle tug and she tips forward, moves closer. The chains around her ankle prevent her from falling and the tape across her mouth makes words unnecessary.

With one enormous hand he cups her face and squeezes, until her features contract and tears form. "I'm going to teach you a fucking lesson, princess. One you won't forget."

The chair creaks and moans beneath him as he leans into it, finding purchase for his heels, knowing what's coming next. The hard skin on his heeling palm feels alien against his pulsating cock; like the hand of a stranger. Not the velvet touch he envisages, but more like that of someone who has toiled, busied themselves with hard labour: a sex slave maybe? He likes the sound of that.

The thought of having sex on-tap excites him further; he has the means and the opportunity, why not? His arousal peaks. Tiny beads of sweat gather on his forehead and across his lip. He picks up the pace and the anticipation of sexual violence is enough to have him gasping and clutching at the threadbare arm of the chair. He's on fire. The scorching sensation comes out of a delirious craving for a solitary person.

"I'm going to fuck you senseless," he declares, believing it to be a statement of fact. He's unaware of the savagery of his self-abuse and pounds on and on, until the image of her wilting body is so intense he cannot contain himself. He comes hard into her yielding core, still unable and unwilling to open his eyes. When he does, his sight is drawn to his bruised and flaccid penis.

"Aren't you a greedy little thing? Can't get enough of Danny boy, eh? This time tomorrow you'll be begging for more."

19

My desire was to stay in bed, but I reconsidered; this is our last day and I want to make the most of it. The shower reinvigorates every part of my body and alleviates the impact of the welts forming on my wrists. I emerge pink and buffed and dress alone in the bedroom, picking up my bathrobe off the carpet by the bed as I go. From it falls the cord, the blindfold and a condom packet, unopened. I gather them up and throw them in the drawer and select my travel outfit. A simple pair of pale blue designer jeans, a white Calvin Klein T-shirt and a matching scarf to go with my navy blazer.

When I step into the lounge, room service are just leaving, having laid out our breakfast selection on the terrace. Ayden is calmly giving a subordinate a series of instructions relating to some kind of merger. It looks like I'll be having breakfast alone today, with only my memories of the past three days for company. I can live with that.

Orange juice from a crystal glass tumbler trickles down my throat, while I gaze out over the now familiar panorama, feeling as if a great weight has been lifted from my shoulders. This day feels special somehow.

Hearing Ayden's footsteps I turn; he's still wearing his bathrobe, un-showered and decidedly unkempt. My mouth twitches as I try to withhold an amused grin. "Is everything okay?" I ask tentatively.

"It is now," he answers rather abruptly, shaking his head from side to side. "I can't believe I lost track of time like that, that never happens."

Well, I'm sorry to have kept you.

I feel affronted. He grabs a croissant with one hand and pours out a cup of coffee with the other. I say nothing and pretend to be reading the newspaper, giving him time to reconsider his thoughtless remark. Becoming aware of my silence, he puts down his coffee and moves over to where I'm sitting. In the same way he did in the cafe, he places his hands on the arms of the chair and leans into me. I lift my eyes to his, waiting for his acknowledgment.

"Good morning." His eyes are a kind of sultry green colour; specks of brown and gold are flickering in his irises like an early morning firework display. They hold my attention. Even though he's unshaven, with two days growth and looks as if he's just rolled out of bed, he's still incredibly handsome.

"Good morning." For all the wrong reasons, I feel a little bashful and self-conscious. This gorgeous man has seen me tied up and entirely naked, and it's that very thought that causes me to blush.

"You've been very demanding, Miss Parker," he admonishes. "So much so you made me miss my nine o'clock call." A feather-light kiss finds my lips. "If we had more time, I would carry you back to bed and take those fifteen minutes back in kind."

I say nothing. I'm too busy trying to conceal my crimson cheeks.

"Is this what they call the silent treatment?" he asks, playfully.

I raise my eyes to his and shake my head: no.

He takes a step back. "I do believe you're blushing, I wonder why?"

Stifling a smile I look away to the left.

"My precious little genie is wishing she could climb back into her bottle right now."

I can't help but laugh. "No, I'm not. I'm never going back. I'm just ..."

" ... Shy about what we got up to."

I nod, yes.

He tips up my chin with his right hand. "Did I keep my promise? Did I take good care of you?"

"Yes, you did." I smirk.

"And do you want to do it again?" His smile is wickedly mischievous; his brows are lifted high for effect. He's simply irresistible.

"Yes please." I whisper softly, pulling his bed-head to mine. "Thank you for taking care of me."

"Always a pleasure and never a chore, Miss Parker." He ends the conversation with a soft, lingering kiss. "I'm going to shower and make myself presentable for you. Can you bear to be away from me for ten minutes?"

"It will be tortuous but I'll soldier on somehow," I tease, pushing him away from me.

"That's the spirit." He tips his head back gleefully and I can hear him laughing as he leaves the terrace. *He's* in a good mood.

I use my time to check my texts and emails. I reply to Charlie and renew my car insurance on line, and that takes all of ten minutes.

Ayden appears on the terrace looking much less dishevelled, still a little tired around the eyes but refreshed and clean shaven. He kisses my hair before sitting down opposite me. "You smell good."

"Thank you. So do you." I pour out another cup of coffee and place it down in front of him but, before I can pull my left hand away, he gently takes hold of it and slots it between his right and left palms.

"We don't have much time, Beth. I want to finalise something."

Oh? Why do I think this is going to be a serious conversation? "About last night?"

"No. Something else."

"OK." I lean further into the table, giving him my full attention, keeping my eyes on his face, searching for clues. I wait.

"Well ... I've been thinking about this for a while and, you know ..."

Whatever it is, he's struggling to get it out. Is he finishing with me? I can't conceal my fear; my voice is a mournful utterance. "Are we breaking up?"

He's shocked at my question and takes my hand to his lips. "Dear God! No! Why would you think that?"

"You ... you can't get the words out and you mentioned finalising something."

"That's because I'm an idiot and I've fucked it up, said the wrong thing, phrased it all wrong." He blows out an impatient gust of air. "What I'm trying to say is ..." He reaches into his left trouser pocket with his hand and lifts out a small blue box.

I can't take my eyes off it, off him, off it. He flips it open. I see what's inside.

"Frances Elizabeth Parker, will you marry me?"

It's embarrassing I know, but my mouth has fallen open, I'm having to cover it with my free hand. I try to speak. This is so unexpected.

"Beth?" He's trying to coax me with a stare but I can't shake my eyes free of the platinum engagement ring. "Do you plan on answering any time soon? Do you need time to think about it?"

"No."

He's taken aback. "No. You won't marry me, or no you don't need time to think about it?"

I start to laugh. "I love you, Ayden, but this has got to be the least romantic proposal ever. What are you like?" I stand, still leaving my left hand in his and slither onto his lap. "Yes, I will marry you and no, I don't need time to think about it." My smile is so wide, my face hurts. I'm beaming.

He reaches around me and removes the stunning ring from the box. "Thank God for that. For a minute there, I thought you were turning me down." His relief is audible.

"Now why would you think that?" I ask, taking his beautiful face in my hands. "You're the man I adore."

"Give me your hand." I outstretch the fingers of my left hand. "If you don't like it, we can choose another, but it matches your bracelet so I thought ..."

I hold it up to the light. "It's perfect." A constellation of sparkling, ice white diamonds frame an enormous sapphire the colour of the night sky, cut into the shape of a heart. Exactly the same colour as the charm on my platinum bracelet. It's gloriously extravagant and must have cost a fortune.

I shift my attention to him. "You didn't have to buy me this, you ..." But, before I can finish the sentence, he grips my head and pulls my mouth onto his, smothering out my words.

Between a passionate kiss he confesses, "Yes I did. You've had my heart from day one."

"Oh, Ayden, that's such a romantic thing to say." I take another look at my engagement ring and a thought occurs to me. "Do you realise what you've given me? It's a heart of stone, it's your heart." I feel tears welling, making it impossible to focus on my future husband. I wrap my arms around his neck and hold on tight. "I love you, Ayden."

"I love you more, Beth and I can't imagine my life without you."

I make him a solemn promise. "You won't have to. I will always love you."

He spends the next twenty minutes consuming two portions of scrambled eggs and bacon. The night and early morning exertions have given him a ravenous appetite. I'm happy to read him the headlines and to listen to him relay details about the Hong Kong merger. His enthusiasm is contagious, even his body language conveys a heightened awareness of all things corporate; he's gesticulating, raising his voice, making declarations about profit margins and productivity. With every new revelation, I feel him slipping away, leaving me for his mistress: A.S. Media International.

I've been spoilt, demanded his attention like a petulant child; but now, for all his wealth and position, spending whole days and nights together has become a luxury even he can ill afford. With the deal done and our engagement 'finalised,' we're about to return home. I have the love of a wonderful man who wants to give me everything and I have the ring to prove it, so ... why then, do I feel like his latest acquisition?

He's instructed the hotel staff to pack our cases and I'm keeping out of the way, but what if they find the blindfold and the cord and the condoms? Shit! And my toys! I'm mortified at the thought.

When I return to the bedroom, they are all but done; clothes folded beautifully, shoes bagged. I make my move. "Thank you for your help, I'll take it from here."

"Very well, Miss Parker. Please call reception when you are ready to have your cases collected." The forty something housekeeper straightens her uniform and exits the room, leaving me to pack our private possessions and toiletries.

It's a five minute job. I take a long, lingering look at the king-sized bed and memories of the night before converge on the golden duvet, jostle for first place and cause a surge of sexual bliss to radiate around my body. I leave the room, wearing a sensual smile, betraying the kind of guilty pleasures which some might consider improper. What do they say, as long as it's safe, sane and consensual?

I go in search of Ayden, to organise our day. I don't have to search very far; he's still in the study with his mistress. And I thought I was demanding. For once he isn't on the phone, he's sitting comfortably in his chair, arms folded, attention focused on the screen of his laptop.

I reposition myself, trying to get a glimpse of what it is that has him so transfixed. The music I added to the slideshow is turned low, but he can hear it perfectly. Katy Perry sings *Teenage Dream* and it's light-hearted enough to make him smile, particularly when it's teamed up with the photo where I'm standing beside a sign pointing out the Trevi Fountain but still focused on my Sat Nav.

Happy days.

Images of the day roll by one after another: so many smiles, so many close-ups and too many of me. I've never looked more alive, he's never looked more handsome.

His finger hits the space bar and I'm curious, why? It's the one of us together at the bottom of the Spanish Steps, obligingly taken by a random tourist. I make a mental note to take a closer look when I have some time to myself. What has he seen?

I cough and approach him from behind, just as the music is fading and hang my arms over his shoulders from back to front. My senses are intensified in response to a powerful cocktail of pheromones and Obsession, how apt. The photographs have triggered a visceral response in him and his arousal is clearly visible, even from where I'm standing.

"Come here, woman of my dreams." He smiles, hooking me into him with his left arm. "Look at you in your tight little jeans." He grins, eying me from head to toe before ensnaring me.

"*You're* in a very good mood," I remark, arranging his hair and avoiding his eyes.

"I'm always in a good mood, when you're around. Can't you tell?" He lowers my right hand from his hair, kisses my palm and rests it on his crotch. "I've only been looking at photographs and

I'm hard for you. Imagine how I feel when you're naked and beneath me."

"I don't have to imagine, Ayden, I just have to remember." I pull back a knowing smile and continue to fiddle with his hair.

"And what a memory," he answers, eyelids heavy and lustful. He doesn't hold back.

This is where our relationship started, physical attraction, sexual magnetism. But I sense his need to talk or share a secret that will begin with playful banter and end with I love you. If he's been half as moved as I was to see the slide show then, I suspect, he needs to talk about that. I'm sitting comfortably across his lap, ready to listen.

Each word draws me closer and makes me want him more, so profound is the sexual chemistry between us. His right hand is stroking my back and his left hand is caressing my hair with so much gentleness, I'm beginning to feel the world fade into nothingness; he has me spellbound.

"Come to Hong Kong with me," he asks, not so much pleading but appealing to my impressible side. He's making it virtually impossible to refuse. "We'll play hooky for a couple of days, see the sights, I'll navigate ..."

His boyish grin sets my nerves on edge; I'm starting to squirm on his lap and he knows it.

"You can tie me up and I'll submit in Chinese, what do you say?"

He must be desperate.

"You're trying to seduce me, Mr. Stone, using your sexiness to get what you want." I widen my stare and caress his lips with the fingers of my right hand. "It's back to business, I have to give you back to *her* now." I offer a smile of resignation.

"Her?"

"Yes, A.S.M.I., your mistress. It occurs to me that our relationship has three components and, if it's going to work, I have to get used to sharing you."

He huffs away a smile. "For you to share me would imply I love you both in equal measure and, that simply isn't the case." He holds my face in his warm hands and meets me head on. "I love you more and I have the photo evidence to prove it." He nods to the screen. "Take a look."

We focus our attention on the first photograph he took of us in my apartment, pre-Titanic and Chinese take-away: one of my favourites. "See, I loved you then and I love you now."

I saw that too

My attention lingers on the photograph. "I loved you then too," I confess, returning my eyes to his. "That was the first time you made love to me."

"Yes, is it any wonder? Look at us together. Just the thought of you turns this heart of stone into a raging furnace." He places my right hand onto his heart.

I'm touched by his honesty, but I can't let his disclosure shatter my resolve or affect his ability to operate independently. I offer a coquettish smile. "It has to, to get all that blood to your extremities."

He grins, my sweet boy again. "Well, my *extremities* are full-blooded now."

Now look what I've done.

"Oh really?" To stir him further, I pull my thumbnail to my mouth and watch his breathing quicken; the glistening flecks in his eyes are darkening into a fiery, navy blue. "And what do you propose to do about it?"

"I propose to make love to my future wife, right here in this office."

He closes the lid of his laptop and places it on the floor just at his feet. The dark, wooden desk has a vacant space, just wide enough to accommodate my slender frame. He taps it with the tips of his fingers.

"Take a seat, Miss Parker." True to form, Ayden can only talk sex for a limited time; having it is a way of ending a conversation. I'm happy to swap discourse for intercourse anytime.

I slide over, lifted by patient hands gripping my waist. "It would be my pleasure Mr. Stone, but isn't this where you spend quality time with your mistress?"

He chuckles. "Fuck that, we'll have a threesome."

Our laughter is smothered by hot, wet kisses and all-consuming passion erupting around us. He's using the wheels on the chair to move closer to me and unbuttoning my jeans. His smiling eyes never leave mine.

"You can't be serious?" I'm stifling a giggle.

"Yes I can, but this is going to be quick and hard, we have a flight to catch." He grabs my buttocks and pulls me to him, leaving me to fumble with his fly, but I can't do it one handed and, suddenly shy, don't want him to see what's in my left hand.

He misses nothing. "What have we here?"

"Nothing."

"You're going out of your way to conceal *nothing*."

I should be used to his authoritative tone by now, but it only makes me tremble with anticipation.

"Show me."

We both look down as he gently peels back my fingers, like the petals of a delicate flower. Sitting in the palm of my hand is our joint present. He's taken aback but utterly bemused.

"Well, aren't you full of surprises?"

I can't look at him, this is beyond embarrassing. What was I thinking, bringing a vibrating love ring to his office? Whatever it was, we're both thinking it now.

He cups my face with his hand and tips up my chin. "I think we should christen our joint gift, don't you?"

My eyes are wide and darting nervously every which way. I nod yes.

"Do you want me to draw the drapes?" What a selfless thing to say.

"No." I place the love ring on the desk and set about undoing his fly, using both hands. My eyes never leave his. I slip my hands inside his boxers; his hot, firm buttocks flex and tense under my fingers, causing my own cheeks to clench with craving. My heart beat is increasing by the second. I lean back. "No kissing, just look at me."

"With pleasure." He does just that. Flickering sapphires hold me in place, stealing the breath from my body. As he inches towards me, his face takes on a pained expression, lips parted, breathing laboured with the intensity of his focus.

He's reaching into his trouser pocket, I assume for a condom and I'm presenting a mocking look of surprise. He catches it and tips his head to the left. No words are needed. He learned never to be unprepared on the flight over. I smile cheekily and raise the level of my own arousal by watching him roll the condom down his rigid cock, and then position the love ring over the crown and then slide it to the base. The black object sits nicely against his pubic bone and nestles in his pubic hair. It's a sight I could never have envisaged seeing, up until a fortnight ago. Now, nothing surprises me, except myself.

He spreads my thighs. "Hard and fast. Ready?"

I've lost the power of speech.

"I'll take that as a yes." He looks positively euphoric. With a groan of surging passion, he slides into me and grasps my waist, pulling me onto him so there is barely a millimetre between us. He clicks the small button on the magical black ring and rests it against my clitoris. He doesn't thrust but rolls against me in tight, little circles, caressing me with the pulsating head of the ring, his eyes never leaving mine. "Miss Parker, you're a very *naughty* girl, and I want you wet."

The combination of words, vibration and penetration set my nerves jangling; he has me fisting his hair. "My God!" I call out, sucking him deeper into me.

"There's the spark. Feel it, Beth."

Under his coaxing, I begin to spasm, feeling an uncontrollable desire to orgasm. My own delicious agony is starting to morph into helpless rapture and his bulging cock is thrusting and lunging, filling me to the point of stretching.

"Too much?" he gasps, dipping his hips to stake his claim.

"No," I pant. "God no." I'm impaled, racing towards orgasm, struggling to inhale between excited cries. "Oh, Ayden."

I convulse around him, tightening, crushing him once, twice, three times until I can hold off no longer. I'm so swept away, I lean back, splaying my hands left and right on the dark wooden desk, taking everything he has to give and wanting more.

From a foot away, I can feel his steaming breath on my face, but it's his eyes that cause my muscles to clench and tighten; from the depths of the darkest place, they consume me, taking away any thoughts I might have of self-determination. I feel possessed, my body is his. I belong to him.

"Come," he growls. "Give me the memory."

His words are my undoing. I pull him to me and wrap my legs tightly, holding him in place, willing the vibrations to turn my insides into molten flesh. I'm rocking and pushing against him, responding to his circular motion, urging me to come.

"That's it ... I can feel you creaming me." He throws back his head, crazy with a savage hunger to ejaculate. "I want to live inside you, Beth."

I'm on the verge of a breath-stealing orgasm and his words are igniting the smoking embers sparking in my groin again and again. I'm losing control. The throbbing is making me shudder, ripping me apart.

I arch my back away from him, but my trembling arms will not bear my weight. He reaches out and his hands spread out across my shoulder blades like folded wings, holding me in place. Fully supported, I fist my hair and pant my way through an earth-shattering orgasm, surrendering myself to the sensation, eyes closed, tears forming.

My God!

There is a rumble of such physical longing it makes me open my eyes. His groans convey so much yearning and helplessness, I want to reach out to him but my need for some degree of self-preservation forces me to stay where I am, at arms' length.

His groans increase with every penetrating stroke, until he reaches that point of no return. His damp hair is tumbling over his forehead, his T-shirt is clinging to his muscular torso and now I'm getting to watch him come inside me.

"Look into my eyes," he snarls, using his hands to pull me onto him, bending at the knees until our bodies are moulded together, filling and spreading me.

"You have all of me. You always have." And with that, the intensity of his bewitching stare fades and softens as he bares his soul to me at the moment of his supreme orgasm. I take hold of his biceps and hold on tight, until his thrusting slows and my internal clenching eases.

The pained expression leaves his face far more quickly than it formed and I have my lover back, a little worse for wear, but back.

"Fuck," he announces, gently easing out of me. "One of these days, Beth, you're going to give me a heart attack." He leans over, takes my face in his hands and sucks on my lip with his hungry mouth.

"You started it," I tease, as he raises his boxers a little, leaving the condom in place. "I only came over to look at a few photographs." I feign innocence.

"Of course you did, carrying this." He slides the love ring off and holds it out in front of me." He grins, in the mood for some self-denigration. "So what are you suggesting? I'm a predatory, over-sexed megalomaniac who takes advantage of you?" He lowers me off the desk, pulling up my jeans tenderly. "No, really, are you okay?"

It feels good to be asked. "Yes. And you?"

"Better now I have my mental picture of *you*." He arches a brow sensuously and I roll my eyes. "Now it will be the three of us in Hong Kong. I got you to come for me and *with* me, didn't I." He laughs adoringly and rubs his nose against mine.

"Bravo, Ayden. You win and I don't even have to endure the jet lag."

"Then it's a win, win outcome."

"Please ..." I nod my head from side to side. *Give me a break.* "Haven't we moved on from the winning, isn't it the taking part that matters?"

"Yes," he states, grabbing hold of my shoulders as I stand in front of him. "It's the *taking* part I'm enjoying the most."

"What about the *giving* part?" I ask cheerfully, waiting for his smart reply.

"I like to think I give as good as I get." He winks.

"This is true," I reply, with one of his stock responses, meeting his relaxed stare. "And while we're on the subject of giving, thank you for this." I hold up my engagement ring. Even in the artificial light the diamonds sparkle and the sapphire is iridescent. "It's beautiful."

"Just like you," he interjects. "I'm not looking forward to us being apart for nearly three days." He takes my hand and we stroll into the lounge, but my legs are still shaky and I'm a little disorientated. He's actually smirking. "Are you alright?"

"After what we just did, you ask me that? What do *you* think?" I punch him in the arm and try to walk or rather stumble away.

"Poor, baby." He picks me up off the floor and throws me over his shoulder, as if I'm a sack of something weightless. "You need to lie down."

"You need to *put* me down!" I call out, half laughing, half shouting. "What are you doing, you'll injure yourself. Put me down you crazy, over-sexed megalomaniac!"

"Here, lie down for half an hour. I'll get the bags taken down." He places me gently onto the enormous bed. "Do you need anything?"

"No, not really. Just you," I purr.

He bends over to kiss me. "You've already *had* me, baby, remember?" He walks away shaking his head from side to side, laughing and pulling off his sodden T-shirt.

"How could I forget?" I call out, following him with lecherous eyes.

"Sleep!"

I feel my eyes flickering as a wave of tiredness washes over me. I really do need to rest.

***

It's 0600hrs and Dan has been awake for nearly an hour, undertaking a virtual tour of apartment 53a; some people count sheep to help them sleep, he counts steps from door to sofa, from sofa to table, from table to bedroom door ...

With eyes shut tight, he revisits the soon to be scene of the crime, a crime of passion resulting from days, months and years of infatuation. The prospect of that gives him butterflies that skip and somersault around his intestines. He uses his heavy hands to massage away the frisky insects with palms that no longer hurt. In fact, they have hardened up quite nicely. From fingers to wrist, the skin is pleated and puckered into neat little wrinkles. They look as if they belong to someone ancient, withered or dead.

Untouched by vanity, he lifts them from under the duvet, switches on the lamp and inspects them. With his fingers splayed, his palms look like huge sheets of sandpaper. Instinctively, his thoughts turn to the love of his life, 'These hands will keep you in place, feel your soft skin, explore your body, inside and out. You won't forget the feel of *these* hands.'

There had been moments of self-doubt this week when he'd seriously thought about throwing in the towel, but not anymore. He's a man who has found his second wind and, even with less than four hours sleep, he's fighting fit.

What usually amounts to a fleeting encounter between flesh and flannel turns into a long, drawn-out face to face between skin and scorching streams of water. For some reason, he feels the need to cleanse himself, of what, he has no idea.

When he steps from the shower, his skin is glowing the former colour of his scorched palms; he scarcely recognises himself in the bathroom mirror. Naturally his face is flushed from the self-inflicted scalding, but there's something about his eyes; they are glistening, alight with lust and brutish thoughts. He's a man who has been raised from the dead: he's alive. The lascivious grin only reinforces the fact he has the upper-hand. He's mentally and physically prepared to fight for what is rightfully his and, when he takes it, to indulge in whatever activity takes his fancy to achieve total, sexual gratification.

In false light, his newspaper free lounge seems dustier than ever. Foot square shapes of brightly coloured carpet have appeared around the walls, reminding him of just how long the hunt for his girl has been going on. It had seemed like an exercise in perseverance, a tour of duty that would never end, but now he is coming home. Or at least that's how it feels.

Breakfast is a simple matter of eating what's edible and throwing away what's not. He sits down by his computer and boots it up, while sipping hot tea from a mug that has the University of Cambridge crest on it. He Googles Heathrow airport and clicks on 'Flight Arrivals.' There are eight flights coming in from Rome, starting at 0945hrs. The last flight is 2200hrs. To be on the safe side, he decides to get to Elm Gardens for 1000hrs, giving him ample time. He'll have to break off to meet Elise, but that won't be a problem, everything is in place and it will simply be a case of retrieval. 'Operation Snatch Back' is good to go.

His rucksack is so light he barely notices the weight of it. He has off-loaded its contents on earlier expeditions and there is little left to carry. He attributes his anticipated success to premeditation, that and ingenuity. He has a date with destiny, and he's making good time.

20

I inhale my prince's provocative scent before I see his face: it's Obsession and he's mine.

"Time to wake up, sleeping beauty. It's 11.30, we need to catch our flight before one o'clock or we'll miss our slot." He brushes away the unruly strands of hair from my face. "Feeling better?"

I turn to face him, unprepared for what I see: he's even more handsome than I've remembered him from an hour ago. He's showered and now he's wearing a tightly fitting V neck, white T-shirt and pale blue jeans. I swear I can see every contour of his perfect body. What a wake-up call.

"Yes, I'm rested. You look and smell scrumptious."

"Good to know." He grins. "Still feel wobbly?" Standing, he eyes my nether region suggestively.

"No, the only thing that's wobbling is my pride." I swing my legs off the bed. "I need to freshen up before we leave, give me ten minutes."

"Sure, take this with you." I take the steaming cup of coffee from him.

What a nice thought.

With nothing left to salvage from my make-up, I shower quickly and reapply some tinted moisturiser, a little mascara and a warm pink lip-gloss. Thankfully my jeans and white T-shirt have survived our sexual encounter better than my cosmetics and I slip them on in a second. With so little time, I scrape back my hair into a decorative clip and saunter out into the lounge, with all my toiletries thrown into an oversized make-up bag. There they sit by my navy blazer, waiting to be packed into our hand luggage.

"All done," I call out to Ayden, but he's disappeared. I take a seat, finish my coffee and catch my breath, remembering to take two travel sickness tablets. I don't want to embarrass myself again. Although the outcome was a lot of fun, as I recall.

I jump up when I hear his voice outside in the hall, preparing to leave and excited at the prospect of another four hours of quality time spent with the man I love.

"All set?" he asks curtly.

"Just my toiletries to pack." He takes them from me and hands the bag to a gentleman in uniform waiting outside the door, who immediately disappears down the hallway. "Where's he taking my things?"

"Downstairs with our bags. The car's waiting."

"Oh! OK."

He's eager to get going. How quickly he loses his holiday spirit; it's business as usual. And, as usual Ayden Stone is impatient and impervious to the needs of others. He's the proverbial one man band and I feel a little like an ex-band member. I can hear drawers opening and closing in each room and wardrobe doors slamming. He's making sure nothing is left behind; either that or he's in a foul mood.

I slip on my blazer and wander out onto the terrace one last time, savouring the mid-morning sun on my face. "Arrivederci Rome."

The sunlight fades as I move away from the French doors towards the elevator, with Ayden a couple of paces behind me. When the door slides open, he takes my hand and we step into the lift together. He's breathing faster than usual and there's no doubting he's a little tense.

I squeeze his hand. "Is there something bothering you, only you seem bit ... off?"

He gives my hand a reassuring squeeze and plants a soft kiss on my left cheek. "No, I'm good, we're running a little late and we need to make that flight so I can attend to a couple of things. That's all."

I nod and present a sympathetic smile, suspecting he's about to walk into a fire storm which may have been averted if he'd been paying better attention. Instead he's been bestowing upon me the most priceless of gifts after his love: his time.

Thankfully, we make it to Fiumincino airport with twenty minutes to spare, but the sprint to the fuelled private jet waiting on the tarmac leaves me exhausted and a little light headed.

By the time we're buckled in and are ready for take-off, I'm shattered. I may just sleep through the entire flight. After enduring a large dose of self-control and endurance, I survive the white knuckle take-off, aware of Ayden's eyes upon me the whole time. I must appear very weak willed to him, but I simply don't understand the physics of the process and anticipate a miscalculation on every flight.

Once we're airborne, I set about making coffee, as much to steady my nerves as to fulfil some sort of function. The two guys up front are flying the plane and he's is conversing with God knows who on the other side of the world. Once again, I seem to have become superfluous.

My phone makes its text received noise. Leaving the coffee to percolate, I reach over to my bag and take a look.

Thanks for delivering the package to L.A. Any chance of an early HK delivery? The shit's hitting the fan here!! Work your magic. J.

Not surprisingly, my face betrays my astonishment and I'm having to think quickly to throw Ayden off the scent.

He looks up. "Bad news?"

"Oh, the usual. Charlie's had a bump in her car. Some buffoon reversed into her new Audi yesterday. She's pissed. I'll give her a call when we land." Feigning indifference, I archive the message, throw the phone into my bag and return to my coffee making duty. For some reason he has taken it upon himself to watch me closely. Does he suspect I was lying?

"Can I help you with something, Mr. Stone?" Sweetly, I tilt my head to the left.

"No, just the coffee for now." He returns to his iPad and breaks off again. "I was picturing you in my kitchen."

What?

"Oh, you thought you'd throw that out there, did you? Okay, it's a swerve ball but I'll run with it. Let me serve coffee first." I wiggle my way to the cockpit and give a gentle tap. "Can I interest you in a cup of coffee gentlemen?" They accept the beverages with thanks and I close the door behind me, and prepare to be reeled in.

"Go on, I'm listening." I hand him his coffee and seat myself opposite on the plush leather chair.

"I'm thinking of putting Stone Heath on the market, my house in Belgravia."

"Why?"

"Because you won't like it."

"That's not very business-like, it's your home. Besides, I might love it. That is, if I ever get an invite." I sip my coffee and flutter my eye lashes at him, stressing the point.

"We'll go there today when we land. You've got everything you need in your case."

That was a quick change of plan, but one I like the sound of. "Alright, but now you've got me hooked." I kick off my flats and pull my legs up underneath me. "Why won't I like it, is it a playboy mansion with a mirrored ceiling in the master bedroom?"

"How did you guess?" My mouth falls open, and he starts to chuckle while still focusing on his iPad.

I roll my eyes. "Dear God, tell me you're joking."

"I'm joking but it's ... how can I put it?"

"A bachelor pad?" I interrupt, helping him out.

"Yes, but an up-market one, as you would expect." Now he's rolling his eyes.

"Naturally." I wouldn't *expect* anything less.

"But, it isn't homely, not like your apartment." A flat smile graces his lips.

I see such an endearing warmth emanating from his eyes that it makes me want to take him in my arms. "My apartment is what an estate agent would call bijou and compact; it's a one bedroom shoe box with a private parking spot in North London."

"Yes, but it's ... cosy."

Why the hell is he so taken with my place? The terrace we have just left had a bigger square footage than my apartment. "Cosy is a polite way of saying *small,* Ayden." He's just being kind.

"Whatever, but I've enjoyed spending time there with you," he says affectionately, reaching out to take my hand.

My heart aches. "Thank you, I've enjoyed spending time there with you too, but ...

"Don't start with the buts, we're going to need more space."

"We are?" Where is he going with this?

"I want us to move in together until we get married, then ..."

"Whoa! Slow down." My coffee cup rattles into position on my saucer. I'm trying to keep up, but he's moving at the speed of light. "If you keep this up, you'll have me dead and buried before I'm thirty." I start to laugh. "Take a breath, Ayden. Think about what you're saying, this is serious stuff."

"Well, why wait? This is a *serious* relationship, isn't it?" He waits for my reply and I actually believe if it wasn't for the sound of the twin turbo engines, we would hear a pin drop.

I don't think I have ever seen him look quite so earnest about anything. He holds me in place with an unyielding stare and I feel the colour draining from my face, not out of fear but more to do with the impact of his conviction. My God, this man is desperate to have me and not just in his bed but in his life, permanently.

"Yes, it's a serious relationship but let's not be hasty, you have more important things to be thinking about than this: the Hong Kong merger for instance." I reach over and kiss him softly and return to my seat.

Whilst he continues to focus on his iPad, I watch as his mouth twitches ever so slightly. "Did you just side-step me asking if you want us to move in together, Miss Parker?"

"You weren't asking Mr. Stone, you were assuming. There's a difference," I reply astutely, playing with my platinum bracelet and keeping my eyes out of range. Now he's smiling and I'm beginning to heat up inside, but that might only be the after effects of the coffee. "You've been doting on me and dealing with your business long distance for the past three days. You need to regroup. I'm not going anywhere."

"Are you done?" he asks sternly.

"No." He gives me a 'here we go' face, but I continue anyway. "If you keep on like this, it will be L.A. all over again." I pause, knowing he'll look at me. "I don't need any more assurances. I'm good, we're good. Do the second thing your good at." I stand and drape myself over his body, forcing him to hold his iPad against his chest, fearing I may break it. "Go rule the fucking world."

He nuzzles his face into my neck and holds me in place with his left hand at the base of my spine. His words, from my lips, have hit home.

"You didn't wash your hair, did you?" He's inhaling deeply and rubbing his nose beneath my hairline.

"No, I didn't have time. Why?"

In a steaming whisper he explains. "Because your hair smells of sex: hot, rough sex."

Holy shit!

I fist his hair with my left hand and slide my other down the back of his sweater and his T-shirt, desperate to feel the heat from his skin on my palm.

"I need *this,* morning, noon and night, Beth. I need you."

I kiss his hair and lean back, taking his stunning face in my hands. "Okay, so I'm a push over. We'll think about moving in together when you get back from Hong Kong."

I'm rewarded with a knock your socks off smile that brings tears to my eyes. "And only because I'm looking forward to seeing your cute arse in the mirrored ceiling." I pull away and begin clearing coffee cups and saucers.

"Then I'll have to get one fitted," he calls out after me, inspecting my backside as I saunter off.

"Get on with your work and less of the seduction. This body is out of bounds." I give him a ballerina swirl.

"Then stop flaunting it." He feigns annoyance, but I know better. Regardless of what comes out of his mouth, his eyes are glowing and I know, like me, he's enjoying our playful banter.

With the recommended dose of two travelsick tablets calming my stomach, I'm feeling no air sickness. I'm enjoying listening to my music, toes tapping and humming to Rihanna singing '*Only girl in the world.*' I keep my happy thoughts to myself and lock them away behind a gentle smile.

"Beth ... Beth." Ayden is calling my name and signalling for me to listen to him. "I have a business proposition for you."

Did I hear him right? "A what?"

"A business proposition."

I pull out my ear plugs and switch off my iPod.

This should be interesting.

"You know when you send me songs, how do you access the music? How do you know which songs are appropriate?"

I glance around the airplane, what a strange topic of conversation. "I don't know, some of them are on my iPod, so I know them, others I remember hearing and get them off iTunes. Over the years they've made coming home to an empty house a little more bearable. Why?"

"It's just I think you could be onto something." He's so animated and enthusiastic, this isn't chitchat. "There must be thousands of people out there like me who don't have your knowledge of music, but still want to communicate their feelings in a not verbal way. Don't you think?"

He's asking me? "Yes, people who are in love or those who have broken up. The forgive-me songs *you* sent me were very special." I smile appreciatively and settle my hand on his knee.

"Yeah right, but it took me all night to find them. No-one has that much free time, and that's what I'm thinking. What if there was a website where you could punch in a type of song like, say, 'forgive me' or 'I love you' or even 'You bastard, I hate you,' wouldn't you use it if it saved you time?"

"I suppose so, it does make sense and people might get back together and fall in love more quickly if they didn't have to trawl the internet looking for songs."

"OK. I'll get a couple of my website designers to look into it, but you think it's doable, right?" He seems genuinely excited at the prospect of getting it off the ground.

"Why not? You could even call it 'HeartBeats'©, say it, sing it, send it© ... or something like that? It's just an idea."

"That's a brilliant idea. I'll give you a million for it." Why is he lifting his brows expectantly? "What do you say?"

I'm happy to play along. "Make it four and you've got a deal." I snigger, not giving any credence to the conversation.

"Alright, I'll meet you halfway. Two million and we've got a deal." He's not smiling. Instead, his eyes are intense, and he's totally focused on me.

He can't be serious?

"We'll shake on it." He takes hold of my hand and grips it firmly. "We have a deal. I'll transfer the two million pounds into your account on Monday morning." He steps up from his seat and heads off in the direction of the wash room.

"Pardon me?"

When he returns, I'm still unsure of what just happened.

"What's the matter?" He sits himself down opposite me and returns to his iPad. He knows perfectly well what he's doing.

"You weren't serious were you, about the money?" I'm trying to catch his eye but he's being purposely evasive.

He launches one of his penetrating stares in my direction. "Of course I was, I'm always serious when it comes to money. Besides, it's a sound business proposition and I already have the skills base to launch something like that." He smiles gleefully. "Did you think I was messing around?"

I nod.

"Well, Miss Parker, you just sold me your idea for two million pounds and I think, quite frankly, you should have held out for more. I'm good for it." He squeezes my knee affectionately. "Now we're business partners with benefits."

"We are?" I smile nervously, nibbling on my thumb nail, "Does that mean you'll want to see my Mission Statement?" I'm feeling playful.

"That's not usually how I operate, but in this instance I think I may be persuaded to take a look at it." He's sitting back in his chair, arms folded, darkening eyes, utterly adorable.

I turn to check out the cloud formations and start to laugh. "You have more money than sense," I reproach him, refusing to believe a single word.

"Be that as it may, give it twelve months and you'll be wishing you'd asked for more." He lifts up his chin and looks confidently around the jet, before settling his gaze on me. "How are you feeling?"

"Rich!" I answer, shrugging my shoulders and sniffing the air.

"I'll get my legal team to sort out paperwork and bike it over to you on Monday. Then we'll celebrate."

"Why not, it will be my treat." I grin from ear to ear. This *is* for real.

"I don't think so, I said I'd take care of you and I meant it." He isn't joking.

"I thought you meant between the sheets?" All this talk of sex and money has me feeling rather needy. I think he can tell.

"I meant take care of you in every way." He's eyeing me so closely it makes me wonder how this conversation will end.

"I see, so the two million pounds finding its way into my bank account was you taking care of me?"

"No, that's the going rate for entrepreneurial ideas. It might make money in its own right or serve as an advertising platform, either way it won't be a loss leader. I'll see to that."

I'm not convinced. "I think you're doing it to make me feel better about being engaged to you and bringing so little to the table, so to speak, and that's okay but you don't have to dress it up for me. I know what people will say: you're a catch and I'm a gold digger." Saying those words saddens me, but it's true.

He's shaking his head from side to side. "Oh, Beth, it's not going to be like that, you'll see."

Why do I think he has something up his sleeve? I squint and tip my head on the side, "What aren't you telling me?"

The fact he's simply holding up his hands like an innocent man facing a firing squad, only reinforces my suspicion.

"Will I like it?" I try a different approach.

"My lips are sealed."

Undeterred, I fold back the small table between us and lean over to him, resting my knees on the floor. "And can your lips be unsealed?" I ask, tracing the outline of his perfect mouth with the fingers of my right hand.

"That depends."

Here it comes …

"On what?" I smirk, feeling his thighs tensing under my hands. *As if I didn't know.*

"On how persuasive you can be." He places his hands either side of my face and slides his fingers into my hair. "I'm willing to trade your mouth for mine."

No way!

"You want a BJ right here, right now?" My voice increases in pitch slightly, revealing not only my surprise but the intensity of my arousal. The idea of being caught at any moment is an enormous turn-on. Is he feeling it too?

"What about Ben and Jerry in the cockpit?" I realise my faux pas the moment the words fly from my mouth.

A flash of a smile appears. "They can get their own blow jobs."

I laugh out loud, and his toothy grin sets my insides alight. "Just as well, I don't think I could manage a hat trick."

"I'm very pleased to hear it." He's blinking and wincing at the thought, and that only makes me laugh more.

Now I'm giggling, a blow job is completely out of the question. "If you keep cracking me up, I won't be able to do it for laughing." I place my hand against his cheek. "I love you."

"I love you more." He pulls my face to his. "Forget the blow job. You've unsealed my lips by making me laugh."

He raises me off the carpet and sits me back in my chair. "OK. Here goes … I've had my people issue a press release, announcing our engagement. It will hit the newsstands tomorrow and the internet news services today. So don't be surprised if you have a couple of press photographers hanging around your apartment this week."

It takes me a couple of seconds to process the information. "Why didn't you tell me you were going to do something like that?" I'm not unhappy about it, but I would like to have been consulted.

"Because you would have said no."

I throw him an indignant look.

"See, I was right, but you have to take into account who I am, Beth, my position. What happens in my life makes the news, we're news. Better to issue a press release and hand over a photograph than wait for some arsehole to make up a story and hide away in the bushes waiting to catch us unawares."

I give him a sideways glance. "A photograph?" He's spoken of his Achilles heel, now he's found mine. "Which photograph?"

"The one of us on the terrace last night, you looked a million dollars."

"Two million dollars," I interject sarcastically, watching the humour fade from his eyes.

"Behave! This is the real world, Beth, I don't make the rules, I just operate in it and so do you now. Get used to it."

He's actually chastising me. "And where's the romance in that?" I demand, feeling the sting of his words blistering my skin.

He takes my hand. "Why are you so upset?"

"Ayden, for such a smart guy you really don't have a clue, do you?"

He's beginning to lose his cool. He shakes free of my hand and begins to pace.

"Do you realise your family and my friends will find out about our engagement from the newspapers; you did all this behind my back and you even set it up last night with the professional photographer, didn't you?" I break away. "We could have planned this together. Anyway ... why didn't you propose then, we had the candles, the stars, poetry?"

"I was going to, that was my plan. I had the ring in my pocket the whole time, but *someone* decided to go and turn themselves into this hot babe and *someone* tied my hands behind my back and my feet to a chair, and fucked the shit out of me."

I'm finding it impossible to keep a straight face, so impassioned is his protestation I'm having to fold my lips into my mouth, to stifle bubbling laughter.

Poor baby.

Slightly out of breath, his rant continues. "I couldn't speak, let alone propose. So it's not entirely my fault." He shares a wicked smile. "But, don't get me wrong, I'm not complaining."

I match his ridiculously hot smile. "Neither am I but ..."

He rolls his eyes.

"... But look at it from my point of view. One of the most memorable events of my life, you proposing, feels like it's been staged; you've had your script and I've just been strung along like an extra. That's why I'm upset." I watch him moving back and forth. For the first time in forty eight hours, his hand finds his neck and he is visibly tense. I've said enough.

"So, alright, I was a little hasty and I should have run it by you, but I wanted to tell the world, is that so wrong? I fucked up the proposal and now I've fucked this up. I'd better just stick to what I'm good at."

I stand, take hold of his biceps, struggling to keep him in one spot long enough for our eyes to meet. "Don't beat yourself up about it, Ayden, you're good at this, at us. You're used to flying solo, I should have realised that." I take his hand "But you have a co-pilot now. You have me. Come and sit down." I lead him to the sofa area and lift his chin, witnessing his disappointment. "I was surprised, but I'm okay with it now. Your intentions were honourable, and you were right to plan ahead."

"You have to keep reminding me to include you; it's a reflex action. Do you want me to try and pull the press release?" He means it.

What a preposterous idea. "No, you've got enough on your mind without that, besides Charlie won't believe her eyes." I force a cheerful smile.

"Alright, but lesson learned. I'll discuss this kind of thing with you next time." He kisses my lips with gentle devotion. "Thank you for letting me off so lightly."

I twist my engagement ring around on my finger. "Maybe I haven't, maybe a suitable punishment will be waiting for my naughty boy who makes me want to do naughty things, when he comes back from Hong Kong?" I fix him with a girly stare which goes some way towards reinforcing my sensual threat.

He kisses my hand and runs it from his collar bone, down to his heart. "You can't go making threats like that, Beth. I won't get through the day picturing you in that outfit with my belt around your neck."

He grins in such a way I feel my insides melting. "Then you shouldn't have been so impulsive," I whisper, brushing my lips over his. "Now we are officially an item, your word for the week and forever is "we." Got it?"

"Yes, Miss Parker." He breathes into my ear, sensuously. "I suppose *we* won't be getting a blow job now?"

I gaze upon eyes that are alive with a mixture of laughter and desire. "I'm afraid not. *We're* about to land."

"Damn! I'll ask them to circle for half an hour," he growls, pretending to leave the seat and holding back a loving smile. "Come on, *we* need to buckle up."

I take his hand and stand by his side, straightening his sweater and smoothing out his hair. "I like it when you say the word 'we,' it makes what we have seem real somehow."

"Oh, it's real, baby, and tomorrow you'll be able to read all about it." He winks and leads me to my seat. "Brace yourself!"

I throw him a baffled stare. Does he mean for the landing or for the press release? Before I can ask him which, the Captain announces we will be landing in ten minutes.

I fumble with the seat belt and distract myself from my least favourite part of the flight by examining this gorgeous man sitting opposite me. He is totally relaxed and utterly fuckable in his slate grey sweater and pale blue jeans, which are just about managing to contain his fading erection. My Mr. P. is the embodiment of male perfection and, by the look on his face, he knows that's exactly what I'm thinking.

"Assessing?"

"Enjoying," I reply candidly.

"Me too."

Like the shutter on a camera, I close my eyes, memorising every inch of him, rescuing my body from his potent stare and mentally preparing myself for the longest three days of my life.

***

The aroma of home-cooked food and Elise makes Dan a little lightheaded. Not because it or she affects him viscerally, but because he hasn't eaten a decent meal since, well, he can't remember when. The whiff of garlic, onions and roast beef tantalises his taste buds while her floral fragrance evokes a memory of wild, open spaces and childhood.

The pub lunch is the least romantic option but it suits them both. They order food at the bar and find an out of the way seat where they can hear themselves speak, yet are still within earshot of the TV. Thinking ahead, Dan wants to avoid any awkward silences and is using the TV as back-up; if all else fails they can talk about the news.

As luck would have it, there is little need of CNN and the conversation is fluid. He embellishes a couple of university anecdotes and she amuses him with stories about viewings and courses she's attended. She talks. He listens and takes it all in.

Twenty minutes in, the food arrives. They tuck into two ploughman's lunches and a basket of chips, hardly noticing the passing of time. The awkwardness that was evident two days ago has merged into a mutual understanding; they're two friends having lunch together and amorous intentions do not feature on the menu. There seems to be a silent arrangement which is allowing them to relax, safe in the knowledge there will be no pressure to perform, neither of them have expectations. It's just lunch.

Elise is visibly relaxing and Dan is happy to watch, commending himself on his judiciousness. She's just what the doctor ordered: a distraction and nothing more.

He knows the next few days will be a test of his skilfulness as a kidnapper and a lover. By this time tomorrow, he'll be able to have his cake and eat it.

By 3 o'clock, they are full to the brim with sticky toffee pudding and lager. A lull in the conversation forces Dan to turn to his back-up for inspiration. "You been keeping an eye on the trouble in the Far East?"

Elise signals no.

"What a bunch of fucking morons, won't be happy 'til they start a war, and then we'll all get drawn into it."

She tucks her hair behind her right ear. "I don't pay much attention to it. I've got enough to think about without worrying about them."

"Right, I know the feeling."

The anchor man appears on screen:

"We've just had word that media magnate Ayden Stone has announced his engagement to an English school teacher ... over to you Bret ... yes, thank you Matt. One of the most eligible bachelors in Europe has announced his engagement today to Elizabeth Parker, a twenty seven year old school teacher from London, England. In a press release today he said, "Beth and I are very happy. After a whirlwind romance, we're planning to get married as soon as possible and build a future together. I'm a very lucky man ..."

Both Dan and Elise look up at the screen, open-mouthed, transfixed. "Fuck!" They say in unison, turning to each other so quickly their heads spin.

"Pardon?" Elise is the first to react. She's frowning and staring at Dan, refusing to release him from her startled gaze.

"Sorry."

"About what? Swearing or having something to say about Ayden Stone?"

Dan's flustered. He picks up his glass and throws back the remaining dregs of golden liquid. "About swearing. It was uncalled for."

"I don't give a flying fuck about the swearing. It's why you did it that worries me. I need a drink." She grabs her purse from her bag and pushes back a chair. "Same again?"

"If you're buying."

With a cursory nod, she strides over to the bar. Dan's brain is working overtime. Has he let the cat out of the bag? What can he tell her? Nothing. Why the hell did *she* swear?

When she returns to her seat, she's bursting to talk. "So, are you going to tell me why you were shocked?" Her unflinching look tells him she's like a dog with a bone. She will not let it drop.

Dan takes the offensive position. "I think you should be the one confessing, Elise. It wasn't a very ladylike thing to do, calling out like that. You must have had good reason?" He drums his fingers on the table, waiting for her reply.

"Firstly, I never said I was a lady, and secondly, I do have good reason." She hesitates, finding it difficult to explain. Dan gives her all the time she needs. "Ayden and I have history. We go way back and, since then, well ..."

Dan cannot conceal his astonishment. "You *know* him?" He cannot put the two of them together, it simply does not compute.

She's offended. "Yes. Why? Is it so surprising that someone like me should know someone like him?" She lifts up her glass and takes a big gulp. "He's just a guy you know, not a fucking God."

"Oh, I know that, but ..."

"But, you can't imagine what he'd see in me?"

Dan prepares to salvage what he can of her ego. "No, it's not that. I'm just wondering why he let you go." Leaving the compliment floating around in the shifting air, he takes a sip of his drink. "He must be a fucking idiot."

Elise is dumbstruck. She had an arsenal of self-defending remarks all loaded up and ready to launch and is grateful for not having to propel a single one. She places her hand on his arm. "Thank you. That's a nice thing to say."

"It's the truth," he lies, thinking she has been so preoccupied with her own outburst that she has forgotten his. He's wrong.

Still deep in thought, she sips slowly and turns to him, leaving the glass in front of her face, "So, that explains my little eruption. What's your excuse?"

It's shape up or ship out time for Dan. He could lie quite easily and spin a yarn about some university visit gone wrong involving Stone. Or he could tell her a half truth. Who knows, she may be a valuable ally?

"My shout out had nothing to do with your ex, it had more to do with his fiancée. I know *her*."

Now it's Elise's turn to be shocked. Her lips are parted and her eyes are large and disbelieving. "You know *her*?"

Dan gives her a reproving look which sears her to her chair.

"I didn't mean it like that." She gives his arm a squeeze. "What I meant to say was, *how* do you know her?" She is still and attentive.

He refuses to feel boxed in. For the first time in his life, he can actually speak her name. "Elizabeth Parker went to Cambridge about six years ago and we got together then." It's not a lie. Merely saying her name out loud causes a stab of that which has no name to circulate his groin.

Elise wants details. "You went out?"

"Yeah."

"For how long?"

"A couple of months."

"Nothing serious then?"

"Not for her."

She eyes him suspiciously. "But it was for you?"

"Yeah, you could say that."

"Have you been in touch with her since?"

"No. She moved away, I don't know where."

"I do." Her face contorts into a grimace. "Right into Ayden's arms, that's where."

"Looks that way."

"Yes it does." She arches her body towards him and leans in so close he can feel her fevered breath on his face. "And what the fuck are we going to do about it?"

Dan's face splits in two. His wicked grin leaves her in no doubt as to his willingness to get involved. "Leave it with me, Elise, I'll think of something."

"Good." She lifts up her glass, expecting him to do the same. "I'll drink to that."

21

L ester is a welcome sight, waiting outside international arrivals. At least his driving will comply with some sort of Highway Code, which is more than can be said for his Italian counterparts.

"Mr. Stone, Miss Parker. Welcome back. I hope you had an enjoyable trip?"

"Lester."

As Ayden doesn't do small talk, I speak for both of us. "Yes we did, thank you Lester, the hotel was lovely and the weather stayed fine."

I notice Lester is smiling politely but shifting from left to right. He knows how Ayden can be. I stand my ground. It costs nothing to be polite.

"How about you? What have you been up to?"

"What the hell. We're losing daylight here," Ayden yells from inside the Rolls Royce.

I accept Lester's apologetic smile and climb inside. "Ayden, sometimes you can be so rude." I turn away to look out of the window. Even though he's tutting and blowing out hot air, I won't let it go. "For someone whose business is communications, you're a terrible communicator." All I'm getting back is a wide stare.

"You'll find people will work harder and be more loyal if you treat them with respect."

"Miss Parker, in business, '... it is much better to be feared than loved,'" he says smartly.

"Oh please, tell me you're not blaming Machaivelli for your rudeness?"

He wraps his left arm around my shoulders and buries his nose in my hair. It feels so intimate and I fold into him. "No, it was just a quote that came to me. I'll bear in mind what you said."

The Rolls pulls out onto the busy lane and picks up speed. In a moment of mental clarity, I recall Jake's cryptic message, *The shit's hitting the fan here* ... What does he expect me to do about it? I can't *make* him leave me and go to Hong Kong. If I tell him about the text, I'll have to disclose my other L.A. arrangement and he'll feel betrayed. If I say I want to be alone, he'll become suspicious and upset. What to do?

I fidget around on the leather seat and try to find a 'painless' position, knowing Ayden will notice my discomfort. He misses nothing.

"What's wrong?"

Here goes ...

"Nothing, I think I need a good long soak in a hot bath." I offer a half smile.

"Are you sore?"

He's genuinely concerned and I'm touched. Not wanting to worry him too much, I play it down. "A bit, but I'll be okay. Don't worry."

"We'll go to your apartment, if you want, if you'd feel more comfortable there. Or we can still go to Belgravia, if you're up to it?" He's tipping his head sympathetically, waiting for a reply.

I hate myself. "Maybe I should go home and let you get on with some work." I drop that suggestion out there, testing the water.

"If I didn't know better, I'd say having had your wicked way with me, Miss Parker, you're trying to get rid of me."

Shit!

Now he's becoming suspicious. I stretch up and kiss his cheek. "Of course not. I just think being on the receiving end of so much ... sex, has its disadvantages."

"Oh I get it, you want me to kiss it better?" He starts to position me in the middle of the enormous leather seat. Now he's kneeling between my legs. "Looks like I'll be ruining another pair of trousers."

So much for my scheming.

He's unbuttoning my jeans. I take hold of his hands and slide them down my thighs. As tempted as I am and as needy as I feel, I have to at least try to get him back on track, but this is proving harder than I thought. "That's a kind offer but I'm afraid I cannot accept it."

An inscrutable look appears like a mist over his face. Either he's worried that I'm rejecting him or he hates the idea of being rebuked. Either way, it's not good.

"This from the woman I spent the last three days fucking."

There's a disturbing shift in tone. I hate it. "Yes, that would be me, Ayden. I'm the one who's sore and swollen and in pain, so consider your words carefully. I don't want you to see how I look at the moment. It's not a pretty sight."

If self-loathing had a face, it would look like the one in front of me. He's unhappy about his lack of sensitivity and, frankly, so am I.

"I'm sorry." His firm hands find their way to my face and slide into my hair, releasing the clip. Still kneeling, he ruffles my hair until it settles on my shoulders, before inching towards my lips. The softness of his kisses and gentleness of his hands massaging my hair, remind me of how close we have become. He's on his knees to me and I feel as if this is the closest I will ever get to being worshiped.

"*We* need to take a time-out, don't we?"

I hear the 'we' loud and clear. How can a single word make my chest hurt? "I think we do."

I lean into him and our foreheads touch. I know if I pull him to me, I'll fold. He knows that too. I glance at his hands shaped into fists, left and right of me on the seat. I attempt to lift him off the floor but he won't budge, his eyes are downcast and his mood is sombre.

"Ayden, look at me." I tip up his chin and hold his face in place with my hands, caressing his cheekbones with my thumbs. "I'm the happiest I've ever been in my life and it's all down to you. You know that, don't you?"

He answers with a slanted smile and a nod.

"I can't keep my hands off you and that's why I'm sore, it's nothing to do with you being rough or too demanding. You've done nothing wrong." I take hold of his fists and try to lift him again. This time he obliges and sits down next to me on my right. "Talk to me." I wrap my left arm around him and rest my head under the crook of his neck.

He clears his throat to speak. "I'm going to fly out to Hong Kong this afternoon."

I don't believe my ears...

"I'll be able to sleep on the flight and get the meeting brought forward, so I only have to be away two days instead of three." He plants a kiss on my head. "When I get back, you can come and stay over at Stone Heath and, if you want, you can move in. I'll arrange to have your things collected and you can either hold onto your apartment or rent it out, whatever you think's best. How does that sound?" He stops to take a breath.

"Like a plan," I state, gazing up at him adoringly. "My Mr. P. is back."

"Baby, I was never away," he assures me, although I suspect he's just being cute.

As we pull up outside my apartment, I notice the wrought iron window dressing and the alarm box flashing on the wall next to the front door. He has kept his promise to keep me safe. Whilst we were in Rome he'd arranged for an alarm company to install, what will probably be a state of the art sensor system.

I edge over and settle myself across his lap; my favourite place in all the world. "Will you be alright?" I ask tentatively, tracing the outline of his jaw with my right hand.

"Why wouldn't I?" he snaps a little too abrasively.

"You know what I mean, after everything. You have no reason to feel vulnerable or unsure, right?"

"Are you trying to tell me how to run my business, Miss Parker?" He rubs his nose against mine. "I only felt vulnerable because I couldn't come to terms with how I felt about you. I know now."

I hold his gaze for as long as he will let me. "And do you still need the lock of my hair?"

He considers the question and twists the forefinger of his left hand round and round in my hair, creating an unruly ringlet. "I'll always need it, Beth, you know that."

I pull on his firm shoulders, trying to break his reflective mood. "So now you have my hair, the visual memory of my noisy orgasm and all my love, you have the best of me." I forge a playful smile when really, with every passing second, I'm dying inside with a single gut-wrenching thought: I've lied to him.

"I do and I can't ask for more than that. All I need now is a kiss and I'll be on my way."

Why am I doing this?

I adopt a serious expression and hold him with a fierce blue stare, changing my position so I can straddle him. I don't care if it's daytime, if the neighbours are watching or if Lester is pretending to read his newspaper. This is what I want to do, this is what he needs. A goodbye kiss he won't forget.

Resisting the need to rub up against him, I grip his outer thighs with my knees and squeeze tight, pinning him beneath me. I might think I'm taking the lead, but he's seducing me with his passivity: darkening eyes and his dextrous hands, that's all it takes.

I'm kissing his neck on the left side, allowing my tongue to taste the warm flesh shifting beneath it, making my way to his chin, taking my time, savouring his delectable face, smothering him with love. His fragrant hair folds and separates around my fingers like strands of liquorish and I feel my breath quickening as his erection presses into me. He raises his hips off the seat in search of a point of contact.

When my lips find his it's like striking gold. Nothing compares to the way this man can kiss. He could make me come with no more than soft words and a wet, ravishing kiss. He doesn't use his tongue to taste and explore, he uses it to make love.

"Ayden," I whisper, fighting for breath. "You're doing it on purpose. You're making me come with a kiss." I begin to moan. This was supposed to be my farewell and here he is, fucking me in broad daylight with his tongue. I can't help myself. I begin to rub up against him, grinding against his erection.

Sensing my impending orgasm, Ayden presses the button in the door for the privacy glass. Now we are soundproofed and shielded on all four sides in our private world, I need not hold back. My hands are fumbling, unbuttoning his jeans. I need to feel him inside me.

"No." He takes hold of my hands and prevents me from unzipping him. I try to shake off his hands. "No, Beth."

"Yes, Ayden, let go of my hands. I want you." I can hear myself shouting, so acute is my craving for him.

"I don't want to hurt you." The look on his tormented face cuts me to the quick, but I cannot help myself, he's just too damn hot.

"You won't, Ayden, I'm so wet." I kiss him over and over. "Please, please."

He releases my hands and holds his own high in submission, allowing me to take out his pulsating cock. I gasp and begin clinching involuntarily, wrapping my arms around his neck and leaning backwards, urging him to come with me, to lay me out on the seat.

In a split second, he has me beneath him and he's tearing at my jeans and my panties, dragging them to my knees and feeling me with his right hand, testing for moisture, making sure I'm ready for him.

"Don't worry, I'm ready," I pant, so wanton I hardly recognise myself, I've never felt quite so reckless. What's got into me? Has the prospect us being parted for three days reignited my sexual appetite? Whatever the reason, my pants are down, his cock is out. If ever I needed to be fucked, it's now.

I watch as he reaches into his pocket and tears off the top of the condom packet with his teeth. I'm writhing, my hands are gripping the edge of the seat and my heart is racing. I'm forgetting my lie.

Looking me in the eye, he rolls the condom down the length of his erect penis. "I don't want to do this," he mutters in a voice coated in anguish.

His words still me. I realise, he's doing this for me, not for himself. In fact, the thought of inflicting actual bodily harm is causing him pain. I sit up, affronted. "Then don't." I pull up my underwear and my jeans.

He can't believe his eyes. "What?" He takes hold of himself with a motionless hand.

"I'm not going to force you to do something you don't want to do, for the sake of my own pleasure. We both have to want this."

He's shaking his head from left to right, screwing up his face and pursing his lips as if he's experiencing actual physical pain.

Dear God! What have I done?

"Don't do this, Beth. I'm about to fly half way round the world and you're mind fucking me." Impulsively, he takes hold of my upper arms and drags me down onto the leather seat. "I'm not going to get on that fucking plane feeling bad about not pleasing you, it's the only thing I want to do, so let's just do it."

Now it's my turn to feel slighted. "How dare you talk to me like that! You're the one who just fucked me with your tongue. I was about to give you a good bye kiss and leave." I'm so enraged, I could spit.

"We both know that's not true. You take great delight in unravelling me and here, in the back seat of my car is your favourite playground. But that's okay because you get off on it."

With that, I slap him hard across the face with my right hand. "That's not true." Tears are filling my eyes, my lower lip is starting to quiver.

He takes hold of my offending hand and pulls it to his lips, angling his face to kiss my palm before raising my arms above my head, gripping my wrists in his powerful left hand. As hard as I try, I cannot break free.

"You drive me fucking crazy," he calls out for the whole world to hear and presses a button on the door behind my head. "Just drive."

I feel the engine starting and the car moving away from my apartment. What the hell is he doing? With his left hand pinning me down, he yanks down my jeans and panties, spreads my legs with his right hand, keeping them parted with his knees. I can't help but be aroused. Just one look into his wild, indigo eyes tells me that he intends to fuck me senseless, and that's exactly what I want.

I feel his fingers stroking and caressing me, feeling every fold and inch of my drenched skin. He slides a warm finger inside and I moan and push into him, urging him to make me come.

His hand stills and I lower my chin and focus on him, gasping at what I see. He's enraged, glaring at me and about to explode.

"You're not sore and you're not swollen, and you look perfect. Why did you lie to me, Beth?"

He inserts a second finger and pushes deeper into me. I'm so turned-on I can barely speak, let alone confess. My body responds. I move involuntarily against his hand, pinioned beneath him with no hope of freeing myself. "Ayden," I call out. "Listen to my body, what's it saying to you?"

He turns away, he isn't listening to me or my body, he's not motivated by a need to please me into submission, he's being driven on by one mindless objective. To get me to the point where I'm so aroused I will say and do anything.

With the swiftness of an athlete, he lifts me from my horizontal position and flips me over so I am lying across his lap, my head on the seat to the left of him and my stomach resting on his knees. I try to push up with my elbows, but he snatches at my hands, and holds them together against my lower back. I know what's about to happen next and the thought of it has me in a sexual frenzy.

He slides his hand over my bottom and slips two wet fingers inside me. I clench onto him, moaning and panting away the feeling of total submission.

"Tell me why you lied to me, is there someone else? Is that why you're in such a hurry to get me out of the way?"

What!

"No, no-one, but I can't say," I moan helplessly, so close to an orgasm that I think I will crush his fingers.

"I need to know why you lied to me. I can take the bullshit off everyone else, but not off you, Beth." He slaps my backside hard. I cry out, feeling the stinging sensation a single second before he sinks his fingers into me again. My body is contorting and I'm fighting for breath, over stimulated and climaxing onto him.

"I'm waiting."

What's he doing to me?

"Ayden, stop!" He slaps me again and this time, so forceful is his thrusting that I come onto his hand again, screaming out his name.

As he massages my tingling cheeks, he continues with his interrogation. "You've been a very bad girl. Why did you lie to me, Beth?"

When his hand slaps my tender flesh this time, he pushes his hand beneath me and focuses his attention on my clitoris, making me wince and convulse onto his knees. I'm fast approaching my limit; I can't take any more. It's too much. Where's the love in this? What started out as an erotic encounter has become terrifying. I don't think he's going to stop until I tell him the truth.

"Romeo," I whimper, sobbing into the seat. He pulls his hand from beneath me and slackens his grip on my bruised wrists. I'm shaking uncontrollably and struggling to catch my breath between sobs. When he reaches over to me, I flinch and pull away until I'm just a small, tightly wound body, lying in the foetal position on the back seat of his silver Rolls Royce.

Minutes pass; they feel like hours.

"Please take me home." I can't even look at him. I pull up my panties and jeans and try to flatten my hair. With little thought, I pull it back and clip it off my face. My T-shirt serves as a cloth to pat my cheeks and to wipe my nose. I look a mess. I feel a wreck.

Ayden issues an instruction: "Back to Miss Parker's apartment." He then turns to me.

He attempts to speak, but is dumbstruck when I raise my eyes and he sees my terror. Both his hands cover his face, more out of shame than despair. There is a metre of space between us, but it might as well be an ocean. I cannot touch him and he doesn't know how to reach out to me.

The car pulls up outside my apartment once again. I make a move to leave and then turn back. He deserves to hear the truth, it won't make him feel any better about what he's done, but it will make my disloyalty a little more bearable. Fighting back sobs I confess.

"Jake texted me today while we were in the air and asked me to get you on an earlier flight to Hong Kong because, quote, 'the shit's hitting the fan' and you need to be there. So I lied to you so you'd leave me, because I knew you wouldn't go unless I had to be on my own for some reason. It was a stupid lie. That's the truth." I brush away my tears, wipe my nose with the back of my hand and take a fortifying breath.

His horror is palpable.

"Bye, Ayden. Have a safe flight."

Just as I'm stepping out of the car he calls out, "Beth! I told you I'd fuck up, didn't I?"

I turn to see his tear stained face.

"I don't deserve you. I never have." He squeezes his eyes shut, barely able to speak. "Tell me truthfully, what we had in Rome was good, wasn't it?"

I lower my head, trying to hold back my tears long enough to get the words out. "No, it wasn't good, Ayden ... it was perfect."

I take the long walk to my security door and then my front door, just about managing to place one foot in front of the other. I knew the next three days were going to be difficult, now they will be unbearable.

***

Every time Dan relives his conversation with Elise, he cannot help but smile. Here they were less than a week ago, total strangers. Here they are now, comrades in arms.

He gets back to his lookout post just in time to spot the return of the 'happy' couple. He checks his watch: 1540hrs. Anxiously, he waits for her to step out of the silver Rolls, crossing his fingers that Stone will leave her to her fate: to him.

He waits.

Thirty minutes later, he's still waiting. With every passing second, he's becoming more agitated; his fingers are twitching, his back is aching from standing. The wait is excruciating, but he cannot tear his eyes away.

Without a word of warning, the car pulls away. He's glancing left and right, listening for the security door to slam shut: Nothing. "What the fuck?" All he can do is pull up a chair and watch darkness fall, he daren't move. He stands. A Peugeot appears and turns around in the cul-de-sac then drives away and, for the next thirty minutes, that's all that happens until ...

Like a glowing metal object moving across the night sky, the silver Rolls Royce glides into view. No one emerges and then he sees her. She steps tentatively out of the car, stops and turns to face *him*, says something.

Through his zoom lens, he focuses on her tear stained face; she's the ghost he has lived with all these years, pale, lifeless. Her clothes are creased and her hair ...

"What the fuck has he done to you, princess?" Dan's left hand grapples with the curtain, screwing it up into a tight ball, rage sweeps through his veins like an avalanche. "I'll make him pay for this."

All his senses are on high alert. He's listening for the security door to slam. There it goes. He's watching the Rolls weave its way around the cul-de-sac and disappear down the road. There it goes. The coast is clear.

Carrying his rucksack, he slips the straps over his gloved hands, pulls his front door to but does not lock it, knowing he may need to return sharpish. With due care and attention, he deploys his best covert skills and descends the stairs, one step at a time ...

***

The emotional torment that comes after a break-up far exceeds any physical suffering. I feel as if my spirit has been broken. I've been violated, all because of a foolish and unnecessary lie. I can't forgive him and he can't forgive himself for subjecting me to sexual torture.

Once inside, I realise all of my luggage is in the boot of his car, but it doesn't matter. I won't be dressing-up any time soon. I click down the button on my Yale lock, resting my hand against the door, trying to hold back the pain; it's impossible, it's inside me, ripping me apart like an exploding firework. All I want to do is climb into bed and sleep. When I wake, all this will have been a terrible nightmare. I'll get up and wander onto our terrace and feast on croissants and fruit while Ayden reads out the headlines.

Please God ...

The car is stationary outside. From behind my curtain, I watch dark clouds forming like a suffocating shroud over my home, over my heart. The elements converge, creating a bleak and sombre backdrop to a make-believe world. But, I'm home now, it's back to reality and what a fucking miserable reality it is.

My laptop sits on the kitchen table. While I've been collecting memories that will live with me forever, it's been collecting dust. I lift open the lid and return to a world I know; a world where music comforts me, offers me catharsis and peace of mind. Right now I'll do whatever it takes to stop this agonising heartache.

But, I'm not prepared for what I see. The desktop picture appears: it's *that* picture. I can take anything but not that. My legs give way and I hold onto the back of the chair for support. Barely able to focus, I scroll down my iTunes library, knowing the exact song I'm looking for. Rihanna asks the question for me:

'What now ...?'

She puts my thoughts to music and I collapse onto the chair, crumpled and misshapen. I look down at my hands, resting my gaze on my engagement ring; a perfect sapphire in the shape of a heart encased in a constellation of diamonds. Focusing on the irony and not its beauty, I pull at it until my finger wriggles free and hold it up to the light between my finger and thumb. It must have cost the earth.

Reluctantly, I place it on the table where it glistens and winks at me with every step I take away from it. I look back, fighting off a magnetic pull, but it has no hold on me now.

The walk into my bedroom is a gruelling exercise in self-control. Putting one foot in front of the other is unbearable, when you know you're walking away from your destiny.

Somewhere out there in a faraway place beyond the planets, two bright stars crossed paths; they came within touching distance of each other and, for a brief instance, they basked in the glow of interplanetary union: two celestial bodies fusing, becoming one. But now, their trajectories have shifted, they have moved on and the space between is infinite. We are those star crossed lovers.

I fall from the sky, come crashing down to earth and descend into a black hole of despair, a solitary figure: I'm alone.

The song ends. I lift my face from the sodden pillow ... was that my doorbell ...?

The Story of Us continues …

TouchStone
for giving©

TouchStone
for ever©

Songs featured in this book may soon be available as a cd.
They are the perfect accompaniment to
The Story of Us

Contact: P.A Ms. J. Watson -
https://www.facebook.com/SocialButterflyBooks?fref=ts
sjpublishing@virginmedia.com

TouchStone Family Circle:
https://www.facebook.com/groups/TouchStoneFamilyCircle/
?fref=ts
Twitter: @SydneyJamesson,
@TouchStoneFans, @ElizabethP1984,
@AydenStone, @CharlieM_TSFP

FB: https://www.facebook.com/Sydney-Jamesson
Website: http://sydneyjamesson.com/
Amazon: http://viewBook.at/B00CW6FNXO

Printed in Great Britain
by Amazon.co.uk, Ltd.,
Marston Gate.